HMS *INFLEXIBLE*

By the same author

HMS *Marathon*
HMS *Crusader*

HMS *INFLEXIBLE*

A. E. Langsford

Oh Lord, when Thou givest unto Thy servants to endeavour in any great matter, grant us also to know that it is not the beginning but the continuing of the same until it be thoroughly finished which yieldeth the true glory . . .

Sir Francis Drake before Cadiz, 1587

ARROW

To my parents and to all the Officers and Men who
served in or with the British Pacific Fleet, November
1944-August 1945, with humility and in the hope that
I have done them justice.

Published by Arrow Books Limited
20 Vauxhall Bridge Road, London SW1V 2SA

An imprint of Random House UK Ltd

London Melbourne Sydney Auckland Johannesburg
and agencies throughout the world

First published in Great Britain by Barrie & Jenkins Ltd in 1991

Arrow edition 1992

1 3 5 7 9 10 8 6 4 2

© 1991 by A. E. Langsford

Printed and bound in Great Britain by Cox & Wyman Ltd,
Reading, Berks.

ISBN 0 09 997070 8

Acknowledgements

This book could not have been written without the help and support of a large number of people. In particular, Captain J. F. T. Bayliss and Mr T. K. Norledge, Technical Information Officer of the Institute of Marine Engineers, devoted much time and effort to answering my queries about naval law and disciplinary procedures and marine engineering respectively. Squadron Leader R. T. F. Lyon and Mr Bernard Thompson provided information on wartime flying training; Commander Frank Bromilow, Lieutenant-Commander Ralph Parkinson, Lieutenant-Commander D. J. Price and Mr W. A. Reeks gave me the benefit of their experiences as observers in the wartime Fleet Air Arm, including, in the case of the last, a graphic first-hand account of his being shot down over Ishigaki in April 1945, which he kindly allowed me to make extensive use of. Gus Britton of the Royal Navy Submarine Museum, Jack Brooks, Al Lever and Tony Tickner all took a keen interest in the book during its development, and gave me every encouragement to continue. Lastly, I owe a special debt of gratitude to Commander C. W. S. Dreyer DSO DSC who read the book in manuscript and made many constructive suggestions, and also passed a number of my queries to Geoffrey Brooke DSC, a survivor of HMS *Prince of Wales* and later a flight-deck officer in both *Indomitable* and *Formidable*. All errors of fact are, of course, my own.

Prologue

The Admiralty, London, March 1944.

'You here again? It hardly seems five minutes since you were pestering me for a ship the last time. And what, pray tell, have you been doing in the interim? – No, don't tell me. I know all about it. I wouldn't exactly recommend a swim in the Barents Sea at this or any other time of the year, but you're looking pretty fit on it. You've had a good leave, you're ready to get down to some work again and you want me to give you another ship.'

'Yes, sir, preferably an aircraft carrier.'

The Naval Secretary paused before replying, his forearms resting on the blotter on his desktop so that the broad band and single narrower ring of a Rear Admiral were on display. 'You've obviously been corrupted by six months with the intrepid birdmen. I've seen it happen before.'

Outside the sky was leaden grey, and fierce equinoctial gusts splattered rain on the windowpanes. In the Naval Secretary's office the lights were on, and a fire burned in the grate to take the damp chill from the air. It was a room with a heavily traditional air, the painting above the fireplace showing a frigate under sail, and a set of engravings of the uniforms of Trafalgar lining the walls; the two telephones on the desk, one black, one red, providing an almost incongruous touch of modernity.

'Hm, I thought you'd have been glad to see the back

1

of carriers. In any case, Thurston, aren't you being a bit greedy? You've had a lot of sea time, and generally covered yourself with glory in the process.' The Admiral glanced at the double row of ribbons on his listener's left breast, which began with the claret of the Victoria Cross and continued with the blue with red edges of the DSO. 'I think it about time you were reminded of what a desk looks like.' His fingers leafed through the pages of the folder which was open in front of him. 'It appears that you haven't had a shore appointment since – let me see – 1936. Eight years ago, which means that you're long overdue for one. In point of fact there are a couple of jobs about to fall vacant in this place.'

'Sir,' the Captain protested, 'my experience would be completely wasted in a shore job.'

'Not at all. You would be a valuable addition to the team here. We have a policy, as I'm sure you're aware, of getting you chaps ashore from time to time so that your experience can be disseminated,' the Admiral seemed rather pleased with the word, 'disseminated among the rest.'

'I believe that it is also Admiralty policy to keep those officers who have proved themselves in seagoing appointments at sea,' the Captain said in quiet, but incisive tones.

Captain Robert Thurston was a tall man, an inch or two over six foot, broad-shouldered and long in the leg, so that he appeared too large for the chair he was sitting on. His face went with his frame, lean and a little angular, and growing more austere with the years; dominated by a high-bridged nose which had been broken when he was a midshipman and had healed a little out of line, the forehead crossed by a long white scar which divided his right eyebrow into two, a second, smaller scar on the left side of his jaw. His hair was dark, greying at the sides now and beginning to thin a little in front; his eyes blueish-grey and set deeply into their sockets.

The Admiral looked disconcerted, realising that the tables had been turned on him in a few quietly spoken words. 'Quite so. But why an aircraft carrier?'

'I've already commanded one, sir. I was given *Crusader* to sort her out. I sorted her out, and I learnt a hell of a lot about carriers in the process. It seems to me that I would be better employed putting that experience to some use.'

'Yes, yes. Bertie Manning-Wilson seems to have been quite impressed with your efforts in *Crusader*. Came down here from the Clyde singing your praises last week, in between trying to persuade me to give him a cruiser squadron.' The Admiral fidgeted with the papers on the blotter once more. 'Good fellow, Bertie; he was in my term in the *Britannia*. Pity about that wretched wife of his . . . And I agree with him. You did a damn good job with her, until you lost her. I mean *Crusader*,' the Admiral added hastily. 'And now you want another ship so you can go and lose her. You're getting rather expensive, you know. That's the trouble with you chaps. You may do a lot of damage to the enemy, but you also keep the dockyards busy. Two sinkings, *Marathon* in dry dock twice, even if you did manage to finish off the *Seydlitz*, which was a damn fine piece of work.' The Admiral saw Thurston's jaw clench, put his hands together. 'No, no, I'm only joking. Go on.'

Thurston shifted the brass hat which was resting on his knee. Brand-new, like everything else. 'We've all been trained to command cruisers, sir, or destroyers or battleships, but there are still very few senior officers with experience of aircraft carriers. I happen to be one of them. I had to learn the ropes as I went along, but I've learnt them now. Things are changing; aircraft are taking over from big guns now. Guns will hit a target up to twenty miles away, if the visibility's good enough to follow the fall of shot. But at Midway the Yanks and the Japanese never even saw each other. It was all aircraft. A bomber can drop bombs on a target two hundred miles away. One radar-equipped Swordfish can keep half a dozen U-boats submerged, because they all have radar detectors and dive as soon as they pick up our transmissions. We proved that in *Crusader*, especially after we started night flying. It's quite true that we only sank a couple of U-boats, but we were there to protect the merchant ships, and by keeping the U-boats down we did just that.'

'Yes, I've heard something of your reports. They make quite interesting reading. You're clearly full of the zeal of the converted.'

'I'd be happy to take another escort carrier. I believe there are a couple more building in America and about to commission.'

'That's quite true, but you won't be getting one of them, or any other escort carrier for that matter.' The Admiral was grinning now, and Thurston suddenly realised that he had been playing a game with him. 'I'm giving you *Inflexible*. You are rather junior still, but, as you say, you do have experience of carriers, which may or may not be an advantage.'

Thurston started to thank him, but the Admiral cut him short. 'Might as well try to put the square pegs in the square holes. But your next appointment will definitely be ashore. It's long overdue. That's not the only thing. I understand you've been doing some illicit flying. One of the things Bertie Manning-Wilson mentioned.'

'Yes, sir, that's quite true.'

'Thought you'd kept that quiet, I suppose. There are no secrets in the service, you should know that by now.'

Thurston decided to take the bull by the horns. 'There is quite a difference between commanding a carrier and a conventional warship. To be able to do the job justice, you really need to be a pilot or observer yourself, preferably a pilot. Only then can you fully appreciate what you're dealing with, both on our side and on the enemy side. I'm not, of course, and that was my biggest handicap in commanding *Crusader*. As yet there are only about half a dozen post captains who are qualified as pilots. But, at least by learning the basics of flying I've gained some understanding of the problems the aircrews are dealing with.'

'Actually, Bertie thought it quite enterprising of you. How much did you do?'

'About fifteen hours in a Tiger Moth at Abbotsinch, sir, three of them solo, and I went over to Lee-on-Solent one day while I was on leave, and got in a couple more hours. But that's only scratching the surface. In point of fact,' Thurston went on, more boldly now that he had the Admiral's interest, 'if I'm going to take over a fleet carrier, there's a strong argument for saying that I should get some experience of modern aircraft. All I've flown is a Tiger Moth, and there's no comparison between that and the things being flown from *Inflexible* and ships like her.'

'Yes,' the Admiral mused, 'I suppose you do have a point.'

Thurston, realising that the Admiral was weakening, continued. 'Midshipmen have an acquaintance course in flying so that they do at least know one end of an aircraft from the other, but post captains are expected to know all about commanding carriers even if they've never been near an aircraft in their lives. We do cover the basics of gunnery and torpedoes in Subs' courses, so there's no particular problem in taking over a conventional warship, but we don't do anything about flying, which can only become more important. The Americans do it quite differently. They insist that anyone who is going to command a carrier qualifies as a pilot or observer, if he hasn't already. I certainly don't think we should follow the Americans slavishly in everything – '

'Certainly not,' the Admiral looked suitably shocked.

' – but this is a case where they do have the right idea, and where we can usefully take a leaf out of the American book.'

'You're coming perilously close to teaching me to suck eggs, Thurston.'

'I apologise, sir.'

The Admiral pushed back his chair, tilted his head in contemplation of his elegant plaster-moulded ceiling for a time. 'All right, you've managed to convince me. I know you young chaps think we're a lot of old has-beens who haven't had an original thought since Trafalgar, but we do have some idea of what's going on. I don't want you doing any more flying on the quiet, and someone might come down very hard on you if they hear that you have been, but I may, and I stress the word *may*, be able to arrange for you to fit some flying in on an official basis. *Inflexible*'s in Boston refitting, and we won't need you over there quite yet, so there's time to fit something in, rather than have you taking it as gardening leave. I'll have a word with the Fifth Sea Lord, it's his pigeon. You'll probably have to do it with the RAF, of course. Now go away and keep out of my sight in case I change my mind.'

Thurston stood up, and tucked his cap beneath his arm. 'Good morning, sir, and thank you.' He started for the door.

'One more thing,' the Admiral called after him. 'I hear you're a father again.'

'Twin boys. Last week.'

'No wonder you want another ship.'

Chapter One

North-west Pacific, May 1945.

'Are you awake, sir?'

Thurston, lying on his bunk, naked except for a pair of shorts, did not respond.

'Are you awake, sir?'

At the repetition of the ritual question, Thurston grimaced, opened his eyes, then rolled automatically on to one side to glance at the course and speed indicators on the bulkhead.

Spencer deposited a cup of tea on the locker top. 'Oh four thirty, sir.'

'Thank you, Spencer.' Thurston extended his arms above his head and for a moment studied the network of grey pipes crossing the deckhead.

'Going to be 'ot again, sir.'

'That much is obvious.' Spencer's round face was already flushed pink, and a single bead of sweat was beginning to course downwards in front of his ear. Thurston sat up, swung his legs over the side of the bunk and reached for the cup of tea. 'You'd be the first to complain if it was any different.'

Spencer grinned. 'Breakfast as usual, sir?'

Thurston grunted a reply as he drank some of the tea. 'How's the marmalade situation this morning?'

''Ave to consult me suppliers, sir,' Spencer said, tapping his nose in a conspiratorial fashion.

Thurston finished his tea, got down on the deck and

pumped out fifty press-ups, then another fifty sit-ups.

Spencer looked up from attaching a pair of rank slides to the shoulder straps of a clean pair of white overalls. 'Wears me out just watching you, sir.'

Thurston stood up, reached for a towel and mopped the back of his neck. 'You'd better be careful, Spencer. It's about time you did something about that middle-age spread of yours.'

'I've had that since *Ganges*, sir.'

Thurston pushed aside the fireproof curtain and went through to the shower. One of the luxuries that went with command of a ship of this size – no, in this climate it was a necessity. Even so, this was one of the few times of the day he could be sure of using it. *Inflexible*'s evaporators had not been designed to cope with the demands of two thousand men in the steamy heat of the Pacific, and the fresh water could only be turned on for limited periods each day. He would turn on the water, duck his head under and wash away the accumulated sweat of his few hours' sleep, knowing that as soon as he was dressed his skin would begin to turn slimy again, and long before noon Spencer's stiff creases would have dissolved and his clothes would be wringing wet.

'Good morning, sir.' The Officer of the Watch made his customary only salute of the day.

'Morning, Carstairs.'

'Course one-seven-oh, sir. Speed fourteen knots.'

'Thank you.'

The exchange had the familiarity of routine sanctified by years of tradition, though Carstairs wore the wavy rings of the RNVR and had sold vacuum cleaners or something until the war came.

On the bridge it was still dark, the eastern sky gradually turning from black to grey with the promise of dawn, the edges of the carrier's flat-iron silhouette sharply etched against the lesser darkness. Other ships of the fleet – *Inflexible*'s sister carrier *Invincible* a mile away to starboard, a couple of the cruisers – gradually came into view as Thurston's eyes became fully accustomed to the dim light. There was movement on the flight deck now as aircraft were brought up from the hangar and ranged ready for take-off, and the dozen fighters of the deck park were trundled out of the way for the first time that day. Fuelling hoses were run out across the deck and swelled with petrol pumped up from tanks many decks below in the ship's double bottom; there were sounds of machinery as the lifts at either end of the flight deck moved up and down and aircraft wings were unfolded.

Voices floated up to the bridge, very clear in the pre-dawn stillness, snatches of conversation. No shouted orders; the aircraft handlers were well practised and knew their jobs. A small group of pilots and observers, rostered for the early sortie and preferring wakefulness to a few more minutes in their bunks, clustered at the doors of the ready room with mugs of coffee. A little apart from them, their air gunners congregated in a similar fashion, parachutes resting against their feet. One of the observers wandered further out on to the deck, stepping carefully in his suede desert boots over a fuel line. 'Gangway, sir!' someone called. The observer stepped aside as an Avenger came abreast of him, big-bellied and ungainly with its undercarriage down.

The engine tests began. Two ratings lay across each tailplane to hold it down, the Corsairs' eighteen-cylinder Pratt and Whitneys working noisily up to full revs, the aircraft butting against their chocks and straining to overcome their brakes. Beside one of the Corsairs two of the air engineer officers conferred in low tones, flicking over the pages of the Form 700 technical logbook. The flight-deck Petty Officer was called over from the other side of the deck, and the Corsair was

9

manoeuvred out of the way and a replacement brought up.

Thurston left the bridge, looked into the Fighter Direction Room and the Plot, then went over the met forecast with the ship's Instructor Lieutenant, declining his offer of a cup of tea. It was all routine, part of a way of life which had become established and familiar in the last few weeks. The night had been quiet, a time for the hangar party to get to work on the routine maintenance of the carrier's aircraft, and for the aircrews to stand down, go below, eat and try to sleep as the steel bulkheads threw out all the tropical heat they had absorbed during the previous day.

Ten minutes until the first serial took off, a shred of the eastern sky beginning to colour, the last stars fading. A mile to starboard *Invincible*'s dark silhouette was following a parallel course, the other two carriers now in sight beyond her. Further off the Fleet's cruisers and destroyers were scattered, apparently haphazardly, but each with her allotted place in the screen. The sea was flat calm, with only the slightest of swells to create ripples on the still-dark water. Thurston took the day's first operation order from his pocket and began to check over its details in the dim light from the binnacle. He felt the first wetness beneath his arms, a trickle of sweat began its course downwards between his shoulder blades. Like everyone whose duties took him on to the open deck, he was wearing full anti-flash gear, mandatory since the Japanese had started their suicide attacks on the British and American carriers. Overalls – white for commissioned officers, warrant officers and midshipmen, blue for ratings, a useful instant recognition mark when everyone looked the same – the legs tucked into his socks, surname stencilled in blue paint over the left breast pocket and the single word CAPTAIN in larger letters across his back, asbestos gloves rolled up in one pocket for the time being, hood pushed down below collar level, and the respirator haversack slung over one shoulder with a blue-painted tin hat hung over the outside. It might protect against the more superficial effects of fire and explosion, but inside it, even before the gloves and helmet went on and the hood went up, you moved in a bath of sweat, the saltiness exacerbating the irritation from the skin rashes and insect bites everyone was suffering from, so that it seemed at times there was nobody aboard who was not constantly scratching.

A signal blinked from the flagship's shaded lamp.
  'Acknowledge.'
  Inflexible's lamp blinked in reply.
  'Execute.'
  Carstairs bent to the voicepipe, made the helm orders.
  'Revolutions for thirty knots once we've turned.'
  'Aye aye, sir.'
  All round *Inflexible* the other ships made the same turn, the destroyers furthest away varying their engine revolutions and advancing or delaying the movement to maintain their places in the screen. The entire Fleet must make the turn into the wind, in order for the four carriers to remain within the protection of its anti-submarine screen and anti-aircraft barrage during the vulnerable period when they flew off their aircraft. The aircrews climbed into their cockpits, fumbled with their straps.
  'Midships.'
  'Midships, sir.'
  Inflexible came out of the turn, and the slight sticky wind increased its strength as the ship worked up towards her maximum speed.
  'Start up Corsairs!'
  Ratings dropped from the wing roots on to the deck. Radial engines coughed, ran roughly for a few seconds,

11

and settled into their noisy rhythm. The pilot of the leading Corsair completed his checks and crossed his forearms in front of his face whilst a rating ducked under the wing, pulled the chocks clear of the wheels, dodged nimbly to one side and jerked his thumb towards the sky. On the bridge the Commander (Flying) dropped his flag, the engine roared and the Corsair began to gather speed up the deck. For those who watched from the bridge, and for the crews of the aircraft waiting their turn, there was always the anxiety that in these near-windless conditions he would not reach flying speed, always the heart-stopping instant when, airborne, the Corsair dropped below the level of the bows and out of sight, the almost palpable relief when the throttle opened and he climbed away to starboard to clear the way for those who followed.

0530. In the quartermaster's lobby the Marine bugler sounded Action Stations. Some of the ship's normal sounds were lost as the ventilating fans were turned off, and almost instantaneously the temperatures below decks began to climb. Parties of men took down the accommodation ladders, leaving only the vertical metal rungs inside the wells up which ammunition was passed to the 4.5-inch guns, sixteen of them, deployed in twin turrets at the four corners of the flight deck. Watertight doors and hatches were clipped shut, dividing the ship into a honeycomb of separate compartments linked only by telephone and voicepipe. The guns' crews closed up, ammunition numbers cradling the rounds in their arms, tin hats on their heads, anti-flash hoods obscuring their faces.

'Change of course coming up, sir.'
    'Carry on.'
    'Port ten,' Carstairs spoke into the voicepipe.
    'Port ten, sir.'
    Inflexible heeled into the turn.

'Midships.'

'Midships, sir.'

'Steer one-five-niner.'

'Steer one-five-niner, sir.'

The zigzag would continue day and night except during the times when the four carriers were flying off or landing on their aircraft. In twelve minutes the officer manning the lot would call up another alteration of course, this time to starboard, then another, after a different interval, and each time the entire Fleet would make the same turn.

The patch of sky in the east turned to pink and the orb of the sun rose out the sea with the suddenness of the tropics. The eastern sky was a brief glory of red and pink and gold. He exchanged a few words with Carstairs, then with the Navigator as he emerged from the chartroom.

'Stand them down from Action Stations, Carstairs. The Japs must be having some extra time in this morning.'

'Aye aye, sir.'

Thurston's eyes stayed on Carstairs for a moment. Carstairs was a full lieutenant, and a fairly senior one by wartime standards, yet he still had a good deal to learn, tended to be a bit careless and to cut corners, and there had been a hell of a row at Trincomalee just after Christmas when a planter who had invited three or four of the young officers to stay for a weekend had come home unexpectedly early from an inspection of his tea plants to find Carstairs in bed with his wife.

Carstairs must have become aware of his Captain's eyes upon him, for he turned his head a little away and looked out over the sea to port. Like most of the young officers, he seemed in awe of him, perhaps even a little afraid of him. Part of the awe was the proper and inevitable consequence of Thurston's rank; a post captain in command had, in theory, the power of life and death over his officers and men. In wartime, with *Inflexible* and her sister ships the favoured targets of Japanese aircraft, this could well be the literal truth. Another part of Carstairs' awe might be reserved for the man who wore the VC and two DSOs, who had survived two sinkings earlier in the war, who had been in command of ships at sea since 1939, and was still, even as the war dragged on through its sixth year. But things were never so simple, so absolute, and there was much which Carstairs did not know, and could not know, unless at some time in the future he commanded a ship himself.

Chapter Two

Sitting in the cockpit of Corsair C-Charlie, Sub-Lieutenant Geoffrey Broome could not contain his excitement. 'You're on the Ramrod this time,' he had been told just before lunch, and there was his name, chalked on the blackboard in the ready room, among the first eight, those who would be making the ground-strafing run over the islands instead of stooging over the task force on CAP. This was it, at last. He was a fighter pilot, about to take off on an offensive sortie against the enemy.

'Start up Corsairs.'

Ahead of him a rating, unrecognisable in anti-flash gear, swung the propeller. It caught, and slowly began to rotate. The rating stepped to one side, pulled the chocks away from the wheels, then dropped out of sight beneath the wing and clear of the undercarriage. Broome released the brakes and the Corsair began to roll forward. He pushed the throttle away from him, heard the engine note increase to a roar and watched the propeller disappear in a blur. *Select fine pitch for take-off, watch Ken Barnes's Corsair lift clear of the deck a few yards ahead. Just a whisper of a crosswind abreast of the island, touch the starboard rudder pedal to counter it. Rising off the deck now, a slight pitching fore and aft, then the uncomfortable drop ahead of the carrier's bows, into shadow for a moment. Pull the stick back, feel the aircraft respond and climb away. Look back at the carrier, already growing smaller, white bow wave creaming back as she steamed into wind at thirty knots, another Corsair coming off the deck.*

Broome turned to starboard to clear the way for him, continuing the climb. The CO's voice came through his headset, telling them to get themselves organised. Broome looked round, located the CO's aircraft with the large white-painted Q on its rudder, slotted himself into position abreast the fuselage, half a length behind, and put the propeller into coarse pitch. They were passing over the outermost destroyers of the screen, lean rakish shapes below them, steaming hard into wind with the carriers.

'Get down. Get down.'

The CO's voice again, and his right hand motioning up and down from inside his cockpit, a conductor's *piano, piano* motion, Broome suddenly thought. Down, down, right down to water level, below the Japanese radar which was sending out its pulses from the islands ahead, which would warn the flak positions of their approach. In training low flying had been anything lower than two hundred feet; now it meant coming down lower, lower, until the tips of the whirling propeller blades could be only inches above the sea, which was no longer smooth, and never still, rising and falling unpredictably with the gentle swell. One blink, or a fraction of a second's lapse of attention, and the propeller tip would touch. At three hundred and fifty miles an hour the sudden loss of forward momentum would flip the Corsair over on to her back, and she would go on down, into the blue water, and somewhere far down the pressure of thousands of tons of water would crush the life out of him. Stay alert, though, and low flying, real low flying in a Fleet Air Arm Corsair, was the most exhilarating sensation in the world.

Broome could not remember a time when he had not wanted to fly. At junior school there were balsa-wood gliders, bought with saved pocket money for a shilling;

friendly rivalry with other boys over which could fly the furthest. He would stand out in the garden and look out towards the gentle swell of the Downs, and dream of flying over them. RAF Tangmere was less than ten miles away; by the time he was eleven he had a bicycle and could spend entire days of the school holidays watching the silver Fury biplanes as they landed and took off. One day, one day. Everything was planned. He was going to Cranwell as soon as he reached the minimum age of seventeen and a half, and one day he was going to be among those nonchalant young men whom he sometimes pedalled past on his bicycle.

On holiday with his parents when he was fourteen, with five shillings in his pocket saved from his birthday, he presented himself at a nearby flying club, and asked if he could be taken up. Five minutes in a Tiger Moth, but that was enough. The war came, and the following summer he could, even from his parents' garden, watch the vapour trails from the British and German aircraft duelling far above. Once a Heinkel crashed into a field half a mile away. It lay on its belly among the ripe corn, propeller blades bent backwards by the impact, its glass nose smashed open. There was a policeman standing beside it and two men in flying kit with their hands above their heads. One of the Germans had blood on his face, both looked dazed, uncomprehending. He was fifteen. Cranwell had shut down because of the war; there were three more years to wait.

He thought only of the RAF, until a lieutenant-commander of the Fleet Air Arm came to his school to give a lecture to the sixth form. The Lieutenant-Commander had flown in Norway, and then in the Mediterranean. There were black-and-white slides of Hurricanes and Seafires taking off from carriers, an exciting account of the Swordfish attack which had destroyed the Italian fleet at Taranto. Broome was swayed, but not entirely won over. As soon as he was eighteen he applied to both the RAF and the Fleet Air Arm. The latter proved to be quicker in dealing with his application, so he found himself inducted as a naval airman second class, kitted out with bell bottoms, and posted to HMS *St Vincent* at Gosport to learn to be a sailor, and then, at last, to Kingston, Ontario, for training as a pilot. The Allies landed at Salerno the day he arrived at *St Vincent* and were slowly pushing their way up the long leg of Italy. The Second Front came as he was doing cross-country exercises in a Harvard. Would he get into action now? Back to Britain aboard a troopship, with one wavy stripe and a pair of bright golden wings on his sleeve. The first deck landings, aboard *Pretoria Castle* in the Firth of Clyde. Then, at long last, out to Australia in a succession of transport aircraft; Glasgow to Gibraltar, Gibraltar to Algiers and then Cairo, Cairo to Bombay, Bombay to Darwin and, finally, Sydney. They gave him a brief conversion course on to the Corsair, told him which ship and squadron he was going to, and put him aboard one of the escort carriers for the final leg of his journey, northwards into the operational zone.

And now, before he had even driven a car, he was flying an aircraft capable of four hundred and twenty miles an hour, with three 0.5-inch machine guns in each wing, with a two-thousand horsepower engine and two-stage supercharger which could pull it up to thirty-seven thousand feet. The Corsair was not a gentleman's aircraft, not like the delicate Seafire, with her elegant elliptical wing and undercarriage which was really too fragile for deck landing, which you were supposed to fly as if she were a beautiful woman. The Corsair was big, powerful, bent-winged and unforgiving. The American Navy had ordered her from her manufacturers as a carrier fighter and had then declared her unsuitable as such at the trials stage, passing her on to the land-based squadrons of the United States Marines and to the

Fleet Air Arm, which had had to prove that the Corsair could be flown from a carrier simply because she was too good an aircraft not to be used for her designed purpose. Even so, there had been many accidents, among both novice pilots flying her for the first time, and among the more experienced who had grown careless; one among Broome's course at Nowra had proved the rumour that the Corsair could not be pulled out of a spin.

Down low, inches above the sea, the CO's hand making its *piano, piano* movement once more, an irregular blur on the horizon ahead. A brief order from the CO, and they were pulling up away from the water. Ten thousand feet, looking down for the first time on the island. Ishigaki, the name which had been bandied about the ready room ever since he had arrived aboard *Inflexible* a week earlier. Now he was seeing it for himself, a place of low brown hills. On the plain between the hills was the airfield from which the Japanese took off to fly against the task force, and the American Marines who were pushing forward, inch by bloody inch, across the island called Okinawa, the last before the British and Americans reached the main Japanese islands themselves. Of course, the Yanks were keeping the business of dealing with the Japs on Okinawa for their own carrier-borne aircraft and had relegated the British to the less glamorous but equally hazardous business of knocking out the Japanese second-line airfields.

At ten thousand feet it was as hot as it had been at sea level, the sun cutting through the wide Perspex canopy a few inches above his head. There was the CO, and beyond him to port the other pair of Corsairs of the flight, Ken Barnes slotted in behind John Tracy as wingman, as Broome was behind the CO. Behind and a little above were the two pairs of the second flight, spread out in the same 'finger four' formation.

Another order, and they were going down again, diving

steeply towards the island. Broome found his mouth dry, and wished he had brought something to drink. He licked his upper lip, but it dried in an instant and seemed only to make things worse. He scanned the sky ahead and above. No Japanese, but the flak was still to come. The Japanese would have them on radar now, and the gunners would be ready at their positions, rounds being rammed into the breeches, belted ammunition laid out in trays, the gunners making the final checks to ensure that nothing obstructed the belt, just as they did at the 40 mm and 20 mm positions aboard *Inflexible*.

Down close to the sea again, that sensation of speed which had been lost at altitude, pulling the nose up slightly as the white curve of beach flashed below, the white changing abruptly to a steep slope of brown burnt grass. Small grey puffs in the sky ahead. The guns had started. Broome felt his stomach knot for a second, then they were past, and he was rising over the crown of the hills and dropping down into the basin beyond. There, through the haze, he could see the wide grey length of the runway, empty now, but no, there, right on the edge of the burnt grass, was the unmistakable shape of a twin-engined bomber.

The CO had slid round to port, lining himself up with the bomber. The guns were firing, a curtain of the grey puffs coming up at them. There were black shapes on the ground, long deadly black needles training towards them, regular flashes of brightness coming out of the muzzles. Broome moved his thumb to the gun button, touched the stick to put him in line with one of the flak positions. Around him he could hear the other Corsairs firing. He pushed his thumb forward, felt the aircraft judder and recoil, saw his own tracer hosing down towards his target. Out of the corner of his eye he saw the CO's tracer striking the metal skin of the bomber, then a sudden wumph, and yellow fire was spreading all around it. Ahead of him he saw something fall away from the gun position, realised with slight surprise that it was a man, and that he himself must have killed him. They reached the end of the runway, stick back once more, another gun firing at them from halfway up the hill, the whitish sandbags showing up sharply against the brown. A final burst at the gun, then they were clear, heading out towards the sea again. He'd done it. He'd ground-strafed Ishigaki and he was going home.

Climbing steeply, the nose pointed up towards the sky and the supercharger engaged. No point in trying to evade the radar; they went home at high level so they could not be bounced from above.

'Have we got everybody?'

One by one they answered, all seven of them. He had ground-strafed Ishigaki, and they were going home with no casualties.

'Keep formation,' came the CO's voice.

Broome's attention had wandered in his exhilaration. A touch of rudder, harmonised with the stick, and he was back in his place. Half an hour out and half an hour back, and a long iced drink when he got back to the ready room.

They passed over the 'veterinary' cruiser, making the required circuit of her while her gunners decided they were friendly. Even though their own aircraft were fitted with IFF, switched on as soon as they left the target area, the task force took no chances, and regarded anything approaching from the west as hostile unless proved otherwise.

There was something wrong as they sighted the main task force once more, a column of black smoke rising from the deck of one of the carriers.

'Is that us?'

One chance in four, but it was *Inflexible*, unless she

had changed her position with one of the others. In confirmation they heard the voice of the Fighter Direction Officer coming up from the ship.

'Can you keep orbiting for the time being. We've got a bit of a mess to clear up.'

The attack came forty minutes after the Ramrod had flown off, just as the Avenger squadron was preparing for its second sortie of the day. The CAPs were airborne; the radar had picked up the enemy while they were still eighty miles away, and so the guns were ready. *Irresistible*'s Seafires got in among them, shot a couple down, but still they came on, a dozen or more twin-engined bombers, and fighters all around them. Some of the fighters had bombs slung underneath and flew in a tight, rectangular formation, other fighters weaving around and above them. Suiciders; the Japanese called them *kamikaze*, the Divine Wind.

'Tin hats on. Pipe all personnel on deck to take cover.'

The ship's main broadcast clicked on, the bored voice of one of the bosun's mates floated out across the deck. 'D'ye hear there. All personnel on deck take cover. All personnel on deck take cover.'

Thurston pulled up his anti-flash hood, picked his tin hat off his respirator haversack and fitted the strap under his chin. The rim rested on the old scar over his eyes and tended to give him a headache after a few hours, but he could not order tin hats for everyone else and not wear one himself. Cotton wool went into his ears; he brought the gloves out of his pocket and pulled them over his hands. Now everyone around him was unrecognisable, only eyes, mouths and noses visible in the circles of exposed flesh inside the white hoods. Down on the flight deck the aircraft handlers were jumping clear of the Avengers ranged ready for take-off, running for the shelter of the island. The twin

40 mm guns on the platform to starboard were tracking back and forth, the Director Layer's head against the rubber eyepieces of his sight, the man indicating to the rest of the crew with one hand. The gunners were standing ready, the breeches open, brass cartridges bright in the sun. The twin barrels found their target, locked on, the movements becoming smaller, more precise.

'Shoot!'

The sixteen 4.5-inch guns opened up, followed a moment later by the close-range weapons. Suddenly the whole world was noise, scarcely muffled by the cotton wool in Thurston's ears. The Japanese were coming in low, a couple of hundred feet above the water. The kamikazes' formation had split up, the pilots selecting their targets: first the carriers, because if they knocked them out the whole fleet would be open to attack, then, a long way after them, the cruisers and other ships. *Inflexible*'s rudders were large, which made her surprisingly manoeuvrable for a ship of her size, and Thurston was taking evasive action, never holding her on the same course or speed for more than a few seconds at a time. It made her a difficult target, but it also made it more difficult for her own gunners to keep the Japanese in their sights. The Corsairs and Seafires were holding off, clear of the barrage from the guns.

Now there were only the Japanese. He saw one of the bombers go into the sea, one engine on fire. At that height there was no chance for them to recover from a hit, to evade further attack and try to limp away on the remaining engine. One of the kamikazes came in ahead of the carrier, growing large in his vision, then she exploded as a round from one of *Inflexible*'s guns detonated the bomb at her belly. No respite, because a second later there was another fighter ahead, another radial-engined Zero. No bomb this time; she must be one of the escorts. Red balls of tracer were rising up towards her, but still she came on, straight toward the

23

bows, little points of flame coming out of her wings.

'Port thirty.'

'Port thirty, sir.'

The Chief Quartermaster was quick, the helm went over sharply and the ship began to turn. But the Japanese pilot was good, and the Zero was turning too, still firing, finding the Avenger which was in position on the catapult for take-off, fully fuelled and bombed up, the crew strapped into their seats, unable to move. Bullets ricocheted off the deck, sending unexpected spurts of dust up from the steel surface.

'Shit!' someone said behind Thurston.

A puddle appeared beneath the Avenger's belly, spreading slowly as more petrol dripped on to the deck, rolling back and forth with the ship, shining wetly in the sun. The ship was still turning. Thurston dropped his head to the voicepipe, snapped out another order. When he looked back there was a patch of flame on the deck, feeding on the petrol dripping from the tank. The Avenger pilot had the canopy open, had released his straps and was beginning to climb out. His head and upper body were out of the cockpit, behind him the observer was doing the same, whilst the gunner had got his turret doors open and was pulling himself out backwards, hands on the Perspex sides and overalled buttocks emerging. The fire was spreading, flames licking upwards to the aircraft's belly.

'Shit!' the man behind Thurston said again.

There was a bang, and yellow flames all round as the fire reached the petrol tank and the tank exploded. The aircraft lifted into the air and came down tipped on to its nose. The gunner was lying on the deck on one side, starting to drag himself away. The observer was sagging backwards, the pilot turning round to pull him away, flames licking at his sleeves. The pilot let go, half climbed, half fell, over the side of the cockpit and on to the wing. The observer slumped back inside, only his head visible as a black object above the flames.

Another detonation, and another, as the fire set the bomb load off, and pieces of metal rose high into the air, flashing in the sunlight. A second later the sound of the blast reached the island. When the smoke cleared, there was nothing left of the Avenger, only a ragged hole in the deck. The gunner's head and upper body lay face down a few yards away, the legs gone, a red stain on the deck where they had been.

The guns were still firing, with no interruption in the barrage, and there were more Japanese aircraft all round the carrier.

'There's another, sir!'

Another Zero, bomb beneath her belly, coming in amidships from the port side, heading for the island.

'Hard a starboard.'

'Hard a starboard, sir.' The Chief Quartermaster's voice was very calm.

The ship began to turn, but the Zero pilot was altering course to follow, his port wing going down and blunt nose moving left. Part of one wing tip disappeared and black smoke began to come out of his engine, but still he came on, filling Thurston's vision, so close now that he could see the pilot's helmeted head black beneath his canopy.

The kamikaze ploughed into the flight deck abreast the island, within ten feet of another loaded Avenger, and the bomb beneath its belly exploded. The deck went up in a sheet of flame from punctured petrol tanks.

Chapter Three

Quite suddenly, the attack was over, the remnants of the Japanese formation turning westwards and heading back towards Formosa. On *Inflexible*'s flight deck the petrol fire burned, licking closer towards the surviving Avengers with their bomb loads and filled tanks.

'Right, let's get started.'

Out there? one of the men thought, looking out from the door in the side of the island at the spreading fire, now blackening the wings of the nearest aircraft.

'Get a move on! Do you want the whole lot going up?' Chief Petty Officer Ernest Pritchard grabbed one end of a fire hose from the spool on the bulkhead and placed the nozzle into the hands of one of the surprised men. 'Now, get started!' He was shouting at them, pulling out another hose, telling them to get a move on. His anti-flash hood covered most of his face, but he could feel the heat of the fire on the few square inches of exposed flesh, the heat which was now coming through the hood and the rest of his clothing. The air itself was hot, drained of its oxygen by the fire which was feeding on it.

'Come on, come on!'

The hoses were unravelling, the first feeble jets of foam coming from the brass nozzles, swamping the edges of the fire so that there was a fringe from which the flames had been beaten back. Rivulets of foam and petrol ran over the deck. A few yards away Lieutenant-Commander (Flying), recognisable by the lettering on the back of his overalls, was manning a hose, playing it over a patch of flame, turning round at the same time to marshal the members of his Aircraft Handling Party.

'As soon as we can get to them, we'll have to get them over the side.' Lieutenant-Commander (Flying) jerked further round, spoke sharply to the Petty Officer at his elbow. 'Go up to the bridge. Ask Commander (Air) to ask the Captain to turn the port side into wind.'

'Aye aye, sir.' The Petty Officer bolted towards the island, secretly glad of a legitimate reason to be out of the fire.

Before those bombs go off, Pritchard thought to himself. One of the Avengers was on its back, resting on its rudder and the top of its cockpit canopy, moving slowly over on to the starboard wing tip. It was incredible that the bomb load had not gone off already.

All the hoses were out, swollen with foam, shooting it out over the fire. They were moving forward, step by step, beating the fire back. But there was still petrol all around, flames beneath the aircraft, the rubber tyres ringed with fire. There was the smell of burning rubber and the petrol itself, overlaid with the fainter but unmistakable smell of burnt flesh which came drifting down the deck from the hole where the catapult had been.

Thurston looked over the side, saw the screen of fire around and between the Avengers, made a brief calculation and came to the same realisation as Lieutenant-Commander (Flying). The wind was northerly; if he brought the ship round to starboard, the flames would blow back towards the island, away from the aircraft.

'Starboard ten.' Not too tight a turn, not with the damaged aircraft balanced unstably on the deck.

'Starboard ten, sir.'

The ship began to heel. The direction of the wind changed, the heat on the left side of his body increasing.

Sweat was streaming down inside his overalls, his mouth was arid, his eyes irritated by the smoke. What were conditions like for the fire party, down there in the fire itself?

A young petty officer from the flight-deck party had appeared breathless from the head of the ladder, was speaking to the Commander (Air). 'Lieutenant-Commander (Flying) says can you ask the Captain to turn the ship so that the wind comes in over the port side, sir.'

'It's all right. I'm already doing it.'

'Aye aye, sir.' The Petty Officer disappeared down the ladder once more.

Down on the deck one man began to cough, turned aside and staggered a couple of paces before he fell forwards on to the hot steel surface. Someone else rolled him on to his back, dragged him away towards the island.

Turning the ship had done its work. The wind was blowing the fire away from the aircraft, the flames still feeding on the petrol which ran across the deck as the ship heeled, but very gradually being beaten down by the blanket of foam which the hoses were spraying. The aircraft handlers were running round the edges of the fire, reaching the aircraft, one man pulling away the chocks, another pulling himself up on to a wing and reaching into the cockpit to release the brakes.

'Keep clear of the guns!' Lieutenant-Commander (Flying) shouted.

Almost at the same moment the ammunition in the inverted aircraft started to go off. One man stood still for a second, reached down towards a thigh which had suddenly turned red, then he was down, more 0.5-inch bullets impacting in his body as the heat of the fires set them off, a pool of blood spreading all around.

The first aircraft dropped into the water with a heavy splash. The aircraft handlers were already at work on a second, others moving the three undamaged aircraft forward towards the lift.

'How are we going to shift that fucker?' someone asked, shielding his eyes as he contemplated the Avenger which was on its back, bullets still coming intermittently from the machine gun in its starboard wing.

They used the boat-deck crane, gingerly attaching strops to the fuselage on both sides of the wing roots, another around the tail, trying to ignore the four five-hundred-pound bombs inside the bomb bay, almost certainly knocked off their crutches and rolling freely inside. The crane operator pulled her very slowly and carefully towards the port side, the metal and perspex of her structure grating on the deck to set their teeth on edge, finally lifted her clear of the deck, swung her over the side and let her go.

The shipwright's party came up from below, mixed a large quantity of quick-setting concrete and poured it into the scoop left in the armoured deck by the kamikaze.

'How long before we can start flying again?' Thurston asked.

The Warrant Shipwright pushed his hood back, reaching under it to mop his brow with a large khaki handkerchief. 'As soon as the concrete's had time to set, sir. About half an hour.'

Lieutenant-Commander Murillo, the American Liaison Officer who controlled a party of half a dozen telegraphists and coders inhabiting a hot little compartment on the deck below, was staring open-mouthed.

'Now do you see why we have armoured decks?' Thurston said to him.

'When we get hit by those things,' Murillo said wonderingly, 'we get six months in Pearl. You talk about flying in half an hour! Jeez!'

The American carriers had wooden decks, which a kamikaze would slice right through, exploding inside the hangar or deeper still. One American fleet carrier had been so badly damaged by a kamikaze that she had sunk in less than an hour, others had suffered heavy loss of life and been put out of action for months. In the past the Americans had claimed that *Inflexible* and her sister ships were a liability in this war because they had insufficient anti-aircraft guns to defend themselves against kamikazes, and that their armoured decks meant they could not carry sufficient aircraft to make their presence worthwhile. But the kamikaze had failed to penetrate *Inflexible*'s four-inch deck armour, all but a few men had heard the pipe and been under cover when it happened, and the damage control organisation had worked. The fire party had gone straight out on to the deck and dealt with the fire, and the aircraft handlers had got the damaged aircraft over the side and the rest out of the way before their bomb loads and full petrol tanks could cause further damage. Even up forward, where the Avenger's two-thousand-pound bomb load had gone off, the armour had absorbed the worst of the blast, so that the damage was confined to the deck and the forward end of the hangar immediately below it. They had lost eight men, but it could have been a lot worse.

'I'm afraid the forrard lift's completely jammed, sir,' the Warrant Shipwright went on. 'The lift itself isn't much damaged. The hydraulics seem all right, but the top surface of the lift and the deck to the port side are so badly buckled that it won't move. We tried shifting it, but it's jammed solid, and even if we did get it to go down, it probably wouldn't come up again. It's a dock-yard job, but we can smooth the bumps out with concrete so the aircraft can go over it.'

The aircraft handlers had begun to trundle the un-damaged Corsairs towards the after lift, one at a time, wearily in the hot sun. Thurston dictated a signal to the flagship, telling the Admiral what was happening, then turned his attention to the aircraft which were still air-borne. The Corsair's fuel tanks held enough petrol for five hours at cruising speeds. Thurston looked at his watch. The Ramrod had now been gone just over two hours. They should be all right.

'They'd better watch their fuel consumption just in case,' said Commander (Air) who had come out on to the main bridge from his own small platform on the port side. 'No playing games with the superchargers. I'll tell Horace to pass the word.'

Horace was the ship's Fighter Direction Officer, a former schoolmaster who cut a comically unmilitary figure in uniform and was rumoured to work on prob-lems in differential calculus at breakfast, in the same way as the more serious members of the wardroom pored over crosswords.

At twenty thousand feet the sky was empty, the sun shining through the cockpit canopy from one side so that inside it was hotter than ever. Sub-Lieutenant Broome was growing bored. A couple of Seafires from *Irresistible*'s CAP had come up and had a look at them, decided they were friendly, and gone away again. They were on a different frequency, so they could not talk to them. The eight Corsairs were circling, throttled well back to save fuel, a wide area of sky, cloudless blue above, a flat sheet of darker blue far below, dotted with the needle shapes of the ships. He was hot and he was thirsty, and if they stayed up much longer he was going to have to use the pee tube which the Chance Vought Aircraft Corporation of Connecticut, USA, had kindly thought to provide in the Corsair's cockpit. He was fly-ing the aircraft with one hand, the other resting in his lap, or drumming occasionally on one knee, the sleeves

31

of his flying overalls pushed up above the elbows, the front zip pulled undone as far as his waist, so that the steel of the parachute release box made a pleasant cool patch against his stomach.

What were they doing down there? Horace had come up on the radio again and told them there had been a kamikaze, and something else as well, but since then everything had gone quiet. The smoke had cleared; there was only a wisp of brownish vapour coming up from the funnel. *Don't go to sleep.* There could still be more Japs, sneaking up while the task force was licking its wounds after the last attack. Perhaps this afternoon he would have been better off on CAP, with the chance of having a go at a Japanese aircraft, instead of ground-strafing an empty airfield. But there would be other chances, there were still plenty of Japs out there, and they all said the Japs would fight for every last inch, even for a couple of square miles of coral, and would not let themselves be taken alive.

'All right, you can come home now.' Horace's voice, sounding a little weary.

Four Corsairs had taken off from *Inflexible*'s deck, climbed to thirty thousand feet as high CAP over the task force, briefly waggled their wings at those waiting to land on, eyes drawn anxiously to the fuel gauges now. *Push the stick forward, adjust the throttle, watch the altimeter unwind and the sea come up, notice the guns on a couple of the cruisers training towards them.* They must know who we are, he thought with a flash of irritation. Down to a few hundred feet now, pulling back the stick to feel the g-forces mash him against the seat as the wings came up. The CO made his approach, landed neatly up the centre of the deck, came to a halt. *Now push the hood back, pull the flaps out, lower the undercarriage and arrestor hook, select fine pitch on the propeller.* He was flying down *Inflexible*'s port side, noticing the empty black hole, three men standing at its edge, where the catapult had been when he took off, and the irregular patch of paler grey beside the island, just to one side of the white square which had been painted to fool the Japs into thinking there was a third lift amidships. *Turn to port, and position the Corsair for the approach*. There was the white ensign streaming back from the mast, dead in line with the ship's course, the batsman on his platform on the port side, orange bats raised ready to guide him in. Left a little. Now he was too low, touch the stick back. The bats were held out at ninety degrees. Bang on! Above the ship's stern now. The bats crossed in front of the batsman's face. Broome shut the throttle, felt the Corsair sink down towards the deck, and the jerk as the arrestor hook found a wire. Then he was down, the wire running out behind, men climbing out of the catwalk to unhook the Corsair.

'Down wires and barriers!'

He was taxying forward, over the two steel mesh barriers which had suddenly dropped to the deck. *Brakes on, press the button to fold the wings, press the release button on the harness and start to climb out.*

Broome went to the ready room for debriefing by the Ops Officer, then found it was six o'clock and flying was over for the day, apart from the CAPs, which were still airborne over the task force. It seemed an anticlimax, to follow the rest of the squadron aft to the wardroom, through the watertight doors which were still shut, seeing the ship's officers and ratings still on duty in their various positions, to order an iced lemonade in the anteroom from the bar steward and sign the usual white chit for it, with his bar number in one corner, one-six seven, and look forward to dinner in a couple of hours' time. He noticed one of the ship's officers standing by himself beside the serving hatch, meditatively sipping from a pint glass of Coca-Cola. He was an RNR lieutenant,

with the purple stripes of an engineer between the in-
tertwined rings on his shoulder straps. He wouldn't
have seen anything of the kamikaze, but Broome found
himself, full of curiosity, asking what it had been like.

'Big clang from up top. Clang-g-g. Made your teeth
rattle. Then the Commander was on the broadcast telling us that it was a kamikaze. That was all.'

The engineer was a muscular-looking man a little
shorter than Broome, with a mop of untidy black curls
and a mashed nose. His accent told Broome that he
came from somewhere up north. Not Yorkshire, somewhere else. Broome could not remember seeing him
before, nor speaking to any of the ship's officers. The
aircrew tended to form a separate group within the
wardroom, and in any case he was only just getting to
know the other members of his own squadron.

'I was flying when it happened. I just wondered.'

'They seem to have cleared up the mess now. I'll
mebbes go and have a look up there before dinner.'

The engineer lifted his glass to his mouth, a sign that
the conversation was over. Broome moved back into
the huddle of pilots around the bar.

'D'ye hear there? This is the Captain speaking. Good
evening. First, I wish to thank you all for your wonderful efforts in dealing with the two attacks on us this
afternoon. In particular, I wish to thank the flight-deck
fire party, who got the fire out, and the aircraft
handlers, who made sure the fire didn't spread to the
aircraft on deck. Because of their efforts, the damage
we suffered, and the casualties, were kept to a minimum. Had things been otherwise, our damage would
have been very much more serious, and we would in all
likelihood be limping home for repairs.'

'Would that we were!' someone said in a fierce
whisper.

'As it was, we were able to start flying again within
two hours of the kamikaze hitting us, thanks to some

further good work by the shipwright's party, and, despite the loss of the forrard lift, we are still able to play our full part in operations.' Thurston found he had run out of words. 'That is all.'

The ship stood down from Action Stations. Thurston handed over to the Officer of the Watch, went down the ladders to the flight deck, where the hangar party was at work among the Corsairs of the deck park, hundreds of rounds of 0.5 link being fed into the magazines in the wings, tool boxes open beneath each fuselage. One engine cowling was off, the squadron Chief Air Fitter talking to one of his men about changing the plugs.

'Good evening, sir.'

'Good evening, Chief. Carry on.'

'Aye aye, sir.'

Most of the men had taken advantage of the stand-down to get out of their overalls and now clambered over the aircraft clad only in boots and shorts, long streaks of oil on their torsos, but taking care to avoid contact with the bare metal, which would still be hot enough to fry an egg for hours yet. Thurston came to the edge of the paler patch, cautiously put a toe on to it and pressed down. His boot left no mark, though the wags had been at work earlier: there was 'Dusty was here' in large letters at one end, and 'Watch out Hirohito' somewhere else.

'Good to see that,' he said to the Chief Air Fitter. It was not quite in accordance with traditional naval discipline, but it was a sign that morale among the flight-deck men, who had been closest to the kamikaze, was still strong.

He went on towards the bow, walking up the great open space ahead of the deck park, trying to remember when he had last come as far from the island as this. It must have been days ago. The distance was little more than a hundred yards, but already the island seemed smaller and far away, casting its dark shadow up the deck as the sun dropped towards the horizon.

The Warrant Shipwright and his party had filled the hole from beneath with a double layer of timbers, one fore and aft, the other athwartships, supported by vertical members and diagonal buttresses inside the hangar below, and were preparing to pour another load of concrete on top. For yards around, the deck was already patterned with the paler grey of the concrete settled into the ripples left by the blast. The wags had been busy again, and there was a large KEEP RIGHT painted on a wooden box lid and stuck up on a post.

'I never thought I'd find myself navvying when I joined,' the Warrant Shipwright said, 'but I'm going to get down on my knees tonight, sir, and thank God and the man who thought of armoured decks.'

Thurston thought of *Crusader*, which would not have stood a chance against one of these. Out here the escort carriers stayed with the Fleet Train, beyond the range of the Japanese.

'We didn't find much to bury, sir. A few bits, all jumbled up. You could fit most of them into a shoebox. And one of Mr Thompson's dog tags, and a bit of someone's shoe.' Mr Thompson had been the Flight Deck Engineer Officer and in charge of the catapult.

Thurston's messenger, Boy Maxwell, began to look a little green. There would be a funeral later that evening, eight canvas bundles at the ship's stern, six of them containing little besides sand, the few anonymous pieces of flesh which had been recovered shared out between them in a curious gesture of propriety, and there would be eight letters for him to write when he got back to his sea cabin, while the incident was fresh in his memory.

He went down the deck once more, reached inside his

overalls to scratch the heat rash on his chest. Dusk had come, with the same suddenness as the dawn, the air definitely cooler, but the heat of the deck still coming upwards through his boots. The paint on the port side of the island was blackened and bubbled, bare metal showing through in a few places. There were splinter holes too, but incredibly there had been no further casualties.

Passing the deck park his foot brushed against something, barely visible in the shadow of a Corsair's wing. He poked it into the light with his toe, squinted at it. It was about two inches long, irregular and charred black. He bent down, dropped on to one knee to take a closer look. There were small white objects along one edge, and something else, dull gold and a little larger, and he realised that he was looking at all that remained of the pilot of the kamikaze aircraft. Part of his jawbone, three natural teeth and a gold crown. Maxwell must have realised what it was in the same moment, for he jerked his head aside, and coughed heavily as though he was about to be sick.

'I'm all right, sir,' he said hastily as he straightened up.

Maxwell was sixteen years old, and had only joined the ship in Australia three months earlier.

For some reason no one wanted to touch the jawbone, though various men came to look at it, standing a little away from it in a kind of superstitious awe, and it remained on the flight deck until the Chief Air Fitter picked it up in an old piece of newspaper and threw it over the side.

Thurston went back up to his sea cabin, stripped off his sodden overalls and stood under the shower, anointed his feet with a fresh coating of Edinburgh cream – the humid conditions had set off a dormant infection and there were raw patches the size of half-crowns on the soles of both feet – then changed into shorts and a shirt. The Japs didn't fly at night, and what was left of their fleet was bottled up in harbour, so that the task force had a few hours' respite in which to prepare for the next day's flying. Later tonight there would be the burials. The padre would do them, but he would have to be there too. Spencer brought his supper, the usual tinned mixed vegetables and beef stew out of a tin, followed by pineapple chunks out of another tin and evaporated milk. The task force had been at sea continuously for forty-five days, broken only by four days at the Americans' advanced base at Leyte in the Philippines, and most of the fresh food had run out weeks ago. Surgeon Commander Grant, *Inflexible*'s Principal Medical Officer, had forecast worsening health problems among the men if the situation was not remedied, but nothing could be done until *Inflexible* went back as far as Manus, or preferably Sydney.

Chapter Four

The burials took place after dark, lit only by the ships'
shielded navigation lights and the faint light of phos-
phorescence coming up off the water. The padre was a
young man, still in his twenties, who had come from a
curacy in a country parish, and his reading of the burial
service was slow and rather hesitant, pausing in the
wrong places and then speeding up, until Thurston
found himself wishing he could take the prayer book
out of his hands and finish it himself.

*'Man that is born of woman hath . . . but a short time
to live, and is full . . . of misery . . .'*

Eight bundles on the deck, the red crosses on the white
ensigns draped over them showing grey in the darkness,
containing all that remained of Lieutenant Thompson,
Flight Deck Engineer Officer, Sub-Lieutenant McCall,
the pilot of the Avenger, and Sub-Lieutenant Bishop
and Leading Airman Jamieson of his crew, together
with Naval Airmen Cooke, Knightley, Martin and Ste-
phens of the flight-deck party. A semicircle of men in
khaki shirts and shorts around them, a shaded green
light at the base of the island which reflected off the
dulled metal of the bolt of a rifle in the firing party, a
Marine boy drummer wetting his lip as his moment
approached, his face in shadow beneath the white-
topped cap which seemed too big for him.

*'Forasmuch as it hath pleased Almighty . . . God of
His . . . great mercy to take . . . unto Himself the souls of
our dear brothers . . . here departed . . .'*

Eight bundles sliding down the chute into the water forty feet below, the ensigns whipped away at the last moment, the distant splashes, one by one, then the Last Post, hanging in the still air for a long time.

'Ready . . . Present . . . Fire!'

The rattle of the rifle bolts, the clatter of brass on the deck, three times, then the brazen blast of Reveille through the stillness. The drummer finished, brought the bugle away from his lips, the mouthpiece angled at forty-five degrees away from him, and then snapped it down to his side. The padre, relieved that the worst was over, rattled through his closing prayers, the men on the fringes of the semicircle already moving away quietly into the shadows.

Back in his sea cabin Thurston took out his pen, rummaged in one of the desk drawers for a writing pad, and made a start on the letters. He had not really known any of the dead men. Three were simply faces among the flight-deck party he would not see again. Of the rest he had met McCall and Bishop when they joined the ship at Sydney, the usual formal welcoming on board, a handshake, where did they come from, where had they trained, how long had they been in the Navy. Leading Airman Jamieson had done a particularly wicked take-off of the Commander (Air) at a concert party in Trincomalee, and Knightley had once appeared before him and been given seven days' cells for trying to smuggle a bottle of whisky on board. Thompson he had come into contact with from time to time, usually when there were problems with the catapult machinery, but with two thousand men on board it was impossible to know more than a proportion of them, or even to be able to put a name to many. So the letters had to be conventional expressions of regret, with a careful use of words to make them appear personal and individual when really they were not. But they had to be done, and done carefully; a letter from the dead man's

Captain was likely to be handed round among friends and other family members, whether by McCall's parents in St Andrews, or by Martin's sister and next of kin in Market Rasen, Lincolnshire.

It was late by the time he had finished, blotting the letters and addressing eight envelopes. He took out the most recent of his wife's letters, one of a bundle of half a dozen which had come up with the last lot of mail. Both the twins were walking now, and Kate had enclosed a photograph of Thomas supporting himself on a chest of drawers, looking slightly startled as Andrew bore down on him from the other side of the room. It still seemed strange, almost embarrassing, to have a son of nineteen who had just been commissioned as a sub-lieutenant, and an eighteen-year-old daughter at medical school, and then two more sons who were only just getting past the crawling stage. He hadn't seen them since their baptism, and he doubted whether he could have told them apart in the photograph, had Kate's letter not mentioned that Andrew was wearing the light-coloured shirt and Thomas the dark. They were supposed to look like him, or was that simply conventional wisdom, that sons were expected to look like their fathers, and daughters like their mothers? In any case they both had hair like Kate's, fair with hints of red in it, rather than the dark brown which George and Helen had inherited from him.

Inflexible had returned to the Clyde for a few days after the refit in America, making final preparations before sailing for an as yet unknown destination, although there had been strong indications that she would be joining the Eastern Fleet at Trincomalee. Kate had come up to Greenock with the twins, a journey which must have been hell, eighteen hours on trains with not just one fractious baby but two, even though Helen was with her. Thurston had rung his father, and asked him if he was up to making the much shorter but equally awkward journey from Langdon. The old man had brusquely replied that nothing was going to stop him from baptising his latest grandchildren as he had baptised the others. The refit had lasted five months and children had been born to the wives of several members of the ship's company in that time, so after Divisions that Sunday morning, there were five or six to be baptised in the ship's bell, on the flight deck in the open air, with a bright sun overhead and a brisk wind coming up the Firth to flutter the blue collars of the men and the black stoles and white surplices of the clergymen. Thomas Henry Thurston, unmindful of the vows taken on his behalf, had duly disgraced himself by yelling at the full pitch of his lungs from the instant the holy water touched his forehead, thereby setting all the others off, so that the occasion lost some of its dignity, but that was the only unhappy note in the day. In the afternoon Thurston and Kate had gone for a walk ashore, then back to Kate's hotel room, where Kate had fed the twins and got them off to sleep, and they had made love, lingeringly, drifting in and out of sleep afterwards; later there had been dinner with Thurston's father and stepmother and Helen, another walk outside under a crescent moon. *Inflexible*'s orders for the Eastern Fleet had been confirmed the next day, and the day after that she had sailed.

Thurston got up from his desk, went up to the bridge for a last look around before he turned in. Bingham, the Signals Officer, was on watch, a regular with four years' seniority as a full lieutenant, and competent despite an air of treating everything as a game.

'Goodnight, Bingham.'

'Goodnight, sir.'

A brief look into the FDR and then the Ops Room, fuggy with stale air and greenish with the light of the radar displays. Everything under control, everything as usual, despite the damage of a few hours ago, now fading away into the past. In Europe Hitler was dead, Goering had surrendered to the Americans and the war was in its dying days, but out here the war would go on, until the last shreds of resistance had been smashed out of the Japanese on their own islands. Aboard *Inflexible* eight men were dead and had been buried, but life, and the war, went on for the rest.

He went back to his sea cabin, took off his shirt and shoes, laid his watch on the locker top and stretched out on his bunk, rolling over on to one side so that his upper body got the full benefit of the stream of slightly less sticky air stirred up by the fan in one corner. Perhaps it had something to do with the losses, but tonight he could not get Kate out of his mind.

Years ago, in Malta before the war, he had come home very late one night; *Retribution* had been at sea on night-firing exercises which hadn't finished until after eleven, and by the time she had got back into harbour and everything was sorted out it must have been nearly two before he was walking up the drive, with on one side the grapevine which never produced edible grapes because the house had inadvertently been built on an ant heap and the ants ate them before they were ripe, and on the other the high wall of local honey-coloured stone. Then too it had been a hot sticky night, with the scirocco blowing out of the Sahara and picking up moisture as it crossed the Mediterranean; he had unhooked the high collar of his whites as he came up the drive, and slapped away a mosquito which immediately homed in on the exposed flesh of his neck. Kate had been sleeping naked because of the heat, with one of the balcony doors open, and she must have pushed the single sheet down in her sleep at some time, so that her breasts showed alabaster white in the moonlight that flooded the bedroom. He had stood looking at her for a

43

time, fair hair spread out over the pillow, looking sensuous yet somehow supremely innocent at the same time. She had stirred sleepily as he got into the bed alongside her. 'What time is it?', 'Just on two.' 'How did it go?', 'All right.' Still half asleep she had rolled over, moved an arm across his back and come to rest against his chest, her nipples growing hard and her mouth moving upwards to find his.

He found himself aroused at the memory, tried to resist the temptation for a moment. There were footsteps in the flat outside, and he turned over to put his back to the doorway, then unfastened the buttons of his shorts and pushed his hand between his thighs as he relived it, wishing that it was Kate's hand on him instead of his own, his mouth opening slightly in a smile as he came. He opened his eyes reluctantly, knowing that Kate was far away, whilst he, his body rank with sweat, was in his hot little sea cabin, five seconds from *Inflexible*'s bridge, under the dull red light from the deckhead which was meant to preserve his night vision, the sticky wetness lying on his stomach, and the usual vague sense of shame, even uncleanness, which always came in the aftermath.

In the carrier's after engine room Lieutenant Frederick Holland made the rounds of the gauges, then dipped an enamel mug into the barrel of salted water which stood in one corner. The thermometer next to it stood steady at a hundred and twenty-eight degrees, not particularly hot as engine rooms went; he'd known the temperature in here get up to a hundred and seventy, when *Inflexible* had been going flat out for longer than usual, just north of Manus and practically on the equator. Who'd be an engineer? The deck officers and the flyers complained enough about the heat out here, but they didn't know the constant steamy heat of the machinery spaces, all day and every day.

Inflexible was steaming at fifteen knots, a comfortable cruising speed, most of her boilers shut down, with variations of only a revolution or two either side as the Officer of the Watch maintained station on the flagship. Her engines could produce a hundred and twelve thousand horsepower, though tonight most of that power lay sleeping. *Inflexible*'s machinery could give her twenty-five knots on two-fifths of her boiler capacity; the remainder was needed to force another five knots out of her to bring her up to maximum speed. A hundred and twelve thousand horsepower, three huge Parsons turbines driving triple screws and nearly seventy men, all, for the four hours of this middle watch, in his charge. In the Merchant Navy, if he'd stayed with the same company, the most he could have expected was to be second engineer of one of their old coal-burning tramps with a single clapped-out reciprocating engine, flogging back and forth across the Atlantic with the slow six knot convoys. And if he had never stuck his neck out in the first place and gone to sea, he might still be nothing more than a fitter at Parsons, married to a typist or a girl who worked in a shop, or still living at home with his parents.

Holland's father had been the bright boy of his family, bespectacled from an early age, and serious. On leaving school at thirteen, instead of going into the shipyards of Wallsend like his father and elder brothers, he had obtained a post as office boy in a bank, walking the three miles to the city centre each morning for a seven-thirty start, and back again at six. Forty years later he was senior clerk in one of the bank's smaller branches, the owner of an immaculately kept 1930s villa in Whitley Bay, a regular worshipper in the Methodist church, and treasurer of a local friendly society. He had hoped, after pulling himself up into the lower echelons of the middle classes, that his only son would follow him into the bank, with the advantages of a grammar school education and a School Certificate in his hand; it was clearly a severe disappointment that his only son's interests so obviously lay with machinery. At the age of eight he had taken his parents' wedding-present clock to pieces and attempted to put it together again, and within a year or two he had, unknown to them, augmented his threepence a week pocket money by repairing bicycles belonging to neighbours. After he had failed the scholarship exam at the age of eleven, the School Certificate was an impossible dream, but there were posts available for boy clerks, and the boy might yet work his way up from the bottom. His headmaster at Whitley Bay Central School for Boys, however, had considered that the obvious place for young Frederick, who was so good with his hands, and in the top two or three of his class in carpentry and metalwork, was in an engineering apprenticeship. Holland junior had made his feelings clear by declaring that he was not going to be stuck behind a desk in a bank for the rest of his life. The headmaster had a brother who was a marine engineer, a few words were said, and the day after Holland left school he had found himself walking through the gates of Parsons engine works to begin his five years as an apprentice.

Parsons built marine steam turbines, and at the end of his apprenticeship it had been the most natural thing in the world to sign on as a junior engineer in a tramp steamer. His parents had, unexpectedly, approved of this; a son who was a ship's officer, even if an engineer, was a considerable improvement on a son who was a fitter, and when the war came, and he had been commissioned in the RNR as a sub-lieutenant, his mother's delight had known no bounds.

But Holland had had enough of Whitley Bay and the desperate respectability of his parents and his parents' friends. As his father had broken free from the Wallsend shipyards, so he had broken away from the world his parents had created. And he did not intend to go back to it. The Navy had been a passport into a different world. During *Inflexible*'s refit in America there had been weekends in gracious houses in Massachusetts, with gracious American hostesses and girls who took no notice of his Geordie accent. Later, in Ceylon, there had been weekends in plantation houses, and once, thrillingly, an expedition into the surrounding jungle after elephant. When the RNR commission went with the ending of the war, so too would all that go, and it would be back to being a second engineer in a third-rate shipping company. Could he stay in the Navy?

It was something he had been thinking about, secretly, for a long time. He could do the job, he'd proved that, through five years of war, but after five years he knew well enough that it was not simply professional competence that the Navy was interested in. Looking around the wardroom it was only too obvious what they expected of their regular officers, all those languid Dartmouth types in the anteroom, one leg with its black glacé half-boot draped over the arm of a chair, leafing idly through a copy of *The Field*, and exchanging remarks in clipped accents. They had all, of course, been to the right schools, had the right parents, and came from the right parts of the country, Sussex, Surrey, Devon, certainly not the suburbs of Tyneside. But surely the war must have changed things? The old order was being swept away, and that must affect even the Royal Navy.

He made his tour of the engine room, glancing at the men in their positions, eyes on the gauges, dipped a handful of cotton waste into a bucket and mopped his face with it, then pushed the wet wad as far down the back of his neck as he could get it. He had once confided his ambitions to the RNR engineer with whom he shared a cabin.

'You, a straight-striper? Fred, you want your head

examining! The pay's lousy, and you'll be up against all those chaps from Dartmouth and Keyham whose daddies were admirals and who know all the right people. What chance have you got among that lot? Even if they did take you, you'd never get beyond lieutenant-commander, and you'd be out on your ear in the first lot of defence cuts. Get yourself into a decent company, and the sky's the limit. And if you want to swank around in uniform, you're better off with the P & O.'

Jim Jennings had said what he thought and most of the non-regular engineer officers on board would have echoed him. But why not, why the hell not?

Chapter Five

From twenty thousand feet Lieutenant-Commander Minoru Terauchi looked down on a flat expanse of blue, quite empty now that the islands had passed away into the distance. Flying eastwards, the morning sun filled his cockpit, so that even inside his thin summer flying suit his body was sticky with sweat. The sea was empty, but the sky held perhaps fifty aircraft, obsolete Zero fighters for the most part, with the modern Kawasaki 100s, like the one he himself flew, ranged around the flanks of the formation.

Each Zero pilot had knelt before take-off for the final blessing from his commander, drunk the ritual cup of sake, and had the headband with its rising sun motif knotted over his brows. All of them had been strangers to Terauchi, boys fresh from training who remained with the unit for only a few days before their missions. They had been prepared and were ready to die for their Emperor, but there had not been the time or the resources to train them fully as pilots, so the course they steered was uncertain, their handling clumsy and lacking the practised grace of the expert Terauchi knew himelf to be. The old Zeros, weighed down by their bomb loads, were slow and unmanoeuvrable, so that the escorts continually had to throttle back to avoid outpacing them and leaving them naked before the attacks of the British fighters, which would soon come, long before the attackers were within sight of the warships.

Terauchi had seen it all too many times. Most of the kamikazes would be shot down into the sea before they reached their targets. They would indeed meet death for their Emperor, but theirs would not be the imperishable glory of a successful attack.

Terauchi had seen the Emperor only once, at a military parade shortly after he joined the Navy and before he finished his training as an officer. Most of his memory of that day was blurred now; the sea of backs and legs parted at ease as they waited for hours in the hot sun, the hard-baked earth and dead brown grass which divided the formations, naval whites close by, the soldiers in khaki further off. Bands played, the formations came to attention, swords and bayonets flashed in the sunlight, and a group of mounted men appeared in the far distance, riding slowly between the files, so far off that it seemed impossible that they would eventually reach his own formation. So the waiting had gone on, a little wind stirring the dust raised by the horses' hooves, the powdery dirt greyish khaki like the uniforms of the soldiers. He did not know how long it was before they reached him, but there, almost unexpectedly, was a slight bespectacled man on a chestnut horse, his eyes almost closed behind the spectacles. For a moment the horse stopped, reined in, and the man, one hundred and twenty-fourth in an unbroken line from the first Emperor, descended from the union of the first Emperor and the Sun Goddess, was looking directly at Cadet Terauchi, studying him, appraising him, and in that moment Terauchi would have died for him.

But Terauchi had not died, then or later. He had flown against the American Fleet at Pearl Harbor, and again at Coral Sea and Midway, where four of Japan's carriers had been sunk. When there were no more carriers left, Terauchi and the remnants of his squadron had shifted ashore, the trained nucleus absorbing green young pilots fresh from training and converting them into veterans. Now there were not enough of them, and insufficient time to train any more, so that all that was left was the pride and honour of the Japanese warrior, which would lead him to smash himself and his aircraft on an enemy's deck for his emperor.

There was a sudden flash in the sky ahead of them, then more, and suddenly the British were there, the bent-winged Corsairs climbing up from one of the carriers, ready to attack. Terauchi spoke briefly into his radio, told the pilots to keep formation, to be ready for the attack. Few of the kamikazes would get through a determined fighter attack. They lacked the skill to manoeuvre their aircraft with the split-second timing and instant decision-making required to evade the fire from the Corsairs. Most had never even fired their guns

Terauchi pulled down his goggles, switched on his gun-sight. The Corsairs were still climbing, blunt noses pointed skywards, white vapour stretching out behind. One of the Zeros was drifting away to starboard, forcing a second to move away to evade a collision. Terauchi spoke sharply into the radio. The first Zero turned sharply back to port, too sharply, for the pilot on his port side, seeing him come close suddenly, instinctively banked away. Terauchi muttered a curse, then pushed his throttle forward, feeling the satisfying kick as the Kawasaki responded with its full power. He picked out one of the Corsairs, brought his aircraft round a little to port to place himself broadside on, and pressed the gun button. The aircraft juddered with the recoil. He saw his tracer passing harmlessly above the fuselage, cursed again, touched the stick forward.

A rush of satisfaction as the bullets struck home behind the cockpit, then he was past the Corsair, lining himself up to attack a second, banking sharply to follow it round to port, pressing the gun button in. Out of the corner of his eye he saw a bright flash of flame, then an aircraft going down towards the sea, the blue and white roundels marking it for a Corsair. One less to prevent the kamikazes from getting through. A second's lapse from concentration had been enough; one of the Corsairs was behind him, opening fire. He jerked the Kawasaki round to port, then to starboard before he was out of the original turn, pulled the nose up, and glanced behind to see that the Corsair had broken off to seek an easier target among the kamikazes.

There below were the enemy ships, the four carriers in the centre of the formation. Terauchi uttered another curse. Yesterday he had gone in low over one of the four, blown up a loaded bomber as it waited on the catapult; one of the kamikazes he had escorted had hit the centre of her flight deck among the parked aircraft. An American carrier would now be limping away badly damaged, out of the fight, but the British ship was still there, steaming parallel with the other three, maintaining her speed and station, more aircraft on her deck. Terauchi ordered his formation into a dive, the Corsairs still snapping at their heels, more aircraft coming up from one of the carriers, Seafires this time. Behind him an explosion shook his aircraft, necessitating some instinctive action with stick and rudder. One of the kamikazes had disappeared, a few dark pieces of wreckage floating slowly downwards.

Down, down, and they were among the guns of the fleet. The fighters did not frighten Terauchi, but gunfire from the fleet did because it could not be reduced or restricted, it simply went on, the impersonal curtain of fire coming up, some of it aimed at an individual aircraft, some indiscriminate. The Japanese formation split, the kamikazes heading for their allotted targets, the fighters following them in, to distract the gunners, draw away their fire, and to deal with the British fighters which could still appear inside their own barrage. Terauchi picked the same ship as yesterday, the second carrier in from the port flank, the one which remained defiantly afloat and operational despite his efforts, her deck marked with irregular patches which had not been there yesterday. Puffs of black smoke hung in the sky above. One round exploded close by and his aircraft rocked again; he could almost smell the smoke. He saw another of the kamikazes blow up, still five hundred feet above the deck of the ship it was aimed at. Terauchi pushed the stick forward, banking to take himself towards the carrier's bow. Nothing on the catapult today, but there were still the aircraft on the deck, loaded with explosive petrol and ammunition, ready to take off to assault Terauchi's own airfield. Sweat prickled his eyelids. He pushed a finger up inside his goggles, massaged the lower lid. Two hundred feet, the carrier's blunt bow ahead, red tracer coming up from the gun positions on either side. Terauchi opened fire, saw his tracer rebound off the armour plate.

A sudden impact, acrid smoke all around, the stick useless in his hand for a second. There was the carrier's bow, his duty calling him to bring the aircraft round a little to port, aim it at one of those gun positions, and push the stick forward into the final dive. But his mind had somehow separated from his eyes and hands. He found himself moving the stick to starboard, away towards an empty patch of sea. The aircraft responded sluggishly, a hole in its wing on the port side, part of the aileron flapping loose, flames spreading away from it. Petrol was running into the cockpit, cold around his feet.

He levelled out, just above the water. It was much rougher than it had appeared from altitude, crests seeming to rise above him. He eased the stick back into the landing attitude, felt the fuselage beneath his feet touch the water. Then the aircraft pitched forward, nose down, going down, down, the water darkening around him. The smell of petrol was making his head swim. He groped for the canopy release, found it at last as the water inside the cockpit rose up past his chest, and groped with the other hand at the release box of his harness. The canopy lifted, he felt the restraining straps give way and lifted up his arms to swim clear. But something still held him back. He pulled again at his flying overalls, found more straps and remembered his parachute harness. *Turn the top of the box through ninety degrees, then bang it.* The box on this harness was stiff, and it always took two hands, so that his head was nearly bursting before he got it to turn, the aircraft going deeper all the time. Both hands pressed on the spring-loaded top. There was a release of tension, the straps fell away, he kicked his legs clear and bent almost double to swim out through the canopy which had half closed on him once more.

The sea's natural buoyancy carried him upwards, and his head broke surface in a trough. He gasped out water and worked away with his legs to keep himself afloat, reaching for the inflating tube of his life jacket. Above him the sky was suddenly emptied of aircraft, only the ships' guns intermittently firing. It took a moment before he realised what had happened to him. Shot down. Defeated in battle. And he had deliberately turned aside from a warrior's death on the carrier's deck to ditch his aircraft on the water and live. Terauchi let go of the inflating tube and reached for the officer's dirk at his waist. It wasn't there. It must have come out of its scabbard as he was struggling in his panic to get out of the cockpit. He swore again, pulled the laces of the life jacket undone and wriggled free from it. Treading water still he said a brief prayer to the gods of Japan, then put his face under, opened his mouth wide and raised his arms above his head to take himself down. But the buoyancy of the water carried him back to the surface each time. He gasped water, then put his head back under, tried again, but still it made no difference. Each time he tried he obstinately came back to the surface, a little more breathless. He saw a boat moving over the water towards him and re-doubled his efforts, lashing out with his arms as the boat's oars came near, trying to fend them off, screaming at the crew in the Japanese they would not understand. Something touched his overalls, moved across his chest and then found a hold.

'Gotcha!'

The thing was pulling him towards the boat. He brought his arms in, tried to get himself free of it, but the men in the boat had stopped pulling their oars and one of them was leaning out from the side, grabbing at his left arm. Terauchi tried to push him away, but the Englishman held on, pulled him in towards the boat so that he was scraping against the high wooden side.

'Come on, Nip. You're not going to join your ancestors this time.'

Terauchi had studied engineering before he joined the Navy, and as part of his degree had spent six months in England at Imperial College; he understood the man well enough. The man's wrist was an inch from his mouth. He moved his head suddenly, and bit in hard. The man uttered a word Terauchi did not understand.

'Ungrateful little bugger, isn't he,' another man said.

Two of them sat on Terauchi as the rest pulled slowly back towards the destroyer. Half drowned as he was, half crushed beneath the weight of two large English bodies, he felt like crying for the first time since he was a small boy, but he was a Japanese warrior, and he would not let them see his distress.

Thurston lowered his binoculars to his chest. 'Yeoman,

ask *Pendragon* to send him across to us. And if he shows any reluctance, tell him, one, we shot the Jap down, two, he was attacking us, and three, we've got a Japanese-speaker on board who can interrogate the fellow straight away.'

A live Japanese prisoner was a rarity, for a Japanese fighter pilot to survive to be taken prisoner rarer still, and much valuable intelligence might be got from him while he was still in shock from his ditching.

'From *Pendragon*, sir. *Will transfer prisoner by jackstay. Beware, this dog bites!*'

'Does he indeed.'

The destroyer closed, altering course and revolutions until she was steaming at the same speed as *Inflexible* and exactly parallel. There was a crack as the line was fired from the carrier's boat deck, a brief scrabbling for it on the other side.

'They aren't taking any chances with this one.'

'Easiest way of keeping him quiet,' drawled Lieutenant Bingham, who was Officer of the Watch.

Terauchi was strapped securely inside a Neil Robertson stretcher, arms against his sides, unable to move an inch in any direction as the stretcher swayed thirty feet above the water, moving gradually upward towards the cavernous opening in the carrier's side, dark in shadow beneath the overhang of the flight deck.

The Englishmen around him were large and fair-skinned, their faces burnt to lobster red by the sun. They smelled of sweat, and they were efficient. They disconnected the stretcher from the jackstay lines, carried it across a dark space below decks, then up several ladders to a hot little cabin inside the island superstructure. They released him from the stretcher, turned him over, and, with someone's knee in his kidneys, handcuffed his hands behind his back. A thin young man with officer's badges stood in the doorway and said slowly and carefully in Japanese that the door would now be locked and there would be an armed sentry outside at all times, with orders to shoot him if he tried to escape.

Shoot him? That was what Terauchi wanted. He should have died with the aircraft, on the deck of this very ship, or else, if the gods had favoured him, he would have drowned before the Englishmen's boat had reached him. When the young officer had gone, and a key had rattled in the lock behind him, Terauchi sat up on the bunk, swung his legs on to the deck and cautiously stood up. The cabin was as bare as a prison cell, containing only the bunk with its mattress, pillow and single sheet, and a chair which was bolted to the deck, Terauchi discovered when he kicked one of the legs experimentally. There was no scuttle, only four empty bulkheads painted a uniform pale green, a ventilator placed high up above the door, a galvanised bucket in one corner, a hole drilled in the door itself, at what must be eye level for the Englishmen, and a metal bracket sticking out over the foot of the bunk where an electric fan must have been. Nothing.

'We've put him in the Navigator's sea cabin, sir,' the Major of Marines told Thurston. 'Locked in, with a sentry outside.'

'I like that,' the Navigator protested. 'Why *my* sea cabin?'

'We've shifted your gear to the chartroom,' the Major of Marines said soothingly. 'Plenty of space there.'

'You're always complaining about the heat in there anyway,' said the Gunnery Officer.

'Just because my sea cabin is a wretched little hole, it doesn't mean I want it taken over by the Imperial Japanese Navy, thank you very much.'

'Has Vickers managed to get anything out of him

yet?'

'Not as far as I know, sir. He's a pretty sorry-looking specimen at the moment. But he's not saying a word, not so far, at any rate.'

'Perhaps he doesn't understand Vickers' Japanese,' Bingham suggested.

In Sydney that February, *Inflexible* had acquired, along with an American liaison officer, signals ratings and various other groups of men with unexpected and slightly nebulous duties, a party of a dozen or so Japanese-speakers, who now stood watches in a particularly hot and airless compartment inside the island, listening in to Japanese communications. Most of the wireless traffic was in cipher, but from the amount and sources of the traffic they could gather a surprising amount of intelligence material.

'He's not talking, sir. I haven't managed to get a word out of him. He's a lieutenant-commander according to his badges, but beyond that nothing, not even his name.' Vickers blushed a little. He was a gawky, narrow-shouldered young man, awkward in tropical shorts which on him were more than usually baggy. He had been an undergraduate at London University, recruited solely for his language skills and put through a crash course in spoken Japanese before being given an immediate commission and sent out to join *Inflexible*.

'Keep on at him. Does he understand you?'

'Yes, I think so, sir.'

'And it must be getting pretty hot in that cabin by now. He should be stewing nicely.'

'Yes, sir.' Vickers looked as though he was feeling rather sorry for the Japanese.

Terauchi lay on the narrow bunk, sweat running off him into the mattress, trying to keep as still as possible and to breathe as little of the stifling air as he could. His watch had been taken from him and he had no idea how long he had been there, only that it must be many hours as the sentries outside had changed more than once. He could hear movements on the deck outside, an occasional crash of boots as the Marine sentry came to attention, brief exchanges in English. Sometimes when he looked across to the door there would be a single eye at the spyhole. It was rarely the same eye twice. Some were brown, some the peculiar washed-out blue common among the English, one had been green. Twice the door had been opened, allowing a blessed gush of less foetid air into his prison. Once the thin young man came in and fired questions at him in uncertain Japanese whilst a Marine, cap peak down on the bridge of his nose so that the upper part of his face was hidden, stood in the doorway, a gleaming bayonet directed towards Terauchi's stomach. Another time a second Marine gingerly released one of Terauchi's wrists from the handcuffs and shackled the other to the metal pipe running vertically down one of the bulkheads while the other covered him with the bayonet. He deposited a tin plate on the bunk and the two went out, locking the door behind them once more. Teruachi looked at the food with distaste: a reddish ooze streaked with off-white fat, stained green by the liquid coming from the pile of peas next to it. An hour later the two Marines came back, looked at the untouched plate.

'This son of heaven don't like corn dog.'

'Don't blame him.'

They handcuffed Terauchi's arms behind his back once more, and left him alone.

The attack had failed. At intervals aircraft took off and landed, there were other sounds of engines being run up and maintenance being carried out, and once the clatter of a spanner falling to the metal deck, its echo very loud. Another time the guns opened fire, the noise reverberating through the island, bringing Terauchi brief hope, but the gunfire had faded away, and there was silence once more. He must wait, and seize his chance.

He must have dozed, despite the heat, for the crash of boot heels woke him, then the familiar triple rattle as the sentry outside presented arms. Another eye at the spyhole, this one grey, the iris rimmed with darker grey.

'Might as well take a proper look at him,' said an authoritative English voice.

'Aye aye, sir.'

The key rattled in the lock and the door opened outwards. Terauchi felt a surge of envy towards the Englishman, the owner of that grey eye, who stood in the doorway, face crinkling in distaste at the smell which lay heavy in the air, envy for that crisply laundered shirt, the sleeves rolled up and pressed into geometrically precise two-inch turns, a single vertical crease running down each leg of his shorts. He was very tall, hawk-nosed and lean and there was a lot of dark hair on his arms and more where his shirt collar opened at the neck – the English were a disgustingly hairy race – whilst a short horizontal scar on one side of his jaw showed very white against a reddish Englishman's tan. Blurred marks of old tattooing showed below one sleeve. Terauchi saw the four stripes on his shoulder straps and instinctively bowed deeply, clumsily because his arms were locked behind his back.

Thurston's initial reaction was surprise at how small the Japanese was. He must be almost a foot shorter than he was, wearing nothing more than a rather grubby loincloth, patched whitish with dried salt deposits, his body unmuscled like a young boy's and almost hairless.

'Ask him who he is,' he told Vickers.

Vickers translated into slow Japanese.

Terauchi remained silent.

60

'Did you check his clothes for labels?'

Vickers flushed more deeply. 'I'm sorry, sir. I've only done *spoken* Japanese. I don't read script, and none of the men do.'

Thurston frowned. 'Ask him again.'

The question was repeated. Terauchi remained silent, features composed into an expression of blankness, trying not to allow his face to betray his understanding of the enemy language. Let the English continue their stupid games. He, Terauchi, would beat them yet, just as the Imperial Japanese Navy would destroy this ship and kill these English officers, perhaps within a few hours, once the new day dawned and the kamikazes returned.

The young officer rattled through the same questions as before. Name? Rank? Where had he taken off from? What type of aircraft had he been flying? They knew that of course, because it was the guns of this ship which had shot him down. The Captain's immaculate shirt was darkening beneath the arms even as Terauchi watched, which cheered him a little. He was standing close enough for Terauchi to read the time off the watch on his left wrist, twenty minutes past nine, thirteen hours since he had been shot down.

'All right, Vickers, leave Tojo to stew a bit longer.'

The two filed out, the Captain first, the other following. The sentry's boots crashed, the key rattled once more.

Twenty minutes past nine. Wait a little longer, until the traffic through the flat outside had ceased with the night, and the sentries were growing sleepy and less alert. Terauchi smiled, manoeuvred himself back on to the bunk and shut his eyes.

Chapter Six

Marine John Wright pulled the barrel of his rifle back towards him and then pushed it away, trying to relieve the cramp which was beginning to gnaw at his biceps. Bloody Jap. If it wasn't for him John Wright would have been where a man should be at this hour, which was in his hammock and making zeds, instead of which he had had to do up his kit, polish his boots, apply a fresh layer of blanco to his webbing and turn to for four hours' guard so that the little bastard didn't top himself. The flat was quiet now, the only sound the whirring of the fans which came through the open doors of the sea cabins, whilst the light from the deckhead bulbs was dark red to safeguard night vision. He shuffled his toes inside his boots, scratched his crotch with one hand – the starch from his shorts was playing havoc with his dhobi itch. If this was tropical paradise, the Japs could keep it.

And he was fairly certain now that Jackie was two-timing him. There had been that Air Force wireless operator sniffing round her the last time he was on leave, and Scampton was a good deal closer to Jackie than the Pacific Ocean. He thought of how Jackie had giggled as they lay at the edge of the cornfield, shaded by a clump of trees, kissing and exploring, how she had moaned and thrashed after he lifted her skirt and went inside . . . 'Oh come on, come on, harder, oh my Johnny, I love your cock . . . ' And now she would be saying the same things to that bloody crab, wrapping her legs round him and pushing on his backside to get more of him inside her. He'd kill that crab if he got hold of him, and then he'd give it to Jackie good and proper, to teach her not to mess with him. She wouldn't like it at first, she'd try to fight him off, but she'd be begging him for more, and he'd give it to her, oh yes he'd give it to her, and no rubbers this time.

Wright noticed a strange gurgling noise coming from inside the cabin. He turned, put his eye to the spyhole. The light inside was very bright, coming from a single naked bulk above the bunk, and it hurt his eye for a second. The Jap was lying on the bunk, his loincloth fallen away, body jerking up and down, white gobs of spittle on his chin, teeth clenched, the strange gurgling coming from between them. Wright vaguely remembered the second or third first-aid lecture of his basic training. *He's having an epileptic fit.*

The keys to the cabin were hanging on the keyboard at the far end of the flat. The Colour Sergeant had told him on no account to open the door when he was by himself, but to call for assistance and wait until it arrived, but the Jap looked like he was choking and there wasn't time to wait until someone came. Wright crossed the flat in a few long strides, grabbed the keys, then put down his rifle, bayonet resting against the bulkhead. The Jap was still jerking, there was more foam around his mouth and the gurgling had become a high-pitched whine. Wright wrenched open the door, moved inside for a moment, then hesitated, suddenly unsure, trying to remember what you were supposed to do with an epileptic fit. Then there was sudden blinding agony as the Jap's bare foot caught him full in the groin, he doubled up, and then there was a second burst of pain beneath his ear as the foot hit him a second time.

The sound of Wright's fall jerked Thurston out of sleep. He sat up sharply, pushed himself off the bunk and reached the open door in time to see a naked shape flash past him. He saw the light glint on the dull metal of the handcuffs behind his back, and gave chase. The ladder to the next deck down was at the other end of the flat, a dark well opening in the deck, with a waist-high metal coaming on three sides. The Japanese had not been blindfolded when he was brought aboard; he knew where the ladder was. He had had a good start, but his strides were much shorter and the inability to use his arms held him back. Without shoes Thurston's feet were sliding on the damp cortecine, forcing him to slow down. In a couple more strides the Japanese would reach the head of the ladder. Desperately Thurston dived at his legs, a fraction too late. He made contact with one heel, but the Japanese kicked back at him and the sweat-slick foot pulled itself clear of his hand. Thurston landed heavily, sliding painfully on his bare chest for a couple of feet. The head and upper body of the Japanese disappeared into the well, his legs rose grotesquely pale above the deck, then disappeared. *Bloody bloody hell*. Thurston got to his feet and turned as he heard footsteps behind him.

The Ops Officer was hastily buttoning his shorts. In the red light his body was flabby and soft, unfit-looking, though he was little more than thirty. 'What's happening, sir?'

'Bloody Jap's just chucked himself down the ladder.'

'Deliberately?'

'I would think so,' Thurston snapped. He went to the head of the well. The Japanese was lying crumpled at the bottom, a dark stain spreading on the deck next to his head.

'Get hold of the PMO, and a stretcher party.'

'Aye aye, sir.'

When the Ops Officer had gone back to his own sea cabin where there was a telephone, Thurston slid down the ladder on his hands, twisting at the last moment to avoid landing on the Japanese. The blood was still spreading, thick and treacly-looking in the red light, which meant he must still be alive. He got down on to one knee, reached out to the Japanese's wrist, thought he found a pulse, faint but still beating.

The Ops Officer came back. 'The PMO's on his way up. I had a look in there on my way past. He must have enticed the sentry in and then clobbered him. There's a bootneck with a very sore head just waking up.' He looked down at the Japanese. 'And with his hands manacled. Makes you think. Must have been a karate expert.'

Thurston wished the Ops Officer would shut up. It seemed hotter than ever, the smell of sweat lying heavy around them. There were sounds of movement on the deck behind, people coming out of the FDR to see what was happening, then going away as they were called back to their duties.

'A depressed skull fracture,' the Surgeon Commander pronounced, after squatting down beside Thurston and running his fingers gently over the Japanese's head. James Grant was an ascetic man from Aberdeen, and his accent always became more noticeable when among his patients. 'Likely mean an operation. Pressure on the brain. Have to get him to the sick bay and have a proper look at him. Did it deliberately, did he?'

'Looks like it.'

'Aye. Funny people the Japanese. Fanatical, some of them. We'll get him below, and see what we can do for him. Not that he's going to show us much gratitude.'

'Keep me informed.'

'Aye, sir.' The stretcher-bearers loaded the Japanese up and took him away. Thurston went slowly back up the ladder.

The Ops Officer was waiting at the top. 'If there's nothing more, sir, I'll go and get my head down again.'

'Goodnight.'

'Goodnight, sir.'

Thurston looked into the Navigator's sea cabin. Marine Wright was sitting on the bunk, another man alongside him. His face was grey and he had been sick down his shirt at some time.

'The Jap looked like he was having a fit, sir. Wright here went in to make sure he was all right, the Jap kicked him in the balls and then clocked him one on the head.'

'The oldest trick in the book, and you fell for it.'

Wright looked up wearily, stiffened at the sight of his Captain. He was probably expecting a court martial for this. His head drooped, and he was sick once more.

'Take him to the sick bay, and he can be dealt with in the morning.'

Thurston went back to his sea cabin, splashed some water over his face and chest, and stretched out on his bunk once more. He looked at his watch: fifteen minutes past two. Almost immediately the telephone buzzed.

'Captain, sir, PMO here. I've got Stockley here, and he agrees with me that we'll have to operate on this fellow. We're just about to scrub up. Stockley's going to do it.'

Stockley was the senior of the ship's two surgeon lieutenants, and the specialist surgeon.

Grant was explaining what he and Stockley were going to do. 'A piece of the broken bone is pressing on the brain, so we're going to lift it to get the pressure off. It's a mite fiddly but it's a perfectly standard procedure, and provided it's done at once there should be no problems.'

'Do you want me to slow the ship down?'

'I think we're all right as we are, sir, but no sharp turns, if you can.'

Thurston put the telephone back on its hook and lay

66

back, listening to the familiar noises, the whirring of the fan and the annoying click it made as it turned on its bracket, reached the end of its traverse and turned back. Precisely six seconds between the clicks. One of the torpedo-men had looked at it, fiddled with the turning mechanism for a time, but had finally said there was nothing he could do about it.

He scratched again at the rash, then held his left arm up towards the light, squinting at the ridge of scar tissue which ran across the untanned inner side of his wrist and the regularly spaced blobs either side where the stitches had gone in. Two and a half years on it was difficult to remember he had done that himself, in the time of despair and desperation after the last Malta run with *Marathon*, difficult now to comprehend what had driven him to it, which was a mark, he supposed, of his recovery. He was over *Connaught*'s sinking now, as much as he ever would be. The bad moments still came, when he was back on the raft with a dead Royal Marine bandsman slumped against his chest, or seeing his dead men filing past him in a long line, each bringing up his right hand in a salute and shouting his name and rate, as they had done the day before sailing from Gibraltar, but the weight of guilt at being alive had lifted, and was now only a shadow in the back of his mind. For the Japanese pilot it would not have been despair but his own country's conception of an officer's duty, a different kind of desperation from his own which had made him throw himself head first through twelve feet of space to split his skull on a steel deck.

He let the arm fall back to his side and shut his eyes. Earlier in the day the news had come through that the war in Europe was over, in the flat unemotional language of an Admiralty communiqué. He should have been elated, or filled with relief at least, but out here, embroiled in another war, the news didn't really register. He supposed George would be celebrating, in the unthinking fashion of very young men. Of course,

George was only just nineteen, able to let off steam and enjoy the comparative freedom of being a commissioned officer undergoing a course ashore after two years at sea as a midshipman, although the submarine course he was doing at the moment did have the reputation of being a fairly exacting one. He supposed also that Edward Masters would be home soon from his prison camp, if he wasn't home already – there had been various bits of news in the last few days about POWs being freed and flown back by the RAF.

When the war's over, Masters had said. Thurston had been due to go across to New York on the *Queen Mary* and take over *Inflexible*, but there had been some sort of delay when he arrived at Gourock, minor engine trouble or something, and he had been told that he didn't have to stay aboard, he could do what he liked provided he could get back within a few hours. Kate was too far away, and Langdon at the extreme limit of his range, but he had taken the risk, thinking that it was a long time since he had last seen his father, and that it could be even longer before he saw him again. Masters had also been on leave, from the staff of the 1st Airborne Division, a lieutenant-colonel now, resplendent in red beret and paratrooper's wings, 'the oldest jumper in the division', or so he claimed. Masters had been a contemporary and close friend of Thurston's second brother, had had his active service in the last war in Palestine with the Desert Mounted Corps, and had stayed with his cavalry regiment for another four or five years before resigning his commission to return to his family acres in Northumberland. A keen Territorial, he had gone out to France in 1939, got back through Dunkirk, and then moved sideways into the infant airborne forces. Masters had invited him to supper – beef, from one of his own cattle ('Cow broke a leg').

After a wet day it was a fine night, a bank of cloud rolling away to reveal a clear evening sky, and Masters suggested they take a turn round the terrace after supper.

'Won't be long now. It's just a matter of waiting for the weather and the tides. We're not involved in this, more's the pity. They're keeping us in reserve for something else, otherwise I wouldn't be on leave now.'

Thurston knew what Masters was referring to. A vast area of southern England seemed to have become an armed camp. Coming away from it on the train, Thurston had kept thinking that he was going in the wrong direction, that he must be the only man in British uniform going north instead of south. George would be in it, if only on the fringes; normal convoy sailings were being suspended and the escorts diverted to close the Channel to U-boats and any other German vessels which might try to get in among the invasion fleet.

'If it comes off as it should do, the war could be over in a few months, and when it's over I'll be needing someone else to run the place. Arthur Ridley's not getting any younger, and really he's just hanging on until there's someone available to take over.' Masters stopped for a moment to light a cigarette, shook the match out and dropped it into the grass, then continued. 'The fact is, Bob, I think you're just the man. The place has been run down since long before the war – it's only because of the war that it's managing to break even and make any money at all. Arthur's done a good job in holding it all together, but what the place needs is someone with a fresh mind, who hasn't any preconceived ideas and who knows how to get the best out of people.'

'My mind's certainly fresh,' Thurston said. 'I don't know the first thing about farming.'

'That wouldn't be a problem. There's plenty of courses at Cirencester which you could go on, and in any case it's not a farmer the place needs, but someone to manage it, who can get the farmers to farm, and the keepers to keep, and the forestry on to a profitable footing. You can run a ship, and how many men is it - two thousand-odd?'

'About that.'

'And you wouldn't expect to be able to do all the jobs aboard. It's not a matter of doing it yourself, but making the men underneath you do it. Think about it. I won't need an answer straight away, that can wait until the war's over. There's a house which goes with the job. Arthur's in it now, but he'll move out to one of the cottages. Salary negotiable, shall we say.'

'What did Masters have to say for himself?' Thurston's father asked the next morning.

The vicar had put down his newspaper, masticated the last of his toast and finished his cup of coffee, signalling that he was now prepared to make conversation. There were only the two of them at the table, at opposite ends, an expanse of starched white damask between them – Maud, Thurston's stepmother, would have breakfast by herself later on.

'He's asked me to take over the Hermitage. When the war's over, of course.'

'He has? I take it you told him it was out of the question.'

'Actually, I told him I'd think about it.'

'That would mean your leaving the Navy.'

'It would.'

His father's manner towards him had remained unaltered for as long as he could remember, and despite the clerical collar the old man remained all too obviously the soldier he had been before his ordination, marked as such by the cavalryman's bowed legs and the military moustache he had retained even in the teeth of episcopal displeasure.

'Good God, Robert,' he finally burst out. 'Do you realise what you're contemplating?'

'I do.'

'You do realise what you would be throwing away?

Dammit, you'll have your flag in a year or two.'

'More likely five or six.'

'Surely not as long as that? Mountbatten's younger than you are, and isn't he a full admiral?'

'Mountbatten's an acting full admiral, and a substantive captain. He's also the King's cousin, and he has the ear of the Prime Minister. There are about a hundred and fifty chaps on the Captains' List ahead of me, and I'm not the King's cousin, so I won't be promoted until I get to the top of the List. And even then there's no guarantee that I will go up, at any rate no guarantee that I'll be promoted on the Active List and not simply put out to grass as a rear admiral.'

'Quite so.' The old man paused. 'But you would nevertheless be throwing away everything you've worked for, everything you've achieved up to now. And to do what? To come back here and gaze at the sheep. That's all very fine for a year or two, but not for the rest of your life. And then you'll just be one of hundreds of war heroes chasing after too few jobs, which is exactly what happened after the last war. You've got a good VC, but it's only going to be a handicap outside. I've seen that happen too often before.'

'*You* sent in *your* papers, Father.'

'I did, but that was in no way comparable. I was a passed-over major then and I wasn't going any further. You might be First Sea Lord yet. You may think I'm exaggerating, Robert, but I'm not, or not very much. It would be a criminal waste, and I mean that, if an officer with your abilities and your experience were to resign his commission, just as he was on the verge of reaching a position of influence in the service.'

It had been a surprise to hear that from his father, nay, completely unexpected. He thought now that perhaps the old man hoped, whether knowingly or otherwise, to gain vicarious success through his only surviving son after the disappointments of his own service career.

Henry Thurston had passed out second on the list from Sandhurst, with the Saddle for the best horseman of his intake, and years later had won a DSO in the Tirah, but for some reason his career had never taken off, and he had never gone further than major.

'And in any case, you owe it to the Navy to stay on,' the old man went on. This was more familiar ground. Responsibility, one of the fundamentals of his father's philosophy; you took what the service had to offer, and you gave them something greater in return. 'They've trained you, and they deserve a return on their investment. They may not let you resign, have you thought of that? But you've never paid much attention to what I've had to say before now, and I don't suppose you will this time.'

The vicar picked up his coffee cup once more, verified that it was indeed empty, reached for the pot and found that it too needed refilling.

The door opened and there was a sound of skirts sweeping the polished floorboards as Maud came in.

'What are you two men arguing about? I could hear you from the landing.'

'We were not arguing, my dear, merely discussing. Robert,' he almost spat the name out, 'has got it into his head that he's going to leave the Navy.'

'Indeed?' Maud said sweetly. 'Then I'm sure Robert is quite capable of making up his own mind. He always has done before now.'

The vicar pushed back his chair, and stood up, tall still, but the great frame made gaunt with age. 'I shall be in my study.'

Thurston had written to Kate, told her of Masters' offer. She had, as he expected, told him it was entirely up to him whether he decided to take it up or not, though he knew she would like to settle down in one place after twenty years of following the Navy, to have a house of her own, even if it was tied to her husband's job once again. There were the twins to consider too, and their education which would have to be paid for when the time came. But the war was not over yet, and there was no guarantee that it would be this year, or even next.

Chapter Seven

Another day had come and Thurston was once more on the bridge when Surgeon Commander Grant came up to make his report.

'We've finished. He should do well enough now. But I'm not going to have Vickers trying to interrogate him, or anyone else for that matter, until I say he's fit.'

'How long will that be?'

'At least a week. *After* he regains consciousness that is. He's had a major operation, which he's not going to recover from overnight. And he may be a little yellow bastard who's been doing his utmost to kill us all, but he's my patient for all that.'

'You'll let me know when he is fit to be interrogated.'

'Of course, sir, but there's no guarantee that you'll get anything useful out of him. There may be brain damage as well as the skull fracture; we can't tell until he regains consciousness, which he may not do for days. And when he does, even if there's no serious brain damage, he'll probably have no memory at all of what he's been doing for the last six weeks.'

Thurston smiled. 'I think you've made yourself plain enough. And what of Marine Wright?'

'He'll be all right.' The expression came out as 'ah richt'. 'He's a bit sore and sorry for himself, and I don't suppose he'll want to look at any young lady for a week or two. The Jap gave him quite a kick, and there's a nice little haematoma to show for it. Lucky for him that he wasn't wearing shoes.'

The sky was overcast, the sun blotted out by cloud, but aboard the ships of the task force it seemed hotter and more airless than ever. Fuel and supplies were low, and this evening the task force would begin to fall back towards the rendezvous with the Fleet Train scheduled for the following day. It would mean a brief respite, relatively speaking, while aircraft from the escort carriers carried out the routine CAPs; anti-flash gear could be shed, and alcohol, strictly rationed to two tots of spirits or two cans of beer per man, would be available in the ships' wardrooms. It was a relaxation of tension, but not a relief, because there were still Japanese submarines at sea, although the rendezvous was out of range of the kamikazes.

But today the work went on. The morning strike went off against the airfield at Ishigaki, and on the flight deck *Inflexible*'s squadron ratings, sweaty and uncomfortable inside their heavy clothing, carried out the routine work of aircraft maintenance. Lieutenant-Commander Terauchi lay in the carrier's sick bay, a bored sick berth attendant sitting next to him, turning the pages of a back number of *Picture Post*, every now and then looking away towards the scuttle.

The morning ended badly for *Inflexible*. One of the Corsairs failed to return from Ishigaki. The flak had got him over the target. The pilot had managed to stay airborne long enough to get out over the sea and ditch. At least, the other pilots thought he had ditched; one of them had seen the Corsair touch down on the water, stay afloat for a few seconds, but nobody had seen a dinghy, or even the bright yellow of the pilot's Mae West. And even if the pilot was in his dinghy, he was close inshore, which meant that the Japanese would probably reach him before the slow Walrus amphibian or the rescue submarine could. An intelligence report had been circulated among ships' captains a few weeks before, written from information smuggled out of one of the Japanese-held islands and unnamed, to protect the agent who had witnessed the event. The report told, in the usual unemotional Admiralty prose and detail which was all the more terrible because of that, of the capture of an Avenger crew from *Irresistible*, their torture – beatings mainly, on the palms of the hands and soles of the feet, but they had also been held forcibly under water until they were three parts drowned, and then beaten about the head with rifle butts – and final beheading in a clearing hacked out of the jungle, one at a time, the Leading Airman gunner first, then the two officers, by a Japanese major using a sword. The last man had still been alive after two blows had left his head only partly severed.

An Avenger bounced heavily on landing, missed the wires and ploughed into the crash barrier. The observer and gunner were undamaged, but the pilot had incautiously failed to tighten his shoulder straps sufficiently and smashed his face into the gunsight. The pilots were tired, and the prospect of a break from operations on the morrow was making them careless, like schoolboys on the morning of a half holiday, knowing that they had only to last a few more hours before a brief taste of freedom.

Lieutenant O'Connell, a schoolmaster from Manchester, was Officer of the Watch. Thurston sat on his bridge chair, struggling to write a letter to Kate, the pad resting on his knee, the ink smearing in the heat. There were so many things which, for security reasons, could not be said, so that writing a letter was always an exercise in self-censorship. He pushed an index finger up inside his sleeve, scratched at the scar on his wrist, pushing beneath the buckle of his watch strap in search of temporary respite from the itching.

Spencer appeared at his elbow. 'Tea, sir?'

'Make it something cold, please.'

'Aye aye, sir.'

It was a familiar exchange, which had taken place two or three times each day since *Inflexible* had reached tropical waters. Spencer had been with Thurston since the week the war began, when he had got his fourth stripe and command of an old cruiser brought out of reserve. Spencer's appointment was supposed to last only a few days, until a temporary lack of stewards had been sorted out, but *Connaught* was long gone, and six years on Spencer was still there. He must know Thurston's habits by now, but except at the times – breakfast, eleven hundred and after dinner – when coffee would be provided automatically, he would always ask him whether he wanted tea, and seem slightly surprised if Thurston asked for anything else.

Spencer reappeared with a tall glass of lime juice, with three ice cubes floating below the lip.

'There you are, sir. Keep the scurvy away.'

Spencer's stomach stretched the front of his overalls so that lines of tension appeared between the buttons, and his face was pink with the exertion of climbing the ladder in the heat.

'Hot, innit, sir.'

'Spencer, you have a genius for stating the obvious.'

Spencer grinned. 'Better'n using the long words some of your lot come out with, sir, so's nobody knows what they're talking about.'

Spencer had known him a long time, knew how far he could go, and his irreverence made a welcome contrast to the deference shown by every other man on board. He could never simply walk into the wardroom and have a drink with the officers. As the Captain he had to be invited, by the Commander as mess president, and though the Commander tried to make those occasions as relaxed and informal as possible, there was always the sensation of everyone being on best behaviour, coupled uneasily with an effort to behave as normal. As a post captain in command Thurston messed by himself, an arrangement hallowed by three centuries of tradition; he had a petty officer steward, a petty officer cook and Spencer to attend to his bodily needs. It was expected of him that he would have groups of officers to lunch and dinner when in harbour, and the midshipmen to breakfast, but otherwise he need never make contact with his officers except in the course of duty. Even the senior officers were distanced from him, fully aware of the invisible line drawn between them which must not be crossed. Thurston might use their Christian names or trade nicknames, but his own name remained unspoken by anyone on board *Inflexible*. He was just 'Captain, sir'.

He sipped at the lime juice, watched the ice cubes gradually diminish in size, irregular areas of clear water appearing around them until the glass was gently shaken, wrote a final couple of sentences of the letter to Kate, addressed the envelope.

Spencer reappeared. 'What would you like for lunch, sir?'

'What is there?'

'Corn dog, sir.'

'As if I didn't already know. What are you doing with it this time?'

Food, at this stage of the deployment, was a preoccupation for everyone on board.

'Corn-dog sandwiches, sir, with onions. Onions are good for the scurvy, same as lime juice.'

'We've still got some onions?'

'We have, sir. Don't know about anybody else.'

'You're going to get yourself arrested one of these days.'

'I'm not worried, sir. They've got to catch me first.'

The dinner hour came. Men were allowed to stand

78

down from their action stations, a few at a time, and eat the sandwiches the cooks brought round, the bread baked before dawn, then coated with margarine and slabs of corned beef added. No one wanted soup in that heat.

Surgeon Commander Grant came up, bundled in unaccustomed anti-flash gear.

'The Jap's dead, sir. He seemed to be doing ah richt, then his blood pressure dropped suddenly, and he went. Stockley opened his chest and tried to get his heart going again, but no luck.' Grant sounded disgusted. 'No fight in him, that's what it was. Just lay there and died, for no good reason. Oh aye, he had a cracked skull, but he shouldn't have died, not the way he did.'

'I suppose that's what he wanted,' Thurston said. 'He went off the ladder deliberately in the first place.'

'Aye, sir, I expect you're right.' Grant shrugged. 'But God knows I hate losing a patient, even if he's not one of ours. We'll have to bury him, of course, before he starts to stink too much. Mebbes we just drop him over the side.'

Thurston thought for a moment. 'Have him sewn up properly, and the padre can sort something out.'

The U-boat whose torpedoes had led to *Crusader*'s sinking had itelf been sunk, and survivors of both had been picked up by the same destroyers. One of the wounded from the U-boat had died later, and the U-boat captain had given his men's parole to bury him. Matrosenobergefreiter Johann Heinrichs had been buried under his own flag, and Korvettenkapitän Lauterbeck had read the Latin burial service over him. But the Japanese were different. It was difficult to feel anything for the Japanese pilot with no name, even though this was for Thurston the closest he had ever been to his enemy.

79

Spencer came back, bearing a tin plate which contained the sandwiches, shreds of raw onion just visible beneath the crusts.

'There you are, sir. Put some mustard in them as well.'

The bridge messenger returned from the galley with lunches for the remaining watchkeepers, and for several minutes everyone turned their attention to eating.

'Wonder what the Jap equivalent of corn dog is?'

'They eat raw fish.'

'Sounds lovely.'

'Might be worth trying as a change from this stuff,' one of the signalmen said in tones of disgust, finally pushing away his plate and muttering that it was too hot to eat.

'Radar . . . Bridge. Large formation of enemy aircraft approaching.'

'Bloody Japs. Don't even let us have our fucking dinner in peace,' muttered the same signalman.

'It's their assault on our morale, Norton,' said O'Connell.

One of *Inflexible*'s Corsair squadrons was providing high CAP over the task force. From thirty thousand feet the Japanese were visible a long way off, silhouetted against the thin grey blanket of cloud which lay below them. Sub-Lieutenant Broome instinctively tightened his shoulder straps, licked his dry lips. There were the usual assortment of aircraft, the bomb-laden Zeros, old and slow and out of date, the half-dozen twin-engined bombers which carried in their bomb bays the stubby-winged things which were nothing less than piloted bombs, and the modern fighters of the escort, weaving above and around them. Once you got through the escort, the kamikazes were sitting ducks for a Corsair. Perhaps today he would shoot down his first Jap.

Horace had vectored them on to an interception course. Now the Japs were in sight, and it was up to them to deal with them. He tucked himself in a little closer to the CO, pulled down his goggles, switched on the reflector sight and checked that the graticules were set for single-engined aircraft. He heard the CO's voice in his headset, moved the stick to the right to follow him round towards the rear of the Japanese formation. For a moment the Japanese continued on the same course as before, then the escorting fighters began to peel off, climbing up towards the British Corsairs.

Briefly the Japanese remained far away, not yet a threat, then suddenly they were right ahead. Broome pressed the gun button, saw his tracer pass harmlessly either side of the Japanese fighter. Too far away! He remembered the instructors on the air gunnery course in England. 'Get in close. You've got to get in close.' But that was easier said than done. The Japs were jinking, never holding the same course for more than a few seconds, and they were firing too.

Where were the other Corsairs? He whipped his head from right to left, and then upwards. No sign of them. Where were they?

Suddenly he was alone among the Japanese fighters. He felt something striking the fuselage behind him, moved his eyes to the mirror. There was the nose and propeller blur of an aircraft, very close, flashes of yellow light coming from the gun muzzles. He pushed his nose down, saw a second Japanese ahead and jerked the stick to the left to take himself clear. The Jap's wing tip seemed to pass only inches away. He remembered something else from the air gunnery course. Turn, keep on turning. You're the one who decides which way to turn, so you will always have the advantage over the pilot who's chasing you. He was trying to put the advice into effect, but the Corsair seemed sluggish, heavy in comparison with the shark-nosed Kawasaki whose pilot seemed to anticipate his every manoeuvre.

For the first time Broome was afraid, the cocky confidence evaporated. There was only the fear, and the need to keep turning, hand pushing the stick this way and that, feet working the rudder pedals in time with the stick. The altimeter needle was unwinding, below fifteen thousand now, the cloud layer much closer. He had forgotten the rest of the squadron, there was only himself, and the Jap who clung to his tail. His overalls were soaked in sweat, and more was finding its way down his face from beneath his leather helmet and oxygen mask. He remembered other advice: never let yourself be separated from your formation; stick with them; never follow the enemy down, because when you think you've got that one, sure as eggs one of his mates will sneak up behind you and get *you*.

Under thirteen thousand now. He wondered how thick the cloud layer was, whether he might lose the Jap in that. He glanced at the mirror. There was nothing there. He kept his eyes on it, thinking as the seconds passed, the longest seconds of his life, that the Jap must reappear. He caught his breath, then moved his head slowly, searching through every inch of his canopy. Far away to starboard, and several thousand feet above, he saw other aircraft, both British and Japanese, a single fighter climbing towards them. Broome straightened up, then brought the Corsair round in a climbing turn to starboard, engaged the supercharger and felt the surge of power.

'Where the blazes have you been?' the CO shouted as he caught sight of Broome. 'I'll see you when we get back.'

The Japanese formation had been broken up, but the individual aircraft were still heading towards the task force in ones and twos, many of them damaged, smoke trailing behind them and pieces missing from the wings, harried by the Corsairs, and the Seafires which had come up from *Irresistible*.

'Got to hand it to the bastards,' someone breathed.

'D'ye hear there. All personnel on deck take cover. All personnel on deck take cover.'

In a moment the flight deck was empty, except for the aircraft parked there, fewer than before since the weeks of operations had left their toll and there were not many aircraft left serviceable.

Tin hats and gloves on, hoods up, the air hot and thick inside.

The Japanese aircraft broke through the cloud layer, the British fighters still following.

'Alarm starboard, commence, commence, commence!'

Noise; the regularly spaced bangs from the guns and the faster rattling sound of the close-range weapons, his own voice, unnaturally steady, rapping out wheel orders to keep the ship manoeuvring, other voices reporting to him, all blurred by the cotton wool in his ears, shading into one another.

There was a Japanese, one of the stubby-winged flying bombs, coming in from the port side, a Seafire from *Irresistible* chasing her, cannon firing red tracer at her wings. *Irresistible* herself was turning to port, evading a Zero which was heading for her stern. Further off the cruisers were firing, *Marathon, Persephone, Agamemnon* and the rest. Thurston was watching the kamikaze, eyes screwed up beneath the rim of his tin hat. Black smoke appeared ahead of her as one of *Inflexible*'s rounds exploded; she dropped, fell away to one side, then recovered and came on. The Bofors on the port side stopped firing to avoid hitting the Seafire. There was sudden silence, broken by the regular bang . . . bang . . . bang from the 4.5s.

'Hard a-port.'

'Hard a-port, sir.'

Turning towards the kamikaze, to present him with the smallest possible target, there was a long second before *Inflexible*'s rudders began to bite and take her round.

The Japanese aircraft ploughed into the sea, and the bombs inside her exploded, flinging a curtain of steel splinters at *Inflexible*'s port side. The Seafire pulled up sharply, passing low over the island. In the same moment there was an explosion somewhere beneath Thurston's feet; the ship vibrated with the impact.

'Where the fuck did that come from?' shouted Murillo, instantly recognisable in his American tin hat.

'Gyro compass gone dead, sir,' the Quartermaster reported after a pause.

The automatic response, 'Very good. Steer by magnetic.'

After the explosion there was silence, and then the port-side Bofors began their rattling again, raggedly, out of time with each other.

Leading Seaman Spencer had been in the galley making a brew of tea. There was nothing much for him to do during an attack, but the blokes were always glad of a cup of tea once it was over. His hood was off, the front of his overalls unfastened to the navel. Inside the island it was less noisy than on the bridge, but the sounds of gunfire reverberated and echoed, so that there was no silence. The fuel had been drained from the galley fires, of course, but there was a pipe which came up from the engine room to provide the galley with steam. You turned a valve and the steam circulated around a large metal urn to boil the water inside. It took only a few seconds. Spencer opened the valve, got out a fresh packet of tea, put four tablespoons into the teapot, watched the needle on the urn climb into the red zone, shut off the valve, put the teapot beneath the hot-water outlet and spun the tap.

The explosion came just as the teapot was full and Spencer was resting it on the edge of the hot plate in order to reach out to turn off the tap. The lights went out, he staggered, felt a sharp pain in his right arm which made him let go of the teapot, and then another kind of pain as tea or boiling water found its way through the lace holes of his boots. He stepped backwards, realised the tap was still open and that the urn was spilling its contents on to the deck, reached out to try to find it, and recoiled again as his fingers made contact with the body of the urn. He didn't have a torch, because he didn't usually need one. With his right hand he pulled the sleeve of his overalls down over the left, stepped well clear of the jet of water, and began the search for the tap a second time. The ship rolled, sloshing the water around his feet, so that he could feel its heat through his boots. The galley, three decks down inside the island and with deadlights in place over the scuttles, was pitch-black. It took a long time to find the tap, following the body of the urn round until it began to curve the other way, the heat coming through his fingers despite the sleeve, then down until he encountered the horizontal pipe which stuck out from it, following it until he was at last able to turn off the flow.

He turned round, blundered into a bulkhead and stopped again to get his bearings. Following the bulkhead round to the left, and the door was there. His arm hurt, somewhere above the elbow, and he could feel a flow of blood inside the sleeve of his overalls. He got out into the passage, stopped again while he tried to remember which way was out. The watertight doors were all shut and clipped into place. He made up his mind, turned right, and almost immediately stopped again when his right boot made contact with something soft.

85

There was a groan at his feet and a gasped expletive. Spencer felt a sudden wave of relief at finding someone else.

'Who's that?'

'Hopkinson, radar mechanic,' the man said in a faint voice.

'You all right, chum?'

'Don't ask such fucking silly questions. I wouldn't be here if I was all right. It's my leg. The left, near the top.' He stopped speaking for a moment, then went on, almost pleading, 'Can you get me out of here?'

Spencer's feet were wet, the water inside his boots still hot, the flesh raw, as if the skin had been scraped away. He bent down, found one of Hopkinson's arms by feel and put it round his own shoulders.

'Come on now, up you come. Does it hurt much?'

'Not really, just numb.'

'Okay then, let's just take it gently, and we'll get ourselves out.'

Hopkinson sagged against him, his weight pulling at Spencer's shoulders. He found himself glad of Hopkinson's company, relieved that there was someone with him to share the search for a way out. They reached one of the watertight doors, and he had to lower Hopkinson to the deck while he wrestled with the clips, four on each side.

'You're going to have to pick your feet up here, Hoppy, just so's you can get over the coaming. Come on, upsy-daisy.'

One of Hopkinson's feet caught on the coaming, he hung back, and eventually Spencer had to drag him through, leaving the door swinging behind.

'Sorry, Hoppy. 'Ope there won't be too many of those.'

In the darkness it was difficult to remember how many more doors there were, and where the ladders were located. Funny that they hadn't met up with anyone else. A thought struck him. 'Hey, Hoppy, what's your action station, and why aren't you there?'

'FDR. I got caught short, and they let me out to go to the heads. With the Japs right on top of us we didn't really need to watch the displays. I haven't got there yet.' Hopkinson sounded embarrassed and very young.

'Well I hope you can hang on to it until we get out.'

The FDR and Ops Room were on the next deck up, and the bridge on the deck above that, which meant there were ladders to be climbed before they could get out. Spencer wondered how he was going to get Hopkinson up there. His feet hurt, and he had had to stop using his right arm, which now hung limp at his side.

'You all right, Hoppy?'

'Yes, I think so.' Hopkinson must have thought for a moment. 'Look, I'm sorry, I don't know who you are.'

'I'm Spencer. I do for the Captain. You call me Spence.'

Spencer wished he had a torch. He should know his way, he had been in the bloody ship long enough, but the total darkness had disorientated him. He smelt smoke and cordite fumes, wondered where that was coming from. He moved on, feeling Hopkinson's weight dragging behind him. They came to an area where the smoke was thicker, catching in his throat. Hopkinson coughed, the sound very loud in the enclosed space. Where was everybody else? The ship had been hit, so there should be a damage control party on the way. All he and Hopkinson had to do was find their way out, or keep going until they met the damage control people. He heard another cough, much further off, perhaps on the deck above. The sound cheered him. 'Nearly there, Hoppy. Soon be out of this.' Hopkinson didn't answer. 'Hey, Hoppy. You still there?'

No reply. 'Christ, the poor bugger's fainted,' Spencer thought to himself. They had been taught first aid at *Ganges* when he first joined the Navy, and sporadically since then, but he thought a little bitterly that he had never been asked to do it in the dark, and after he'd been hit himself. He let Hopkinson down on to the deck. Top of his left leg, he'd said. There was a shell dressing in one of his pockets – standing orders. He tried to think of what he could use as a tourniquet. His lanyard would have been ideal, but you didn't wear it with anti-flash. His hands were moving down Hopkinson's body, finding the right leg, intact and solid as far as he could reach from the position he was in. The left leg. His hands moved down, felt wetness which must be blood, then his left hand sank deep into a warm tangled mess of flesh. He recoiled in revulsion, pulled his hand away, wiped it on the front of his overalls in an effort to clear the contagion. He heard Hopkinson groan, then slumped against the adjacent bulkhead, sliding down into a sitting position, faint and sick now, and content to wait for the damage control party.

The explosion had taken place right inside the island, the projectile bursting in the flat alongside the FDR and separated from it by only a thin steel bulkhead. Steel splinters, ranging in size from a few thousandths of an inch to three feet, scythed in every direction whilst flames began to devour the layers of paint and the electrical wiring which followed the underside of the deckhead. Inside the FDR the radar displays disintegrated, flinging up miniature spears of glass to join the steel, short circuits within creating more fires. The men inside stood no chance. Most died instantly, one or two, shielded from the worst force of the blast by the wooden tables and equipment mounted on them, lingered, deaf and blind in the darkness, long enough to realise what had happened. One man managed to begin a slow crawl towards the doorway, leaving a long slick of blood stretching back from beneath the table, where an able seaman from the damage control party found him.

Training, once more, had its effect. The fire party,

bullied and cajoled by its petty officers, moved inside the island by the dim light of torches, unfurled their hoses, connected them up the fire main and directed a torrent of water on the flames until the fire was beaten down.

'Right, let's get in there and see what's what!'

The Petty Officer swung his torch over the black space in front of him, and recoiled, crashing into the man closed up behind him.

'Get back!' His arms went out sideways, holding the rest back. 'Get back! There's no fucking deck!'

He shone his torch again, more slowly this time, saw a curve of metal ahead of him, ending in a jagged edge, just where he had been about to place his foot. Beyond the edge a dark void, into which the torch beam barely penetrated.

He was thinking the problem through. 'We'll have to get some beams. Bridge over the gap.'

'What for, PO?' someone asked.

'To get to the other side, of course! There were men in there. *Men*, not brainless babes in arms like you!'

The torch moved again, located a six inch lip of metal which was still intact, running along the base of the bulkhead opposite. The Petty Officer put his back to the bulkhead and began to inch his way very gingerly along it, the torch held in his teeth and casting unearthly shadows all around. The other men stood silent, watching him, and he wished they wouldn't, feeling uncomfortable with their eyes upon him. He reached the door, realised he was going to have to make a turn, stopped, very deliberately took the torch from his mouth with his right hand. He turned his head slowly to the left, saw almost with disappointment that the ledge continued into the doorway, and began to shift his feet, shuffling, an inch at a time, trying not to think of the empty space below. The worst moment came when he was at right angles to the bulkhead. He risked a bigger step, lost his balance for a second, swayed outwards, and would have gone down into the void had he not got the hand which held the torch around the edge of the doorway. He completed the turn, the sweat on his face running cold, got a good grip with one hand, found solid places for his feet, and leant in through the doorway.

'Oh, sweet Jesus.' It was almost a sigh.

Inflexible was still steaming at twenty knots, maintaining her station parallel to *Irresistible*, her nerve centre smashed, but her hull and engines and flight deck undamaged. O'Connell was conning the ship, absorbed in the task of maintaining station, all the time wondering what on earth had happened.

Chapter Eight

'I'm afraid there's no doubt about it, sir.' The Major of
Marines was standing in front of Thurston, his white
hood pushed back and his ruddy face shiny with sweat
and black-streaked from the smoke. The blackening
had affected one side of his moustache only; the other
remained reddish, giving a faintly comic effect which
was out of keeping with what he had to say. The thing
he held up to the light was a piece from the base plate
of a shell, blackened and bent out of shape, but marked
with a figure '5', a decimal point and part of a '2'.

'Thank you.' There was nothing more to say, beyond
the ritual 'Carry on.' He looked out over the sea to
port, at the cruisers deployed around the carriers.
Marathon, his old ship, *Bellerophon* and *Persephone*,
her 'chummy ships' from the Mediterranean, *Agamemnon*. All had 5.25-inch guns. The round must have
come from one of them. The FDR had gone – there was
no chance of restoring even limited functioning – and
twenty-three men with it. The aircraft already airborne
had been diverted to the other carriers. The damage
control party had got to work, bridged over the hole in
the deck and brought the bodies out on stretchers, one
at a time, balancing precariously on the beams, feeling
their way across. They had found more bodies, men
dead of splinter wounds, and one man stripped naked,
without a mark on him, but blood had come out of his
ears and dried on his neck and he was dead. They had
found men wounded too, Spencer among them, huddled in a corner with another man who was even now

on the operating table under the surgeon's knife. The mess was being cleared up, the water which had quenched the fire being mopped up with buckets and bundles of rag.

The Commander came up from below. 'The FDR's a complete write-off, sir. We knew that at the beginning. I think we can patch the Ops Room up and get things working again, but it's not going to be a five-minute job. More like a couple of days. The torpedomen are working on the lighting – part of the ring main was cut by a splinter – and they should have a jury rig working fairly shortly. We're going through the roll now, to see who we've got and who we haven't.'

Commander Howard Dent was thirty-six, on the young side to be already inside the zone for promotion to captain. Commander of a battleship or fleet carrier was very much a promotion job, which meant that Dent should be good. So far, he had proved himself to be so, but this was likely to be the biggest crisis he had yet had to deal with.

'Is it true that it was one of ours, sir?' The Commander's voice was lowered very slightly.

'It looks like it. There's nowhere else it could have come from, even before this turned up.' Thurston took the shell fragment from his pocket, held it in his palm while the Commander peered at it intently.

'That's bad. That's very bad.' Dent looked out towards the four cruisers. 'Do we know which one yet?'

'Not yet. I suppose they were all firing, and we would need to compare the logs and work out who was firing on that bearing at the critical moment.' Thurston was surprised to find himself thinking so far ahead. There would be a Board of Enquiry, perhaps also a court martial, but none of that would undo what had already been done.

In the sick bay camp beds had been set up to supplement

92

the eight cots which were already occupied by the most serious casualties, a row of them lining each of the side bulkheads. The deadlights were open, and late-afternoon sunlight streamed in now that the cloud had begun to break up. In several places torpedomen stood on ladders and boxes, and black lengths of cable bearing naked bulbs hung down in long loops from the deckhead; Thurston found himself bending automatically to pass beneath them.

'Can you not stretch them a bit tighter?'

'I'm just working on that now, sir,' the Leading Torpedo Operator said from the top of his ladder, indicating a line of bright new metal staples which already anchored part of the cable to the deckhead. The man wore spectacles, and sounded calm and highly competent, his open toolbox on the deck at the foot of the ladder showing a collection of small rubber-handled screwdrivers and miniature coils of fuse wire.

Surgeon Commander Grant was standing at the far end of the sick bay, wiping his hands on a large wad of cotton wool which smelt of alcohol, giving instructions to his Sick Berth Chief Petty Officer.

'Nineteen, at the last count, sir. Stockley's got one on the table at the moment, and there are two more in the queue after him. The rest won't come to any harm if they wait a bit.' Grant's sleeves were pushed up, and there was a long streak of dried blood which he had missed on the inside of one forearm, more on the front of his overalls.

One of the torpedomen began a tuneless whistling, and stopped just as suddenly when Grant's cold stare fell on him. A second leant out a little too far from his ladder, wobbled dangerously as the ship rolled, gave up the struggle for balance and dropped to the deck, shaking up a metallic rattle from his toolbox. Grant glared again.

'Man, this is a sick bay,' he sighed.

The slow walk round the sick bay, still in his anti-flash gear, cap under his left arm, his messenger two paces behind, stirring memories of *Marathon* after the Italian torpedo had got her. There were the same buckets of used dressings, white streaked with dark blood, the smell compounded of vomit, excreta and ether, all overlaid with strong disinfectant, the sick-berth attendants moving silently in gym shoes. Time was supposed to heal all wounds, but this was something he would never get used to.

One man, head bandaged so that only a single eye glared out of his face, and a black hole where his mouth was, his bare chest angry with sunburn.

'Telegraphist Diamond, sir,' the PO Sick Berth Attendant read from his list.

Thurston found himself wondering how Diamond had come by that sunburn when he would have spent the daylight hours under cover in the wireless office.

'Hello, Diamond.'

Diamond shifted, instinctively straightening towards the position of attention. The black hole changed shape, the bandages moved a little around it, but only a croak came out.

'It's all right, Diamond. Don't try to talk.'

He was still for a moment. His right hand was also bandaged, resting on his stomach above the hem of the sheet, parts of the bandage tinged yellow with some unguent. Then his left hand came up from his side, opened out. Thurston found himself taking hold of it, feeling Diamond's grip, unexpectedly strong, and aware of Boy Maxwell's puzzled eyes on him. The grip relaxed. He let go, and straightened up, heard the Petty Officer say something encouraging to Diamond, then moved on.

'Hello, Spencer. How are you?'

'Hello, sir.'

Spencer lay on one of the camp beds, his right arm in

a very clean white sling, both feet bandaged so that only the toes peeped out.

'It looks as though I'm going to have to make my own tea for a week or two.'

He had meant it as a joke, but a single tear ran from the corner of one eye and down Spencer's cheek.

'I'm sorry, sir.' Spencer sniffed, then turned his head away.

'It's all right, Spencer,' Thurston said, knowing the words to be inadequate. Boy Maxwell had also turned away, teeth set and jaw muscles standing out in harsh ridges.

'Hoppy, sir.'

'Who?'

'Hopkinson, sir. He was with me . . . I was trying to look after him.'

Thurston turned to the Petty Officer, who shook his head silently.

'I'll tell him, sir.'

The temptation was clear. It would be so easy to walk out of there, leave it to Petty Officer Cheetham, who was used to this sort of thing. But he got down awkwardly on one knee beside Spencer, took a deep breath.

'Spencer, Hopkinson's dead.'

'Yes, sir.' Silence for perhaps a minute. 'Sir, I was supposed to be looking after him. He wanted me to get him out. He asked me to. . . ' Spencer rolled over towards the bulkhead, eyes screwed up to hold back the tears.

'Spencer, this isn't like you.'

'I know, sir. . . I'm sorry, sir.' He rolled back towards him, his face relaxing so that the tears began to flow in earnest.

'It's all right, Spencer. At times like this it doesn't matter.' He might have reminded Spencer that he had blubbered himself, in the aftermath of that Malta convoy with *Marathon*, and it had been Spencer who had found him then, slumped across his desk, blubbering for the first time since his boyhood, but in the public atmosphere of the sick bay, with Petty Officer Cheetham beside him and Boy Maxwell at his back, he could not. He found a crumpled handkerchief in his pocket, pressed it into Spencer's hand.

'Now you get yourself back on your feet, Spencer.'

'Will you be all right, sir?' The tears were coming silently, between noisy breaths.

'Don't worry about me, Spencer. I can manage for as long as it takes you to be fit again.'

'Aye aye, sir.'

'Shock, sir,' the Sick Berth PO said. 'He'll be all right in a couple of days.'

Murillo was on the bridge when he returned, helmet still in place.

'Expecting any more?'

'Just taking what you people call proper seamanlike precautions.'

It was something the British officers ragged Murillo about. The British only wore tin hats when absolutely essential, and went back to their ordinary caps as soon as an attack was over; Americans wore theirs at the slightest excuse, to prove that they were fighting men, or so the British claimed.

'Have you heard about the *Bunker Hill*, sir? Kamikaze hit her. It came up on the radio just now. Over three hundred guys killed, and another three hundred wounded. She's on her way back to Pearl.'

Bingham had taken over the watch from O'Connell. He stretched his arms above his head. 'Thank God for armoured decks.'

'Yeah,' Murillo said briefly.

Dusk had begun to fall. The Fleet had secured from Action Stations and movement was beginning on

Inflexible's flight deck as the hangar party started work on the remaining aircraft.

'I'm going below to clean up. Call me as usual.'

'Aye aye, sir.'

'And ask my secretary to come and see me in fifteen minutes.'

'Aye aye, sir.'

Thurston reached his sea cabin, hung his cap on its peg and sat on the bunk to unlace his boots. Almost immediately there was a knock on the bulkhead.

'Come.'

A very neat young man in steward's whites slid soundlessly through the door.

'Steward Dunhill, sir.'

'Oh yes. Of course.'

'The Commander (S) told me to come to you, sir.'

'Yes. . . Thank you.' At the moment Dunhill was not important.

'Is there anything you need, sir?' Dunhill enquired.

The sea cabin was lit by one of those naked bulbs suspended on a length of black cable. There was a hole in the bulkhead above the bunk, the jagged edges of metal bent inwards.

'You could find me a clean shirt. There should be some in that drawer there. And if the water isn't back on yet, you can draw me a bucket of sea water.'

'Aye aye, sir.'

The shower emitted only a trickle, and then died. Dunhill went away, and came back with a bucket which was still three-quarters full. Thurston stripped off, stood in the shower cubicle and sluiced himself down, finally emptying the bucket over his head. The water gurgled away down the plughole, greyish in the dim light.

A fresh set of khaki drill was lying on the bunk, and Dunhill was attaching the blue and gold rank slides to the shoulder straps. The splinter hole, seven inches long and two and a half wide, was just above the pillow. It took little imagination to visualise what the splinter would have done to his head if he had been in his bunk at the time. But he hadn't been there, and never would be while the ship was at Action Stations. Dunhill buttoned the second shoulder strap and handed the shirt over.

'Is there anything else, sir?'

'Not at the moment, thank you, Dunhill.' Thurston felt a surge of dislike towards the steward. But that was unfair to Dunhill, who was simply doing as he had been trained, and had come at a bad time.

Dunhill went out, to be followed within a few minutes by the Captain's secretary. *Inflexible* had been in the operational zone, thousands of miles from her base, for more than three months, and operating her aircraft at full stretch for most of that time. Nevertheless routine administrative work went on, could not be left until the ship was in harbour but had to be dealt with, so that a session with his secretary was part of Thurston's evening routine after the stand-down from Action Stations. Thurston sat down on the chair, manoeuvred his legs beneath the desk.

'What have you got for me tonight?'

Scott deposited a sheaf of letters in front of him, each paperclipped to its envelope. 'If you could just sign these, sir, they'll be ready to go with the mail tomorrow.'

Thurston uncapped his pen, skimmed rapidly through the pile, signing, initialling the carbons, rejecting one or two and moving them to one side.

'This list of radar spares is a bit out of date now.'

'Yes, sir. But we do still need them.'

'And a few hundred others.'

Scott grinned. He had been Thurston's secretary in *Crusader*; they had got on well then, on a professional level, and so Thurston had asked the Second Sea Lord's branch for him again when he was appointed to *In-flexible*.

'Is the list ready yet?'

'It's being typed, sir. I'll bring it up as soon as it's finished.'

The list set out the names, ranks or rates of the dead, and the names and addresses of their next of kin, taken from the cards they had all filled out on joining the ship. Their deaths had already been recorded in the log by the Midshipman of the Watch, each name suffixed 'DD' for Discharged Dead – bureaucracy was para-mount, even in death. But that bureaucracy, like his sit-ting at his desk signing the letters which must go with tomorrow's mail, was a means of not thinking too deeply about the losses, which would be faced later, one at a time, when he wrote the next-of-kin letters, twenty-nine of them, in alphabetical order, beginning with Mrs C. E. Adams, wife of Leading Coder A. W. Adams, P/JX 437166, and ending with Mr R. D. Wat-kin, father of Radar Mechanic R. D. Watkin, who had only been identified by the Chinese dragon tattooed in coils around his left bicep.

'A bad business, sir.'

'It is.'

'The Plot's just about straightened up now – except for the new air conditioning!' It wasn't a very good joke, but they both laughed; it was another part of the defence mechanism. 'Schooly was telling me that he didn't really see much. Just a big bang and all the lights going out. Then he found a torch and someone started complaining that everything had been knocked off the Plot and he didn't know how effing long it was going to take to put everything back in the right place!'

Once again, as only a few days earlier, the stretchers on the flight deck, three rows of seven and one of eight, and this time one stretcher in the shadows apart from the rest, containing the body of the dead Japanese pilot. In the heat they were already beginning to smell. Once again the ship, and the rest of the task force, slowed to half-speed, with the ensign at half-mast, the semicircle of men around the stretchers, separated from them by a zone of empty deck into which only those actually involved in the ceremonial would move. Some men in khaki, some, spared temporarily from the repair parties, still in overalls and streaked with oil and water.

They had had to use all the ship's white ensigns and union flags, including the smaller boat ensigns which were only large enough to cover the head and upper body, and left the canvas on view below. The last bundle was without a flag and a little apart from the rest. Once again the padre's hesitant reading of the burial service. '*Thou knowest, Lord . . . the secrets. . . of our hearts . . .* ' His head down and voice half-muffled in the prayer book. '. . . *For as much as it . . . hath pleased. . . Almighty God . . .* ' He seemed to take even longer than the last time. The burials, too, took much longer, because there were more of them, the bodies disappearing one by one over the edge of the deck, a long pause with teeth clenched, and the distant splash as each hit the water forty feet below, to be carried on down by the firebars sewn into each canvas bundle. 'And good riddance to the bugger,' Thurston heard one of the Marines say out loud as the dead Japanese went over the side. The drummer sounded Last Post and Reveille, the firing party fired their three volleys.

There was the desolation, more marked now than the last time, for it was not even those men's enemies who had killed them, but also the message of hope, in the stark words of St Paul, *For as in Adam all die, even so in Christ shall all be made alive. . . The last enemy that shall be destroyed is death*, and in the simple affirmation of the hymn which someone must have asked for and which was spontaneously taken up by dozens of male voices in the darkness, tenor, bass and the drummer's unbroken treble:

> *I fear no foe with Thee at hand to bless,*
> *Ills have no weight and tears no bitterness.*
> *Where is death's sting, where grave thy victory?*
> *I triumph still if Thou abide with me.*

Chapter Nine

'*Repair on board . . .*'

Thurston had been expecting the summons to the flagship, knew that the meeting with the Admiral would not be an easy one, but the phrasing of the signal gave it an ominous ring. It was a little after eight o'clock, the task force had made the rendezvous with the Fleet Train an hour before, and the transfer of fuel and stores had already begun.

Again the morning was overcast, but this time the cloud dragged lower over the sea, turning the whole world dull grey and bringing a sharp drizzling rain which was too warm to be refreshing. Thurston walked across the flight deck, carrying parachute harness, Mae West and flying helmet, feeling the rain work its way through the toes of the suede desert boots he was wearing, seeing for the first time the hole the shell had left in the port side of the island, whose paint was still blackened and peeling from the kamikaze hit, only a few days before, but now faded into history. A single Avenger was in position ready to take off. Wearily, he fastened the tapes of the Mae West, slotted the straps of the parachute harness one by one into the release box, climbed up on to the wing, pushing his feet into the toeholds in the fuselage concealed by spring-loaded metal plates, and got into the narrow space behind the pilot, made smaller still by the radar and radio equipment on either side. One of the mechanics followed him on to the wing, leaned into the cockpit to help him with his seat harness. There was a large eagle, wings outstretched, tattooed across his chest. Thurston looked round to make sure the parachute was in its rack behind him, ready to be clipped to the hooks on his chest. The gunner had wormed his way into the turret behind him, and was going through his checks, traversing in each direction and taking the guns to the limits of their elevation and depression.

'Ready, sir?'

'Ready.'

The pilot pressed the starter, ran the engine up, signalled to the mechanic, who pulled the chocks away and disappeared from sight beneath the wing. The Commander (Flying) lowered his green flag. The Avenger began to move forward. The take-off run seemed very short, the aircraft had hardly got up speed before they reached the end of the runway, lurched into the air, the pilot fighting to keep her airborne as she dropped towards the water before climbing slowly away.

'Bit dicey without the catapult, sir,' he remarked. 'Especially when there's a full load on board. Still, we'll have one coming back.'

He was one of the older pilots of the Avenger squadron, an RNVR lieutenant named Monk, and one of the few pilots aboard who could boast of a previous operational tour, flying Albacores and then Barracudas. The Avenger, he claimed, was a Rolls-Royce by comparison.

The rain stung on the cockpit canopy, ran down it in streams. The concrete which had patched *Inflexible*'s decks was very obvious from the air, creating a surreal effect against the darker metal. They were beginning to descend already, overflying *Invincible* and dropping towards the flagship. She was making a lot of smoke; Thurston thought to himself that if that were *Inflexible* he would give the Commander (E) some explaining to do.

The Avenger bounced once on the flagship's deck, came to a halt at the limits of the arrestor wire. Thurston unstrapped himself, retrieved his cap from the chart pocket at his side and set it on his head. The Admiral's Flag Lieutenant, standing on the deck to meet him, led him, not towards the island as he expected, but to the Admiral's main cabin right aft. After *Inflexible*, heavily damaged and with temporary repairs going on everywhere, the flagship seemed strangely ordered and secure. There was a Marine sentry on duty outside the cabin, presenting arms with a crash of boots and a clatter of working parts which suggested that the loosening of screws required to produce that impressive level of noise had rendered his rifle incapable of being fired.

'Captain Thurston, sir,' the Flag Lieutenant announced.

The Admiral was on his feet in the centre of the carpet, directly beneath one of the deckhead fans, taking short puffs from the cigar he held in his left hand.

'Ah, morning, Thurston. Glad you could come across at short notice.'

That was simply politeness; he had intended the signal to be acted on immediately, and had probably been impatiently awaiting Thurston's arrival from the moment it had been sent.

'Hello, Bob,' the Flag Captain said, getting up from an armchair on the Admiral's right. Edward Strickland was several years older than Thurston, and almost at the top of the Captains' List, with crinkly iron-grey hair and a misshapen ear from boxing.

'Coffee? It's a bit early in the day for anything else.'

'Thank you, sir.'

The Admiral nodded to a petty officer steward who

had been standing quietly in his place at the pantry hatch. Though Rear Admiral Charles Winthrop was very short, under five foot six, he was not small but broad-shouldered and stocky, bulging a little over the waistband of his shorts, his cheekbones bearing the un-shaven tufts of hair that were known as bugger's grips. The coffee arrived. The steward poured Thurston a cup, manoeuvred the tray for him to add his own milk and sugar, then moved on to the other two.

'Thank you, Pettigrew. I shan't need you again for now.'

'A bad business, Thurston,' the Admiral said after another pause. 'How much damage is there?'

Thurston went through it, briefly. No FDR, the Ops Room badly damaged, both gyros toppled, extensive damage to the electrical circuits, twenty-nine men confirmed dead, nineteen wounded and one unaccounted for who had to be presumed dead.

'What exactly happened?'

Thurston waited, and took a pull at his coffee before replying.

'I can only tell you, sir, what I know did happen. I don't yet know *how* it happened. I turned the ship hard a-port to evade a kamikaze which was coming at us from the port side. That was at 1322 – the time of the turn is in the log – and a 5.25-inch shell hit us from the same side.' In the background, half in shadow from the closed deadlights, the Admiral's assistant secretary was taking down his words in rapid shorthand, the point of his pencil scraping audibly on the pad which rested on his knee.

'You're quite certain it was a shell?' Strickland asked. 'That it couldn't have been a Jap bomb?'

'Quite sure. To begin with, there were no enemy air-craft in the right place. There weren't any right over-head. There was a Zero heading for my stern, firing cannon. I'd just turned to port and he'd gone past us.

Then there was the kamikaze I was busy evading – one of those piloted bomb things – but he was heading towards the port quarter, not the island, when we were hit, and I would think he was still a hundred or so yards away.' He was surprised now that he remembered so clearly, but his mind seemed to have taken a quick mental snapshot of the kamikaze at the moment before the explosion. 'Secondly, whatever it was went through the side of the island, not the top, and it hadn't bounced off the deck. Thirdly, the damage control party found this.' He brought out the fragment of base plate from his pocket.

The Admiral took it from him, turned it over in his hands, then passed it to the Flag Captain. 'Hm, that seems fairly conclusive. It's what we thought. There'll have to be a Board of Enquiry, of course. Possibly a court martial, once we find out who it was. Bad time to lose a carrier of course. You'll have to go back to Sydney, that's quite obvious – you're not much use to me with no radar.' He turned to Strickland. 'Do you have anything more to add, Edward?'

'No, I don't think so, sir.' The Flag Captain put down his cup with sufficient force to rattle the spoon in the saucer, making it clear that he had heard all that was necessary and intended to return to his bridge.

'You realise that none of this can be allowed to get out, Thurston. You can imagine what the gutter press would make of it.'

'Only too clearly, sir.'

'The very last thing we need is some overpaid scribbler spreading it about that we can't be trusted to fire our guns at the enemy instead of our own people. Especially when we're having trouble enough with the Australians already. This business mustn't go outside the service.'

'The men are likely to talk, once they get ashore and they've had a few.'

'Yes, there is always that danger, and I'm relying on

106

you to stamp on it.' The Admiral turned his hand over so that the butt of his cigar was pointed directly at Thurston's chest. 'You can warn them, *before* you reach Sydney, that careless talk of any kind will be most severely dealt with.' The Admiral inhaled deeply from the cigar, idly scuffed the pile of the carpet with one foot. 'Pity about that Jap you lost. We might have got some useful intelligence out of him. I take it you've dealt with that idiot of a sentry.'

'I will, sir, once he's fit.'

'Did you get anything out of the Jap at all?'

'No, sir. Not a single word My Japanese speaking officer tried several times, but the Jap just kept silent.'

The Admiral grunted. 'All right, Thurston, that'll be all, thank you.'

Strickland stood up, reached for his cap. 'I'll see you over the side.'

'It's his bloody reputation he's worried about,' Strickland said when they were outside the cabin. 'Of course we have to keep the press out of it, but that's to save his face as far as he's concerned, not the service's. Bloody man. He keeps telling me how I should run *my* ship. And he a jumped-up ruddy desk wallah!'

Thurston had heard that Winthrop and Strickland were not on the best of terms, but he had not expected such direct evidence. He didn't even know Strickland all that well; they commanded ships in the same squadron, that was all.

'Still, I don't suppose I'll have to put up with him for much longer, whatever happens.'

Strickland did not elaborate, but Thurston caught his tone of voice, tried to keep his reply light. 'Don't go doing a *Royal Oak*.'

They were crossing the flight deck now, the rain still coming down, harder now, so that large drops were penetrating Thurston's shirt. 'I shan't. He hasn't called the bandmaster a bugger. Yet. And he's not worth scuppering my career for, much as I'd like to tell him what I think of him.'

They stopped alongside the Avenger. Someone came forward with Thurston's Mae West. The pilot and gunner, warned of his approach, were already on board.

'Well, here's your chariot of fire, Bob. Remember me to the sheilas.'

'I will. Any particular sheila?'

Strickland laughed, aimed a mock buffet which Thurston sidestepped neatly. 'I should have seen that coming.' Then he grew serious again, his voice lowered. 'How many was it that you lost, did you say?'

'Twenty-nine.'

'Too many. Far too many.'

Aboard *Inflexible* the news was greeted with cheers and relief.

'Sydney. And about fucking time! How long is it since we last saw a fucking woman, even those native bags at Manus? Some of them weighed sixteen stone if they weighed an ounce! And had the chance of some real food, instead of this shit?' The man stirred the mess of meat and vegetables on his plate. 'No wonder that bloody Jap topped himself, having to eat this muck.'

'How long will we get this time?'

'Not long enough, that's for certain. Depends how long it takes to patch the old girl up. And that depends on the Aussies. Here's hoping their dockyard mateys decide to go on a nice long strike!'

Inflexible fuelled and took on stores, the tanker steaming on her port side, joined to her by the flexible hoses through which precious fuel oil streamed into her hungry tanks, an elderly freighter flying the Norwegian flag to starboard, the necessary items coming across by jackstay. Stores assistants with clipboards checked numbers painted on the crates, cursed as pencils ripped through rain-sodden paper, whilst chains of ratings shifted the crates below, their contents to be stowed in the appropriate places.

'Sardines for supper,' one of the signalmen said cheerfully.

It was one of those odd little customs, one which had grown up over the last months, that sardines were on the menu, half a can per man, on replenishing days. There would be a long queue at the Naafi when it re-opened, the men eager to buy the sweets and chocolate which had had to be rationed since the last replenish-ment. More cigarettes would be smoked than usual, until the men began to realise that their supplies were not unlimited and either cut back or ran out com-pletely. But that would not happen this time, for in little more than a fortnight the ship would reach Syd-ney.

The more seriously wounded were transferred to a hos-pital ship, the stretchers with their burdens swaying sickeningly over the grey water, on which a heavy swell was now running, splashes of white foam showing in the gap between the two ships. There were mixed feelings at seeing them go; on the one hand the knowledge that the other ship had better facilities for treating them, on the other the sense that they were losing some of their own people, who, whatever the outcome, were unlikely to return to the carrier.

'Boat ahoy?'
'*Persephone!*'
'Wonder what he wants,' said Carstairs.

Thurston sent Boy Maxwell to his main cabin for his telescope, left the bridge and went aft to the quarter-deck, from which the jumping ladder had been hastily rigged. The side party were in their places, awaiting the unexpected visitor, the air of excitement almost pal-pable. No outsider, apart from a Seafire pilot who had force landed on her decks, had come aboard *Inflexible* since the two days at Leyte, half a lifetime ago across the events of recent weeks. Boy Maxwell doubled up, Thurston took the telescope from him and pushed it under his arm, feeling the coldness of the metal barrel through the damp cotton of his shirt. *Persephone*'s seaboat, an eight-oared cutter, was rolling over the waves, raising patches of foam as the oars cut through the water, their rhythm a little ragged.

'Out of time,' the Bosun's mate muttered.

There were small grins among the side party, which meant, '*We* can do better than that!'

The boat disappeared out of sight beneath the ship's side.

'Toss oars!'

Feet rattled on the ladder. The Bosun's mate brought the silver-plated call to his lips, and the pipe shrilled over the grey water. *Persephone*'s Captain reached the head of the ladder, right hand raised in salute. The pipe finished. Thurston came forward, shook his hand.

'My sea cabin's this way.'

In the maze of compartments and passageways below the hangar there was little sign of the explosion, but once inside the island the signs of recent damage were plain to see: the scorched paintwork, marked by the water which had been used to put out the fire, the torpedomen still at work in odd corners, the detour made necessary by the damage to the deck outside the FDR. The Captain's face was set; he said nothing.

'Thank you, Maxwell, that'll be all. Drink?'

'I shouldn't at sea, but I will have something.'

'Gin, Dunhill, and a ginger ale for me.'

'Aye aye, sir.' Dunhill looked slightly surprised.

'My regular servant's in the sick bay.'

'That's what I came about,' the other man said uncomfortably.

Captain William Stanley was only thirty-seven and therefore one of the youngest captains in the service; *Persephone* was his first command. He was reputed to be something of a high-flyer, and known to have considerable private means. Thurston had met him only once before, at a reception in Sydney when the task force was assembling. He had been quite different then, smiling, with an overdressed woman on his arm, and, Thurston had thought, rather full of himself.

Stanley waited until Dunhill had brought the drinks and he had taken a long pull at his gin. 'There's no point in beating about the bush. We did it. At least it was my guns. We were following the kamikaze that was heading for you, and held on for a fraction too long. How many?'

'Twenty-nine. And nineteen wounded.'

'Seriously?'

'Some of them.'

'I couldn't be more sorry. That's all I can say.' There was a slight pause. Stanley had been sitting at the side of the bunk opposite him, his eyes on Thurston's feet. Now his head came up a little, the tone of his voice altered. 'Your servant, is he badly hurt?'

'No, just very shocked.'

'Tell him I hope he's better soon.'

Thurston supposed that this was the simple human level, that of the single individual or small group of individuals, where the extent of the losses could sink in. *If you want me to tell you that I forgive you, that it was simply one of those accidents that can happen to anybody, I can't, but I do know that it was one of those things which can happen, all too easily, in wartime, and that Hopkinson and all the rest were casualties of war as much as if it had been a Japanese or German shell which killed them.*

'I will. It might cheer him up.'

'It was quite obvious, as soon as it happened. My

111

Gunnery Officer was following the fall of shot.'

'Are you quite sure?'

'Yes. None of the others were firing at that aircraft and on that bearing. I suppose there'll have to be a court martial.'

'There may be. I don't know.'

A court martial, Stanley well knew, would probably be the end of his career, even if he and his Gunnery Officer were to be acquitted. His career might well not recover even without one.

Stanley finished his glass. 'I've taken up enough of your time.' He began to get up.

'That's all right.' He had not been aboard more than ten minutes in any case. 'If there's anything I can do . . .'

It was said for form's sake, because there was nothing. Thurston noticed that his own glass was still full, untouched.

As Stanley went over the side Thurston noticed that the atmosphere had changed. Strange how something could have got about so quickly. He supposed Stanley's boat's crew had let something slip.

Once again it seemed a long way back to the bridge, across the flight deck and past the men working on the aircraft, then through the door at the base of the island and up inside. He saw again, as if for the first time, the chaos the explosion had made, strangely lit and shadowy under the emergency lighting, festoons of electric cable hanging from the deckhead. The smell of burning hung around him, though the scuttles were open and the fans forced a draught of fresher air through the passages. Two men were at work with brushes and buckets on a section of bulkhead outside the Ops Room, one of them whistling tunelessly through his teeth, water running down to form a dirty puddle on the deck, taking with it shapeless gobbets which could only be human flesh. Thurston thought of the missing man, could not prevent himself from wondering whether those fatty lumps had been part of him until the explosion blew his body to nothing.

He turned aside into his sea cabin, gripped his hands into fists and slammed first one and then the other against the bulkhead. Such a bloody bloody waste. They were all his men, and thirty of them were dead because some bloody fool hadn't checked firing when he should have done. Thirty of them, some only kids, a year or two out of school, alive one day and now dead, each leaving an empty space which could never be filled. He moved up against the bulkhead, rested his brow against the hard metal surface, screwed his eyes shut so that he could not betray himself. *Oh God, why did it have to happen this way? Why them?* and the old familiar litany, *I should not be here. I should be dead with the rest of them.* He opened his eyes, stepped back from the bulkhead, uncurled his hands.

'Captain, sir, is there anything you want?'

He turned on Dunhill, all the rage and grief exploding into two words: 'Get OUT!'

It was late afternoon by the time the fuelling was finished and the hoses disconnected so that the tanker could turn away to join her consorts. The huge assembly of ships began to separate once more into its component parts, the task force, which would turn north-west once more and be back on station in the operating zone before dawn, and the Fleet Train, which would head back towards Manus to take on more stores, ready for another replenishment twelve or fourteen days hence. *Inflexible*, and the two destroyers which had peeled off from the screen to act as her escort on the passage south, now belonged to neither, and a sense of separateness from the rest had developed during the long day, reaching its height as she turned away from the task force and the men on the upper deck could watch the other warships recede into the greyness and the rain.

Chapter Ten

The cloud broke and the sun came out once more, drying the wet decks in a matter of minutes. Working
parties chipped the blackened and peeling paint off the
port side of the island and replaced it with a fresh coat
of light grey, though the splinter holes remained, providing, as the wags kept saying until it grew monotonous, 'a bit of light and air in there'. Air patrols flew
during the daylight hours; there were still a few
Japanese submarines at sea, and if one got within range
a fleet carrier would provide a tempting target.

But with *Inflexible* and her escorts making twenty-
five knots and steaming directly away from the operational zone, thoughts of the Japanese were receding
and on board a holiday atmosphere was becoming apparent. The ship went over to tropical routine, all work
done in the forenoon as far as was possible, so that
most of the men, except those actually on watch, were
off duty after midday. Shirts came off and men lingered
on the flight deck to work on their tans for the benefit
of the sheilas when they got to Sydney, so that broadcasts had to be made to make it clear that anyone who
rendered himself unfit for duty through sunburn would
be on a charge.

A deck hockey league started again in the Dog
Watches, and after weeks in which they had been too
occupied with other duties even to think of music, the
band began daily practices. Camp beds appeared on
deck after dark as men came up from below to sleep,
though it was after eleven before the steel finally re-

leased all the heat absorbed during the day. Thurston started to run once more, to the mild amusement of the less energetic among the men, a dozen circuits of the flight deck immediately after Dawn Action Stations, before the heat got too bad. The padre held a belated thanksgiving service for Victory in Europe, though this had a slightly hollow ring, for the war *Inflexible*'s men were fighting was still very much on.

Spencer, and others less seriously wounded, lingered in the sick bay, half empty and restored almost to normality now that the worst cases had gone.

'I have to admit, sir, I'm not very happy about young Spencer.' Surgeon Commander Grant was in the habit of referring to anyone younger than himself as 'young'. 'He's normally a cheerful sort of fellow, is he not, and I'd have expected him to buck himself up by now. I'll hang on to him another day or two, until he's ready to start using that arm again, then perhaps you'd have him back on light duties. That might help. Give him something to do, and less time to think.'

Grant was right. All Spencer's bounce, all his usual cheerfulness and cheek seemed to have been knocked out of him. He moped listlessly around the sick bay, getting up when he was told to, and going back to his cot without resistance. Even a pile of letters from his wife and stepdaughters had failed to excite his interest. He was no trouble, the PMO told Thurston, 'but I'd be happier about him if he was giving me cheek the way he usually does. Still, it's early days. I expect he'll buck up soon enough.'

It was midway through the afternoon watch, too hot as close as this to the equator, for those off watch to do anything more than sit in the shade, either below or on deck in the narrow zone where the shadow of the island fell and the benefit of the twenty-five-knot slipstream could be felt. They stretched out on blankets and hammock mattresses to protect themselves from the hot metal deck, working their way through some of the dog-eared paperbacks constantly circulating the mess-decks.

'There's someone who fancies himself as a thinker,' said Thurston after studying someone's reading matter through his binoculars.

'*The Intelligent Woman's Guide to Socialism and Capitalism*,' read the Torpedo Officer – who was Principal Control Officer and would be responsible for the ship in Thurston's absence from the bridge – after making similar use of his binoculars.

'I don't like the sound of that,' said the Navigator, 'though I suppose it could be worse. It might be *Das Kapital* or even *Mein Kampf*.'

'I don't think we need worry too much about *Mein Kampf*, in the light of recent events,' said Thurston.

'In any case,' said the Navigator, 'it's supposed to be absolutely unreadable. Some Jerry professor described it as "sixty-four thousand offences against German grammar".'

'And ended up in a concentration camp,' chimed in the Midshipman of the Watch, before remembering where he was and turning his eyes to the deck in embarrassment.

'*The Intelligent Woman's Guide*,' mused the Navigator. 'Is there such a thing as an intelligent woman?'

Thurston pulled himself up on to his bridge chair, taking care not to let bare skin make contact with the metal. He thought suddenly of Kate. Their twentieth wedding anniversary was in a fortnight's time, and would be the sixteenth they had spent apart.

Ten months now since he had last seen Kate, in that hotel in Greenock which had seen better days. His images of her, when she came into his mind, lying on his bunk at night, or during these quiet times on the

117

bridge, were strongly sexual, concentrating on her breasts and the triangle of hair between her legs, bringing the unwelcome arousal and reluctant recourse to the lonely solace of his midshipman days. This phase would pass eventually, he knew from experience, and for days and weeks he would barely think of her in those terms, until another of the phases began, and he would find himself thinking of her again with half-closed eyes, and the heaviness in his loins.

They had breakfasted in company, but afterwards Thurston's father and stepmother had quietly recognised that he and Kate would want to be by themselves for a time and had gone out for some fresh air, taking Helen with them.

In a short time all traces of their presence would have been cleared away. Kate's suitcase was packed and labelled, an old stirrup leather buckled around it for extra security, the twins' paraphernalia consigned to another bag which rested on top of the suitcase. Everything of his was already on board *Inflexible*, apart from the few requirements for an overnight stay ashore, which were stowed away in his briefcase. Kate was feeding the twins, in the hope of getting them off to sleep for the first stage of the journey at least, sitting on an upright chair opposite him, her back to the window, supporting one child to each breast – she had decided, after some experimenting, that it was both quicker and less fraught with difficulty to feed them together, rather than leave one howling in his cot while his brother was dealt with.

He and Kate did not say much; they always ran out of things to say on these occasions, once the usual trivialities of 'Have you got everything?' and 'Don't forget to pay the gas bill', had been gone through. Soon a taxi would arrive to take Kate to the station, and then there would be nothing more to keep him here, nothing to hold him back from the walk to the pier where Petty

Officer MacLeod and the Captain's motorboat would be waiting for him, but in this brief interval there was Kate, and the two small bundles clinging determinedly to her, Kate's cheek resting on one downy head, a serene smile on her face and in her eyes.

'Can you take Andrew for a few minutes, while this greedy little pig has his fill?'

Kate looked indulgently down at Thomas, then detached the second bundle and passed it across. Thurston settled the child on his knee, steadying him with his arms, uneasily conscious of what Andrew might do to his trousers at a singularly inopportune moment; looked down at him, at the blue eyes as yet no different from any other infant's, the rounded unformed face with its blob of a nose which might one day become the hawkish Thurston features. Andrew put out his hand, seized Thurston's index finger in his tiny fist, the whole of his hand shorter than that one finger of his father's, each digit a perfect miniature, complete with nail and tiny creased knuckles and already bearing its own unique print. Opposite, Thomas was still sucking on his mother's breast.

Kate smiled, 'He takes after his big brother.'

Kate always said of George that his first complete sentence had been, 'Mum, I'm hungry,' and that he had been saying it at half-hourly intervals ever since.

'I suppose I'd better get moving.'

The greedy little pig had had his fill. Kate got up, deposited Thomas and Andrew in their carry-cot.

'It's been lovely seeing you again.'

'And you. And the boys.'

'Despite the racket they make.'

'It beats me how something that size could make so much noise.'

Then it was as it had been at the beginning of the war, standing on *Connaught*'s quarterdeck with George, dressed in his new cadet's uniform before leaving for his first term at Dartmouth, knowing that it would be years before they met again, wondering whether he would ever hear George's unbroken boy's voice after this. *Inflexible* was destined for the East Indies. Next time he saw Thomas and Andrew they would not be babies but small boys, walking, talking, and he would be a stranger to them.

If he accepted Masters' offer it would mean an end to the long separations from Kate, and he would be able to see more of the twins as they were growing up than he had of George and Helen. Their lives would be settled instead of being punctuated by upheavals every two or three years, each time with the business of finding somewhere to live. He and Kate had begun their married life in furnished rooms; when George's arrival had drawn near Kate had moved back to her parents' house, staying there and having Helen while Thurston spent two years on the China Station. There had been a cottage with no electricity and a roof which leaked a forty-minute motorbike journey away when he was a Term Officer at Dartmouth – Kate had considered it quite ridiculous that married officers were required to live in and were forbidden to have their wives living within thirty miles of the College. It was followed by a pokey flat in Greenwich when he was at the Staff College, then a series of houses gradually increasing in size as he rose through the ranks to Commander.

It struck him that he had no idea what he would have done had he not chosen to go to Osborne and into the Navy at the age of twelve and a half. There had been the Geddes Axe of the early 1920s, during which one-third of the Navy's lieutenants had found themselves compulsorily retired in the cuts which had followed the last war. Some had used their gratuities to fund themselves through university and had carved out careers in law or medicine, some had emigrated, and others had found the world outside the services had little use for them; they had gone from job to job, each a little worse paid and a little more insecure than the last, had sunk any savings in abortive business ventures and usually acquired wives and children along the way who had to be provided for somehow. And those who had been axed had been in their twenties, without family commitments, not forty-five as he was, with three children still dependent on him.

On a still, suffocatingly hot morning, *Inflexible* came into Manus, a fringe of low coral islands linked by causeways rising only a few feet above the water which circled the harbour which had become the advanced base for the British Pacific Fleet. The harbour gave the place its importance. The islands had been captured from the Japanese fifteen months before, and as soon as the fighting was over the American Navy had sent in their Construction Battalions – the Seebees – who had hacked an airfield out of the jungle which extended as far as the water, laid on electricity and piped water, and built a complex of administrative and accommodation blocks, with the ubiquitous PX and suppliers of Coca-Cola to serve the Fleet which was now moving the battle forward towards the Japanese mainland. Manus, though utilised by the British, was unquestionably American territory. The base was dry, with severe penalties for being caught in possession of liquor, except in the small areas which the Royal Navy declared to be their own. American sentries patrolled in white-painted steel helmets, American jeeps travelled on the right-hand side, an American radio station broadcast American music over loudspeakers.

Thurston was in his main cabin aft, for the first time in weeks shifting into tropical whites, and thinking that the trousers were quite definitely looser than when he had last worn them. Odd, considering the stodgy food and lack of exercise of the last weeks. His face, too, was

121

thinner, all the features more sharply etched, and the creases around his eyes a little deeper.

Inflexible would be in Manus for only a few hours, long enough to pick up mail and top her oil tanks, but the formal call on the American Admiral was part of the required routine of entering a foreign port; the service expected it, and the Americans expected it.

Thurston heard a noise behind him and turned his head to see Spencer standing in the open doorway of his sleeping cabin.

'Morning, Spencer. Come to make sure that Dunhill's been looking after me properly?'

Spencer was also thinner, and his face bore a sick-bay pallor. He was wearing his seaman's cotton flannel and white shorts, a bandage peeping out below one sleeve, and there were gym shoes on his feet.

'I'm excused boots, sir.'

'How are your feet?'

'All right. It was mostly the tops that was burnt so they're all right to walk on. Long as I don't wear boots.'

'And the arm?'

'That's all right too, sir. It wasn't nothing much to start with. Didn't really need to be in the sick bay.' Spencer had not yet looked up from the carpet, and his voice was a low monotone.

'So you're ready to take over again, and Dunhill can go back to the wardroom?'

'S'pose so, sir,' Spencer said after a moment.

Thurston moved past Spencer to the door. Dunhill was waiting outside. 'Dunhill, I shan't be needing you for the time being.'

Dunhill looked surprised, and did not move.

'Dunhill, you heard me.'

'Aye aye, sir. I'll be in the pantry, when you need me.'

'No, just go and find yourself something else to do for half an hour.' Thurston realised suddenly why it was

122

that he disliked Dunhill. He didn't trust him, and Dunhill wanted Spencer's job too much.

'Spencer, what on earth's got into you?'

Spencer was still standing in the middle of the carpet, gym shoes planted side by side, staring down at the pale geometric pattern, regularly spaced on the wine-red background.

'Don't know, sir.'

Thurston sat down on the end of his bed, unhooked the high collar of his whites, his fingers sliding sweatily over the starched drill.

'This isn't like you. I've never known you like this before.'

'No, sir.'

'Is there anything wrong at home?' It didn't seem likely, but . . .

'No, sir.'

'Rosie and the girls are all right?'

'Yes, sir.'

'And your mother?' Spencer's mother lived by herself in Portsmouth, and had been bombed out earlier in the war.

'Yes, sir. She's okay.'

'Go and make us both a cup of your infamous tea, Spencer.'

'You're supposed to be goin' ashore, sir.'

'That can wait. He's only a *Yank* Admiral after all.'

It wasn't much of a joke, but Spencer, encouragingly, managed a ghost of a smile. He turned, and walked slowly away to his pantry.

'Kettle's on, sir. Do you want it in here, or next door?'

'In here, Spencer.' His sleeping cabin was more private, less formal than the day cabin it opened off.

A few minutes later Spencer came back with the tray, held carefully in both hands.

'Can you manage that?'

123

'Yes, sir. The doctor said I was to just keep using me arm like I always do.' He placed the tray on the locker top next to the bed. 'It wants a couple of minutes to brew, sir.'

'Sit down, Spencer.' Thurston indicated the chair opposite him. Spencer looked uncomfortable, but sat, on the edge of the chair, gym shoes planted squarely side by side. 'Now, what's the matter?'

Spencer said nothing, looking away from Thurston towards the photograph of Kate on the locker top, his face twisting up with misery and uncertainty.

'That tea should be about ready now, sir,' he said eventually. He stood up, reached for the teapot, and carefully poured two cups.

Thurston shifted, felt a trickle of sweat run down between his shoulder blades, unfastened a couple of buttons and twisted his body to gain maximum benefit from the fan in the corner. Large damp patches had already spread over Spencer's flannel. Both scuttles were wide open, and the air which came in was heavy and humid.

'Rotten climate here.'

'Yes, sir.'

'Are you looking forward to Sydney?'

'S'pose so, sir.'

'You don't sound all that keen. Would you rather be back home with Rosie?' He was fishing, trying to persuade Spencer to talk about something so as to make him open up. He reached for his cup of tea, drank some of it. 'There's nothing wrong at home?'

'No, sir. Rosie and the girls are fine. So's me mum.' Spencer looked round, turning his head to look out through one of the scuttles, seeing nothing but the head of a palm tree somewhere ashore. 'Nothing wrong with them, sir. It's just me.'

'What do you mean?'

'Well, sir, you know how it was when I got this?' His eyes moved to his bandaged arm.

'I've got some idea.'

'Well, sir, I was trying to find the way out, and to help Hoppy. I knew he'd got it in the leg, but I didn't think it was anything much, something like what I'd got in my arm. He sounded like he was all right. And . . . well, sir, he wasn't. And if I'd done something, got one of those things – tourniquets – on his leg and stopped the bleeding, he'd have been all right. And I didn't, and now he's dead.' Spencer snivelled a little through his nose, screwed his eyes up and looked away.

Thurston passed him his cup of tea. He took it, but made no move to drink it, continuing to look away.

Thurston was trying to think of what to say. Perhaps Hopkinson would have lived had Spencer got a tourniquet on him, perhaps not. He tried to remember Hopkinson, but he was just another of the anonymous majority on board. Radar Mechanic First Class Anthony David Hopkinson. He had written the usual letter to his wife, Mrs June Hopkinson, whom Hopkinson had married on 19th August 1944, just before *Inflexible* sailed from the Clyde.

'Spencer, it probably wouldn't have made any difference. He didn't die from loss of blood; they tried to operate on him and he was too shocked to stand the anaesthetic.'

'Yes, sir, but if someone had done something earlier, if I'd have found the way out, and got him to the sick bay.'

'Spencer, you were wounded yourself, and you did your best for him.' Spencer would have done, he was quite sure of that. He thought for a moment of what it must have been like, the darkness and the disorientation, staggering on his scalded feet and supporting Hopkinson's dragging weight alongside him, wondering where the way out was, if there was still a way out, remembering his own angry helplessness on *Connaught*'s raft as one by one he watched his men die, and further back, in the dark recesses of memory, the claustro-

125

phobic terror in the wreckage of *Warrior*'s forward turret.

'I keep thinking, sir, that if I'd tried a bit harder I'd
have got him out all right. You know, sir, if you're trying hard enough you'll do it, like you did with Mr
Vincent in *Crusader*.'

That had to come, his own record thrown back at
him. Yes, he had kept Vincent afloat in the water when
Crusader went down, for as long as it took *Vittoria*'s
boat to reach them, but that was a different matter; he
was a good swimmer and had simply done what he had
been trained to do, before he had taken the time to
think about it. But Vincent, unlike Hopkinson, had
survived, though, with double pneumonia coming on
top of exposure and near-drowning, there had been a
long period when no one thought he would.

'Spencer, I don't suppose you'll believe me when I
say this, but you've no need to reproach yourself about
Hopkinson. You did what you could for him. It wasn't
because of anything you did or didn't do that he died.'
('You could not prevent the sinking, but afterwards you
did what you could for your men. You cannot carry the
whole world on your shoulders. That some of your men
died despite your efforts to save them does not destroy
the validity of those efforts.') 'You were there, and you
made the effort, you didn't just walk past him and leave
him to die alone down there.'

'No, sir.'

The ridiculous thing about all this was that Spencer
was far better at this sort of thing than he was. Spencer
could unselfconsciously put his arm round someone,
pat him on the shoulder, tell him, 'Come on, mate, it's
not as bad as all that,' where all he had were awkward
words and long pauses while he tried to think of what to
say.

'Does that help?'

'A bit, sir.' Spencer sounded brighter, and he was
looking towards Thurston once more. 'There's another

126

thing, sir. It's been bothering me a bit lately.' Spencer stopped, lifted the teapot and weighed it in his hand. 'Want some more tea, sir?' He poured two more cups.

'Go on.'

'Well, sir, the thing is, Rosie's girls are gorgeous, and they call me Daddy and everything, but it's not like having one of my own. And, well, sir, nothing's happened yet.'

'Spencer, don't forget you've been out here since last August.'

'Yes, sir, but we had long enough before that to get something started. You know what I mean, sir, Rosie's already got the girls, so maybe there's something wrong with me.'

'Spencer, you didn't have time to give yourselves much of a chance. How long have you and Rosie had together – a couple of months?'

'About that, sir. I didn't warm the bell with her – Rosie's not that kind of girl. We had a couple of weeks for our honeymoon – Rosie's mum and dad had the girls – and then we had that time when you was off flying with the Brylcreem boys and I was in Pompey barracks. And we was doing it just about every day, well, night – couldn't do much with the girls around – so that should've been enough. I mean, you and Mrs Thurston seem to have managed it quick enough.' Spencer's face had turned very red, and he was looking down towards the carpet again.

'It doesn't always happen as quickly as that.' Thurston felt that his own face was beginning to colour, and cast about in his mind for an example. 'My wife's sister and her husband had been married over two years before they had their first, and her husband's a farmer so he's always at home.'

'Yes, sir, but . . .' Spencer was struggling for words. 'When it's yourself . . . Me mum says she fell for me the first time she ever did it with me dad, and that was the first time she done it at all, so there wasn't anything else

127

she could do but marry him.' Spencer's father had been a stoker in one of Fisher's battle cruisers, but had stayed with Spencer's mother only long enough to see his son born, before deserting both the service and his wife. ('Mum still don't know what happened to him. She thought he might turn up one of these days, but she gave up that idea a long time ago. Didn't want me going in the Andrew, all the same.')

Thurston remembered Rear Admiral Manning-Wilson in Greenock ('We had some rather embarrassing tests done, and it turned out that I was the one who was sterile'). 'Have you had mumps, Spencer?'

'Yes, sir. Had 'em when I was seven, both sides and chickenpox at the same time, so I looked absolutely lovely.'

'Then you should be all right. I believe it can affect you if you get it later on, after your balls have dropped.'

'Yes I know that, sir.'

'Anyway, there's nothing you can do about it from here, so you wait until you get back to Rosie.'

'She won't know what's hit her, sir.'

'And my wife and I will come to the christening.'

'I'll want you to be godfather, sir, especially when Mrs Thurston couldn't make it to the wedding.'

'I'll hold you to that.'

''Course, sir.' Spencer looked hard at Thurston for a moment, his face twisting in distaste. 'Gawd, Dunghill didn't make much of a job of that ice-cream suit. There's a double crease in them trousers I could drive a train down. Give 'em here, sir. You can't go and see an Admiral looking like that, even if he is a Yank!'

Chapter Eleven

RAF Tern Hill, Shropshire, August 1944.

The Fifth Sea Lord did not believe in wasting time. Three days after their meeting, a letter arrived summoning Captain Thurston to the Admiralty for a second time.

'You'll be glad to hear that the matter has been under consideration, and it has been decided, in view of the fact that you are going to take over a fleet carrier – and for this reason alone, I must stress – that there is sufficient justification for your having some flying training. There's about six or seven weeks before you're needed in *Inflexible*, and we've arranged with the RAF that, subject to your satisfying their doctors that you're fit to fly, you can spend the time at a place called Tern Hill, which is somewhere near Shrewsbury, where I believe they fly Harvards. Ever heard of them?'

'Yes, sir, and thank you.'

'Don't thank me. You're only doing it because the service stands to benefit, and don't forget that. We've arranged for you to start on Monday, and if you can get yourself across to Kelvin House for 1400 this afternoon the quacks will give you the once-over. The RAF are insisting you pass their flying medical, as you're about twice the age of the chaps they usually train as pilots. It's only going to be a six-week course, we can't spare you for any longer, so you won't get wings for it, of course, but it should be enough for your purposes.'

The RAF did not waste time either. A set of instructions arrived two days later advising Captain Thurston to report to 5 Service Flying Training School, RAF Tern Hill, by 2359 on the Sunday, ready to begin his flying course at 0800 on the Monday, together with a letter from Group Captain J. C. Atkinson, Station Commander, suggesting that he take the train which was due to arrive at Market Drayton at 1810, where there would be transport to meet him.

Tern Hill was a peacetime RAF station, built in the last few years before the war over a bare rounded hill set in rolling farmland a few miles from the Welsh border. There were signs of the war in the armed sentries and barbed wire coiled around the main gate, but these came second to the impression of lush green landscape and ordered routine.

'Group Captain said to take you to the mess, sir,' the driver said.

The car stopped at the gate. A corporal in a white-topped cap with a service policeman's armlet came forward. Thurston handed his identity card through the window. The corporal saw the navy blue, a look of surprise and puzzlement crossed his face, then he recovered himself, handed the card back, stepped a pace back and snapped off a salute.

'We don't get too many naval blokes here, sir,' said the driver as he moved off, stating what had already become obvious.

The Officers' Mess was a red-brick building, clearly based on the same design as the barrack blocks and administration buildings which were visible further off. There was a deep-reddish carpet with a geometric pattern in the entrance hall, and spring sunlight streaming in through the sash windows. A Wing Commander emerged from the anteroom to one side, where he had obviously been awaiting Thurston's arrival.

'Captain Thurston? I'm Charles Palmer, Senior Technical Officer and PMC. The Station Commander asked me to pass on his apologies for not being here to welcome you. He's been called away to Group unexpectedly, but he expects to be back in time for dinner.'

The speech had the air of being rehearsed, and was made a little quickly, as if the speaker was slightly nervous. It was strange that the station commander of a training station should have been called away on urgent business on a Sunday evening, but perhaps it was not so surprising. Thurston was senior to the Group Captain in terms of time in rank, and so his presence on the station as a student pilot would be awkward at best for the Station Commander, and without goodwill and common sense on both sides, could easily turn out to be an embarrassment.

Palmer led him away from the reception desk, through the door of the anteroom. The large room was deserted, apart from one young officer curled into a leather chair, legs over one of the arms, engrossed in the Sunday newspapers. He looked up, then started, and got to his feet, his face colouring a little.

Thurston came to his rescue. 'Do please sit down.'

The young man resumed his reading, now seated square in the chair, feet side by side on the floor.

'Dinner's at 1930, sir,' Palmer continued. 'I expect you'd like to freshen up after your journey, so I suggest you come back to reception when you're ready, and I can take you into the bar for a drink and introduce you to the Wing Commander Flying – Wing Commander Garden. Then when the CO arrives we can all go in to dinner together.' He hesitated for a moment, as if he had finally reached the point where he must bring up something which had been hanging over him until now.

'There is a slight problem, sir, which I hope you don't mind me raising. We don't normally have anyone as senior as yourself living in the mess. It's really rather

131

unusual. We do have a number of suites – bedroom and sitting room – which we give to squadron leaders and above who are living in, and we would normally have given you one, of course.' Palmer was clearly trying to express himself as tactfully as possible. 'However, they're all in use at the moment, and it would mean a fairly major reshuffle.'

Thurston caught his meaning immediately. 'That's quite all right. I'm only here for a short time and as a student anyway.'

The PMC looked relieved. 'The single rooms are quite comfortable, sir,' he hastened to add, 'and a good size, and if you're quite happy . . . '

'I should think that after a sea cabin I could make myself comfortable almost anywhere.'

'If you're quite sure, sir . . . '

The WAAF corporal from the reception desk escorted him upstairs. The room turned out to be approximately the same size as the one he and Kate shared at home. It contained a single bed, fitted wardrobe and chest of drawers, and a small bookcase, all of similar design to those found in warships and made of the same dark varnished wood, as well as a washbasin with a glass shelf and mirror above it. The room was in one corner of the building and so had windows in two of its walls, one looking out to the airmen's barrack blocks some distance away, the other over a sports field towards the airfield. A young Waaf was unpacking Thurston's suitcase and stowing its contents away.

'I'm Abbott, sir. I'm your batwoman. Unless you've brought anyone with you.'

He hadn't. Spencer had finally married his Rosie only a fortnight ago, and in any case tended to regard all uniforms except those of the Royal Navy as red rags to a bull.

'Will you be wanting a bath before dinner, sir?'

'Please.'

'I'll just go and start it running.'

Abbott went out, set off a distant sound of running water, and came back.

'Bathroom's two doors down, sir. Breakfast starts at 0700, and most of the officers get called at about that time unless they're on early flying.'

'I don't think that should cause any difficulties.'

'Very good, sir. I'll call you with your tea at 0700, and then take your shoes away and clean them. How do you have your tea in the morning?'

'Milk, one sugar.'

'Yes, sir.'

It was not so unlike the mess in a naval shore estab lishment, but there was an unfamiliarity about it as well, symbolised by the way Abbott had said 'Yes, sir' and 'Very good, sir', not 'Aye aye, sir'. Abbott was looking at his white shirts as she put them away in a drawer, fingering the stiff collars.

There was the same strangeness the next morning. Abbott left his battledress out for him, freshly pressed – 'That's what everyone wears here, sir, except in the mess at night' – then breakfast at a long table in the dining room, with WAAF mess waiters moving soft-footed with racks of toast, and silence behind news-papers. Most of the faces were new, most shoulder straps bearing the single thin ring of pilot officers; he remembered a commotion late last night as a crowd of them must have arrived back from weekend leave. There were glances at his navy blue, unspoken questions of what he was doing there. He tried to work out how long it was since he last messed with other people instead of alone in his own cabin.

Strangeness too, in walking with Palmer from the mess to the Station Commander's office in one of the administration buildings, passing and being passed by airmen and Waafs on foot and on bicycles, each face showing varying degrees of surprise at the sight of this strange senior officer in the uniform of another service, and at their salutes being returned palm down, naval fashion.

The Station Commander was in his office, Wing Commander Garden sitting on a chair to the right of his desk. Palmer stayed for only a moment, and then left. There were the usual polite enquiries. Had he slept well? Was the accommodation all right?

'More than adequate.'

'Yes, it's not a bad mess, and it's big enough not to get too crowded. Charles Palmer will be relieved, though. He's been having kittens about where to put you ever since we knew you were coming here.'

'Then I had better make it clear before we go any further that I'm here purely and simply to learn to fly. I neither want nor expect any special privileges.'

'Of course.' The Group Captain smiled. 'That's as we expected.'

But they all knew this to be an impossibility. No other student pilot was going to wear four stripes on his arms and the ribbon of the VC on his coat. They had all looked at the ribbon for a moment, in the mess bar the night before, as if to satisfy themselves that it was real, then had pointedly ignored it.

The Group Captain nodded to Wing Commander Garden, who took over the conversation.

'How much flying have you done, sir?' he asked without any preamble.

'Just over fifteen hours, three of them solo. All on Tigers, and quite unofficial – my Commander (Flying) in my last ship had a pal at Abbotsinch who was a QFI and I went up with him.'

It sounded very little.

'That's rather less than I expected. I had a rather garbled telephone call from the Admiralty, that's all I had to go on. You'll need at least another ten hours on Tigers before we can convert you on to the Harvard.'

'Will that cause any problems?' the Group Captain asked.

'Shouldn't do.' He began speaking to Thurston again. 'We've a Tiger here we use as a hack. I'll arrange for you to have the use of that. And we've an RLG – Relief Landing Ground – over at Chetwynd, which we use for training. I'll arrange for it to be open from 0700 to 0800 for you, and again in the evening from 1800 to 1900, after regular flying finishes. That means you'll have the place to yourself and your Tiger flying won't get in the way of normal Harvard training. Once you've got enough hours on Tigers, we can integrate your flying programme with the rest. Obviously, we can't cover the whole Harvard syllabus in six weeks, so we'll have to be a bit selective in what we cover with you. Do you have your logbook with you?'

'It went down with my last ship.'

The Group Captain looked a little uncomfortable. He was a smooth faced man of medium height, balding from the front, a little younger than Thurston, too young for the last war and probably too old to have done much flying on operations in this, although he, like Garden, wore a DFC ribbon.

'Oh well,' said Garden, 'I expect you can remember what you've covered up to now. I'm going to attach you to 3 Squadron for admin purposes. They're the junior course here at the moment, started last week. There are actually three squadrons here, doing an eight-week course. I'll put you with 'F' Flight, but that won't mean all that much as far as flying is concerned, since you're effectively a course of one.

'It may not have been explained to you that we mainly carry out acclimatisation training for the chaps who've done their *ab initio* flying training overseas. Until a couple of years ago we took our student pilots from EFTS – Elementary Flying Training School – after

135

they'd soloed on Tigers and done about thirty hours' flying in all. Now most of our training, apart from the very early stages, which are done here mainly to check that the chaps really have got enough aptitude to be worth persevering with, is done overseas. At the end of the EFTS course the students are divided between single-engined and multi-engined training, mainly on aptitude, but partly on what the service is most in need of at the time. The budding single-engine pilots go on to Harvards, and the rest go on to Oxfords, and fly twins from then on. That stage lasts eight months, and they should do about a hundred and twenty hours in the air. They get their wings at the end of it, and at one time they would have gone straight on to Operational Training Units to fly the aircraft they'll fly on ops. These days, however, all the training up to wings standard is done overseas, particularly in Canada and America, but there's also a school in Rhodesia and a couple in South Africa. The OTUs were finding that the chaps could fly all right, but they'd learned all their navigation over prairies and the like, and couldn't cope with the conditions back here. So, the single-engine chaps come here for a short course to get the hang of flying over here.

'Normally, one flight in each squadron will fly in the morning and the other in the afternoon, and they do some ground school work, mainly refresher work because they've covered it for the wings exam, when they're not flying. You'll have to do some ground school as well as flying, and I've got OC Ground School thrashing out a programme for you at the moment, but we'll keep that to a minimum, and as your time here is so short, you'll fly morning *and* afternoon to begin with. But we've found from experience that no one will absorb more than about two hours' flying instruction a day – after that it just doesn't go in – which means that the most we'll manage in six weeks will be sixty hours or so, and that's not allowing for bad weather.

'Now, if you come with me to my office, sir, I'll introduce you to your instructor.'

Garden climbed into the driving seat of a blue-painted jeep which was parked outside.

'My Flying Wing offices, and Tech Wing's for that matter, are down in what we call the Sunshine Hangar – it was blitzed in '40 and still has a big hole in the roof. Normally we all get about by push-bike – the Station Warrant Officer will issue you one later today. I've arranged for Flight Sergeant Lines to fly with you. He's an A1 category instructor, very experienced, and if you really do want to be treated like any other student, then he's your man.' Garden looked at his watch. 'I told him to be available at 0900 hours, so he should be there when we arrive.'

Garden drove rapidly along the narrow roads towards the airfield, manoeuvring around various cyclists and pedestrians, and talking over his shoulder 'It was a bit of a surprise when we heard you were coming, sir. Chap from Command rang to say the Admiralty were asking whether we could fit "one of their chaps" in for some fairly basic flying training – we do get chaps coming for some refresher flying before they go back on ops, if they've been stuck on the ground for a long time, and I should imagine that's why they thought to send you here – and would I speak to him. I rang the fellow at the Admiralty, and of course I rather put my foot in it by asking what was stopping this chap of his from learning to fly in the normal way. I got one of the bigger shocks of my life – roughly comparable to finding a 109 on my tail for the first time – when he said you were a four-ring captain and a VC to boot!'

Once in his office Garden spoke into his telephone. A moment later a smartly dressed NCO marched in and saluted. This was another difference which Thurston had already noted; the RAF, unlike the Navy, did salute superiors who were bareheaded.

'Captain Thurston, Flight Sergeant Lines, who'll be flying with you while you're here. Flight Sergeant Lines, Captain Thurston.'

Thurston put out his hand. 'How do you do?'

'Good morning, sir.'

Lines was small and wiry, with sandy hair and a neatly clipped moustache, dapper in his grey-blue battledress, which he wore with the indefinable but instantly obvious tautness of the regular senior NCO. There was the diagonally striped ribbon and silver rosette of the Distinguished Flying Medal and bar beneath the pilot's wings above his left breast pocket. Lines had a senior NCO's ageless face, but Thurston guessed him to be about thirty.

'What do I call you?' Thurston asked as they were leaving.

' "Flight", sir, unless you want to be very formal, when it's "Flight Sergeant".' Lines' voice had a slight underlay of Liverpool.

Lines asked him about his flying experience, listening in silence as he went through it.

'We'll go over to Chetwynd this evening, sir. With any luck we'll have the place to ourselves by then. Just see how you get on. That gives us the rest of today to get all the kit you'll need, and for me to show you where everything is. When did you last do any flying?'

'About a fortnight ago.'

'And that was after your sinking?'

'Yes.'

'That should be all right then.'

He knew what Lines meant, that the sinking might have affected his nerve for flying.

'Better draw your flying kit to start with, sir. Then I can show you your locker in the Flight, and we can leave it there while we go and pick up everything else you need.'

The stores proved to be deserted. Lines went to the counter, banged on it with his fist. 'Corporal Tyler!'

There was a long pause, and at length a man shuffled out from behind the row of shelves, a pencil tucked behind his ear, his untidy form draped in a long brown coat.

'Took your time.'

'What do you expect with my feet, Flight? I'm excused boots on account of my bunions, marching, PT . . . ' The Corporal had a mouthful of uneven yellow teeth. 'What do you want?'

'Brought one of my students to draw flying kit, if you can be persuaded to let anything out of your clutches.'

The Corporal seemed not to have noticed Thurston, who was standing a little way back from the counter, leaving the talking to Lines. 'He's a bit bloody late. Should've been here a fortnight ago with the rest, and he should have had his flying kit when he came here! What's he done with it, flogged it on the black market?'

Lines looked briefly at Thurston, and grinned at him. 'This chap's a wee bit special, Corporal Tyler, and he's lost all his kit.'

'I hope he's got a bloody good excuse then, if he's not going to pay for it!' The Corporal looked past Lines for the first time, his mouth slowly dropping open as he took in Thurston's gold lace and medal ribbons.

'Got a perfectly good excuse, Corporal Tyler,' said Lines. 'Kit's at the bottom of the Arctic Ocean.'

Corporal Tyler shuffled back behind the shelves, could be heard shouting at some unseen minion, and returned with a pile of flying suits and a couple of sheepskin Irvin jackets. 'Try these on, sir, see if they fit. What size shoes do you take? And what size hat?'

The Corporal took the business very seriously, bidding Thurston to walk up and down in his new flying boots and getting down on his knees to prod the toes with his thumb, asking anxiously, 'Do they fit right, sir?'

'Makes a change,' said Lines. 'Getting kit from him is like getting blood out of a stone, and as for kit that fits, you can forget it. If you can get it on, it fits, as far as he's concerned.'

The pile of kit mounted on the counter: flying suit, Irvin jacket, boots, goggles, two flying helmets, one with Gosport tubes for the Tiger Moth, a second for the Harvard – 'You'll need an oxygen mask to go with that,' Lines said. 'We get that in Safety Equipment when we go for your parachute' – long brown leather gloves with silk inners.

Corporal Tyler turned to the paperwork. 'Sign that there, there and there, sir.'

Thurston signed in the places indicated.

'Now, what's your last three?'

'My last three what?'

'Your last three! What's your number, sir?'

'I don't have a number.' The Corporal looked astonished. 'Naval officers don't have numbers.'

With a look which clearly meant 'we've got a right one 'ere', Corporal Tyler seized his book of forms, sucked the end of his pencil for a moment before printing 'NO SERVICE NUMBER' in the appropriate places, then slammed the book shut and shuffled back to his peaceful lair behind the shelves.

'Nice to put him in his place once in a while, even though the effect won't last beyond tomorrow,' commented Lines when they were outside once more.

Next came the parachute store, where a WAAF corporal of an entirely different stamp looked him up and down. 'How much do you weigh, sir?'

'Thirteen stone, or just under.'

'That's lucky. If you're more than fourteen stone you have to have a bigger canopy, otherwise you'll hit the ground a bit hard, and all ours are out at the moment.

Got some very hefty blokes on the latest course.'

Then the business of fitting the harness, the Corporal moving close around him, hauling the various straps as tight as they would go, the familiar litany of time-worn jokes coming strangely from a woman. 'This has to be as tight as you can get it, sir, because if it isn't you're going to come down singing "Oh For the Wings of a Dove". And when you jump, if the parachute doesn't open, you come back here and we'll change it for a new one.'

The day went on. Into the room next door for the oxygen mask. 'You won't actually be flying on oxygen while you're here, sir, but the R/T microphone is inside the mask, which is why you have to have one.'

Then to the Station Adjutant to fill in the next-of-kin card (*Mrs Katharine Elizabeth Thurston (WIFE), 6 Eastfield Road, Emsworth, Hants*); to the Station Warrant Officer for a bicycle, of a very basic four-square flat-handlebarred kind, with the RAF roundel and number 208 painted on the rear mudguard; a meeting with OC Ground School, a bespectacled squadron leader whom Thurston suspected had been a schoolmaster in civilian life.

'Wing Commander Garden has spoken to me already, and we've worked out a programme for you. Obviously, there isn't time to take you through the full syllabus, and quite a lot of it will be superfluous to your requirements anyway. You'll be concentrating on Principles of Flight, Aircraft Construction and Engines. You'll also be doing Navigation and Meteorology. No doubt you'll have covered a lot of that before – I believe you're a nav specialist in the Navy – '

'A navigator, yes.'

' – So we'll be concentrating on the air aspects in both cases.'

At last, in the evening, as most of the airmen were

mounting their bicycles and streaming back towards their barrack blocks, the Tiger Moth. It was one of the few familiar things Thurston had found that day, though this one differed in small ways from the one he had flown at Abbotsinch. The paint inside the cockpit was a different colour, the rubber grip on the stick had recently been renewed and the ridges on it were still clear and unworn.

'Chetwynd's only about six miles away, so we'll see it when we get to circuit height. Will you do the cockpit check, please.'

It took a moment to begin the cockpit check, but then it came automatically once more: fuel – check the gauge; magneto switches off; harness tight; intercom; instruments – altimeter set to zero, airspeed-indicator reading approximately zero; compass grid ring rotating freely; controls – full and free movement; unlock slats; trim wound fully back for taxying. An airman came up and swung the propeller and the engine coughed into life on the second swing.

'You won't need him once you start flying the Harvard. It's got an electric starter.'

Switch the magnetos off one after the other, check that the mag drop on the RPM gauge was less than fifty. Switch them both back on, open the throttle as far as it would go, check the oil pressure.

'Everything all right?' Lines asked from the front seat.

'Yes.'

'Okay, sir. I'd like you to do the take-off, and then I'll direct you to Chetwynd where we'll try some circuits and bumps and see how you get on.'

Look around, make sure the way ahead is clear. Signal the airman to pull the chocks away, then open the throttle and begin to taxi forward, zigzagging using the rudder alone. A change in sensation with the aircraft leaving the grass surface for the tarmac runway. Another strangeness; Abbotsinch was a grass field. Look around again.

'On the Harvard you'll be using the radio and taking your orders from the tower, but for now you just have to keep your eyes skinned. The circuit here is pretty busy, and there are also a lot of other airfields around, so you need to keep your eyes open all the time. Don't let your attention wander, even for a second, because if you do you're likely to end up on the coffin table, and so will the chap you should have spotted.'

Lines had shown him the coffin table, resting on its trestles at the back of the hangar, stark and solitary on the oil-splashed concrete floor.

'You tell me when you see another aircraft and I'll tell you when I see one.'

Turn into wind with the rudder, set the trim forward in case the engine fails on take-off, mixture to rich, check the oil pressure a second time. Open the throttle, feel the slipstream begin to buffet. The aircraft came clear of the ground. Ease the stick back, climb to five hundred feet, turn crosswind and continue climbing.

'Now if you look over towards nine o'clock,' Lines said as the altimeter needle went through nine hundred feet, 'there's Chetwynd.' A larger area of ripe green amid the patchwork of fields. 'Take a good look round and turn towards it.'

He looked round, then made a careful turn to port, straightening out just in time to see a Harvard flash past.

'See what I mean, sir? You've got to keep looking *all* the time. You'll be turning your head so much that you'll be needing a bigger size in collars by the time you finish here. Builds up your neck muscles like nobody's business.'

Chetwynd was indeed deserted, simply an open grass field with an orange windsock rising and falling gently in one corner. Beyond the hedge white-faced

Herefords chewed the cud, jaws working from side to side in monotonous rhythm, and bees buzzed where the first flowers had appeared in the hedge itself.

'Like I said, sir, nice and quiet.'

But within minutes of arrival it was clear that there would be little time to enjoy the peace of the country-side. Lines, for all his quiet voice and measured de-livery, proved an exacting taskmaster, expecting pre-cisely rectangular circuits; each turn was made above the same point on the ground as on the last circuit, the exact same speed and rate of climb maintained during take-off and when climbing to circuit height. And there was the landing, something Thurston thought in the back of his mind that he had never properly grasped before going solo. Once Lines did the approach and brought the Tiger Moth in to an immaculate three-point landing, the wheels seemed to brush through the grass for a moment before settling almost imperceptibly on to the ground, talking through the Gosport tubes all the time. 'Get your landing speed on and fly her down towards the ground, then ease the stick back as the ground comes up and you can see the individual blades of grass, until the aircraft is in the landing position, and just let her sink down gently. None of this wing and a prayer stuff, that's just for the American films.'

'Basically, sir,' Lines said when they had landed once more at Tern Hill and were walking back towards the hangar, 'your flying's not too bad. Obviously, your lack of hours shows, but you've got a nice light touch on the controls, and you don't need to be told anything twice. Do you ride?'

'Almost from the pram.'

'I thought so. I can usually tell who's a rider and who isn't. The ones that do ride are normally better co-ordinated and less heavy on the controls. They used to think that if you could ride, you could fly. It's not absolutely true, but it gives you a bit of a start when you're learning. Your landings tend to be a bit bouncy – you're holding off a touch too high, so you come down a bit hard – but better that than leaving it a bit late and splintering your undercarriage. Tomorrow we'll have an early start, do some more circuits, stalling, and see if you can remember how to get out of a spin.'

Spinning was something he remembered clearly from the lessons with Squadron Leader Reynolds at Abbotsinch. It was April and not December, but even so Thurston was glad of the extra warmth of his Irvin jacket as the Tiger Moth climbed up towards five thousand feet.

'Take a good look round. Don't want to run into something on the way down.'

Tern Hill with its runways was clearly visible, a couple of Harvards in the circuit, a third Harvard much closer, heading northwards.

'That'll be the early detail, one of 2 Squadron's blokes on a solo cross-country. He's all right, he's well clear of us. Now this time I want you to spin her to port, do four turns and then bring her out. I'll just sit back and leave you to it.'

Thurston tightened his straps, took a final look round. The Harvard was disappearing northwards, a couple of thousand feet below them. He closed the throttle, took a deep breath, and pulled the stick slowly back into his stomach. The horizon disappeared, and there was almost no noise, only Lines' breathing through the Gosport tubes. He pushed his left foot forward and the aircraft lurched to the left, the nose suddenly dropping so that through the blur of the propeller the ground began to rotate. There was the urge to make the recovery now, before completing the four turns Lines insisted on, the irregular impacting against the straps as the Tiger Moth cartwheeled on one wing tip. Three, four turns. *Right foot forward as far as the pedal would go, a slight cramping in the mid-thigh. Pause. Move the stick forward. No weight on it; it could simply be fastened to the floor by a hinge, not attached to any of the control cables.* Then relief as the aircraft shuddered and responded, the nose dropping and the stick becoming heavy in his hand. *Centralise the rudder as soon as the rotation stops, open the throttle and ease the stick back into straight and level flight.* It was all as he remembered.

'Not too bad. You lost just under eleven hundred feet. But remember, the time you're most likely to spin is when you're throttled back coming in to land, you're thinking of tea and toast in the mess and you let the nose come up on your final turn, you haven't the height to recover and in you go. Makes a bit of a mess on the runway. And the Harvard has a fairly vicious spin compared with this thing. You'll see that when we come to it. All right, sir, drop me off on the field and you can take her up by yourself.'

Chapter Twelve

Lines kept him flying circuits for most of the first week, in the beginning mainly dual, later more often solo, going over ground covered at Abbotsinch, with occasionally a more complicated exercise interspersed. Steep turns, sideslipping to lose height, an exhilarating sensation near the ground, the aircraft moving sideways in a straight line, the nose yawed one way, the opposite wing down, the slipstream blowing across the cockpit from the side, then levelling the wings, centralising the rudder and gliding in for the landing. Halfway through the week Lines began directing him to take off and land crosswind, out of the line indicated by the windsock.

'Once we start flying from Torn Hill, we'll be using the runways, and we can't guarantee that the wind will always be blowing straight up and down. So it's worth getting some idea about operating out of wind in an aircraft you're used to, instead of trying to get the hang of crosswind landings and a new aircraft at the same time.'

Loops. Unpleasant, the first time, with Lines demonstrating, to see the patchwork fields appear above his head and know that there were only the three-inch wide webbing straps to save him from a fall through five thousand feet of space. After that the unpleasantness diminished, with Lines instructing him through the Gosport tubes and his mind occupied with the detail of flying: 'Line yourself up with the Newport road when you go into your dive, and if you do it properly you'll still be lined up when you come out. Keep your wings

level. Now just touch the rudder to keep her straight.'
And finally, late one evening as a red sunset gathered in
the west, there was exhilaration and a touch of pride at
producing what Lines termed *a proper rounded loop*,
solo, without the familiar sight of the back of Lines'
head in front or Lines' voice to prompt him. Not quite
on the line of the now familiar road which lay a couple
of fields away from the boundary of the airfield, but
only a couple of degrees off to starboard.

'Not too bad, sir,' Lines said laconically when Thurston landed once more to pick him up before flying
back to Tern Hill.

'See you on Monday, sir,' Lines said on Saturday morning. 'And you won't be needing your Irvin – it gets
pretty warm inside a Harvard.'

An awkward train journey home to Kate, Helen and
the twins, arriving just before midnight after three
changes, and having to set off back to Tern Hill after
lunch on the Sunday. His flying course had, inevitably,
upset Kate. She had been prepared to have him go to
Lee-on-Solent for a few hours a day, and come home at
night, but this time, coming hard on the heels of *Crusader*'s sinking and when the twins were only ten days
old, he had gone too far.

'Will you *never* be satisfied? You've been torpedoed
twice and you've already got all the medals that are
going, but you have to keep going on and on. Any normal man would be glad of a shore job after all that, but,
oh no, you have to have another ship, and when you get
the chance of some time at home you won't take it, you
have to go and learn to fly, just to satisfy your own inflated ideas about duty. You've said yourself that most
carrier captains don't fly, and *they* seem to manage.
Why do you have to be so different? For God's sake,
Bob, you're forty-four, not twenty-four, and you don't
have to do everything just because you expect your

subordinates to do it!'

It was something which had exercised his conscience already, but he could not pass up the opportunity. There was Mrs Crosby, the daily woman; he had found a monthly nurse for Kate and the twins on someone's recommendation; and he had promised faithfully to come home every weekend and to telephone. But he knew what she meant. Always there was the double pull of his duty to the service and his duty as a husband and father, and it was always the service which had to come first. Kate knew that, but she also found it hard to bear.

Aircraft – Harvard FH273; Pilot – F/S Lines; 2nd Pilot – Self; Duty – Type familiarisation.

Thurston had seen Harvards all week, in the air or on the ground in the hangar, but this was the first time he had been close to one out on the tarmac, with time to take everything in. At first sight it seemed the aircraft had almost nothing in common with the Tiger Moth he had been flying up to now. The Harvard was a metal monoplane, with a radial engine which gave it a purposeful, almost pugnacious look, a retractable undercarriage and an enclosed cockpit with a short radio antenna sticking up from the fuselage behind. Other aircraft were spaced about the tarmac, each with an instructor and student alongside, the students uniformly wearing the thin single stripes of pilot officers or sergeant's chevrons, very obviously brand-new. He could recognise one or two now from mealtimes in the Officers' Mess, but this was the first time he had gone flying at the same time, gone to his locker for his flying kit alongside them, listened to their banter about their girlfriends and their hangovers.

Inside the cockpit it was equally strange. After the

Tiger Moth's seven instruments – altimeter, airspeed indicator, compass, cylinder-head temperature and oil-pressure gauges, rev counter and turn-and-slip indicator – the Harvard had a positive battery of black-and-white dials and small metal plates bearing warnings and instructions.

'And the Yanks have thought of everything, sir,' Lines told him. 'There's even a pee tube!' Lines leant into the cockpit and fished under the front seat, showing Thurston a long rubber tube with a chromium-plated funnel on the end. 'And don't go upsetting the ground crew, because if you do, you'll come to use it and find they've tied a knot in it. If you get yourself strapped in, I'll start her up this time.'

Thurston dealt with his straps as Lines climbed into the cockpit behind him. Again this was new, a clear view ahead of him, obstructed only by the nose and propeller while the aircraft was on the ground, and the stout metal frame of the canopy, instead of the upper wing and cat's cradle of rigging wires beyond, broken by the back of the instructor's head.

'The thing to remember about the Harvard is that she might appear much more complicated than the Tiger when you're trying to get used to a retractable under-carriage, brakes, radio procedure and everything else she's got that the Tiger hasn't, but those are just frills. She's just as easy to fly, and, because there's a bit of poke in that engine and she's a much more advanced aircraft to begin with, she's much more fun. Now, make sure your radio lead's plugged in, and we'll make a start. And can you lower your seat a bit, or all I'll be able to see once we get airborne is your shoulders.

'As this is your first trip in a Harvard, I'll do the take-off and landing on this one, but I'd like you to follow me through. Ready, sir?'

'Ready, Flight.'

'Two-five: Clear taxi, over?'

Two-five was Lines' call sign. His own would be

eight-seven, when he went solo.

'Two-five, you are clear to taxi.'

He felt the movement through the soles of his flying boots as Lines let the brakes off, allowed the aircraft to roll slowly forward, zigzagging with the rudder because the nose blocked out the view ahead, and turned into wind at the end of the runway. The Harvard's tail wheel, Lines had already explained, was only steerable to a limited degree, twenty-five degrees either side until the aircraft was moving sufficiently fast for a touch on the brakes and full right rudder to persuade the wheel to jump over its cam and become free castoring. Brakes – something else that was new.

'Not many aircraft in the service with foot brakes, but this is one of them. You need to make sure your tail wheel's straight, sir, before you open the throttle, or you could find yourself running off the runway before you get airborne. I'll be doing the take-off, but now I'd like you to go through the vital actions.'

Go through the mnemonic, out loud as Lines required:

'H – Hydraulic lever; set forward.'

'We have to leave that until this stage, sir, because the circuit will start to idle after a couple of minutes and then you'll find you can't get your undercarriage up, or worse, you can't get it down again when you need it.'

'T – Trim; set for take-off.

'M – Mixture; set fully rich.

'P – Propeller pitch; set fully fine.

'F – Flaps up.

'F – Fuel; cocks on, enough in the tanks.

'S – Ignition switches on. Mag drop on run-up not over one hundred.'

'Two-five clear line-up?'

'Two-five, you are clear to line up for take-off.'

Engine checks before take-off, the stick fully back and both brakes full on, the engine roaring all round and the open canopy rattling on its runners. Another of the Harvard's peculiarities was that it was the noisiest single-engined aircraft in service. He turned off each of the magnetos in turn, watching how far the rev-counter needle dropped.

'That looks all right, sir. I have control.'

Feel Lines let the brakes off once more, then open the throttle, and hear the engine roar once more as it works up to full power. Right rudder, to counter the swing to the left from engine torque, a little more, to overcome the push in the same direction from the crosswind. The stick easing forward in his hand to bring the tail wheel off the ground, Lines' voice in his headphones.

'Let her get up to seventy-five, sir. Then she should just ease herself off the ground.' A final bounce on the main wheels, then the Harvard was off the ground. 'Aim for a hundred and ten, pull up your undercarriage and continue climbing towards your circuit height. There's another Harvard at ten o'clock on his crosswind leg. See him?'

Thurston hadn't. He'd been concentrating too hard on the handling.

'Two-five: Airborne.'

'Two-five: Roger.'

'There you are, sir. You have control.'

'I have control.'

Pull the undercarriage up in response to Lines' prompting, select coarse pitch on the propeller, climb to five hundred feet, the Harvard already much faster and more responsive than the Tiger Moth. Turn ninety degrees to port. Continue climbing to one thousand feet, another ninety-degree turn to port, ease the nose down and aim to be at five hundred feet to turn crosswind before landing.

'Now your landing checks, sir, then I'll take her.'

'H – Hydraulic lever; set forward.

'U – Undercarriage down; green lights showing.'

A sudden sluggishness, and change in the Harvard's attitude as the undercarriage went down.

'M – Mixture; fully rich.

'P – Propeller pitch; set fully fine.

'F – Flaps down.

'F – Fuel; cocks on, enough in the tanks.'

'I have control, sir.'

'You have control.'

But despite Lines' advice, flying the Harvard was quite different from flying the Tiger. With its greater speed – over two hundred miles per hour – everything happened so much faster; he was at the turning points in the circuit before he expected to be, and there was so much else to think of, so much the Tiger Moth had not had, which needed to be dealt with at the correct points in the circuit and in the correct order. Try to take off in coarse pitch, for example, and it might not be the coffin table, according to Lines, but it would almost certainly be the operating table. Then there was the art of landing with the engine, trying to judge the right moment to use the throttle and the amount of throttle to be used.

Even getting the engine started was a knack which took a long time to come. Lines had been through the starting sequence beforehand, and had made it sound and appear quite simple, but starting the Harvard's six-hundred horsepower Pratt and Whitney Wasp proved an awkward and frustrating business. *Open the fuel cock on the left tank, make sure the brakes are on, put the generator and battery switches on, give six shots of neat fuel into the cylinders with the ki-gas primer, look round both sides to make sure no one has walked into the propeller radius, then switch on the ignition and start working up the fuel pressure with a hand-operated wobble pump.*

Hold the stick back between the knees, press and hold

*in the starter switch with the right hand while working
the wobble pump with the left. Wait for the hum of the
flywheel to work up to its maximum, then move the
starter switch to engage.*

The propeller began to move, slowly, reluctantly.

'She hasn't caught yet. A touch more on the ki-gas.'

Two more shots with the ki-gas primer, sometimes
rewarded with a cough from the engine, and a billow of
white smoke from the cowling, the propeller turning
more rapidly as the remaining cylinders fired.

'Normally, I just tell my Commander (E) I want
steam for such-and-such a time and he rings me on the
bridge and tells me when he's done it,' Thurston once
told Lines in exasperation, as they were still stranded
on the concrete apron and two other Harvards had
already taxied past.

'It'll come, sir. You'll soon get the feel of it. It's no
worse than getting a car to start on a cold day.'

The syllabus allowed between three and five hours'
dual before flying the Harvard solo for the first time,
but the five hours passed, then six, and he seemed no
nearer to going solo. In the mess the talk was all of flying, the young pilot officers noisily 'line shooting' in the
bar each night, recounting their experiences when
training in Canada and America, looking forward to
the aircraft they would fly at OTU and on operations.
Thurston, because of his rank and belonging to a different service, was cut off from the rest of the mess
members to begin with. In the years of messing by himself he had lost the wardroom habit of easy familiarity;
the only senior officer who lived in was Palmer, and he,
like the rest, was deferential and inevitably distant. In
flying he might have found a degree of common
ground, but that too was lacking at the moment.

'You know what your trouble is, sir?' Lines said as they
were walking back to the hangar on the Thursday after-

noon, carrying their parachutes. 'You're trying too hard. You're starting to get strung up about not going solo and it's showing in your flying, particularly in your landings.' Lines stopped speaking for a moment, getting his thoughts into order.

'Don't forget that you're more than twice the age of the rest of the students we get, and it's inevitable that it's going to take you more time to get the hang of things. You *can* teach an old dog new tricks, but it's always going to take longer. You've got what it takes – your co-ordination's all right, and if there was anything wrong with your eyesight or reactions you'd never have got through the medical. Forget about trying to keep up with the syllabus, which is much tighter for time than it was when I did my flying training, anyway. We're not trying to make you a pilot as such, simply to give you some insight into what your pilots will have to cope with for when you take over your carrier, and you're the one student pilot who's not going to be chopped for going over the hours. *We* can take as long as we need. Best thing you can do, sir, is to forget about flying until tomorrow and get a few beers down your neck in the mess tonight.'

But on Friday the weather closed in. Cloud blotted out the Welsh mountains twenty miles to the west, barely dragged over the closer seven-hundred-foot hills. Gusts rattled the ill-fitting sash windows in the Officers' Mess, rain ran down the panes, finding its way through any gaps on to the inner sills, more water dripped off raincoats hanging on their pegs and puddled on the polished floor beneath. All flying was cancelled. Those students who were scheduled to fly in the afternoon filled the anteroom chairs after lunch, cups of half-drunk coffee at their elbows, occasionally getting up to replenish them from the percolator on the sideboard at the far end of the room. The ground officers had long gone back to their offices after lunch; the atmosphere was one of frustrated idleness, boredom and cigarette smoke, the only sound the ticking of the large wood-cased clock above the fireplace.

Thurston was sitting in a chair near the window, leafing through the bound volumes of *The War Illustrated* he had found in one of the bookcases. It was too wet to go for a walk. He had arranged a game of squash with one of the flight commanders, but there was a long dead interval to be filled before that. The clock chimed the half-hour, he glanced at its hands, decided that in a few minutes he would go back to his room and read. The volume he was looking at covered the summer of 1940; there were many pages showing groups of young pilots gathered around their aircraft, or portraits of other young pilots with sidehats worn at rakish angles, the silver wings prominently displayed. He turned a page and came across another assortment of tousled heads, silk scarves, unbuttoned tunics and Mae Wests, the Squadron Commander standing in the centre with his hands in his pockets. And there, standing to the right of the Spitfire's propeller but separated a little from the rest, was Lines, a sergeant then, cap in place, only the unfastened top button showing him to be a fighter pilot.

He was walking along the corridor towards the stairs when he remembered that there was something he could do.

'Certainly, sir. Come up here by all means. We'll be glad to see you. I'll ask one of my chaps to show you round,' Palmer's voice said at the other end of the telephone. Thurston collected his raincoat and bicycle and pedalled soggily to Technical Wing. Like those of Flying Wing, the Technical Wing offices were in the brick-built row which ran along the side of the Sunshine Hangar nearest the airfield, but Thurston, except when Lines had shown him round the station on his first day, had not yet crossed the invisible dividing line.

On his own ground Palmer seemed more at ease than in the mess, calling to his WAAF corporal clerk to bring two cups of tea.

'Corporal Gunn claims to make the best tea on the station. I can only say it's unique.' The Corporal grinned; this was evidently a well-worn joke.

'I take it you haven't had much experience of aero-engineering, sir.'

'None at all. I'm just an ignorant fish-head.'

'Palmer smiled. 'Not as ignorant as all that, I'm sure, sir. I've asked Flight Lieutenant Dixon – he's in charge of the Aircraft Servicing Flight – to show you round. He should be here in a moment.'

Corporal Gunn returned with the tea, carried on an old tin tray decorated with a picture of Edinburgh Castle and criss-crossed with old scratches.

'The system is basically two-sided,' Palmer went on, leaning back in his chair and nursing his mug of tea in both hands. 'The day-to-day work – which we call first-line servicing – fuel, oil, tyres and the like, is dealt with by Flying Wing tradesmen belonging to each of the squadrons. Other work on the aircraft is handled by us in Technical Wing, and we have a regular servicing routine for each of the aircraft which is intended to pre-empt any technical problems before they become serious. Ah, here's Dixon, he'll explain it all as you go round.'

Flight Lieutenant Dixon was young, pink-faced and very earnest. Unlike Palmer, he wore no wings, but instead the brass lapel badges of the RAF Volunteer Reserve.

'I'd just finished my first year reading mechanical engineering at Imperial College when the war started. They let me finish my second year, and then I got my call-up papers. I volunteered for aircrew, but my eyes

157

weren't good enough, so this was the obvious thing. I think we'll start with Mr Trimble in Eng Records, as he's just along the corridor. It's also a logical sort of place to begin.'

Mr Trimble was a grey-haired warrant officer with a colourful splash of campaign ribbons on his uniform.

'Despite all the rumours which go round Flying Wing, there's absolutely no mystery about what goes on here, sir. A simple Kardex system, that's all.' Mr Trimble indicated two oblong metal boxes which rested on the grey blanket covering his desk. 'One Kardex tray for each aircraft. We keep a running total of the hours each aircraft has flown, which is updated each day, plus other essential information such as the mods the aircraft has had. The aircraft all have a daily inspection each day – you'll know all about that. They also come here for a primary inspection every fifty hours, a minor inspection every hundred hours, and a major inspection after eight hundred. For each of those there is a set servicing routine we go through.'

'For a major, we practically take the aircraft to pieces and rebuild it!' Dixon said, then coloured a little.

'I think you've been flying 273, sir. Just a moment.' Mr Trimble reached into one of the boxes and pulled out a tray. 'She's a fairly new aircraft, done a hundred and twenty-three hours up to this morning, so she's not long had her first minor, and will be due for another primary in twenty-seven hours' time – about another week at the current rate. The cards simply tell us when anything's due; the full aircraft servicing records – the F700s – are kept in those filing cabinets there.' He gestured towards the filing cabinets lining the wall opposite him.

Thurston and Dixon went out into the rain which beat against their faces, half an inch of water covering the concrete, splashing their trouser bottoms with each step. An airman cycled past, head down, raincoat skirts flapping open in the wind. Even though it was only mid-afternoon it was already twilight; lights shining from the windows of the offices.

'Beast of a day.'

'Yes, sir.'

It was a relief to be out of the rain once more, listening to its distant beating on the steel roof of the hangar. In a couple of places water was coming through in heavy droplets, falling into strategically placed buckets which were already half full, or running into the oil patches on the floor. The great steel doors were open, but away from the entrance lights had to be kept burning, so that the aircraft and the men working on them stood out in sharp silhouette, the men standing on the wings or on short stepladders, each absorbed in his task. One Harvard had both its side panels removed, the internal framework of the fuselage and the control wires on view, an airman kneeling on the wing root with his head and shoulders inside the fuselage and blue-clad backside sticking out. The atmosphere was one of quiet concentration. There was, Thurston realised, a discipline there, of a kind which he had seen before in ships' engine rooms, the product of the mutual trust and confidence of men who knew their jobs and would do them without an officer, petty officer or NCO standing over them and watching to make sure they did. Once he went up one of the ladders, to stand precariously alongside an airman who insisted there was enough room for two, while the airman rummaged deep inside the engine to extract each of the plugs, drop them casually into a bucket beneath, and replace them with new ones, whistling an unrecognisable tune all the while, overall sleeves pushed back, hands and forearms streaked with oil.

'Quite impressive,' Thurston said to Palmer afterwards.

'Yes, I often think I could go away for a couple of

159

months and come back to find everything ticking over happily just as I left it.'

'A sign of good organisation.'

'Thank you, sir. That's what I like to think myself. But I'm lucky in my chaps. I've some good officers, and two excellent warrant officers – Mr Trimble, and Mr Ball in Station Workshops – and a very good team of NCOs. The aircrew all like to think of themselves as the pick of the service, but engineering tradesmen know better.' Palmer gave a mischievous smile. 'It takes a year to train a pilot from scratch, and a navigator about the same, but most of my fitters came in through Halton, which is a three-year apprenticeship, with a competitive exam at School Certificate level to get in at all. And then they need a couple of years to get experience before they start to be really useful. They tend to get very protective of their aircraft. *Their* aircraft, as far as they're concerned. They only let the aircrews fly them on sufferance, and woe betide them if they do any damage. But there's a pretty good rapport between the flyers and the ground crews – you'll find it on most stations. The flyers soon come to realise that they depend on the ground crews for keeping the aircraft up to the mark. Ultimately, their lives depend on it.'

'Heard you went round the hangars yesterday, sir,' Lines said the next morning. 'Not a bad idea. Helps keep them sweet. And it's true enough that we rely on them, and on a few other people too. If Blondie from the parachute section is busy dreaming about the corporal from the plug bay instead of keeping her mind on the job, then when you have to bale out you'll find yourself with a Roman candle and be on the way to a three-foot coffin instead of a six-foot.'

'You never told me you were a Spitfire pilot, Flight.'

'You never asked me, sir! Oh yes, I flew Hurricanes in France for a bit, then got posted to 610 Squadron and flew Spitfires from Biggin Hill during the Battle. There

160

wasn't much left of my original squadron after we got out of France, five or six aircraft left flying and just about everything else left behind, so the powers that be split us up among other squadrons. 610 had had quite a few losses over Dunkirk, and being auxiliaries they had less experience than the regulars, so another sergeant pilot and I from Number 1 were posted in to give them a bit of stiffening. I stayed with them until about February '41, when someone remembered I'd applied for an instructor's course before the war, and sent me on one. Trouble is, once you're a QFI they like to keep you instructing. I write a letter to the Wing Commander every couple of months – *Sir, I have the honour* and so on. He must have enough to paper the wall by now, but still no luck. The Wing Commander's doing much the same thing himself. He'll let me go when he gets back on ops. He was in the Battle, on Hurricanes, baled out twice in one week.' Lines grinned. 'And I've looked you up too, sir. *You* sank a German cruiser in the Denmark Strait, and I don't know how many merchant ships in the Mediterranean, and covered yourself with gongs and glory in the process.'

Aircraft – Harvard FH298; Pilot – F/L Crowe; 2nd Pilot – Self; Duty – Flt Cdr's check.

'Flight Commander's going to fly a couple of circuits with you now, sir.'

Lines went away towards the hangar, a small upright figure striding across the concrete apron, leaving him alone with the Flight Commander. Crowe was fair-haired, and framed by the leather flying helmet his face still appeared absurdly young. The battledress beneath his flying suit was bare of medal ribbons; Lines had mentioned that Crowe, like most of the commissioned flying instructors, was a 'pure instructor', having been creamed off to go on an instructor's course straight from SFTS instead of going on to operational flying.

It was Saturday morning. The rain had finally stopped a few hours earlier and the cloud base had lifted sufficiently for flying to begin again. The hangar stood black and stark against the grey sky, the pitted concrete darkened by water, separated into great slabs by shiny convex streaks of bitumen. Earlier in the week he had purchased a second-hand motorbike from an instructor about to be posted to Egypt, and had got hold of a supply of petrol coupons. In a few hours he would be on his way back to Kate, and could forget about flying until Monday morning.

Crowe finished strapping himself in, and plugged in his radio lead. 'Start her up, then taxi out, and do me one circuit and landing please, sir.'

Now when it did not matter the engine fired and the tail wheel obligingly jumped over the cam at the first attempt. Throughout the HTMPFFS checks, Crowe sat silent and watchful in the rear seat.

'Two-one: Clear line-up?'

'Two-one: Runway not clear. Hold.' There was another Harvard ahead of them, one of the sergeant pilots by himself in the cockpit. They waited, Thurston looking down at his knees encased in the grey legs of his flying overalls, the inner sides of his black boots showing in shadow beneath the instrument panel, resting clear of the rudder pedals. The Harvard ahead of them took off, the main wheels retracting neatly inwards a few feet off the ground.

'Two-one: You are clear to line up for take-off.'

'Two-one: Roger.'

He moved his feet on to the pedals, took hold of the stick, and started to taxi forward. A slight bump as the Harvard left the grass surface and went up on to the tarmac once more. He brought the aircraft round to port, making her face up and down the runway. *Run the engine up for the second time, let off the brakes and let*

162

the aircraft move forward. Stick forward to raise the tail wheel off the ground. The view ahead suddenly appeared beyond the propeller, the control tower over to port, and the grey-green hedge almost a mile away at the far end of the field. *Feel the pull to the left, and push the right rudder pedal forward to keep her straight. Seventy-five, ease the stick gently back, feel the Harvard bounce once, the ground falling away. Undercarriage up, get up to a hundred and ten and continue climbing. Look round.* There was the Harvard which had taken off ahead of them, flying crosswind at ten o'clock, another on his downwind leg, his undercarriage going down in readiness for landing.

'Yes, sir, I've got them,' Crowe replied, speaking for the first time.

On round the circuit, finding strangely that he was enjoying himself, that suddenly it had all clicked into place, that it was almost true that the Harvard was no more difficult to fly than the Tiger Moth.

'Not bad, sir,' Crowe said on landing. 'Let's go back up and see if you can do a couple more like that.'

Round again, twice more, realising now that this was a serious check, so that, inevitably, he was more conscious of every small imperfection in the circuits, a couple of bounces when landing for the first time, and a swing when the crosswind caught her that took a lot of rudder to correct, a turn on the second that was more a hundred degrees than ninety. He hardly dared to hope, but Crowe climbed out afterwards and began securing the straps in the rear cockpit.

'One circuit and *one* landing, sir, and don't break anything.'

The shower which had threatened for the last half-hour came suddenly, heavy droplets bouncing off the windscreen, more coming inside the cockpit where the canopy was open, working gradually through the knees of Thurston's flying suit and battledress trousers.

'Better just wait a couple of minutes until this goes off, sir.'

Crowe was standing on the wing root, right hand resting casually on the canopy, flying helmet off and hair blowing about in the slipstream as the propeller idled. The sky above lightened, and a small patch of blue appeared over the hangar gable. Crowe gave him a thumbs-up sign, dropped down off the wing and began to walk away, to where Lines was waiting on the edge of the apron.

'I told you, sir. All you had to do was relax and stop trying.'

Chapter Thirteen

Another routine was established. Abbott brought his tea at 0700, then breakfast, and out to F Flight for an eight o'clock start. An hour's flying, then ground school for the rest of the morning, sometimes by himself, at other times in the company of bored young pilots who had covered the subjects once already. More flying after lunch – and more of the exercises on the list pasted into the front of his logbook ticked off – first demonstrated by Lines from the back seat, then practised dual, and then solo. At first it was a repetition of things he had already been through in the Tiger Moth, but soon the exercises were entirely new: climbing turns, forced landing practice – picking a field, making the approach, then opening the throttle to overshoot at the last moment – then the strange experience of a simulated engine failure on take-off.

'The most important thing to remember, sir, is *never* turn back. There've been more good blokes killed because they turned and tried to make it back to the field than for any other reason. And that goes for experienced pilots who should have known better as much as for sprogs like you. In fact, the sprogs usually have the sense to do it the way their instructors tell them. Let's think it through logically. You've just got off the ground, you're climbing through two hundred feet, and your engine dies on you. What attitude are you in?'

'My nose is up, and I'm only about ten knots above

the stalling speed.'

'Miles per hour, sir! But correct. So what's the first thing you're going to do?'

'Get the nose down.'

'Why?'

'Because if I don't the aircraft will go into a stall, and there won't be enough height to recover.'

'Correct. Stick forward, then check your altimeter and work out where you're going to land. And don't even think about how you're going to take off from some handkerchief-sized field afterwards, or how much you're going to be spending on drinks in the mess. We can always dismantle the aircraft and bring up a tractor to get it out, but there's not a fat lot to be done except play the Dead March if you and the aircraft are strewn about the downwind boundary in little pieces because you tried to make it back to the field. As it happens, we've a nice big field here, so there's enough room to land straight ahead. I'll let you get off the ground, then I'll simply shut the throttle and it's all yours.'

He was waiting for the engine to stop, and it seemed to take a long time to happen. Seated directly in front of Lines as he was, he could not hope to see Lines' hand move towards the throttle lever, he could only wait for the engine pull to die away.

But it all came automatically, proof that all Lines' instruction over the past weeks had been absorbed. *Stick forward.* A little too far as it turned out, so that he had to ease it back quickly to prevent the Harvard from diving at the ground. *Look at the altimeter on the left side of the instrument panel. Two hundred and fifty feet, a large green field on the other side of the boundary hedge opening out ahead. Go through the landing sequence, HUMPFF, more quickly, much closer to the ground than usual, the aircraft slowing, descending more rapidly as the undercarriage goes down. Eighty miles an hour, the greenness all around, begin to ease back on the*

166

stick and put the aircraft into a three-point attitude for the landing itself. The wheels touched down, bounced once, and settled back on to the ground. Brakes on, he brought the Harvard to a stop.

'Well, sir, I think we might have a few bits to pick out of the radiator. Just about ran out of field there.' The hedge was less than fifty yards away. 'All right, sir, taxi her back round the peri track, and we'll try a couple more.'

It was a now familiar litany. However well or badly Thurston carried out any manoeuvre, it was always 'try a couple more', and then a couple more, until Lines was finally satisfied.

Flying again on Saturday morning, then after lunch a hasty motorbike journey to spend thirty-six hours with Kate, getting up at four o'clock on the Monday morning to be at Tern Hill for eight.

Lines, too, was married. He had remarked casually one morning as they moved out of the circuit northwards, 'See that row of three cottages at ten o'clock, sir? Just alter course a touch and dip your wings as we go over,' and a few days after rather shyly showed him a photograph of a young woman with a small boy who looked the image of his father in her arms. 'She used to be a Waaf here, but she had to leave once John was on the way. She comes from just over the border in Montgomeryshire, so this was a nice posting for her.'

Aircraft – Harvard FH273; Pilot – Self; 2nd Pilot – None; Duty – Cross-country Tern Hill – Sealand – Valley – Tern Hill.

It was a bright morning, the kind to be enjoyed while it lasted, a few white puffs of cumulus cloud at three thousand feet, and more than pleasant to be flying away

167

from the immediate vicinity of Tern Hill by himself for the first time, cockpit canopy slid back, map board resting on his knees. Lines' instructions had been clear. 'Once you get to Sealand, go straight up the Dee Estuary and follow the coast round. Don't on any account let yourself drift over towards the Mersey. Your people are a trigger-happy lot and they shoot first and ask questions after. Keep your eyes skinned for other aircraft. There are several other flying stations around Sealand, and their blokes will all be doing their cross-countries on a day like this. You shouldn't get lost. There are plenty of good landmarks, even if you haven't got your sextant.'

Interesting, to see the silver barrage balloons glinting in the sun high above the smoky haze which hung over Liverpool, then to watch, over to starboard, a convoy arranging itself into a single column to enter the Mersey, the smaller escorts scurrying about like sheepdogs among their flock, and finally to set a compass course over Snowdon and the higher peaks of North Wales towards Tern Hill.

The weather began to deteriorate as noon approached, clouds gathering in the south-west as a warm front came in. The wind had backed, so that the windsock at the corner of the airfield buffeted at thirty degrees to the main runway. Round the circuit he was inevitably thinking that he should be in nice time for lunch in the mess as he checked the landing area was clear. *HUMPFF. Turn in for the final approach, put on a little left rudder to counter the crosswind. Ease the stick back for the round-out, keep her straight with the rudder.* He just had time to realise that he had held off a touch too high when the port wing dropped sharply. He whipped the stick over to the right in an effort to prevent the wing tip from hitting the runway. The port wheel hit the ground, engine torque continuing to pull the aircraft round to the left, the starboard wheel still eighteen inches above the surface. Another bump as the port wheel went off the runway, then it hit a tussock and there was a rending of tortured metal as the undercarriage leg finally collapsed and the aircraft went down on to its belly. Thurston's head, the only part of his body not braced on the controls or restrained by his harness, jerked violently forward and then back again, a delayed shock of pain travelling upwards through his neck. The Harvard continued to move very fast, ploughing noisily across the short grass, still turning left. Thurston's upper body was thudding against his straps, his neck apparently six inches longer.

The aircraft finally came to a stop, the visible propeller blade bent back almost at a right angle. It was suddenly very quiet. He switched off the engine, rested his elbows on the cockpit sides, noisily let out the breath he had been holding in for the last few seconds, turned his head carefully both ways, and found where the pain began. He sniffed, then again, harder. Petrol! And the engine manifold was hot. His right hand dropped back into the cockpit, found the triangular safety pin of the Sutton harness and yanked it out. Then the parachute harness, turning the front of the release box through ninety degrees and pressing it inwards with the heel of his hand. He stood up, placed his hands on both sides of the cockpit rim and pushed. Something was still holding him in the aircraft. Radio lead! He reached back inside, followed the lead to its anchorage and pulled the jack plug out, then took his weight on his arms, swung his legs out and on to the wing, the leg straps of his parachute harness pulling away. The wing was angled sharply downwards. He half slid, half fell off it, picked himself up again and started to run.

Fifty yards away he stopped, heard for the first time the clanging of bells as the fire tender which normally lived next to Air Traffic Control raced up the runway, the crash ambulance close behind. The fire tender's crew wore red-painted tin hats, two of them standing up in the back, holding the nozzle of a hose, waving and laughing. Thurston unfastened the strap of his flying helmet, pulled it off, feeling a trickle of sweat emerge from beneath.

The fire tender stopped. Someone shouted, 'Another one in the club!' There was more shouting, a rush of well-practised jokes. Thurston pulled down the zip of his flying suit a few inches. Someone saw the navy blue battledress beneath, a hint of the gold lace on the shoulder straps, stopped almost in mid-sentence.

'Sorry, sir,' he muttered, crestfallen.

A sergeant with medical collar badges dismounted from the ambulance. 'Come on, sir. Let's get you across to sick quarters.'

'I'm all right.'

'Standing orders, sir. If you have a prang you have to go to sick quarters.'

'What a bloody waste of time.'

'Sorry, sir. Standing orders. The MO won't make any exceptions.'

Lines appeared, breathless after running from the hangars.

'Are you all right, sir?'

'Quite all right, Flight.'

Lines looked at the medical sergeant, then back towards Thurston. 'Better get in the ambulance, sir. Quicker we get you to the MO, the quicker you'll be flying again.'

The Harvard rested on its belly in the field, innocuous now.

'She'll patch up easy enough, sir. Just needs a new undercarriage leg.'

Thurston walked back to the aircraft, climbed back

on to the wing and lifted his parachute from the cockpit. It felt much heavier than when he had taken it from his locker only a couple of hours earlier.

'Well, you showed quite a turn of speed there, sir.'

'I thought I could smell petrol,' Thurston told him, slightly shamefaced now that everything was quiet again and the Harvard was still intact.

'Everybody does, sir! They forget that there's always a smell of petrol in the cockpit, and they're out of the aircraft so fast that Jesse Owens couldn't keep up with them. But it's the right thing to do, sir. As soon as you're down, get yourself out and well clear of the aircraft; you get a good dose of adrenalin up the backside to make sure you do.'

'This is all a complete waste of time,' Thurston told the MO. 'I'm perfectly all right.'

'Are you?' the doctor replied. 'Are you quite sure?'

'Quite sure.'

The MO was a middle-aged wing commander with an air of having heard it all many times before. 'Then you can hardly object if I just give you a quick going-over to keep my paperwork in order,' he said mildly, before commanding, 'Shirt off.'

The MO saw Thurston wince as he moved his head back to pull off his tie. 'No, you're not all right, are you?'

'My neck got a bit of a jerk when the undercarriage went. That's all it is.'

'Just turn your head as far as it'll go . . . Now the other way.'

The rest of the examination was perfunctory. 'All right, you can get dressed.' The MO rapidly filled in a chit. 'We'll just run you down to the cottage hospital and get that neck X-rayed.' Thurston began to protest. 'Can't

171

be too careful with necks, or anything between the coc-
cyx and the top of the cranium for that matter. The
ambulance will take you.'

Lines went with him to the hospital. They were shown
to a waiting room, where they waited for a long time
among other victims of petty injuries and minor ill-
nesses. Thurston was still wearing his flying kit, and
found himself feeling foolish and out of place among
the mashed fingers, the boils and the small boys with
gravel in their knees. He was thirsty and once got up to
buy himself and Lines cups of tea from a nearby trolley,
only to be shooed back to his seat by one of the nurses.
'No, you can't have a drink until after you've seen the
doctor.' The X-ray was done at last, and then there was
another long wait for the result.

'No serious damage. You've just stretched it a bit too
far. But don't do anything strenuous for a few days.'
The doctor seemed to notice the flying kit for the first
time. 'What exactly were you doing?'
    'A heavy landing.'
    'Ground loop? We used to get them in here all the
time a couple of years ago. Aren't you leaving it a little
late to be learning to fly, and in the wrong service?'
    'Neither the Navy nor the RAF seem to think so,'
Thurston said a little stiffly, 'and neither do I.'

'Did they ground you, sir?'
    'No.'
    'Then we'd better get back to Tern Hill and see if
they've left us any lunch, and after that we'd better get
you airborne again. We can sort out the accident report
later.'

'The MO's got a thing about necks,' the ambulance
driver said cheerfully. 'Ever since he had a bloke go to
him with a stiff neck after a prang. MO sent him away

with an aspirin, and he woke up a couple of days later paralysed from the neck down.' The man grinned, with the familiar gallows humour of men for whom violent death was part of life.

Thurston was strapping himself into the cockpit of another Harvard when Lines mentioned the accident directly for the first time.

'Forget all about it, sir. There's only two types of Harvard pilot. Those who have ground looped and those who are going to. Now you've got yours out of the way, and you've probably learnt something from it. You got away with it, that's the main thing. Don't worry about keeping a lookout if you can't turn your head properly. I'll look after that.'

Lines' matter-of-fact attitude was reassuring. Thurston realised that for the RAF accidents in training were a part of life, as deck landing crashes were for the Fleet Air Arm. You pranged, and provided you were fit, you flew again. There was no point in making a big thing of it; it was just one of those things.

It cost him a certain amount of mild leg-pulling from the more senior officers, and a round of drinks in the bar after dinner.

Wing Commander Garden presented him with an ornate certificate, and with mock solemnity swore him in as a member of the Bent Undercarriage Club, and entitled to claim a pint of beer from each new member after him.

Because Thurston couldn't turn his head more than thirty degrees either side for several days, Lines wouldn't let him fly solo, which meant that they were marking time as the six weeks' flying drew towards its end. Lines used it to introduce Thurston to instrument flying, a black cloth hood secured over the front cockpit so that all the pupil could see was the instrument panel in front of him.

'The thing to remember, sir, is that the instruments are right and you are wrong. When you're flying blind you can get yourself into entirely the wrong attitude without realising it because you've no horizon to relate to. Concentrate on what the instruments tell you, and if your sensations tell you something different, as they probably will, follow the instruments.'

It was difficult to remember, the first time, with darkness pressing down within inches of his head and only the rings of yellow light breaking the all-enveloping black, his body saying one thing and the luminous needle points another, that this was simply a form of exercise and that behind him Lines had his canopy open and his head out in the afternoon sun. Lines did the landings, and after struggling round repeated circuits it was a relief to hand over control and follow Lines through as he came in for one of his daisy-cutting landings, the first contact with the ground almost imperceptible. Night flying, when it came, was much easier, for the darkness was never so complete, even over the blacked-out countryside; there was starlight, a thin crescent moon, and the faint gleam of water far below in the pond near the airfield.

There was a Guest Night in the Officers' Mess, with the station silver brought up from storage and spread out over the dark polished tables where it caught the subdued light from the walls, and the station volunteer band puffing away industriously. There was a sprinkling of other non-RAF uniforms at the table, the Lieutenant-Colonel in command of a nearby anti-aircraft regiment on Thurston's left, and on his right a Home Guard brigadier, an ancient civilian in a dinner jacket who was apparently a judge on circuit.

Thurston was a long way from the sea, the Colonel remarked; he didn't realise there were naval establishments in these parts. Thurston explained that he was at Tern Hill on a flying course, and found it strange to realise that he felt himself part of the place now, a member of the mess and not simply a guest. His orders to proceed to Boston to take command of *Inflexible* had come through that morning, almost as a surprise. In the last weeks he had found he was flying for its own sake; his original purpose had slipped to the back of his mind. And there was regret, too, that in the days when he could have gone into the nascent Fleet Air Arm as a pilot he had not done so, choosing instead the more traditional field of navigation and its more certain prospects for command and career success.

Aircraft – Harvard FH289; Pilot – Self; 2nd Pilot – None; Duty – Cross-country test Tern Hill – Sealand – Woodvale – Walney Island – Valley – Tern Hill.

He went to Safety Equipment beforehand, to pick up a Mae West and Verey pistol – 'If one of your lot does start firing at you, fire the colours of the day and get yourself out of their range as fast as you can, though their shooting's so bad you're probably in more danger if they're firing at something else' – then a long flight over grey water, the flat Lancashire coastline grey and misty in the distance, seeming to come no nearer, finding himself tensing for the slightest change in the Harvard's engine note. The water looked very cold, and it was little more than two months since he had been struggling in another sea. He could not restrain a shiver, when he remembered it, but that was behind him now, and he was going on to take command of another and greater ship.

Wing Commander Garden signed his logbook, scrawled, quite unexpectedly, 'High Average' in the spaces reserved for assessments.

'That stands on its own, sir. It doesn't just mean

you've done well considering your age; it's measured against an absolute standard.' Garden was looking pleased with himself. 'What it boils down to is good hands and a willingness to listen to your instructor. I think it's safe to tell you now that Chiefy Lines was a bit wary of taking on someone as senior as you to begin with.'

'I couldn't have had a better instructor.'

'He's good, isn't he. He's keen to get back to ops, as I think you know, but he's far too valuable as an instructor. I keep trying to persuade him to take a commission, but he won't hear of it.'

'Happy where he is.'

'Exactly.' Garden turned back to more serious matters. 'The Admiralty have asked me to write a report for them and I'm recommending that you be given every opportunity to keep in practice. I don't know this will actually work once you're back at sea. Presumably you'll just have to grab the chance whenever there's a suitable aircraft available. But if you ever find yourself with time to spare in the future we'd be delighted to have you back.'

The Group Captain agreed to let Thurston have the use of his staff car and driver on his last night so that he could give Lines and Flight Sergeant Kennedy, 3 Squadron's ground crew chief, dinner in a hotel a few miles from the station which the Group Captain had recommended. The two NCOs were guarded to begin with, polite and very correct, unsure of themselves away from their own spheres and dining with a senior officer, even though they and he were in plain clothes. There was still the divide between the fifty-shilling tailor and Gieves' pre-war worsted. With food and wine inside them they relaxed a little, told stories of the kind common to all servicemen, of naïve young officers and foolish recruits, of stores which were never available when needed, all with the regulars' contempt for civilians and non-regulars, and anyone who was not part of their own half-enclosed world.

Lines and Kennedy had both joined the RAF as Halton apprentices. Lines had spent a couple of years as an engine fitter before applying successfully for pilot training, but Kennedy had gone out to India at the age of eighteen and spent the next seven years overseas, surviving the Quetta earthquake of 1935. 'The first shake woke me and some of the other fellows up, and we thought we'd be better off outside if it went on, so we went. We hadn't been outside more than a couple of minutes before the big one hit us, and the block we'd been in, and all the others, were nothing but rubble. I can't remember how many days it was that we kept digging through that rubble, mostly with our hands because there weren't the tools – most of them were under it all – trying to get the water supply sorted out, and all the rest of it. Most of the native city was wrecked, and the natives were coming up to us begging us to give them what we had, not that there was very much until the army got the supply side organised. The Quit India lot went very quiet while all that was going on.'

'Pity you couldn't have stayed a bit longer, sir. You'd have been solo at night in another hour or so, and you'd have got your wings with no trouble if you'd been able to do the full course. Once you got off solo, sir, you were all right. It often happens.' They were standing on the gravel forecourt in front of the Sergeants' Mess. Kennedy had said his goodnights and gone inside, leaving Thurston and Lines by themselves. 'But it'd be a waste of all our efforts if you don't keep it up. Any chance you get.' Lines stopped speaking for a moment. 'Well, goodnight, sir.' He snapped to attention, waited for Thurston to make his reply, then marched briskly away.

Chapter Fourteen

'Delighted to see you again, Thurston,' the Commander in Chief told Thurston, managing to sound as though he meant it. 'Allow me the honour of a short inspection.'

The Commander in Chief had a reputation for the common touch which seemed fully justified as he moved along the ranks of men drawn up to receive him, stopping for a word with every third or fourth man, giving him his full attention, so that in that short interval the seaman or marine he was speaking to was the only man present, the smiles and occasional laughter showing that this was an inspection in name only. It seemed strange to see the men in blues after so many months of tropical rig, their mahogany faces ill-suited to them and out of place. They looked different in other ways which Thurston could not pin down; tired certainly, some young faces seeming older than their years, marked by the experiences of the last few months.

The Commander in Chief, for good practical reasons, had his headquarters ashore, and four thousand miles from the operating zone of his fleet, but earlier in the war he had commanded the Home Fleet when it had caught and sunk the *Scharnhorst* in gales and icy darkness in the Arctic seas beyond the North Cape, two months before *Crusader* was torpedoed and sunk in the same seas.

'A bad business, with *Persephone*. I'm convening a

Board of Enquiry, of course. I've really no option in the circumstances. But don't lose any sleep over it. It was one of those things, but we need to find out exactly what happened, and to minimise the chances of it happening again. Anyway, that won't happen for a day or two yet, and I'd say your lads have earned a spot of leave. Do you realise that no British fleet has been continuously at sea for as long as this since Nelson's day, with all that implies?'

'I have to admit I hadn't, sir.'

The Commander in Chief was sitting in one of the armchairs in Thurston's day cabin, nursing a gin which Thurston's PO steward had produced for him. 'Been too busy doing it, of course. Two days at Leyte since you left here at the end of February, and that's all. Makes a change from when you and I were snotties, when we were coaling every five days, and couldn't steam above twenty knots for more than a few hours because the stokers couldn't keep up that sort of effort any longer. And the fact that we're managing to do it at all is a credit to everybody concerned.'

'Thank you, sir.'

'I don't just mean your chaps of course, before they get too cocky. And let us not forget the Fleet Train. Again, we've never even tried to operate one before.'

'We haven't needed to.'

'Exactly. The Yanks know all about operating at long range because they don't have the colonies we have and therefore don't have the bases. They've had to develop a system for supply at sea which we've never needed. You won't have seen their Fleet Train?'

'Only on radar from afar, sir.'

'It's all very nice modern ships; fast, designed for the job, with crews under naval discipline. Very impressive.'

'While we've had to manage with whatever we can get.'

'I think at the last count we had ships sailing under

eleven different flags and men speaking a dozen different languages, with all the problems that engenders. It works, but only God knows how!' The Admiral finished his gin. Thurston's PO Steward appeared, soft-footed, and silently placed a second at his elbow. 'Thank you.'

'But seriously, Thurston, you've all done a wonderful job in very difficult circumstances, and I've brought you back here so that you can repair your damage and go back to the task force to carry on doing a wonderful job. The dry dock's all ready for you, and you'll go in there first thing tomorrow morning to get your bottom scraped. They'll start work on your flight deck and island at the same time.'

'That's going to be quite a job, sir. We've poured the best part of a ton of concrete into the dents in the flight deck and it'll all have to be chipped out and replaced with armour.'

'Yes, the dockyard are aware of that. But, thank heavens you've got armour. The Yanks were claiming that our carriers would be a liability because they couldn't carry enough aircraft, and that all the heat being absorbed through the armour would make the living conditions in the tropics unendurable.'

'They have been pretty grim for the troops, sir.'

'But you've risen above all that. Halsey and Nimitz have been very impressed.' The C in C moved abruptly back to the question of repairs. 'I've also made it clear to the Australians that I want your repairs and re-plenishment completed in four weeks or less. Keep this under your hat, but the rest of the task force will be back here for repairs and replen fairly shortly, and I can't have this ship clogging up the dry dock any longer than absolutely necessary! How long it actually takes all depends, of course, on the Australian unions; I sometimes think they're almost as big a menace as the Japanese. Anyway, while you're here you're all going

180

to get yourselves some leave, and some real food under your belts, and relax and try to forget about the war for a while. You've all earned it.

'But, I'm afraid, Thurston, that I'm going to ask you to do a little work, you personally, that is.' The tone of the Admiral's voice changed. 'As I've mentioned, we've been having a lot of trouble with the Australian unions, and the Australians in general need to be convinced that this is *their* war. They know all about their own chaps fighting in New Guinea, and the Yanks fighting in the Pacific, but they tend to forget about our task force, as do our own people back at home. The impression I'm getting from our political masters is that everyone in England has decided that now Germany is defeated and Hitler dead, the war is over; they've forgotten the war that's going on out here. I expect you want to know what this is leading up to.'

'Yes, sir, but I think I can guess.'

'That sounds ominous. *Inflexible* is the first ship of any size that's been into Sydney since *Illustrious* left in April, and we need to make sure the Australians know about it, and know what you've been involved in. I appreciate that you won't be all that keen on the idea, but I'm going to put you on show a bit. I'm going to send you off to a few factories and have you talk to the managers, and I might ask you to do something for the wireless. It won't just be you, your brother captains will be doing exactly the same thing when they get back here, though it's probably a good idea to start with you. You're our resident glamour boy, after all!' The Admiral's eye settled on the red ribbon for a moment, and he did not notice Thurston's grimace. 'Stokes will brief you. In fact, Stokes is keen to get started, and he's organised a small press conference after lunch. He'll sit in on it, and come to your rescue if you need it, but I don't suppose you will. And I'm sure I can rely on you not to come out with anything which might constitute a breach of security.'

'It seems I have little choice in the matter,' Thurston said heavily.

'Are you registering a protest?'

'Yes, sir.'

'I thought you would. But, unfortunately, in the present climate it's going to be necessary. Cheer up, it can't be worse than taking on the *Seydlitz*.'

'I'm not sure I would have taken on the *Seydlitz* if I'd known the press would lay siege to me afterwards, sir.'

The press conference took place at 1400, with four reporters, three male, one female, occupying chairs in Thurston's day cabin and provided with coffee by PO Steward Hardcastle, with Stokes, an RNVR commander dignified by the title of Fleet Public Relations Officer, sitting silent and watchful in another chair.

'How do you feel about being in Sydney again, Captain?' the woman began brightly.

'Personally, or as a ship's captain?'

'Oh, both,' the woman said equally brightly.

'Personally, I'm very pleased to be in Sydney again, and I think most of the men will be glad of an opportunity to get ashore again after a long spell at sea.'

'You're here for repairs, I believe,' one of the men said, taking the woman's place. 'Can you tell us what type of damage it is?'

'Damage to the flight deck, caused by a kamikaze which hit us amidships, and bomb damage forrard. Fortunately the deck is armoured so the blast didn't penetrate it, and we were able to fill the dents with concrete and continue operating.'

'I see your island's pretty badly shot up as well. Was that from the kamikaze as well?'

Thurston looked round towards Stokes before answering. Stokes said nothing.

'No, that was a separate incident.' He saw Stokes' fingers tighten on the arms of his chair. 'Another bomb, a few days after the kamikaze hit us, which exploded inside the island and wrecked our aircraft direction systems, and caused fairly heavy casualties.' He was aware that he sounded exactly like one of the Admiralty spokesmen who occasionally appeared on the wireless.

'Serious casualties?' someone asked.

The speaker was young and pink-faced, and could never have worn a uniform in his life.

'When a few hundred pounds of high explosive goes off in a confined space it does tend to cause serious casualties. There's not usually very much left of anyone who was unfortunate enough to be in the way.'

The young man blanched and looked away. Stokes' fingers tightened again, and he moved forward in his chair. 'I have the figures here. I'll give you them when we've finished.'

There was an awkward silence, then one of the other men began again. He was balding, with freckles visible on his scalp where the hair had disappeared. 'But the men are holding up well?'

'Morale on board is excellent.'

'Even after incidents like that?' the woman came in again.

'I think we all recognise that we have a job to do, and that we have to keep on doing it, whatever the circumstances. We can't afford to be sentimental in the midst of a war.'

It was all coming out, but only part of what he meant, exactly like one of the model answers the directing staff turned out at Staff College. *Ship's captain interviewed by newspapermen bursting for a story will say . . .* He was aware of the immeasurable divide between these civilians, Stokes, a serviceman in name only, and himself, as the fighting man who had seen and experienced the things of which they were speaking.

There were more questions, each answered in the same manner. Stokes had relaxed now, legs crossed so that one of his trouser legs had ridden up a couple of inches to reveal distinctly non-service maroon socks. And then the more general enquiries. What part of England was he from? He fought down an urge to say the North-West Frontier Province, and replied Northumberland. How long had he been in command of *Inflexible*?

'And are you married, Captain?' the woman asked as brightly as ever.

'I am.'

'And how many children do you have?'

'Four.'

The woman looked delighted. 'And how old are they?'

'Nineteen, eighteen and fourteen months. The two youngest are twins.'

'Oh, how lovely.' The woman smiled as she scribbled in her notebook, obviously with a beatific vision of impeccably behaved, identically dressed and above all silent babies.

'You should ask my wife about that.'

'Are the other two in the services?' someone asked hopefully.

'My elder son is a sub-lieutenant in submarines. My daughter is a medical student.'

'You must be very proud of them,' the woman gushed.

Stokes began to get up. 'Well, I think that's everything. Do you want any photographs before we finish?'

'Yes, I think we should have a few.'

Thurston groaned inwardly.

'Can we go up on deck?' the third man, who had not so far spoken, asked. 'I think it would be appropriate to show you on your flight deck rather than downstairs under cover.'

'I think you mean below.' Thurston's tone was acid, betraying his impatience with the whole ridiculous business.

'Yes, I think that would be sensible,' said Stokes.

There was a brief hiatus while the photographer picked up his bag of equipment and Thurston his cap and telescope, and then they all climbed the ladders to the flight deck. Through the hangar, empty now that all the surviving aircraft had been flown off to the air station at Nowra, echoing and much larger than it normally appeared. The reporters asked more questions, to which Stokes gave practised answers. The flight deck too seemed larger than normal, with the aircraft of the deck park gone. The concrete and the splinter holes in the island were very obvious. Leave had been piped on the ship's arrival, and most of the men not actually required for duty had long gone ashore. A working party was busy with stores at one end, and a few men were desultorily playing deck hockey amidships. The woman scribbled in her notebook, two of the men discussed their next appointment.

It all took a long time while the photographer fiddled with exposures and different lenses. The reporters stood in a huddle chatting to Stokes, and the men scattered over the deck tried to look as though they were not watching with interest.

'That may be a woman over there, and you may not have seen anything female which isn't a cockroach for the last three months, but that doesn't mean you stare at her as though she's Jane from the *Mirror* without her clothes on! Get on with what you're supposed to be doing,' Thurston heard a petty officer shout to one of them, and was almost pleased to see the woman blush.

'Just a couple without your cap, and that'll be the lot.'

Finally the photographer was satisfied, and the newspaper contingent trooped down the gangway.

'That's all for today, sir. Obviously I'll see the copy before it's printed, and make any adjustments which are necessary. It's all intended to chivvy the Australian

185

war effort along a bit. I expect the Commander in Chief has mentioned that we're arranging for you to go round a couple of factories while you're here.'

'He did.'

'It's all quite simple. You go and talk to the directors and the managers, and a couple of your pilots will talk to the workers on the shop floor. If you can find a couple of reasonably articulate ratings to go along with them, then so much the better. We've found that it works better that way. As a captain you're always going to be a bit remote from the ordinary worker – they'll regard you as one of the bosses and won't appreciate that you face the same sort of hardships and dangers as your men do – but you obviously have a lot in common with the chaps at senior management level. You talk for half an hour or so, answer questions – they always like to ask lots of questions – and then they'll give you lunch. You write your own script. I expect you know the sort of things to leave out, but I've got a list here I'll give you. Or I can write it for you, if you'd prefer. Try to slant it towards your particular audience. Tell them your aircraft would never get off the ground without their spark plugs, or they make the best tyres, or whatever it is they produce. Let them know what's really happening out there, so they can feel involved in the war.'

Thurston thought of the burnt-out island, only a few yards from where they stood, and the long succession of stretchers which had come out of it, each bearing part of a man's body, thought he could still smell the death smell which seemed to have hung over the ship ever since, and wondered whether factory managers would really want to know what kind of war the munitions from which they made their fat profits were going to.

'Today's Tuesday, we'll start you off on Thursday – that should give us a chance to sort out what you're going to say – if you're agreeable.'

'It seems I have little choice,' Thurston said for the

second time that day.

Stokes finally left and Thurston went into his sleeping
cabin, suddenly finding himself at a loose end now that
all the official visitors had gone ashore, and it was still
only the middle of the afternoon. The Report of Proceedings had been dictated, typed, corrected and re-
typed during the voyage south, and the correspondence
had already gone ashore. His in-tray was full, but that
could wait until the morning. On his way to the bathroom he noticed a small black object curled up on the
blue counterpane which covered his bed. The object
opened one eye, stretched its front paws, then opened
its mouth in a mighty yawn.

'Spencer, what is that?'

Spencer bustled in from his pantry. 'It's a kitten, sir,'
he said with a perfectly straight face.

'I know it's a kitten. But where did it come from, and
how did it come to be asleep on my bed?'

'He's one of Captain Flint's latest, sir.'

One of *Inflexible*'s American acquisitions, during her
refit in Boston, had been a black and white cat who had
immediately been christened Captain Flint, and had
then confounded everybody's expectations a few weeks
later by producing five kittens.

'He came exploring and his little legs got tired, so I
put him up there for a rest.'

'Do you honestly expect me to believe that,
Spencer?'

'Not really, sir.' Spencer was quite unabashed.

'Spencer, I think you're back to your usual self.'

'Yes, sir. And Rosie and the girls are fine. Elizabeth's been learning to swim, and she can do a length of
the baths now without touching the bottom, and Dot-
tie's done a picture of me at school which she's going to
send with the next letter.'

Thurston reached out his hand and rubbed behind
the kitten's ears with an index finger. The kitten arched

his head back, uttered a small but surprisingly deep purr, then rolled on to his back to reveal an expanse of white underparts.

"'E likes you, sir. I'n't he gorgeous.'

Thurston felt himself weakening.

"'E likes a drop of rum too. I let him have sippers from my tot, just to keep his strength up.'

'Spencer, you're corrupting the young.' He looked from Spencer to the kitten, still purring under his hand. 'Oh, all right. He can live in the pantry, but you'll have to look after him properly. No more sippers.'

"'Course I will, sir. What are we going to call him?'

Thurston thought for a moment. 'He's one of Flint's crew, and he's got a taste for rum. Call him Billy Bones.'

'Aye aye, sir.' Spencer changed the subject. 'Bet you're glad to get rid of that lot, sir.'

'And how.'

'Don't worry, sir. You had them twisted round your little finger.'

'You've been eavesdropping from the pantry again.'

'Yes, sir. Had to keep my eye on things, 'case they wanted another lot of coffee.'

'Spencer, you are incorrigible.'

'Yes, sir,' Spencer said, as if this was a compliment. He picked up the kitten, pressed him against the opening of his blue jean collar. 'Come on, Billy, you're a matelot now, so I'll have to rig you a hammock. You can't sleep on the Old Man's bed all the time.'

Thurston went ashore, and walked for a long time along the waterfront. In four months this was only the third time he had set foot on land, and at Leyte and Manus there had not been civilians, women, private cars, or anything which had not been put there by servicemen for service purposes. Sydney had not been bombed from the air, nor blockaded. The nearest fighting front was two thousand miles away in New Guinea;

there was no rationing, no blackout; and the service-men in the streets were outnumbered by civilians. In the bars and brothels of Kings Cross *Inflexible*'s men, Spencer among them, were slaking four months' thirst for alcohol and the other illicit pleasures which had been denied them in that time, the officers making for slightly less dubious establishments with the same intentions. But for Thurston it was enough to be by himself for a while, away from the responsibility of his command, a private citizen responsible only for himself. He might stay ashore and have a meal somewhere, then go on to the Senior Officers' Club, which was not subject to the peculiar Australian licensing laws, or he could simply go back to the ship, dine on board and get his head down early.

But it was only a respite and would not last long. He was in uniform, and even in plain clothes the zone at the top of his forehead which his cap had kept untanned, the rolling gait of the seaman newly come ashore, and the clipped vowels of Dartmouth would have marked him for what he was. He had been in the Navy for thirty-three years, having gone to Osborne at the age of twelve and a half; he had joined his first ship as a midshipman six weeks before his fifteenth birthday in another war. The service and its ethos were entrenched now, and must come first, last and always. He could have told those newspapermen, and that smooth PR operator who masqueraded as a naval officer, to go hang, but he could not, because this was something the service required of him, just as it required that he sail two-thirds of the way round the world, fight and, if necessary, die to defend his King against his enemies; and that was something so deeply ingrained that he rarely thought consciously of it.

Chapter Fifteen

The dream came again, the old nightmare in which he was struggling to break free of the tangle of twisted metal around his legs while beside him Lieutenant York's eyes, glassy with death, bored into his, accusing, a tide of damply glistening intestines disappearing into the shadows on the far side. *Flood the magazine or she'll go up!* He kicked outwards, trying desperately to free himself, warm blood running into his eyes, but the wreckage gripped his ankle like a vice. The deck beneath was growing hotter. He tried desperately to reach the voicepipe to give the order, but it was beyond his reach. A hand reached out to his shoulder, the fingers charred into four blackened talons, the dead man's eyes blazing out of a skull from which all the flesh had burnt away.

Thurston awoke, as he always did at this point, gulping in air as if he had been under water, aware from the dryness in his throat that he had been shouting, his feet showing palely at the bottom end of the bed where he had kicked the bedclothes off. He got out of bed, went through to the bathroom and splashed cold water over his face. He wondered how many times he had had the dream, had relived the hit on *Warrior*'s forward turret in this distorted form. It must run into the hundreds by now, but each time it was as if it was the first. He heard movements outside, the rattle of the metal rings as the dividing curtain was pulled back.

'Are you all right, sir?'

He straightened up from the washbasin, saw Spencer standing in the doorway, wearing only his vest and underpants, Billy Bones' dark shape cradled against his stomach.

He grinned, almost sheepishly. 'The usual thing, Spencer.' Some of the water had run down his neck and inside his pyjama jacket, and he could feel its cold dampness against his flesh as he moved.

'I could do you a cup of cocoa, sir,' Spencer offered.

'No, Spencer, it's all right.'

At these times he wanted to be alone, even though Spencer had seen it all before. Spencer was still standing there, the tattooes on his arms standing out against the paleness of his flesh. Billy Bones began to purr as Spencer rubbed his ears, the sound very loud in the darkness and the silence.

'Goodnight, sir. See you in the morning.'

Spencer walked away, talking to the kitten in tones too low to be heard. Thurston went back to the sleeping cabin, glanced at the clock on the locker top, then pulled his trousers and greatcoat on over his pyjamas. On the flight deck it was raining softly, enough to damp down the concrete dust from the repairs which crept through every aperture and settled as a thin grey film on any horizontal surface. *Inflexible* had been manoeuvred into the dry dock that morning, after all the remaining ammunition had been laboriously manhandled off the ship and stowed in boxes on the dockside, a red flag flying while this was done and all smoking banned on board and for hundreds of yards around. The dockyard mateys had started work in the afternoon, making the deck reverberate with the noise of pneumatic drills and filling the air with the fine grey dust from the concrete.

He walked to the edge of the flight deck, where it overhung the dockside, saw a bored gangway sentry pacing up and down the concrete, rifle slung on one shoulder. The dream, when it came, was unsettling, a reminder that the ghosts were not yet exorcised and that the shadow of his breakdown still lurked. Seven months of hospitals and sick leave, two operations on the wrist he had slashed at his lowest point, and then three months of frustration on light duties while My Lords Commissioners of the Admiralty debated what responsibilities he could be trusted with. He had got back to sea after that, with his medical category restored, and the mere fact that he was in command of a ship like *Inflexible* showed that Their Lordships had regained their confidence in him. Officially it was all behind him, and for long periods he could forget it had ever happened, but the breakdown would be remembered. 'Thurston? That's the fellow who tried to top himself.' In the way of things there would have been a grudging respect if he had succeeded.

The coldness of the rain was steadying. He gripped the topmost rail with his left hand, the wire damp and a little greasy to the touch, reached inside the sleeve to scratch the scar where it had begun to itch again. Dammit, he was all right. It was the usual thing after a long spell at sea, the pressure was off but he could not let go.

'You've got to learn to relax,' Campbell, the psychiatrist in Alexandria, had told him over and over again. 'You're far too tense; you don't even know what it's like to be really relaxed. You're always going to be under a lot of pressure in your job, and although you can't do much to change the pressure which comes from outside, you can do something to reduce the pressure from inside, which is that puritanical conscience of yours. You must make a conscious effort to switch off whenever you get the chance. Listen to some music, get drunk, provided you don't feel guilty about it, go for a walk in the rain, masturbate if you like – it doesn't make you go blind. Anything, provided you can forget all about the service when you're doing it.'

But that, along with many other things, had been easy for Campbell to say and much less easy to put into practice. *Inflexible* might be in dry dock, but the responsibility for the ship and her men remained. There was also the programme of official events at which he, as *Inflexible*'s Captain, was required to appear and make himself agreeable to the Australians, and there was Commander Stokes and his talks to the profiteers ashore.

The sentry was moving back towards the gangway, head hunched into his collar against the rain which was beginning to fall more heavily. Thurston turned away from the rail, began walking aft towards the ladder, crossing a patch of concrete where the kamikaze had dented the deck, and into which someone had etched NEXT TOKYO in a gesture of defiance.

'Fred, I keep telling you, you want your head examined. The heat in that bloody boiler room must have finally got to you.'

Holland said nothing. His mind was made up, his letter of request written, sealed into its envelope and about to proceed on its way to the Captain. He pushed the letter into a side pocket, went out of the cabin, pulling the curtain closed behind him.

The Captain's secretary was in his office, a cramped little compartment below the waterline, made even smaller by the presence of four large angle pieces which riveted the watertight bulkhead at one end to the decks above and below, several large filing cabinets, and the PO Writer and two Leading Writers who dealt with most of the Captain's routine correspondence and kept all the ship's records.

He knew the secretary by sight, an efficient young man with an Edinburgh accent, regular Navy, from

Dartmouth. Another one.

'We don't often see you in here. What brings you to this spot?'

'Could you see the Captain gets this.' Holland was standing in front of the secretary's desk, rather awkwardly, reaching into his pocket for the envelope, praying that it hadn't become dog-eared or bent during its journey. He noticed one of the Writers look up briefly, then go back to the file he was dealing with.

'What is it, a billet-doux?' the secretary enquired cheerfully.

'No, of course not!' He found that he was reddening, clenched his fists until the nails dug into his palms.

'All right, keep your hair on. I'll see the Captain gets it.'

Scott reached for the paper-knife on his desk, an ornate little object shaped like a naval officer's sword, casually slit open the letter, unfolded it and read through it rapidly. 'I thought most of you chaps couldn't wait to get back to civvy street. Has the Commander (E) seen this?'

'No.'

'Well, strictly speaking, this should go to the Captain through him. But leave it with me. I'll sort that out.'

The Commanding Officer
His Majesty's Ship Inflexible

Sir,
I have the honour to request that my name be forwarded to My Lords Commissioners of the Admiralty for consideration for transfer to a permanent commission.

I have the honour to be,
Sir,
Your obedient servant,

F. D. Holland
Lieutenant (E) RNR

194

'Holland. Do you know him, Scratch?'

'Not really, sir. I had to stop to work out who he was when he brought this thing to me.'

Thurston thought for a moment, trying to visualise the man behind the name, the man whose carefully written epistle he now held in his hands, couched in immaculate service prose on a sheet of writing paper with the ship's badge at the head. 'Boxer, isn't he?'

'Yes, sir. Middleweight, I think. Won his weight in Trinco.'

He had Holland now, an elaborate silk dressing gown flung carelessly around his shoulders, hair glistening with sweat as he stood in front of him to receive his prize. There was blood on his face from a cut over one eye, running down from beneath a pink strip of plaster which was already coming unstuck at one end, a triumphant, rather cocky grin from knocking out his Marine opponent in the final seconds of a fight which could otherwise have gone either way on points. He couldn't remember speaking to him on any other occasion.

'Then we should be seeing him again before long.' The Commander was organising a boxing tournament for the ship's spell in harbour, along with football and rugby matches against various local navy, army and air force units. 'You say he brought this to you directly.'

'Yes, sir.'

'Then Chief probably doesn't know about it. I'll have a word with him about Holland, see what he has to say about him. Meanwhile, could you dig Holland's personal file out so that I can have a look at it. I thought they were all demob happy now the war in Europe's over, itching to get out, not trying to stay in.'

'No, sir, I didn't know about this, but I'm not unduly surprised. I can't say I was expecting it, but if you'd asked me which of my Reserve Officers would want to stay in the service, I'd have picked Holland.'

'What do you think of him, Chief?'

'As an engineer, sir, he's very proficient, one of the best I've got. He's been very useful to me on a couple of occasions when we've had trouble with the machinery because he actually served his time at Parsons and really knows his way around the engines. Doesn't need to bother with the drawings and handbooks, most of the time.'

'But you've got reservations about him all the same.'

'I don't want to scupper his chances, sir, but I have to say yes. He's a good lad, and it's difficult to fault him as an engineer, but . . . It's hard to describe. I've always got the feeling that he's trying to prove something to the rest of us. You might say he has a bit of a chip on his shoulder, in the sense that he's determined to prove himself a better man than the rest. But more than likely he'll grow out of it. He just needs to grow up a bit.'

Holland had obviously prepared himself carefully for the occasion. He wore his best uniform, which had been pressed by his Marine servant and then brushed until every trace of fluff had been removed, his cap placed beneath his left arm by the brim so that no fingermarks had been left on the black patent peak, the seam of the white cover centred exactly above the badge, hair carefully combed into place and secured there with hair oil, not too much, but just enough.

'Sit down, Holland.'

Holland sat, on the edge of the chair, carefully moved his cap to his knees and arranged his legs so that his feet rested parallel to one another on the carpet, pointing directly towards his Captain.

Holland was aware that his accent came out more strongly under stress. It was happening now, just at the time when it would be most to his disadvantage. He could hear it now in his replies to the Captain's questions, contrasting with the Captain's measured bass voice and Dartmouth accent. All the advantages, he thought a little bitterly. Right parents, right school, right everything.

'I see you're from Whitley Bay.'

'Yes, sir.'

'I'm from Northumberland myself. Up near Wooler.'

The Captain was obviously trying to put him at his ease. But Wooler was not Whitley Bay, and in any case the Captain probably owned half of it.

'A place called Langdon, where my father was parson.'

Perhaps he didn't own half Northumberland. But to be the son of a parson was acceptable to the Navy, more than acceptable. After all, Nelson had been the son of a parson.

'What does your father do?'

Background, the thing which was all important. He gave his father an undeserved promotion. 'He's a bank manager, sir.' It was the best he could do.

The Captain was asking him about his boxing the Chief had warned him to expect this – and that was better. His eyes strayed towards the corner where the Commander (E) was sitting, but he could not have seen him without turning his head. It wasn't too difficult to talk about how he'd started in the boys' club at home, gradually worked his way up to win the schoolboy championship of the North of England just before he left school, the training he was doing now that they were out of the operational zone and he had time to get down to some proper training – yes, he had put his name down for the boxing tournament while they were in Sydney – and how he'd started helping some of the boy seamen out; he didn't really think he could call it proper coaching, it was mainly sparring and some fitness work. The Captain seemed to know something about boxing – well, he'd have boxed at Dartmouth at least, but that broken nose of his could have come from

197

a punch, a right-hander, coming up from below instead of straight across.

'The Commander (E) seems to think highly of you as an engineer.'

'Yes, sir.' That was a relief. The Commander (E) was regular Navy, of course, and must have gone in through the usual engineers' route of the Royal Naval Engineering College at Keyham. He had taken Holland aside the day before. 'You know that this request of yours should have gone through me. I'm not going to stand in your way, but I've told the Captain what I think, and whether your application goes up to Their Lordships is up to him.'

'You did your apprenticeship at Parsons, and then what?'

He'd been paid off the day he finished his time, because that was how most engineering firms worked. He could have gone into the drawing office, or found a place as a fitter, but he had elected to go to sea as a junior engineer. By the time the war had come he had had his second engineer's ticket and was therefore eligible for an RNR commission. He had spent a few months in the engine room of an armed merchant cruiser, until she was consigned once more to the Merchant Navy as being too slow and too vulnerable for a warship, followed by two years in a cruiser of the Home Fleet, before being appointed to *Inflexible*.

'Why do you want a permanent commission, Holland?'

'I want to stay in the Navy, sir.'

The Captain gave a slight smile. 'That much is obvious. Why, when everyone else is only too keen to get back to civilian life?'

Holland had thought about it, but he knew that the best answer he could give was inadequate. 'I like it, sir. It's what I've always wanted to do, be a marine engineer.'

'You can be a marine engineer without staying in the

198

service, as you yourself were before the war.'

'Yes, sir. But . . . Well, sir.' To his embarrassment, the word came out as 'sor'. 'It's not the same outside. This, well, it's more important. It's what I like doing, and I want to keep on doing it.'

The Captain looked across to the Commander (E). 'Have you anything to add, Chief?'

'No, sir.'

'Then I think that's everything. Have you anything more you wish to say?'

Holland's mind was blank. 'No, sir.'

'I have decided to forward your request to Their Lordships, with my support.'

'Thank you, sir.'

'This doesn't mean that anything will happen in the next five minutes, you understand.'

'Yes, sir.'

'You will be reported on half-yearly by me, until such time as Their Lordships convene a selection board to consider your case. I must tell you that this will not happen until the ship returns to home waters, unless, of course, you leave her before that.'

'Yes, sir.'

'All right, Holland, that'll be all for now.' The Captain looked at his watch. 'Have you and Holland time for a drink, or do you have to get back to the engine room?'

The newspapers published their stories, each illustrated by the same photograph of Thurston standing on his flight deck, back to the damaged island, telescope under arm, gold lace and red ribbon on display, not smiling, but thoughtful, reserved and serious. *Captain Robert Thurston VC DSO and Bar, of HMS* Inflexible. *Captain Thurston, a father of four from Langdon, Northumberland* (that had the woman reporter's hand in it) *won fame in sinking the German pocket battleship* Seydlitz *in the North Atlantic on 8th July 1941 while in*

199

command of the small cruiser Marathon. Wrong again, as usual. The press had a strange obsession with pocket battleships. *Seydlitz* had been a cruiser, a cruiser nearly twice the size of *Marathon*, but a cruiser nonetheless, and *Northumberland*'s role was, once again, ignored.

The telephone rang on the Friday afternoon. 'Answer that, would you, Scratch and if it's Commander Stokes I'm not available.'

Scott spoke briefly into the telephone. 'Someone called Roper, sir. He says he's a friend of yours.'

'Bob? Jack Roper here. Must say you're a hard bloke to track down. First the operator, then your ADC. Anyway, we heard you were back in Sydney.'

'You could hardly have missed it.'

'Oh, the papers, you mean? I did see something. Anyway, if you're free this weekend would you like to come over? We'd be glad to see you again.'

The Ropers were friends of friends of friends, with a dairy farm about fifty miles away in the foothills of the Blue Mountains.

'You won't need to get the train this time. I've got to be in Sydney first thing tomorrow morning so I can pick you up.'

'Yes, of course. I'd love to.'

'That's settled then. I'll come round to the dockyard and pick you up about eleven.'

Thurston thought for a moment. 'Could you make it nearer twelve? I'll have to do Rounds tomorrow, and in a ship this size it'll take most of the morning.'

'Stand-by-your-beds stuff? No problem. Eleven's probably cutting things a bit fine for me anyway.'

Thurston put the telephone down with a pleasurable feeling of anticipation. He had now addressed two different lots of factory managers, who had listened attentively, asked strings of questions, and provided a large and somewhat indigestible lunch. At the Ropers' place he would be out of reach of Commander Stokes and his publicity schemes, and could enjoy a couple of days' peace and quiet.

'I'm going to be away from lunchtime tomorrow until Monday morning, Scratch.' Thurston wrote a few lines on the pad at his elbow. 'There's the address. Make sure the Commander in Chief gets the usual signal. I'll brief the Commander, myself.'

'Aye aye, sir.'

'And you seem to have joined the army. You're now my ADC.'

'And been demoted, sir.'

'S'pose you want your riding boots cleaning, sir.' Spencer brought them out of the wardrobe, pushed a hand inside one of them and pointed the toe towards the light. 'One thing you won't get me doing, riding a horse. One end kicks, the other end bites, and you have to watch the bit in the middle because it's doin' it's best to get you off.'

Chapter Sixteen

Saturday forenoon meant Captain's Rounds, for no better reason than that Captain's Rounds had always taken place on a Saturday morning. In fact, in a ship as large as *Inflexible* it was necessary to inspect half of the ship on the Friday afternoon, otherwise the whole of Saturday would be taken up with Rounds.

A few minutes after 0800 Thurston emerged from his cabin, preceded by a Marine drummer and attended by the Commander, the First Lieutenant, his 'doggie', Midshipman Anderson, the Master of Arms and Boy Maxwell. The procession wound its way through the passages beneath the hangar, the sound and vibration of the pneumatic drills clear from many decks above, the drummer sounding a brief warning before the Captain entered each compartment, calling the men within to attention. A quick glance around, taking in the overall impression, then asking for a locker or stowage to be opened, apparently at random, running a finger along an unseen surface above head level, paying special attention to compartments which had been unsatisfactory on a previous occasion, Midshipman Anderson making notes in a black-bound notebook.

'Given that we've been at sea for over three months, and we're in the midst of repairs at the moment, it's not too bad. However, the same things keep coming up over and over again, and in the same places. If 2D mess are going to keep pin-ups on the bulkheads and take them down before I come round, they should remember to scrub off the Sellotape marks.' It was the usual way, to begin with the minor, rather amusing discrepancies, and then move on to the serious matters. 'As we were going round I found at least four fire extinguishers which weren't full, and there were no extinguishers at several places where there should have been.'

'The men use the stuff in them to get stains out of their clothes, sir. They've been warned over and over again, but they go on doing it.'

'Yes, Howard, I'm quite aware of that. How often are the extinguishers checked?'

The Commander had to think rapidly. 'Once in three months, sir.'

'That's just not good enough. You'd better make sure we've got our full complement of extinguishers, filled, and in the places where they should be, and have them checked every fortnight in future.'

'Aye aye, sir.' The Commander made a note on his pad.

'And while we're on this subject, this is a good opportunity for a thorough review of our fire-fighting organisation and damage control in general. Could you arrange a heads of department meeting for Tuesday – that'll give everybody time to canvass opinions in their departments. We've got the opportunity, while we're here, to get hold of everything we need, so let's not waste it.'

The Commander made another note. 'Tuesday at 1100, sir?'

Thurston nodded. 'We've got four or five weeks here, and the resources of the dockyard to draw on, so let's get everything sorted out before we go back. I'm not going to accept any discrepancies which have any bearing on our operational efficiency or damage control capability. The rest is icing on the cake. Efficiency comes first, and when time and resources are at a premium, something else will have to give.'

'Yes, sir. I'll get everything sorted.'

'Before Rounds next week,' Thurston chaffed the Commander gently.

'Aye aye, sir.'

As the Commander left, Billy Bones emerged from the pantry door and rubbed himself against Thurston's ankles.

'Sorry, Billy, you'll have to stay behind.'

Spencer picked up Thurston's bag and followed him out of the cabin. Tradition forbade an officer to carry bags or packages when in uniform.

At the stroke of twelve the pneumatic drills had stopped and the dockyard mateys now clattered ashore until 0800 on the Monday morning. There was an audible sigh of relief from all over the ship at the cessation of the noise and vibration, which seemed, for a moment, to leave a strange emptiness behind. A make-and-mend had been piped and the men were on their way ashore, dressed in their Number One suits with gold badges; officers leaving the ship from the after gangway, also in uniform. Lieutenant Bingham was Officer of the Watch, sword belt under his reefer, showing at his left side, telescope under his left arm, pacing the confined quarterdeck with Midshipman Holt.

'Drawn the short straw, Bingham?'

'No, sir. I'm going ashore later.'

Jack Roper was waiting a few yards up the road from the dock gates, behind the wheel of his Ford V8.

'Hello, Bob. Good to see you again. Sling your things in the back, if you can find a space. Who's this?'

Thurston briefly introduced Spencer.

'Have a good weekend, sir. Don't do anything I wouldn't do.'

'That leaves me plenty of leeway, Spencer.'

Spencer thought for a moment. 'Then don't go doing nothing silly, like falling off no horses, sir.'

'See you on Monday, Spencer.'

Thurston returned Spencer's salute, then watched him walk away towards the ship.

'That fellow seems to have quite a rapport with you, Bob.'

'He's been doing for me since the war began. He was supposed to fill a gap for a couple of days and I still can't get rid of him.'

Jack laughed. 'I had a batman just like that in France. He'd been a baker before the war and every time we were out of the line he'd get busy. Don't ask me where he got the stuff from, but he used to make the most wonderful bread rolls for breakfast every morning.'

'That sounds like Spencer. I don't ask him where he gets hold of anything.'

'He was killed in the Salient in '17,' Roper said more thoughtfully. 'Shell got him in the communications trench as we were going back up the line one night, him and a lot of others.'

Jack Roper looked almost a caricature of an Australian farmer, a lean, sinewy six foot four, with massive corded forearms now hidden beneath the sleeves of his city suit. He took one hand off the wheel, extracted a packet of cigarettes from his jacket pocket and flourished it at Thurston. 'Oh, you don't, of course.' He pulled out a cigarette, lit it with a battered brass lighter, exhaled a cloud of smoke and took the cigarette out of his mouth once more.

'Been in to see my solicitor. Couple of things that needed to be sorted out. Well, Mary and I aren't getting any younger, so I'm making a new will. It's about time. The old one's a bit out of date now. I actually made it in a trench at Gallipoli, on the form in the back of my paybook, and solicitor was telling me that it's still quite valid, even though it wasn't witnessed or anything.'

'Privilege. We have it too, provided you're on board ship, or joining a ship, when you make it. But I got my solicitor to sort mine out after the twins were born.'

'It's because of Alan really. Well, not knowing whether he's coming back or not.'

'Still no news?'

'No, and I don't suppose there will be until the war's over now. They say the division was virtually intact at the time of the surrender, so the chances are that he was taken prisoner, and we just have to go on hoping. Not a word about those lads since Bennett got back here making excuses for leaving them behind. Well, there's been a few got away, in the early days, and I'm sure if any of them had known Alan there'd have been a message for us. But he wouldn't have tried to get away himself unless he could have got his men, his platoon, away with him. He knew that much. Matter of fact, you'll be meeting our daughter-in-law, Jane, Alan's wife, while you're with us this time. She had the morning off work, so she came over on the train last night. She got a job in Sydney after Singapore, so we don't see her as much as we'd like to.'

They had left the city behind, the land now dotted with large commercial greenhouses and market gardens. To the west lay the distant slopes of the Blue Mountains.

'Nice morning. Bit cooler than when you were last here.'

'And cooler than where I've come from. Hundred and twenty degrees on the bridge, ninety-odd per cent humidity, and wearing full anti-flash gear most of the time. And the engine room temperatures got up to a hundred and fifty at times.'

'Rough.'

'You could say that.'

'Still, you're all out of it for a bit, and Mary's got

206

lunch waiting for us.' Jack Roper pushed his foot down a little harder on the accelerator pedal.

Mary Roper was in the kitchen, hands streaked white with flour, putting the finishing touches to a large apple pie at the scrubbed wooden table in the centre of the room. 'Oh, you've timed it very nicely. This is just ready to go in the oven, and the meat will be ready in about ten minutes.' She, like her husband, was in her early fifties, but his physical opposite, comfortably plump, and almost a foot shorter. 'Bob, I've put you in the same room as last time, the one at the top of the stairs. Jane's in the room next door; I hope she won't disturb you.'

'Oh, I can sleep through anything,' Thurston assured her.

'I'm not sure where she is at the moment, though she does know it's nearly time for lunch.'

'She can't be far away then,' Roper said cheerfully.

Thurston picked up his bag and went upstairs to the room which had been made ready for him. It belonged to the Ropers' younger son, who was in England as an RAF navigator, and signs of his missing presence were still there in the aircraft models which hung from the ceiling, dusty now in the more inaccessible places, and the pile of copies of *The Aeroplane* on the chest of drawers, the most recent four years old. A photograph next to them showed a Lancaster and the seven men of her crew, Geoff Roper the third from the left, wearing the dark blue battledress of the Royal Australian Air Force and a Pathfinder badge beneath his single wing. Thurston shifted into plain clothes, a Harris tweed jacket which had been made for him on foreign service leave at the end of *Retribution*'s commission just before the war, grey flannels, a wool tie in greens and blues, and brown brogues which Spencer had boned to a deep reddish sheen, then stowed the bag away in the bottom

207

of the wardrobe below Geoff's civilian clothes, still there, though Mary had admitted at the time of Thurston's previous visit that none of them would fit him now. He had been eighteen when he enlisted; he was twenty-two now, and claimed in his letters that his parents wouldn't recognise him.

He went across the landing to the bathroom to wash his hands. Returning, he noticed the door of the neighbouring bedroom open, and stopped for a moment. A girl came out, pushing her hair from her face. No windows opened on to the landing, so that the light was a little dim, and she did not appear to see Thurston until she had almost cannoned into him.

'Oh, I'm sorry. Did I startle you?'

'No, no. I've been asleep. I've only just woken up. Silly of me. I must have just nodded off.' The girl collected herself. 'You must be Captain Thurston.'

'I am he. And you must be Jane Roper.'

'Yes I am.'

'How do you do,' they said simultaneously.

'Come on down. Lunch is ready,' Mary Roper called from the bottom of the stairs.

She was a young woman rather than a girl, about twenty-seven or twenty-eight, with fair hair cut in a bob and very blue eyes. Though it was the Australian winter and she worked indoors, she still had a faint tan, and a scatter of freckles across the bridge of her nose which Thurston found rather attractive, in pleasant contrast to the heavily made-up faces he had seen on the streets of Sydney. In the course of conversation it came out that she worked in Sydney for the Australia and New Zealand Bank, where she was secretary to one of the branch managers, had a small flat, which she, in the Australian way, called a 'unit' on Sydney's North Shore, and left the city to stay with her husband's parents about one weekend in four.

'Well, Bob, I'm sure you're itching to get your leg

across a saddle again.'

'I am. I haven't been on a horse since I was here last, and that's far too long.'

'That's the only reason you come here.'

'Not at all.'

'There is Mary's cooking,' Jack said, looking towards his wife at the other end of the table. 'I've got a few things to do round the farm this afternoon, but Jane'll go round with you.'

Jane had been concentrating on her piece of the apple pie. She jerked her head up, away from the plate. 'Yes, of course.'

'You should have time to go up the ridge this afternoon.' Jack turned to Thurston. 'You get a wonderful view from up there on a day like this. Anyway, that's just an idea. Jane knows her way around. You'd better take Sultan again, Bob. He hasn't been out for a couple of days, so he'll be needing the exercise.' He pushed his chair back, stood up, and initiated a general movement away from the table.

Sultan was a rangy chestnut thoroughbred, who had run a couple of races as a two-year-old before breaking down. He had had several owners since then, before Jack Roper had paid fifteen pounds for him in a sale a couple of years earlier. He was very fresh, tossing his head and prancing sideways as Thurston strove to bring him under control and point him towards the farm gate.

'You'd better go in front. Trouble with him is that he won't stay behind anyone.'

Jane had changed out of her blouse and skirt into jodhpurs and a polo-neck sweater, and was sitting astride the bay gelding which her father-in-law used around the farm. Sultan was still sidestepping, half walking, half trotting, throwing his head upwards in an effort to get away from the bit. Thurston was having to work to keep him into the side of the roughly metalled track which was dignified by the name of road.

209

'Are you having problems?' Jane called out.

'Not at all. He'll be all right once he settles down.'

'We can give him a gallop when we get away from the road. That should calm him down a bit.'

'Get some of the nonsense out of him.'

'Up there,' Jane said, indicating with one hand.

To the left there was a narrow drainage ditch, and a wire fence running along the edge of one of Jack Roper's pastures, where a couple of dozen shorthorns grazed contentedly. Beyond that the river ran in lazy meanders towards its confluence with the larger river which would eventually merge with the waters of Sydney Harbour. On the other side of the road the ground rose more steeply, into green hills which turned to purple and blue on their higher slopes. The point Jane was indicating was another track, running up towards the head of the valley, a slash of pale brown amid the green of the pasture land.

'Through that gate on the right,' she told him.

Thurston brought Sultan to a halt abreast the gate, leant out from his saddle to open it, pushing his left knee into Sultan's side and laying the reins against his neck to keep him from sidestepping away. He was getting Sultan's measure once more, running his free hand along the horse's neck and talking to him softly. 'Easy now. Jack's going to have to cut your oats.' He closed the gate behind Jane, turned Sultan round and let him go forward into a trot. Abreast Jane and her steadier mount for a moment, he could see that she rode well, hands well down and barely moving as she rose and fell with the horse's motion, hair blowing a little in the wind.

The track was climbing gradually up the hillside, a narrow stream dropping more steeply a few yards away. The afternoon was warm, Thurston beginning to sweat a little inside his jacket. He thought suddenly of the ship, a dead world now, with most of the men ashore and the dockyard mateys gone until Monday morning. There would be a few men aboard, those for whom one foreign port was the same as any other and who had all they desired on board, or who had simply decided that going ashore was not worth the effort of cleaning and pressing their Number One suits and falling in to be inspected by the officer of the watch before they were allowed to leave the ship. They would be sprawled about their messes now, reading the tattered paperbacks from the ship's library, occasionally rousing themselves to move as far as the galley for hot water to make cups of tea, or perhaps simply asleep.

They breasted a slight rise, and the ground opened out ahead, level, green and inviting. He turned his head to shout back at Jane. 'Going to canter.'

Sultan needed no urging. Thurston felt the slipstream as the speed increased, heard the bay's hoofbeats as Jane came up alongside. Sultan was pulling, his head jerking forward as he tried to get the bit between his teeth. The bay was beginning to pull ahead, obviously going flat out now. Jane was smiling, urging him on, hair flying back in the wind. Thurston let an inch of rein through his fingers, let Sultan have his head. He began to overhaul her, the powerful muscles of his quarters bunching to drive him forwards. Sultan's head came level with the bay's girth, then he was past, leaving them behind, the bay's hoofbeats fading. At the far end of the field the ground rose steeply once more. Thurston reined Sultan in, turned him to wait for Jane, patting his neck as the horse got his breath.

'You left us behind,' Jane protested.

She was laughing, running the back of her sleeve across her forehead to dry the sweat from her face.

'You said yourself he won't let anyone in front of him.'

'He can fly, can't he. Not like this fellow,' she laughed, running her hand along the bay's neck. 'He's just a plodder, aren't you.'

Thurston let go of the reins, held Sultan with his knees as he pulled off his tie, rolled it round one of his hands and put it away in his jacket pocket. 'I hope you don't mind.'

'I'm a bit hot too, after all that.'

They continued up the path, more sedately as it grew steeper, began to zigzag up the hillside, crossed by bands of bare rock and flanked by occasional boulders. Sultan was quieter now, and it was possible to keep him alongside the bay. They passed through a belt of trees smelling of eucalyptus, insects buzzing around the horses' girths. Sultan swished his tail and began to prance again, sidestepping to bring Thurston's leg briefly against Jane's, causing another frisson of excitement, as there had been when he first saw her on the landing.

'Not much further.' Jane cocked an eye at the sky. 'It should be pretty clear today. It'll start to get a bit narrow in a minute, so you'd better go ahead again.'

It was nearing five o'clock now and the sun was beginning to shine across and into Thurston's eyes, making him squint around it to see where he was going.

'Stop when you get to the top, otherwise you might go over the edge, which isn't recommended.'

They were going up a steep section, leaning forward in their saddles and letting the horses pick their own route, reddish boulders on either side, the scent of eucalyptus all around, heavy in the air. The ground levelled suddenly, and Thurston halted Sultan hastily as he realised that they were almost on the edge of a cliff which dropped vertically into a valley filled with the dark green of eucalyptus, a waterfall plunging down the cliff opposite, the rock deeply fissured and eroded into pinnacles at the summit, the white water turning silver in the stream far below and then white again as it ran

212

over a belt of rocks which uncounted ages of the stream's flow had failed to wear away.

'I love it up here,' Jane said. 'It's so quiet. All you have to do is sit and look. I always try to come here when I'm at Jack and Mary's.'

Thurston had edged Sultan a little to the right to make space for Jane and she had come up alongside him. He thought for a moment that he should have brought his sketch pad with him, but this view, like so many others, was one which could not be captured either on film or paper. It could only be seen, the eye taking in the subtle gradations of colour and texture which the camera would miss, the view changing every moment as the light and shadow changed with the coming of evening, a thin tracing of mist softening the outline of some of the pinnacles. Thurston felt almost as though he was an intruder in this perfect creation of nature, undamaged by man, unaffected by the war he had come to fight. Jane was silent beside him, drinking it in. Sultan's head was down and he was pulling at the tussocky grass in jerks.

'We'd better get back,' Jane said at last. 'Otherwise it'll be dark before we get there.'

They began the long descent, the shadows lengthening now, the horses tiring, but their ears pricked now they had turned towards home. The sun dipped below the ridge, throwing the whole area into twilight. They could see the lights of the Ropers' farmhouse, and another light by itself in the cowshed. No blackout here, the lights acting as beacons in the gathering dusk. Thurston and Jane kept to single file, speaking little, both comfortable with their horses, listening to the hoofbeats on the firm ground, the slight creaking of the saddles between their knees and the metallic jingle of the bits.

'Good ride?' Jack Roper asked as he emerged from the

213

cowshed at their approach, dressed in the old brown coat he wore for milking.

'Very good. You're right about the view from up there.'

'And how did this fellow behave himself?'

'He didn't,' Jane said.

'He was a bit full of himself.'

Thurston dismounted, took the reins over Sultan's head and started to take the saddle off.

'Jane didn't get you lost?'

'Of course not. I've been going up there since I was a kid.'

'And your father and I had to go up and find you then.' Jack jerked his thumb towards the ridge. 'She'd have been about eight or nine, and decided to go off exploring on the pony she had then. Didn't tell anyone where she was going, and when it started getting dark, her dad got worried. Half the neighbourhood turned out to look for her. I found her eventually, on the road going back to her father's place. "I've been up the ridge," she says, cool as you please. What time was that, Jane?'

'About midnight. I hadn't got a watch, and I lost track of the time.'

There was a teasing affection between Jane and her father-in-law, a mutual respect beneath the banter.

Mary Roper put her head around the kitchen door. 'Tea'll be ready in a few minutes.'

'She's really been pushing the boat out, Bob. Hardly stopped baking since she heard you were coming.'

'I used to dream about Mary's pies when we were up in the operational zone and Spencer put yet another plate of corned beef hash in front of me. My PO Cook did his best, but there were only so many things he could do with the rations.'

Lying in Geoff Roper's bed that night he was wakeful for a time, thinking over the events of the day, and almost guiltily of Jane a couple of feet away on the other side of the wall. Geoff Roper's mattress was less firm than he was used to. She was awake too; he heard the creak of springs as she turned over. He wondered what she thought of him. Her manner towards him had betrayed nothing, but there had been the moment that afternoon when Sultan had pranced sideways and his leg had made contact with hers; she had blushed a little then, and cast her eyes away from him. He told himself not to be a bloody fool, pounded the pillow into a more comfortable shape for his head, turned on to his left side, wondered whether she could hear him, then dismissed the thought once more.

Sunday passed quietly, getting up early and going for a run along the riverbank, then to church with the Ropers in a white wooden building on the outskirts of the village a couple of miles away. He was struck, as on his last visit, by the absence of men of military age in the congregation. Apart from himself there was only a young soldier, very obviously fresh from basic training, who blushed and stared at the hassock beneath his knees as the vicar read a prayer on his behalf. 'Jim Jordan's boy,' Jack Roper whispered. 'On embarkation leave for New Guinea.' It was all familiar, even in this strange setting, Matins from Cranmer's Prayer Book, with a brief celebration of Holy Communion, a choir of men and young boys with carefully parted hair in surplices and blue robes, a soft rain drumming on the wooden roof, but with the Australian accents of the congregation in the responses. He thought of his father, who would be making his way to the Norman church at Langdon in a few hours' time, not to celebrate any more, but to stand in the congregation alongside his wife, with a critical eye on his successor's performance in the pulpit. A few words with the vicar afterwards, then back to the farm for lunch.

In the afternoon he and Jack Roper rode round the

215

farm, one of the dogs following behind, in the rain, the pasture land lush and startlingly green at the wettest time of the year, the cattle standing out sharply in their blacks and browns. Thurston found himself paying more attention to the talk of farming than on his last visit, thinking of Edward Masters' offer. Sitting on the back of a horse, listening to Jack Roper talk about his milk yields and the rotation of his herd between the various pastures, it was a tempting prospect, to be free of the upheavals of service life, the long separations from his family, to be able to settle down at last instead of being always on the move. When the war was over, then he would have to decide one way or the other; while the war was on it could only be an idea, a prospect for the future.

Another of Mary Roper's enormous teas, trying to toast crumpets in front of the drawing-room fire and producing more in the way of burnt fingers, then a slow, rather sleepy evening, punctuated every now and then by someone getting up to change the record on the gramophone, writing letters to Kate, George and Helen, drinking a glass of whisky with Jack. Jane's fair head was bent over a book, *South Riding* by Winifred Holtby, her right hand turning the pages in a regular rhythm which suggested absolute concentration. Tomorrow, he had to return to his ship and be the Captain again, ensuring that the repairs were done, that the correct stores and equipment came on board, and the men were kept occupied, bringing *Inflexible* to a proper state of preparedness to go back to the war.

Eleven o'clock came and Jack Roper got up from his chair. 'Better get up to bed. The cows'll want to be milked in the morning.'

Jane was on the stairs ahead of him, the book under her arm. She stopped at the top, outside the door of her bedroom. 'Goodnight, Captain Thurston.'

His mind had been working around the idea since yesterday, now he seized the opportunity which presented itself. 'If you're not doing anything one night when you're in Sydney, would you like to have dinner with me?'

She smiled. 'Yes, that would be lovely.'

It was a conventional response, much as he would have expected. He ran mentally through his diary. 'Tomorrow?' He had nothing official to go to, and there would be a choice between going ashore for a drink somewhere and staying aboard looking at the four steel bulkheads of his cabin.

'No, I'm sorry. There's an evening class I go to on a Monday.'

His excitement faded.

'But I could manage Tuesday. Would that be all right?'

'Tuesday then. I'll pick you up at half past seven. You'll have to remember to give me the address.'

'I'll write it down for you, before I forget.'

She went into her room, and came back a moment later with half a page torn from a shorthand pad and bearing an address and roughly drawn map.

'Thank you. Goodnight, Jane.'

'Goodnight, Captain Thurston.'

He went into his own room, began to undress, and wondered why it was that he felt twenty again.

Chapter Seventeen

The taxi driver found the address quite easily. Thurston told him to wait, then knocked on the front door. It was an old house by Sydney standards, built perhaps at the turn of the century and later converted into flats, with a row of bells on the left side of the front door. Thurston rang the one marked 'Roper' and heard a window open directly above his head.

'I'll be right down.'

He was perhaps a little early, but she was dressed and ready, and looked as though she had been waiting some little time. She was wearing a blue dress, of almost the same colour as her eyes, with white at the collar and cuffs, and a gold bracelet on one wrist, her wedding and engagement rings in place.

'Where are you taking me?' she asked, after the taxi had started to move.

'You make it sound as though I'm kidnapping you.'

'Sorry.' She reddened a little, and for a moment looked very young.

'Doyles. Someone recommended it to me.'

'Yes, I've heard of it. Down on the waterfront at Vaucluse. But I've never been there.'

'I haven't either, but the chap I spoke to swore that it had the best crayfish in Sydney.'

'If you've room for any more food after a weekend with my mother-in-law!'

She blushed again, as if she had suddenly decided that she should not be so light-hearted with a naval captain seventeen or eighteen years her senior.

He offered her his arm as they went into the restaurant. After the slightest of hesitations, she took it, very lightly, merely laying a hand along the sleeve.

'Would you like a drink before we order?'

'Please, but just a small sherry.'

She was shy with him, and he had the impression that it was a long time since anyone had taken her out for a meal. Of course, her husband had been a POW for more than three years, and might well have been overseas for much longer than that. He too was unpractised; it was more than eighteen months since he had last taken Kate out properly, just the two of them by themselves, and far longer since he had dined with any other woman.

'What are you studying at your evening class?'

'French conversation, I'm afraid. Nothing very exciting. I did French at school, of course, but I haven't really kept it up. And then I found I was getting into a rut. I was at home every night, just looking at the four walls, and I decided it was time I did something about it. Don't get me wrong, I didn't go into it to find a replacement for Alan. In any case, most of the other people in the class are coming for the same reason as me, and the only man among them must be about sixty. He's a widower, with no family, and he goes to a different class every night, just to get out of the house and keep himself occupied. It's rather sad really, as he's a nice old chap, even though his accent's *atrocious*.' She had opened the menu, and was studying the pages. 'I really don't know what to have.'

'Have whatever you like.'

'Are you sure?' She was thinking of the bill.

'Of course. I don't have the chance to do something like this very often.'

'All right.' She squinted at the menu which rested in her lap. 'Could I have the famous crayfish?'

'Of course.' Thurston looked down the list of dishes,

219

his eyebrows drawn together in an expression of concentration. 'The chap who recommended this place told me that Sydney rock oysters are as famous as the crayfish, but I'm not all that keen on oysters, so I'm going to have the salmon. There're one or two things among the main dishes I don't recognise. Could you tell me what barramundi is?'

'It's a tropical fish. They usually serve it as steaks. It goes very well with a hollandaise sauce, which is how they do it here I'm told. In fact, could I have it, please?'

'Then I think I'll give it a try too.' Thurston caught the waiter's eye.

'Yes, sir?' He had seen the red ribbon and had been hovering at a discreet distance.

'Could we have the crayfish, and the salmon for me, and we'll both have the barramundi.'

'And wine, sir?' He was a man in his early thirties, and it crossed Thurston's mind to wonder why he was not in uniform. He looked across to Jane, who said nothing.

'A bottle of the Chardonnay.'

'Yes, sir. Your table will be ready in a few minutes.'

After the food arrived she was more relaxed, began to talk more easily, first about her job and her boss at the bank who sounded a bit of an ogre, then moving on to her as yet brief marriage to Alan Roper.

'I've known him all my life. We played together as kids. You know, we played football in the yard, Alan, my brother Joe and me. Geoff's quite a lot younger than Alan, and there weren't many other kids the same age nearby, so we all spent a lot of time together. I taught him to swim – there's a deep pool in the river where you can get out of your depth. He was always there. When he joined the army and went away, though, it was different. He started taking me out when he came home on leave – proper taking me out, dancing and things like that. Then he was commissioned, and he knew he was going overseas, and he asked me to marry him. He got forty-eight hours' leave to get married, and he came back again three weeks later on his embarkation leave, and that was that.

'My father died a few months later – he'd lost an arm in the last war and all the effort of running the farm was too much for his heart. Joe was already in the army, so Jack found us someone to manage the farm, and I went down to Sydney and found a job. I'd done a secretarial course when I left school, so it wasn't all that difficult to find something. And I've been at the bank ever since.' She put down her knife and fork, and changed the subject abruptly. 'I've seen your ship from the ferry. She's absolutely huge. How do you manage to run something that size?'

Thurston poured some more wine. 'I don't do everything myself. It's more a case of the Captain says "Jump" and everybody jumps. In point of fact, most of the organisation and admin is done by the Commander. He's the one who serves six years' hard labour while the Captain does twelve years' solitary confinement. It's really a matter of getting the best out of everybody aboard. They're all trained in a particular sphere, some of them to a very high level, and the essence of command is getting it all to fit together and make everything work. Everything's interdependent, because the finest gunnery department in the world isn't much use if the engines don't work, or the navigator hasn't navigated the ship to the right place, or the wireless office hasn't picked up the signal telling us the position to intercept the enemy cruiser which is trying to break out, or the wireless office has picked up the signal but the cipher officer was half-asleep when he deciphered it. In a carrier there's all the flying side of things to consider too. And finally, there are nearly two thousand men aboard a ship like *Inflexible*, and they all have to be fed and clothed and sent on the courses they're due for, and kept busy when things are slack, and they've wives and mothers and children, and when things go wrong at home they affect a man's performance in his job and that has to be sorted out . . . Sorry, I'm on one of my hobbyhorses and it must be boring for you.'

'Oh no, it's very interesting. But how do you do it?'

'Training, in a word. You get broken in very gradually. You don't suddenly find yourself in command of a ship the size of *Inflexible*.' His tongue had also been loosened by the wine, and he could see the interest in her face. 'It really starts when you're a midshipman. You're given charge of a boat, and a boat's crew, and in the beginning the boat's crew know far more than you and they keep you out of trouble. My boat's crew in my first ship in the last war were all reservists and twice my age, and they looked after me. I'd be standing at the wheel of my picket boat, looking as though I was doing it all, and the coxswain, Petty Officer Drake, would be standing next to me, not saying anything, but surreptitiously putting his foot on top of mine when it was time to turn, or cut the engine, or whatever. But all the time you were picking up experience, learning the ropes, so you didn't need to be looked after so much, though if they decided you were getting above yourself, they'd land you in it, just to put you in your place. Actually, my boat's crew were very good to me and only did it the once.' He broke off suddenly. 'I'm not sure I should tell you this, it's a bit indecent.'

Her face was flushed a little from the wine. 'Oh, go on. It takes a lot to shock me.'

'All right, but you have been warned. During the Gallipoli campaign we spent a lot of time running boats to and from the beaches. We'd be away from the ship all day and quite often most of the night as well, and we got to be rather a law unto ourselves. In fact, we looked like a bunch of pirates at times – my crew, being reservists, all had beards. Anyway, we used to spend quite a lot of time waiting between trips, and I used to do a lot of swimming. I'd just strip off and go straight in over the side. The men thought it was a bit strange as none of them could swim. It wasn't part of the training at the time they joined, and most of them had the idea that if you're going to drown, you're going to drown, and being able to swim will only delay the inevitable.

'Well, it was a particularly hot afternoon, and we were secured to the jetty on one of the beaches, waiting to take on stores which were supposed to be moved somewhere else. I went straight over the side and was messing about underwater. The water was incredibly clear and you could find all sorts of things on the bottom. Of course, I didn't see anyone come up the jetty towards the boat, and the chaps didn't bother to warn me. Then I came back to the surface, looked over towards the boat and saw a most beautifully boned pair of riding boots on the very edge of the jetty, and a staff colonel covered in red tabs talking to Drake. I jumped out pretty quickly, of course, and the Colonel looked me up and down and asked me whether I was in charge of this vessel. So I said, yes, sir, I was, and he looked me up and down once more, spluttered a bit, said, "Good God, shouldn't you be at school?" and asked me whether I would mind taking him up to Anzac. Not surprising really, I wasn't shaving then, and my voice hadn't broken properly, so I suppose I must have looked a bit young and innocent standing there in my birthday suit. Anyway, Drake came up and handed me my cap – my cap you note, not my trousers – and we got on with it. But it was quite a while before they let me forget the business with the Colonel. "Oh, Mr Thurston, you went bright red all over!"'

He stopped speaking, aware suddenly that the atmosphere had become charged with sex. 'Sorry. Talking too much again.' He dropped his eyes back to his plate, concentrated on finishing the last of his fish.

The waiter appeared at his elbow.

He looked across at the table towards Jane. 'Would

you like anything else?'

'I shouldn't,' she began.

'Could we see the menu again?'

'I'll bring the sweet trolley, sir.'

It arrived with a squeaking of wheels as it moved over the carpet.

'Oh gosh, it all looks wonderful, but I don't think I could manage another thing.'

Thurston studied the array in silence for a few moments. 'Why not have the sorbet? You should be able to find room for that.'

'All right. It would round things off nicely.'

'The sorbet, please, and the fruit salad, and then coffee.' The waiter glided away.

'How old *were* you?' In the candlelight she looked infinitely desirable.

'Fifteen, rising sixteen.'

She digested this. 'But that's terrible. My father was at Gallipoli – he and Jack joined up together and were in the same platoon, and that's where he lost his arm – but he never talked about it at all, it was so terrible for him. Even Jack only talks about the funny things that happened.'

'It was terrible at times,' he said slowly. He thought of Arthur Hancock, his leg shattered, the kneecap hanging from a ligament, and Tich Blake, who had boasted that he made too small a target to be in any danger, shot through the head by a sniper below Achi Baba. 'But, in comparison with the men ashore we really had a cushy time. They were up in the trenches for weeks on end, with the flies, the rotten food and lack of water, while we went back to the ship every night, or nearly every night, with gunroom dinner in full whites, as a midshipman, that is, white cloth and silver on the table, and three glasses put out in your place.' Jane looked puzzled. Concentrating on the lighter side of war was a refuge from his conflict of feelings about her. 'One for the white wine, one for the red, and one for the port. Not that we could afford wine more than about once a week – the pay was one and nine a day, and most of that went on the basic mess bill before you had any drinks.'

He was talking, she thought, as though he had been a grown man at the time instead of a boy.

'But fifteen? What were you doing there in the first place?'

'The Reserve Fleet was brought out of mothballs at the beginning of the war, and needed midshipmen. The powers that be cleared Dartmouth of cadets, I was a bit young, I know, looking back. I wouldn't have wanted it for my son. But none of us thought so at the time. You see, we'd all been brought up on *Treasure Island*, G. A. Henty and the rest, so fifteen was probably *the* age for climbing the Heights of Abraham with Wolfe, going on crusades, any other deeds of derring-do you could think of.

'And then we'd all been through Osborne and Dartmouth. It was what we were trained for, why we were in the Navy in the first place, and it was, quite simply, the greatest thing that had ever happened to us. We were going to sink the German fleet with one salvo, steam into Kiel in triumph and make the Kaiser walk the plank for all I knew. In fact, when questions started to be asked in the House we thought it was very unfair, since nobody questioned the right of boy seamen to be there, and they were about the same age as us. Aboard my ship we all decided that if Their Lordships sent us back to Dartmouth we'd all desert and join up on the lower deck under assumed names. I even had my assumed name ready, but in the event Their Lordships realised after a couple of months that the war wasn't going to be over by Christmas, and confirmed us all as midshipmen.'

She put down her empty coffee cup, the spoon rattling

225

a little in the saucer. 'It's been a lovely evening, Captain Thurston.' Her use of his rank and surname, as she had several times in the course of the evening, jolted the mood away from candour, reminded him once more that he was seventeen years older than her, married with a family, that in a way he was betraying Kate simply by being with her. 'Jane, I think it's time you stopped calling me Captain Thurston.'

He wondered what her reaction would be.

'Bob then. Or do you prefer Robert?'

The answer was practised. 'Bob or Robert, but not Bobby and never Robin.'

She giggled, her head going down towards her chest so that most of her face was hidden.

'I think you're much too formidable to be called Robin.'

The giggle brought him down to earth, seemed to clear the wine from his head. He stretched one leg out under the table, and then the other. 'Would you like to go straight back?'

She thought for a moment. 'Not just yet, if that's all right. It's a fine night and it would be nice to walk for a while, to let all that food go down a bit.'

'We could start walking back towards the city, and flag down a taxi when you've had enough,' he suggested.

He paid the bill. Leaving the restaurant, they crossed the road and turned right, following the pavement as it curved along the waterfront. The tide was in and the sea lapped the stone barrier only a few feet below, reflecting the light from the streetlamps in long white and yellow trails, flickering a little with the slight motion of the water. There was a light breeze, cool on their faces after the heat of the restaurant, bringing a fresh salty tang in from beyond the harbour mouth.

'Could you slow down a bit, please.'

He shortened his stride and slowed his pace to what

he thought she could manage.

'That's better. I was having to work a bit to keep up.'

'My wife complains that she has to take two steps for every one of mine.'

'What's your wife like?' she enquired a little later.

'That's a very difficult question to answer.' Kate was his wife, and the mother of his children, which made it impossible to describe her in a few words. 'She rides about as well as I do, but plays the piano a great deal better. She does some painting – did, rather, because the twins keep her fully occupied at the moment.'

'How did you meet her?'

'Playing tennis, I'm afraid. Kate's people had a tennis court; our Torpedo Officer was asked over there one Saturday and to bring a friend. You know the sort of thing. I wasn't doing anything else that day, so I went. In fact, I nearly didn't get there at all. I had a rather unreliable motorbike in those days, and it got up to its usual tricks on the way out there – the place is about fifteen miles from Plymouth; Kate's mother still lives there – and finally gave up altogether when I still had a couple of miles to go. I could usually get her going again, but this time she simply refused to budge. I was late already and was going to be very late by the time I got there, but it was a long way to push the thing back to the ship, and I thought I might be lucky enough to find someone who could sort it out.

'I pushed the bike the rest of the way, and I was pushing it up the drive, fairly well covered in oil though I'd got the worst of it off, when who should appear but Kate. She's a very good organiser, Kate, in an unobtrusive sort of way, and she showed me where to clean myself up, got her father's driver to deal with the bike, we played a couple of sets of doubles and that's how it all started. Her parents weren't very keen to begin with, once things started to get serious. They thought we were both a bit young, which was probably quite true, and we'd only known one another a few weeks. Six, to be precise. My father didn't approve either; not only was I too young, but I should be concentrating my energies on the service. But we insisted, and eventually they all came round. Kate won my father over. My stepmother invited Kate and her mother to stay for a few days and Kate had the old man eating out of her hand in no time, even though he thought her riding astride was nothing short of a scandal.'

'Your father sounds very old-fashioned.'

'He is. He is a man of firm principles, and nothing and no man will deflect him from them.'

She giggled. 'Let me think. Your father's an admiral, your grandfather was an admiral of the fleet, and your great grandfather served under Nelson at Trafalgar.'

'I'm not as old as all that!'

'Sorry, I didn't mean that.'

'And you're wrong on the other counts as well. My grandfather was in the Guides Cavalry, and so was my father until he resigned his commission to go into the church.'

She reddened as she had done earlier, remembering the stripes on his arms and the difference in their ages.

'Have you had enough yet?'

'Oh no, I like walking at night. Somehow you always seem to make much more progress than you do by day.'

'I've noticed that too. I don't know why it should be.'

The road climbed a few feet further above the water line, passing over a low outcrop of rock before dropping again. The lights of the North Shore were visible a mile or more across the water; much closer another group of lights marked the passage of one of the harbour ferries.

They walked on, mostly in silence, keeping step with one another, enjoying the night air and the exercise after the day spent under cover, passing a few other couples, slouch-hatted soldiers with arms around their girls, a blue-clad rating locked in an embrace against the railing with a girl who shivered in a thin cotton dress. She was leaning back so that her head and body above the waist were over the water, the dress stretched tight over her breasts, the man's hand moving in rhythmic circles over her back.

'I think I'd better get you home,' Thurston said eventually. A taxi passed with its light on. He flagged it down, told the driver the address.

'Thank you for a lovely evening,' she said at the door, rather formally, like a child after a birthday party.

He wondered how she would react if he kissed her, whether she would respond as the girl with the sailor had, pressing herself against him, putting her arms around his neck, or would simply push him away. He could find out quite easily, simply make one step towards her, bend down towards her face and take her hands in his. Don't think about it, he told himself sternly.

But he wanted to see her again. 'Would you like to come to the theatre or something one night?'

She thought for a moment. 'What I would like is to see your ship.'

'I couldn't let you do that. She's not at her best at the moment.' He sensed her disappointment. 'Could you get away from work one afternoon?'

'I think so. I'm not that busy at the moment, and Mr Bush does owe me for all that extra time I've put in. What have you in mind?'

'Would you like to come sailing in my gig?'

'In your what?'

'My pulling boat.' The possessive was automatic. 'Six-oared, but you can step a mast and haul up the sails. It comes with the job, but it doesn't get much use in wartime. There's a fast motorboat I use most of the time.'

'I'd love to. But I don't think I could manage tomorrow; I ought to give Mr Bush a bit of notice. But Thursday should be all right.'

'Two o'clock?' He looked at the dress she was wearing. 'You'd be better in trousers if you've got any.'

'I'll smuggle them into work with me,' she giggled.

'We'll meet you at the ferry landing, on the other side if you're coming straight from work.'

Lying in his bed his mind went over the events of the evening. Outwardly all had been as it should, but there had been all the time the unspoken current between them, the heady excitement he could remember from his early days with Kate. Kate's photograph was on the locker top a few inches from his head, invisible in the darkness although his mind could conjure up the likeness exactly.

Kate was his wife and the mother of his children. She had put up with a lot over the years; all the periods apart when he was at sea, the difficult early days when he had gone out to China for two years, leaving her, with one child and another on the way, to manage on a lieutenant's pay and no marriage allowance. She had coped with his black moods and ill temper when he was at home after his breakdown, and had then accepted his decision to go back to sea. Kate represented security and permanence, Jane something quite different. He was standing on the edge of the unknown, looking towards something of which he had no experience, where the ice was thin and the currents deceptive. He should not, but, dammit ... He liked her. She was good company, interested in his job but quite separate from the Navy, and he was sick of the sameness of periods in harbour. Go to official functions as a representative of the Navy, talk to businessmen who found the war a means to handsome profits, and their overdressed, over-made-up wives who always contrived to stand a little too close to him; go ashore and drink with other captains, and talk shop, or with the more senior staff officers who moaned about their shore jobs and wished they were back at sea, and talk shop. And she had enjoyed his company, he was sure of that. Jack Roper had said that she was lonely, too, living by herself and working at a job which was not what she would have chosen, and that she had had a hard time of it, losing her husband and father in rapid succession.

Dammit, he had to see her again! But she was a married woman, assuming that somewhere in Malaya Alan Roper had survived three years in Japanese hands, and seventeen years younger than he was.

You will take her sailing, because you said you would take her sailing. You will have MacLeod and Spencer with you to make sure you behave yourself. And you will exercise proper restraint or you will not see her again

Something landed heavily on his chest and a rough feline tongue began to lick at his chin.

'What are you doing here, Billy? Spencer didn't shut the pantry door properly.'

He sat up, feeling the claws take root in his pyjama jacket and the kitten's weight hang from them, lifted the four paws one by one and carried him through to the pantry. He opened the door and pushed Billy through with his foot.

'Good run ashore, sir?' Spencer asked from his hammock.

Chapter Eighteen

The telephone's ringing cut into his unconsciousness, once, twice. At the third ring he came reluctantly to the surface, dully realised what the noise was, reached out an arm to the bracket next to his head.

'Captain.'

The voice at the other end did not reply immediately. 'Who's that?'

'Officer of the Watch, sir. Sub-Lieutenant Broome.'

He had to think who Broome was. One of the Corsair pilots, who had been left on board when the rest of the flyers went to the air station at Nowra because there were so few aircraft left serviceable, and who was only qualified to stand watches in harbour.

His other hand found the light switch, turned it on. His eyes screwed up automatically against the brightness. 'Yes, Broome, what is it?'

He probably did sound testy, and it was not surprising that Broome was nervous. 'There's been an incident ashore, sir. Some of our ratings met up with some of *Persephone*'s. Apparently one rating's been stabbed.'

'Have you informed the Duty Lieutenant-Commander?'

'No, sir.'

'You should know by now that as Officer of the Watch in harbour you answer to him.'

'Yes, sir. I'll ring him straight away. I'm sorry to have disturbed you, sir.'

Thurston rubbed one eyelid with the knuckle of an index finger. 'Well, Broome, I'm awake now anyway. I might as well come up and see what's going on.'

'Should I still ring the Duty Lieutenant-Commander, sir?' Broome queried.

'Yes, Broome, of course you should.'

He swung his legs over the side of the bed, registered the time on the clock which stood next to Kate's photograph. Ten minutes past two. A fight in an out-of-hours bar, a stabbing, and an inexperienced Officer of the Watch who wanted someone else to take over the responsibility. He wondered why he was going to the trouble of seeing the thing for himself; the Navigator, who was the Duty Lieutenant-Commander that night, was quite capable of dealing with the matter, and the Commander could brief him about it in the morning. Ten to one there was nothing more that Broome could tell him; if the civil police had dealt with the incident the full details would not be made known before the morning, and there would be nothing to be done until then. He reached for his clothes, began to dress, wondered why it always took him so much longer to wake up for an emergency call in harbour than at sea.

Sub-Lieutenant Broome was waiting in the quartermaster's lobby, standing next to his Midshipman of the Watch, who appeared to be enjoying the excitement.

'All right, Broome, what's going on?'

'We've had a report of a disturbance ashore, sir, at one of the bars in Kings Cross.'

'It's called the Southern Cross, sir, in Milton Street,' put in the Midshipman.

The Navigator arrived in response to Broome's summons. 'Morning, sir.'

'Morning, Pilot. How much has Broome told you?'

'I would imagine as much as he's told you, sir.'

'Go on, Broome.' Thurston drew back into the corner of the lobby, left the Navigator to get on with it.

'Apparently some of our chaps ran into some of

Persephone's, sir.'

'Probably went looking for them,' said the Navigator. He too had dressed in a hurry, and there were several inches of bright orange pyjama leg showing below one of his trouser bottoms.

'The civil police have arrested eight of our chaps, and some of *Persephone*'s as well, and two men are in hospital, one with stab wounds.'

'One of ours or one of theirs?'

'One of theirs, sir. The police weren't quite sure at first, but they think he's from *Persephone*.'

'Serious?'

'They didn't say, sir.'

It was just the sort of sketchy report, full of imprecision and half-truths, that could be expected in these circumstances. The civil police had been called to the incident, against the wishes of the landlord who would no doubt wish to avoid a prosecution for selling alcohol after hours. They had got there ahead of the shore patrol, separated the combatants, arrested a representative number of them and despatched any who were obviously injured to the nearest hospital. Those arrested had been pushed into the cells at the police station to sleep off the effects of an evening's hard drinking, and any questioning, beyond ascertaining their names and ships, which must already have been done, would wait until the morning.

'What time did all this happen?'

'The police say they were called to the incident at 2305, sir,' the Midshipman reported. It was Jacobs, the ship's senior midshipman, well known to Thurston from standing watches on the bridge, and no doubt far more experienced in these matters than his superior officer. Jacobs was in any case a bright lad, who had successfully negotiated four years at Dartmouth in the face of a barrage of puerile ragging occasioned by his being Jewish ('You can't eat that corn dog, Izzy, it's not kosher.' 'I suppose you think the Law of Moses gets you out of standing watches on Saturdays').

Three hours ago. That also fitted into the pattern. Things were quietening down ashore, and the police had time to write up their reports, and inform those concerned of what was going on.

'Anything else?'

'No, sir.'

'All right, we're unlikely to hear anything more tonight. But keep me informed if anything does come through.'

'Aye aye, sir.'

'Who's your relief?'

'Carver, sir.'

Sub-Lieutenant Carver was another pilot without an aircraft.

'Make sure he knows what's happening.'

'Aye aye, sir.'

Thurston and the Navigator moved away, beginning the walk aft to their respective cabins. Around them the ship was quite silent, apart from the low hum from the machinery spaces which was so much a part of the background that it was only in these dead hours, when everybody apart from a small watch on deck was asleep, that it was noticed.

'Isn't this typical, sir,' the Navigator said without preamble. '*Persephone* hasn't been in harbour twelve hours and already one of our lads has stuck a knife in somebody.'

'I'm not all that surprised, Pilot. Are you?'

'No, sir.' The Navigator sighed. 'To say I was expecting it would be going too far, but I'm not surprised. Feeling has been running pretty high. Nothing said, but it's all been simmering away under wraps. I'd like to know how they all know it was *Persephone*. Nothing's been said officially, of course. All that happened was

235

that her Captain came to apologise to you.'

'The buzz always gets around.'

'And we never know how it starts. I wish we had some more details about this one, sir. I don't like the sound of it at all. I know "stabbing" could mean anything from a scratch with a blunt knife-point to disembowelling, but I've got a feeling in my water about this one.'

'I think if the chap was dead we'd have been told about it.'

'Yes, sir.'

But Thurston too found himself uneasy. No purpose had been served by Broome calling out the Captain, but because he had done so, there now seemed little prospect of the incident ashore resolving itself into a minor scuffle.

'Goodnight then, sir.'

He could still taste the wine in his mouth from the evening with Jane Roper as he climbed back into his bed and put the light out once more. But it was a long time before sleep came again.

Thurston had barely finished his breakfast when the Commander arrived.

'What news?' He stood up, moved away from the dining table and went to his desk. 'Sit down.'

'Thank you, sir. The NPM's just been on. Apparently the chap our man's supposed to have stabbed is in a bad way. He thought we should know that before he tries to sort things out with the Aussies about jurisdiction.'

'Do we have any names yet?'

'Signalman Norton, sir. He's the chap they're holding on the stabbing charge. Six others. Fighting, drunk and disorderly, the usual things. I've got all their names. They're also going to have the landlord up for breach of the licensing laws.'

'I'm glad to hear that,' Thurston said drily. 'How do

they know it was Norton?'

'According to the police, they got in there and found him standing over the follow – a Stoker Cassidy – holding a flick knife. There was blood on the knife,' Dent said with a suggestion of relish.

Commander Dent was shorter than Thurston, with hair so unexpectedly black and shiny, without even a hint of grey, that Thurston occasionally wondered whether he dyed it.

'Do we know exactly what state Cassidy's in?'

'No, sir, not yet.'

'Then we'd better find that out before we go any further. Do we know which hospital they took him to?'

Dent had that written down. Thurston pressed the buzzer on his desk.

Thurston was restless. He had arranged to go out to the air station at Blacktown, a few miles outside the city, to do some flying and was reluctant to abandon the opportunity for the sake of something which Dent and Scott were quite capable of handling.

'Could you get me St Anthony's Hospital?' Thurston told Scott when he arrived.

Scott spoke into the telephone, first to the ship's switchboard operator, then to the civilian operator ashore.

'Who do you want me to speak to, sir?'

'Find out what ward Cassidy's been put on and get hold of someone in authority there.'

'Just a moment, sir.'

Scott was standing at one side of the desk, head cocked towards the telephone receiver, talking in his usual measured Edinburgh tones.

' . . . Thank you. Just a moment.' Scott put a hand over the mouthpiece. 'I've got the Sister of the ward Cassidy's on, sir, but she's refusing to tell me anything.'

237

'Why not?'

'Because I'm not a relation, sir.'

Thurston was growing impatient. 'I'd better have a try.'

Scott handed the receiver over and moved to one side.

'Ward Seven, Sister speaking,' said a female voice. 'Can I help you?'

'Is there a doctor available?'

'The houseman is at breakfast. Mr Ogilvy does not begin his ward round until ten o'clock. Is there anything you require?'

'I'm enquiring about one of your patients, a Stoker Cassidy. I believe he was admitted last night with a stab wound.'

'Yes,' the woman said guardedly, 'we do have a patient of that name. Are you a relative?'

'No, I'm not.'

'I'm sorry. It's the policy of this hospital not to give information about our patients except to relatives, unless the patient gives his permission.'

'Madam, Stoker Cassidy's relations are twelve thousand miles away.'

'So I understand. May I have your name please?'

'The Captain of HMS *Inflexible*.'

'I see.'

'Madam,' Thurston began again.

'There is no need to shout at me. If you were from his own ship I might be able to make an exception. However . . . '

Thurston could almost hear the crackling of her starched linen. Sarcastic bloody bitch, he said to himself.

'Madam,' he said a third time. 'It is alleged that Stoker Cassidy was stabbed by one of my men.'

'I see.' There was an audible crackle as the Sister drew herself up to her full height. 'And this is the reason why I have two policemen cluttering up my ward in their big boots, demanding to interview Mr Cassidy, who is in no fit state to see anyone, and the Naval Provost Marshal – I believe that was what he called himself – arriving in the midst of my bedpan round asking the same question, and I have a very sick ward as it is!'

'The man who stabbed Cassidy will answer to a murder charge if he dies. Therefore, you had better tell me whether there is any likelihood of that happening.'

The Sister must have pursed her lips. 'Mr Cassidy is in a serious but stable condition.'

'Thank you.' He put the telephone down. 'That tells us a great deal.'

'I wouldn't like to be one of *her* patients, sir,' said Scott.

'Probably Australia's secret weapon in the fight against disease. One look at her and you recover on the spot. I don't suppose we're going to get any sense out of her, but there must be somebody else on duty. Keep trying and see what you can get out of them.'

'I could go over there, and see if I can catch someone when that dragon isn't about?' Scott suggested.

'Do that, if you think it'll work.'

'I will, sir.' Scott looked as though he might enjoy the challenge.

'You know where I'm going to be this morning, if anything does come up.'

'Yes, sir.'

'I'll be back before lunch.'

'Yes, sir.'

'You're looking forward to this, Scratch. I suppose you're going to borrow a white coat from the sick bay and become a mysterious expert from Edinburgh.'

'Well, sir, when I was about eight or nine I read the story of Dr Crippen and decided I was going to be a detective when I grew up. I didn't, of course, but I've never quite lost the desire.'

On the deck above a pneumatic drill began to cut into the concrete.

'Here we go again.'

'Did you have any success?'

'Yes, sir.' Scott was looking pleased with himself. 'I went round to the hospital about 1100; went up to the ward – just tried to look as though I was there officially and no one tried to stop me. Some consultant was parading about with his acolytes, so I didn't go in, but I managed to have a word with one of the nurses as she was going out of there with a message. Apparently, Cassidy's got a punctured lung – Norton, presuming it was him, knifed him in the chest. About there.' Scott indicated a place halfway down his right side. 'He'd lost quite a lot of blood before the police got round to calling an ambulance, and even more before the quacks got him on the table and did something about it. She couldn't tell me much more than that – she hadn't been looking after him or anything like that. But it looks pretty serious. The girl I spoke to said that there was a nurse with him all the time and he was having blood transfusions.'

Scott stopped speaking for a moment, and resumed his professional manner when he began again. 'As far as the charges are concerned, it'll be grievous bodily harm at least, if he pulls through, possibly attempted murder, but in that case we'd need to prove that Norton actually intended killing him.'

Thurston was sitting at his desk, drinking a cup of coffee which Spencer had placed in front of him. 'Or murder, if he doesn't. Have you ever been involved in a court martial for murder, Scratch?'

'No, sir. I've left murder to my father up to now.' Scott's father was an advocate at the Scottish Bar.

'Neither have I, and I don't fancy breaking my duck at this stage.'

'It may not come to that, sir.'

The Commander arrived, reported that Norton and the

other ratings were back on board.

'The NPM managed to sweet-talk the civil police into accepting our jurisdiction in this – he said there was no difficulty about it, though if Norton had stabbed an Aussie civilian there would have been – we sent an escort and they were all back on board and in the cells before 1200.'

'Good. They've all been put on Commander's Report, I take it?'

'Yes, sir.'

'Then we've got until the day after tomorrow to decide what to do with them. Except Norton that is. I could weigh off the rest of them with ninety days, if they've done anything serious enough to warrant that, but Norton's case will have to go to a court martial. Grievous bodily harm must be worth six months at least, even before we start thinking about murder or attempted murder.'

'We're assuming it was Norton, of course, sir.'

'Did he tell the civil police anything?'

'From what the NPM told me, Norton was practically incoherent, but kept telling the policeman who arrested him that he hadn't meant to do it, the chap had walked into the knife, or some such.'

'Of course he'd pulled out the knife in the first place, which won't help him.'

'There's no suggestion that it wasn't his knife, sir.'

Thurston stretched his arms above his head and then out sideways. 'All this is conjecture at this stage. We'd better put a lid on it until Friday when we investigate the thing properly. Unless Cassidy dies in the meantime, when the fat will really be in the fire.'

'We'll just have to hope he doesn't, sir.'

'For Norton's sake as well as everyone else's.'

'How did the flying go, sir?'

'Very well. They've cleared me to fly solo, which will be useful when I need to go up to Nowra.' He knew the Captain of the air station slightly from the

241

Mediterranean Fleet before the war, when the Australian had been on secondment to the Royal Navy, so it had been a matter of producing his logbook for scrutiny, and doing an hour's dual with the Commander (Air) there. 'But you needn't worry, they haven't cleared me to take passengers just yet.'

The Commander smiled. 'I'd better not say I'm relieved to hear that, sir.'

Chapter Nineteen

Thurston had said 'we', but Jane Roper found herself obscurely disappointed to see two other men in the gig as she approached the ferry landing.

'Nice,' the man standing nearest her said laconically.

The gig was painted black, with a single line of gold below the topmost strake, the sails white, filling in the breeze as she tacked back and forth.

'Mummy, can we go in that boat?' a small child wearing red wellington boots said loudly.

'No, you can't, darling. We'll go on the nice ferry.'

'I want to go in that boat,' the girl said more loudly.

An argument developed between mother and daughter, broken suddenly by a sharp slap and a high wail.

The gig came to a stop at one side of the landing stage, where a flight of wooden steps led down to the water, one of the sailors holding her steady with a boathook. Jane found that the eyes of the waiting ferry passengers were upon her as she descended the steps, dressed, as Thurston had advised her, in slacks and an old blue shirt of her brother's, as well as the most solid pair of walking shoes she possessed. The lower steps were slippery with water, and the gig rocked with the sea's motion, so she was grateful and a little relieved when one of the men put out his arm and handed her over the gunwale.

'My coxswain, Petty Officer MacLeod, and Leading

Seaman Spencer, who looks after me.'

The two men said their hellos standing in front of her and smiling. They were physical opposites: MacLeod slight and dark, with a soft Hebridean accent, obviously a quiet man by nature; Spencer with hair, what little showed beneath his cap, of no particular colour, and a beer belly which strained the front of his jersey.

'Carry on, sir?' MacLeod enquired.

Thurston said something to him, then turned to Jane. 'This gig is MacLeod's pride and joy. He doesn't like me using it without him there.'

MacLeod smiled a slow smile, and the three men moved the gig away from the landing. Once out of its shelter the breeze was sharper and colder, although the afternoon sun was warm on her back.

'Put this on if you need it. I told Spencer to find you one that would fit.'

'This' was a blue seaman's jersey like the ones Thurston and the other two were wearing.

'Thank you.' She pulled the jersey over her head.

'Looks better on you than on me, ma'am,' Spencer said.

'You have to watch out for Spencer. I wouldn't trust him further than I could throw him.'

'Yes, sir,' Spencer grinned, showing uneven teeth.

'And don't look so proud of it.'

'No, sir.'

Spencer grinned again, and MacLeod smiled his slow smile. They were clearly chosen men, and there was an air of comfortable understanding between them and their Captain.

Out in the harbour the gig's motion was noticeable, and she began to feel a little queasy, wondering fleetingly whether her stomach would let her down. She sat on one of the thwarts, looking over the side, watched the water a couple of feet below, the trail of white bubbles the gig was leaving astern. The grey shapes of the

244

warships which had come into the harbour the day before were closer now.

Thurston came up beside her, lowered himself on to the thwart, began to point some of the shapes out to her.

'Those are the battleships. *Duke of York*, the Fleet flagship – you can see the Vice Admiral's flag at the masthead.' A red St George's Cross, with a single red ball in one canton. '*King George V, Anson, Howe*. Then *Imperious*, the flagship of the carrier squadron, and *Irresistible*, our sister ship. That cruiser there, the second in line, is my old ship *Marathon*. She looks a bit different now – she had a very extensive refit after I left her.'

'Where's *Inflexible*?'

'Still alongside for repairs.'

Thurston put a pair of binoculars into her hands, waited while she adjusted the fit. She followed the line he indicated; at first all that was visible was water, then the carrier jumped into her vision. Previously, all she had seen had been the high-sided silhouette with its overhang of flight deck, the island superstructure pushed over to the starboard side. Now there were the projecting sponsons from which gun barrels peeped, the netting running along the edge of the deck, life rafts hanging vertically below, groups of men in overalls at work, two men in officers' uniforms walking up and down the deck, one with a sword belt at his side and two gold stripes on his arm, the other much younger-looking, with maroon patches on either side of his collar.

'Officer and Midshipman of the Watch,' Thurston explained.

'Would you like to try your hand at the helm?'

Jane stood up, moving to the stern, feeling the gig rocking unpleasantly beneath, finally almost falling on to the thwart rather than sitting on it. MacLeod moved away to give Thurston space to sit beside her.

'The main thing to remember is that the tiller goes the other way from the direction you want. So, if you want to turn to starboard you move it to port – towards you – and if you want to go to port you move it to starboard – away from you.'

She put her hand on the smooth rounded wood of the tiller, and Thurston let go.

'The wind and current are setting easterly so you'll need to keep the tiller over to starboard to stop her from drifting to starboard.'

She looked at the compass set into the transom. Three hundred and fifteen degrees. But the needle was moving all the time. Three hundred and twenty, three hundred and thirty. She tried pushing the tiller away from her, the gig lurched awkwardly to port.

'Don't bother with the compass. Look for a landmark on shore - there's a nice clump of trees in just the place we want, just above those rocks, one tree sticking up over the top of the others. Line yourself up with it, and use the tiller to keep in line. And feel how the wind's blowing on your cheeks, and keep it blowing the same way.'

She found the trees he was speaking of, let him bring the gig back on course towards them, and took hold of the tiller once more. This time it was much easier. She began to enjoy herself, the queasiness gone now that she had something to distract herself from it. After a time MacLeod took over the helm once more and Thurston took her forward and explained the rigging, showed her how the sails went up and down, let her try it for herself while the two ratings looked on.

'I had a look at the chart before we left the ship, and there's a nice-looking little cove over there I thought we could go into and have something to eat. Spencer insisted on bringing food. It's all in there.' Thurston indicated a large wooden box stowed beneath one of the

246

thwarts.

'You'd be the first to complain if I didn't let you have enough to eat, sir.'

A few yards offshore the gig grounded in the shallows. The men began to take off their boots and socks and roll up their trouser legs. Jane let go of the tiller and bent to untie her shoelaces.

'Don't bother with that. We'll get you ashore dry shod.'

Thurston and MacLeod dropped into the water, one on either side of the bow, and Jane came forward. 'Ready, MacLeod?' A brief charge of excitement as Thurston's arm went round her shoulders, lost when MacLeod's arm came up on the other side and she was swung out over the bow amid laughter and carried the few paces to firm sand, a little lopsidedly as Thurston topped MacLeod by a good six inches.

'Thank you.'

'All part of the service.'

MacLeod waded out once more to help Spencer with the box of food. It seemed very heavy.

'What on earth have you got in there?'

'Ah, you'll 'ave to wait and see, ma'am.'

They pulled the gig well up the beach. Spencer produced a towel from somewhere and for several minutes there was a collective drying of feet and hairily masculine legs. Then they all spread out and began to search for wood to build a fire. There was little driftwood in the cove but a few minutes' work revealed a good supply of dead branches beneath the trees which fringed the cove at the landward side. Thurston and MacLeod got the fire going, while Spencer rummaged in the box and brought out a couple of pounds of sausages and several large potatoes, already scrubbed, which he wrapped in greaseproof paper and buried in the base of the fire.

247

'Those'll take a while to do, so I'll get a brew on to keep us going.'

He produced a billycan, filled it from a water bottle he had with him, and suspended it over the fire on a long stick.

Eventually, the water in the billycan boiled, and Spencer brewed tea in four battered enamel mugs, then handed round hunks of fruit cake cut with a seaman's clasp knife to go with them.

'I know you're supposed to have the cake after the spuds and the sausages, but I don't suppose anyone can wait that long.'

'What you mean is, Spencer, you can't wait that long.'

'That's true, sir, but I don't suppose anyone else can either.'

Jane swallowed a mouthful of cake. 'This really is delicious. Did you make it yourself?'

'Yes, ma'am, but I won't tell you what's in it. Trade secret.'

'Oh, go on, Spencer, you can tell me.'

'Well, there's a bottle of Guinness goes in it, but that's all I'm telling you.'

'So that's it,' Thurston said.

'There's a few other things as well, sir, but that's the main one.'

They toasted the sausages on the ends of sticks, talked, tried the sausages, blackened on the outsides, still half raw in the centres, ate the blackened parts and put the raw parts back over the fire and tried again. Spencer brewed more tea, tasting of woodsmoke and not properly boiled, cut up more of the fruit cake and handed it round on the lid of the tin it had been kept in. Eventually, they decided that the potatoes had had enough time, brought them out of the embers and ate them in their fingers with handkerchiefs wrapped round. Spencer produced butter, salt and pepper from the recesses of the wooden box, they talked some more, a rambling collection of sailors' stories. The shadows lengthened, Spencer produced a mouth organ and played a few tunes, then MacLeod sang a haunting unaccompanied air in a language Jane assumed to be Gaelic.

'You're privileged,' Thurston said. 'MacLeod only sings in public when he's in the mood to, and it doesn't happen all that often.'

MacLeod blushed a little, looked at the flames flickering in the fire, red and orange and yellow, tinged with harsh bright blue where the wood was resinous, greyish smoke curling upwards into the sky.

She and Thurston walked up the curving strip of beach in the fading light, the setting sun sending bars of light through the trees behind them and lengthening their shadows over the sand.

'Better than being at the bank?'

'Yes.'

'You didn't have any trouble getting away?'

'No, Mr Bush was very decent about it. He even said a bit of sea air would do me good.'

'I thought he was supposed to be an ogre.'

'He can be. The trouble with him is that he's absolutely black or white. He's either very pleasant, charming with all the customers, and quite easy to work for, or he's storming about like a mad bull. There's absolutely nothing in between.'

'I've known a few like that.' He looked at his watch. 'I'd better get you home.'

'Already?'

'Haven't you noticed how the wind's dropped in the last half-hour? It generally does around sunset. We may just have to pull all the way back if it drops much more.'

By 'pull' he meant row. It was another of the pieces of naval language she had picked up during the

249

afternoon.

They turned, and began to walk back towards the boat. Jane reached out to slip her hand into Thurston's, but stopped herself before he could realise what she wanted, knowing instinctively that he would not have countenanced such a thing under the eyes of his men. She watched him beside her, his long legs striding easily over the firm sand at the edge of the water, his feet leaving sharply defined impressions behind them, dark hair tousled by the wind – it was a pity he had to keep it so short – eyes screwed up against the sun so that they almost disappeared into the crow's-feet at the corners. Nice eyes, she thought once again, slate grey, but changing to blue when the light was right, fringed by long lashes which were an unexpected feature in the weathered masculinity of his face.

'I like Spencer and MacLeod.'

'Spencer and MacLeod, always that way round. Spencer's the one everybody remembers. He's a rascal, and he's cocking a snook at the service at least part of the time, but he's been with me a long while and I wouldn't be without him now, though you'd better not tell him I said that! MacLeod's actually quite a live wire, though you don't notice it to begin with. He's still only about twenty-two and a substantive petty officer already. He was one of my boat's crew in *Marathon* when he was an AB; he'd just been rated acting petty officer in *Inflexible* when I took her over, and I needed a coxswain, so that was that.'

Once clear of the shelter of the cove it was obvious how much the wind had dropped. Before long there was insufficient left of the breeze to fill the sail. They lowered the sails, brought out the oars, and the men began to pull while Jane took the helm once more.

'Head back towards the ship. I'll shift out of this rig

when we get there and get you a taxi back.'

'I can find my own way quite easily.'

'I'd rather see you safely back at this time of night,' Thurston said in a way that convinced Jane that there could be no argument.

It was quite dark now, a lantern at the head of the gig's mainmast, and a mass of streetlights visible on both shores of the harbour. With only three oars instead of six the journey back to *Inflexible* took a long time. Jane found herself lulled into a half-doze by the gentle rhythm of the gig and the darkness, watching the loom of the oars working back and forth, the practised working of arms and legs and backs in unison ahead of her, whitening knuckles and sleeves pushed up to reveal muscled brown forearms, filmed with sweat and gleaming as light passed over them.

'Aren't you lucky, ma'am. Got three galley slaves all to yourself.'

She offered to help with the rowing, but Thurston declined the offer when she confessed that she had never done it before.

'We all need the exercise. It might even take something off Spencer's beer gut.'

The gig came to a gentle halt against the long stone pier.

'Wait here, Jane. I shan't be long.'

Feet passed above her head, servicemen's boots with steel plates at toe and heel which scrunched on the gravel, talking and laughter as men made their way to a night's shore leave. The stone face of the pier was sheened with water, more dripped from fissures between the stones, wearing depressions beneath. Green weed grew in the larger spaces, large dark clumps of it. A few yards away *Inflexible*'s bow jutted towards them, a stripe of darker paint visible above the water line, the flight deck overhanging everything.

251

'The Old Man won't be long, ma'am.'

Spencer offered her a cigarette.

'No thank you. I don't smoke.'

'You don't mind if I do, ma'am?' He took out a cigarette from the crumpled packet and lit it, expertly shielding the flame with his hand. 'Not supposed to smoke in boats,' he explained. 'But Mac here won't cut up awkward, will you, Mac?'

MacLeod said nothing. Jane supposed that Spencer's irreverence was the reason why he was a leading seaman while MacLeod was already a petty officer.

More footsteps on the pier.

'Be the Old Man,' Spencer said, stubbing out his cigarette and dropping the butt into the water.

It was Thurston. Jane wondered how Spencer was able to tell.

'Goodnight,' Thurston said at the front door of Number 6 Collingwood Street. But he did not move away immediately; he did not wish the evening to end, and as he looked at Jane, continuing to stand on the step and not even beginning to look for her keys, he sensed that she did not mean it to end either.

He changed his mind and paid off the taxi driver, then came back towards Jane. She was standing on the lowest of the three steps, their risers painted white to save the unwary from falling over them, still wearing the slacks and seaman's jersey, her hair attractively disarranged by the breeze of the afternoon. Behind him, the taxi driver let in the clutch and moved away from the kerb. He moved forward again, once again aware of her as a woman. She must have sensed it too for her mouth turned upwards toward his, their eyes held one another's for a moment, and the wondering how she would react was ended as he kissed her. Her lips were very soft, and a little damp, as if she had run her tongue around them a moment before. His hand moved round to the small of her back, pressed gently so that her body came against his. Her mouth opened beneath his, her tongue running over his lips.

'You taste of burnt sausages.'

'So do you. And smoky tea, and Spencer's cake.'

He was stroking her hair, the wisps which grew down her neck, her mouth joined to his, her rounded breasts against his chest.

'I've been wanting to do this all afternoon.'

'I've wanted you to do this since I first saw you.'

It was a long time since he had kissed outside like this, in the shadows cast by a streetlamp; a reminder of the days before he and Kate were married, those passionate fumblings round the side of her parents' house after a blameless evening of bridge or a visit to the theatre, both oblivious to the cold and the rain which dripped from the leaking gutter above, to be followed by a bumping motorbike journey back to virtuous solitude on board ship.

Footsteps turned the corner. Thurston looked past Jane's shoulder, took in a soldier with a young girl clinging to his arm. Jane's mouth broke away from his, she turned, and fumbled in her pocket for her door keys. He pulled himself away.

'I'd better go.'

'No.'

The front door opened. He followed her inside, and they were kissing again, as if without a break. The hallway was in darkness, white banisters climbing in a curve above their heads. His steel-tipped heels clicked on the floorboards. There was a faint but obvious smell of furniture polish. His hands roamed over her back, finding the straps of her bra beneath the jersey. A small voice inside his head was telling him to push her away, to make his excuses, to leave now and not see her again. He tried to ignore the sensations which were building at his groin, but he felt himself stiffen and grow hard despite everything. She moved away and began to go up the stairs. He could call a halt to this, but . . . The hardness was almost painful.

He followed her up the two flights to the door of her flat, waited for her to open the door, then kissed her again inside the narrow hallway, his hand moving to meet her breast. The light was on; he could see that she was smiling in a way that Kate did some afternoons when he arrived home from work, what he called her Mona Lisa look. His hand moved inside her jersey, squeezed her nipple gently between finger and thumb. The voice inside his head was still there. He let go, stepped back once more. She moved towards him, her eyes strayed downwards.

'I want you too.'

'Jane, you know I'm married.'

'Yes, and I don't care.'

And she too was married and her husband a prisoner of the Japanese, but he no longer cared either. Gently he raised her arms above her head, lifted the jersey off, unfastened and removed her shirt and bra. Like Kate, she was pale where the wind and sun had not reached, marked red where the straps of the bra had cut in, her breasts rounded and firm, her nipples already erect. She unfastened the brass buttons of his reefer, her hand sliding inside.

'I haven't got anything with me.'

'It'll be all right. It's a safe time.'

She opened the door of her bedroom, led him inside, shut the door behind. It was a small narrow room, dominated by the double bed pushed against the far wall. There was a bookcase beside it, a large old-fashioned wardrobe and a chest of drawers with a mirror above. He took off the rest of her clothes, slowly, carefully, then undressed, piling his clothes on the chest of drawers, watch and identity discs on top, placing his shoes soberly side by side on the floor in front.

She began rather shyly to caress him, hands moving over the taut muscles of his back. Her fingers slid into the depression at the base of the shoulder blade; puzzlement registered on her face.

'Was that from the *Seydlitz*?'

'Yes.' He turned to show her the scar, blue-white and roughly in the shape of a four-pointed star.

'Didn't it hurt terribly?'

'Not at the time. Later on it wasn't so good.'

He silenced her questioning with another kiss, slid his hand over her stomach and into the cleft between her legs, feeling the lips grow slippery beneath his fingers. She touched him, her fingers encircling his erection as it butted against her stomach in a careful manner which suggested that this was all new and strange, and it crossed his mind to wonder whether Alan Roper had actually had her before he went overseas.

The first coupling was brief. He had wanted to take it slowly, reminding himself that she was a young girl and inexperienced, that he must treat her gently, but the long months of monastic continence were too much, he came suddenly, driven to thrust ever more deeply inside her pelvis and then exploding.

'Are you all right?'

It was a strange question to ask, as if she was not sure what she should say.

'Sorry. I'm not usually as quick as that. Are *you* all right?'

She was equally surprised at the question. 'Yes, of course.'

He rolled himself off her, wondered what he should do now. If either of them had been a smoker he supposed this would now be the moment for the cigarettes to be lit.

'Don't go yet. Stay and talk to me.'

She was lying on his chest, her legs trailing away beside his, one arm thrown across him.

'Tell me about the *Seydlitz*.'

'You can read all about that in the newspapers.'

'I know. But the newspapermen weren't there, and you were. What was it really like?'

'Do you really want to know? It's not a pretty story.'

'Do you mind talking about it?'

'Not really. Not now.'

He pulled himself up a little on the pillows, got himself comfortable, and then began. 'It wasn't anything like the newspapers made it out to be. I got the medal because I was the Captain and they couldn't give it to everybody on board. I didn't really think about actually sinking her – *Seydlitz*. All I was concerned about was stopping her getting out through the southern end of the Denmark Strait and into the convoy lanes. That's what we were there for, nothing more than that. *Northumberland* – an eight-inch cruiser – was at the other end of the patrol beat; as it happened we were about as far apart as we ever were when *Seydlitz* turned up. *Prince of Wales* and *Renown* were at Hvalfjord. But we could keep her busy until they could get there, perhaps damage her enough to make her turn back towards the Norwegian fjord she'd come out from. You see, we'd been in the *Bismarck* chase only a couple of months before and we'd seen then what it took to find her and finish her off once she was out in the Atlantic. The Denmark Strait is confined, relatively speaking, and we could keep her in sight and keep her busy. We didn't have radar in *Marathon* then – we got it in the course of the repairs – and there was quite a lot of mist in patches. If we'd tried to shadow her out of range of her guns, we'd probably have lost her in a few hours, so there wasn't much alternative.

'*Seydlitz*, despite what the papers claimed, was nothing like as formidable as the *Bismarck* had been, but she was still a match for anything smaller than a battleship. The only way we could achieve anything was to keep her guessing. We had a knot or two extra speed over her, and better manoeuvrability, and that was what saved us. We got hit early on – a round exploded on the four-inch mounting below the bridge. Fortunately, it exploded where it hit and didn't penetrate the deck. But it caused a lot of damage and casualties, me included.'

He gave a wry smile. 'I suppose now that I could have broken off the action then, but it honestly didn't occur to me at the time. After what *Seydlitz* had just done to my shiny new ship, I wasn't going to let her get away with it. It wasn't really like the newspapers claimed. It was just a slogging match after that, hanging on until *Northumberland* got there. The mist helped us, we kept dodging and got off a few salvoes whenever we got the chance. Our Gunnery Officer, Jack Barnett – he was killed in the Mediterranean later on – didn't put a foot wrong. He managed to get quite a few hits on her, slowed her down and knocked out one of her turrets. I got him a DSC for that, which really should have been a DSO. The part about me writing my orders on a signal pad is more or less true. I couldn't talk properly after I'd been hit.' He pointed to the scar on his jaw. 'A fairly small bit went through there, broke my jaw and knocked one of my teeth half out, and a rather larger piece got me in the shoulder and came out at the back, which meant that I couldn't use that arm either. So that was the only way I could do it.'

He felt Jane shudder, tightened his arm around her, then she found his hand and squeezed it. She moved inside his arm, so that there was another frisson of desire as her nipples brushed his chest and she kissed him gently on the lips. 'It really sounds worse than it was. I wasn't actually in all that much pain, certainly not at the beginning. Everything went numb – I'm told that's what often happens – and it took quite a while for that to wear off. My face was a mess and I couldn't talk, and I kept having groggy spells, from the loss of blood I suppose. My first lieutenant, a very good chap named James Ffrench – with two fs for some reason of his own – was on the bridge with me and he did most of the work. I think I was getting a bit groggy towards the end, because I don't remember all that much about it once *Northumberland* arrived. Her Captain was senior to me, so he took overall command.'

'Just because he was senior? But that's crazy.'

'That's the way it's always been done, as they say. *Northumberland* had eight-inch guns, and once we'd forced *Seydlitz* to split her fire we were able to do her a lot more damage. Eventually, she was on fire and she must have been hit in the boiler room because she was practically stopped, with a column of steam rising up over her. We finished her off with torpedoes – *Northumberland* gave us the honour. The torpedoes must have touched off a magazine, because she just blew up. Dr Goebbels did try to claim that the German crew had scuttled her, but I've seen a magazine explosion before, and it couldn't have been anything else. They would claim that the scuttling charges had touched off the magazine, I suppose. We did start to look for survivors, but *Northumberland* picked up a contact which they thought was a U-boat, so we didn't stay around any longer. I'm supposed to have handed over to my Commander and walked off to the sick bay, but I don't remember that either, though Spencer tells me that he followed a couple of paces behind in case I keeled over – he claims I wouldn't let him help me.'

The contact with her body had reawakened desire. He stroked her hair once more, and kissed her forehead, then raised himself off the pillows, kissed her breasts and felt her hand move tentatively down his stomach and into his lower hair. He plunged into her, less urgently now, so that she began to move in response to him, moaning, and her eyes finally opened wide in a kind of wonder, before he balanced for a second on the brink, let go, and shot into her.

Chapter Twenty

When Jane awoke the space beside her was empty.
'Bob?' But there was still a faint warmth in the sheets
from another body, and a naval officer's blue jacket
hung reassuringly over the back of the chair. She got
up, belted her dressing gown around her and went
through to the bathroom.

Thurston looked around from the washbasin, his face
glistening with droplets of water, and smiled. 'Morning.'

She wasn't sure what she should say. 'Morning.'

'I was trying not to wake you.' He saw her face
change. 'Trying to sneak away before the milkman, I'm
afraid.'

Uncertainty was cloaked in an attempt at humour,
and then in practicality. 'The milk isn't delivered anyway. There is a razor if you need it. I use it for my legs.'

The bathroom was very small, and even after he had
moved to one side there was little space for two. She
rummaged in the cupboard above the basin, found the
razor among the soap and bath salts people had given
her as presents from time to time, and handed it over.
Thurston found the catch, took the blade out and
pressed the ball of his thumb very gently against the
edge.

'Have you got any spare blades? This one hasn't
much of an edge.'

She had. There was one left, still wrapped in its

paper. He took it and slotted it into its place. 'I don't suppose you keep a shaving stick for your legs?'

'I'm afraid not.' She wondered rather desperately whether the shop on the corner was open yet.

'No matter.'

He dipped the bar of soap into the basin and rubbed it vigorously between his hands, spread the lather across his face.

'Do you mind if I watch?'

He didn't answer, already absorbed in the task, but smiled again through the lather. She stood in the doorway, leaning against the frame, watching Thurston's repertoire of grimaces which stretched the skin, and the clean strips appear as the razor gradually cleared a way through the white froth. There was something reassuring about watching a man shave, go through this daily ritual which truly marked the male from the female. As a small child she had stood at the door of her father's bedroom to watch him, seemingly oblivious to her presence, shirt off, legs encased in whipcord breeches, long socks pulled up over the bottoms, her eyes drawn furtively to the misshapen stump which was all that remained of his left arm. Then he would turn from the mirror, and she could see from his face that he had known she was there all the time. He would squat down and put his arm briefly around her shoulders, then tell her gently that it was time to get ready for breakfast.

Thurston shook the razor in the basin, turned on the cold tap and splashed water over his face. He reached for the towel, held its white expanse in both hands. She could wait no longer and moved towards him. His face was still wet, there was a smear of white high on one cheekbone where the water had failed to reach it. She came up against him, rested her head on his chest. He put an arm round her, kissed the top of her head, feeling protectively solid against her.

'Can I see you again?'

261

She was surprised at the question. 'Yes, of course.'
She thought rapidly. 'Would you like to come round
tonight? I could cook you something.'

She thought immediately that she was being too forward, expected him to decline the offer, politely, as
always, but putting an end to the brief friendship he
had given her.

'Yes, I'd enjoy that.'

She made rapid calculations. She got home from
work just after six. Allow an hour to cook and to get
herself ready, and a bit more in case of accidents.
'About half-past seven?'

'Yes, I can manage that.'

He pushed some of her hair back from her face and
kissed her on the lips. Her fingers reached up and
touched his cheek, still damp, but absolutely smooth
from the razor.

'I'll have to get back to the ship. I've got a Board of
Enquiry starting today.'

She let him go, and followed him back into the bedroom.

'What exactly is that?' she asked as he began to button his shirt.

'A Board of Enquiry? It's an enquiry into a particular
incident – a loss or an accident usually. Not necessarily
anything very serious – I've sat on Boards enquiring
into the loss of a pair of binoculars before now. The
Admiral convenes a Board if he thinks the circumstances warrant it, and the Board investigates the incident and reports on it. The Board's brief is normally
to find out what happened, and what went wrong, to
make recommendations to minimise the possibilities of
it happening again, and to apportion blame, if any.
That's the official position; the cynics say that it's all a
matter of finding someone to pin it on.'

'Is it all right to ask what this one's about?'

'An accident we had on board.'

She sensed that he was keeping something back, but

it was clearly something he would not tell her about, so she did not press him. 'Are they going to blame you?'

'No, I'm just a witness.'

'But what if they did?'

He was standing in front of the mirror, knotting his tie. 'The Board's report goes to the Admiral and he could convene a court martial, if he thought me sufficiently culpable, or he could just make sure I was shunted into a backwater out of harm's way. But, as I say, I'm just required to be a witness at this one.' He pulled the knot up against his collar stud, and began to put on his jacket.

'So this is something serious?'

'Yes.'

'Would you like some breakfast before you go?'

He looked at his watch. 'Thanks, but I'd better be off. I'll see you tonight.'

She was disappointed, but at the same time relieved. She hadn't managed to go shopping yesterday and the only thing she had appropriate to breakfast was a packet of cornflakes.

'How will you get back?'

'Oh, I'll walk down and get the ferry.'

'Do you know the way?'

He smiled that slightly crooked smile of his. 'Sailors can always find the way to the water.'

He was fully dressed and ready to go, buttons fastened, cap in his hand. She went with him to the door, still in only her dressing gown, wondering if there would be anyone to see her like that.

'I will see you tonight.'

He kissed her again before he left, a brief peck on his cheek such as he might give his wife as he set off for work. She listened to his shoes go down the stairs, then went back into her flat, opened a window and let the cool morning air come in, watched his tall form stride purposefully away, turn the corner and be lost to sight.

Outside it was still very early morning, the sun just rising out of the sea and turning the waters of the harbour to pink and gold, only a few people about. Workmen in overalls and carrying metal sandwich boxes and flasks of tea heading for the dockyard, a few men in suits who must be making an early start in their offices, small boys on bicycles delivering newspapers. It was going to be a busy morning; first the Board of Enquiry, followed by Captain's Defaulters, which would include Norton's offence. Then he would be seeing Jane again. He sighed. It would be better if he did not, for her as well as for him. He had compromised her more than enough already, but the lure had once again been too strong, and he had said yes before he had really thought about it.

'Morning, sir. Double fried as usual?'

The cabin had not changed in the twelve or so hours since he had left it, yet there was a strangeness about it, a strangeness even to Spencer's bustle and Billy Bones's rubbing his small body against his legs. But he was the one who had changed, in a way that he could not yet pin down. There were no messages, no signals that had come in overnight and waited on the desk for attention. A quiet night, nothing out of the ordinary, except that for the first time since his marriage he had slept with a woman who was not his wife, a woman whom he had known for only five days – it surprised him when he thought of it – had made love to, not once but twice, and spent the rest of the night entwined in sleeping intimacy with before stealing away with the dawn.

Thurston's PO Steward put a plate of bacon and eggs in front of him.

'Three eggs, Hardcastle?'

'Board of Enquiry today, sir. Thought you could do with something solid to set you up.'

Spencer walked past as Thurston picked up his knife

and fork and began to eat, a smirk spreading across his face. He went into his pantry, picked up the frying pan, and began to feed the scraps of cooked egg white which had stuck to the pan to Billy Bones. Three eggs, and a good pile of bacon, done crisp at the edges the way the Old Man liked it. That'd make sure there was enough lead in the pencil all right. About time the Old Man had a woman. He'd had a hard time recently, what with all the bombing and the kamikazes, and he deserved a bit of fun when he had the chance; it didn't do no good to abstain in a hot climate like this anyway. That Mrs Roper was nice and she'd do him good, help him forget about the ship and the war for once. And she wouldn't come to no harm with the Old Man. He'd treat her right. She could do a lot worse, and so could he.

Spencer began to whistle cheerfully as he put the pan into the sink and turned on the tap.

'Yeah, Billy, the Old Man's getting his rocks off at last.' He picked the kitten up and rubbed between the ears. 'S'pose when you're a bit bigger you'll be looking out for some tabby cat to screw, won't you.'

Billy Bones opened his mouth in what Spencer interpreted as a smile. 'Getting the idea, aren't you, Billy. I'm going to have to keep my eye on you.'

The Board of Enquiry took place in one of the classrooms at the Royal Australian Navy shore base, HMAS *Kuttabul*. There were armed sentries in the corridors and large notices warning BOARD OF ENQUIRY IN PROGRESS – NO ENTRY.

'Captain Thurston, sir? In there, sir, please.'

The Petty Officer ticked Thurston off on his board and reached out an arm to open a door labe WITNESSES NOT SEEN.

It was another classroom, with the desks remov the chairs pushed to the sides and set out in lo facing inwards. *Inflexible*'s witnesses sat on o

Persephone's on the other, facing one another in silence. Thurston saw a dozen faces look up, felt all the eyes upon him as he walked down the centre of the polished wooden floor, nodded a greeting to Captain Stanley, and sat on an empty chair close to, but not among, *Inflexible*'s officer witnesses. He took the *Sydney Morning Herald* out of his briefcase and began to read, but in the pregnant atmosphere of the room it was difficult to concentrate on the news. Opposite him, Captain Stanley was talking in low tones to the Lieutenant-Commander sitting next to him, obviously his Gunnery Officer. Stanley's left leg was crossed over the right, revealing polished mess wellingtons on his feet, which contrasted with Thurston's own regulation black lace-ups, but one hand was clenched around part of the chair frame to betray his tension.

'This Board of Enquiry has been convened by Admiral Sir Bruce Austin Fraser GCB KBE, Commander in Chief British Pacific Fleet, to investigate the incident which took place on 19th May 1945 in which HMS Inflexible *was hit by one 5.25-inch High Explosive shell fired from HMS* Persephone *during a low-level attack by aircraft of the Imperial Japanese Navy, to allocate responsibility, to apportion blame, if any, and to recommend the implementation of measures necessary for the prevention of similar incidents in the future.'*

The President of the Board finished reading from his terms of reference, and removed his spectacles. He was one of the Commander in Chief's Assistant Chiefs of Staff, the most senior Captain available. He was flanked on one side by a Commander who was the Gunnery Officer of one of the battleships, and on the other by an RAN Commander who was the Board's ship-handling specialist.

'You are Captain Robert Henry Maitland Thurston, Royal Navy, Commanding Officer, HMS *Inflexible*?'

'I am.'

'This is purely a fact-finding procedure, and it is my duty to remind you that, although you are not on oath, as a person subject to the Naval Discipline Act you are required to answer all questions put to you. However, any self-incriminating evidence which you may give cannot be used in any subsequent proceedings against you.'

'I am aware of that.'

'Very well. Will you tell this Board in your own words what happened on the afternoon of 19th May 1945.'

He had read through the notes he had made at the time, the ship's logs and the Report of Proceedings written on the passage to Sydney, and it was difficult to differentiate between his memory of the incident and the bald written record. His voice went on through its tale, in an unemotional professional manner, divorced from the excitement, the horror and terror of the moment, from the initial radar report of the Japanese formation approaching, the time and position recorded in the log in Midshipman Jacobs' handwriting.

Yes, the ship had already been at Action Stations, all damage control parties had been closed up, and he had ordered all personnel on deck to take cover. It was difficult to describe the sheer confusion of a low-level attack, aircraft appearing from different directions, their aircraft, and our aircraft which must on no account be fired at, the time to recognise reduced to a split second, and noise all around from the guns, inside and outside your head, your ship and other ships manoeuvring in the restricted space. There was the sharply remembered vignette of the Japanese flying bomb coming in from the port side, *Irresistible*'s Seafire chasing her, and red tracer impacting on the wings. He had put on full port wheel to evade the kamikaze, successfully, because the Jap had gone into the sea, the bomb splinters flung up by the impact wounding two

267

men at one of the pom-pom mountings. Then there had been the explosion inside the island, while the ship was still turning. He had ordered the wheel put amidships but *Inflexible* had not yet come out of the turn. He hadn't known then what had caused it, but afterwards, when they had had time to draw breath and think, they had begun to be suspicious, and then one of the damage control parties had found a piece of the shell's base plate, which put an end to any doubts.

Plans of *Inflexible* were produced and he was asked to indicate where the round had gone through the plates. The explosion had destroyed the FDR and put the Ops room out of action, caused a serious fire inside the island which had taken some hours to put out, left thirty men dead, including the missing man whose body had never been found (Able Seaman C. M. Gaunt, Official Number P/JX 468501), and a further nineteen wounded. The following damage control actions had been taken: the fires put out, the holes in the deck boarded over, temporary repairs made to the electrical circuits, the wounded taken to the sick bay and treated, and the dead buried at sea at a position recorded in the log.

'Any further questions to put to this witness?'

There was a low murmuring between the three members of the Board, a shaking of heads.

It was not over yet. His evidence had to be transcribed from the shorthand writer's notes, checked for accuracy and any discrepancies cleared up. But the worst was over. Thurston found his attention wandering, even as he answered the further brief questions put to him by the members of the Board, back to Jane and the night he had spent with her. He had not intended it, and, he was sure, neither had she, but it had happened, as something quite natural, an inevitable follow-on from the afternoon they had spent sailing. It had been good, too good for his peace of mind now.

'Thank you, Captain Thurston.'

He stepped back from the table and walked towards the door which the sentry flung open, once again the sound of his footsteps the only thing breaking the silence. The Board would go on taking evidence for at least two more days, from *Persephone*'s Captain, Commander, Gunnery Officer and the Officer of Quarters and crew of the turret which had fired the round, and would take several days after that to produce its findings, but his own part in it was over.

He went back into the classroom to pick up his briefcase, noticed Captain Stanley move towards him as he straightened up.

'I thought you might like to know that Stoker Cassidy's off the danger list.'

'Thank you, I'm glad to hear it.'

'I just thought you would like to know.'

'Yes.'

There was nothing more to be said, and in any case it was obvious that Stanley could not think of anything more. The Board of Enquiry would shortly decide his fate, and his mind was concentrated on that. At the far end of the classroom a petty officer began calling the next witness.

'Good luck.'

'Thank you.'

'Signalman Robert James Norton, Official Number P/JX 485106, sir, was guilty of an act prejudicial to good order and Naval discipline in that he did commit an assault occasioning grievous bodily harm contrary to Section 18 of the Offences Against the Person Act 1861 and Article XVIII of the Articles of War, in that he did cause grievous bodily harm to Stoker First Class William Cassidy, Official Number C/KX 377971, of

HMS *Persephone*, with intent to cause him grievous bodily harm in the Southern Cross bar, Milton Street, Sydney, Australia, on 2nd June 1945, sir.'

The Master-At-Arms finished reading the charge sheet and stepped one pace backwards. Standing between the two Marines of the escort, wearing his Number One suit, with the signalman's crossed flags but no other insignia, Norton looked diminutive and very afraid, as though he did not know what was going to happen to him.

'Do you understand the charge, Norton?'

Norton said nothing, simply looked down towards the deck.

'Answer the Captain.'

'Sir,' Norton said with an effort.

The Commander went through a summary of his own hearing of the case the day before. 'I concluded that there was definitely a case for Norton to answer, sir, and, in view of its seriousness, I placed him under close arrest and in your Report, sir.'

'You may wish to know, Norton, that Stoker Cassidy is now off the danger list,' Thurston said when the Commander had finished.

Norton's eyes still looked down to the deck, but his shoulders gave a slight twitch.

'Norton, stand up straight!'

The Signalman jerked upright, teeth set and a muscle jumping in one cheek.

'I am going to investigate this case only. If I find that there is a case to answer, I shall remand you for trial by court martial. Do you understand?'

'Sir.'

'You will have the opportunity to give your account of what occurred after the witnesses for the prosecution have been heard. You will be able to ask questions of the witnesses called in person, or your divisional officer may do so on your behalf. You do not have to say anything in answer to the charge, but anything you do say will be taken down in writing and may be used in evidence at subsequent proceedings.'

'Sir.'

The formal preliminaries completed, Thurston turned to the Senior Engineer, who had been deputed to take the summary of evidence. 'Carry on.'

The witnesses appeared one by one, the statement taken from Stoker Cassidy was read out, and the shape of the incident began to emerge. It was a commonplace story, no different from dozens of similar episodes except in the result. Norton and half a dozen others from his mess had gone ashore when leave was piped, found a bar and stayed there until it closed at the end of the two hours permitted by the Australian licensing laws. They had bought fish and chips, and had then wandered around King's Cross until they found a bar which, illegally, remained open, stayed there for another hour or so, until the landlord shut the place. Someone in there – an Australian rating, they thought – had mentioned a third bar which would stay open all night if there were enough people there drinking, and they had gone on there with him.

By this time they had been drinking steadily for three hours, and so no one could remember the name of the bar or the route they had followed to get there. Someone had thrown up in the gutter, and he and another man had decided that they had had enough for one night and were going back to the ship. The remaining hard core found the bar, purchased another round of drinks and had settled down to drink them when another group of ratings arrived. For a few minutes it had been all backslapping and drunken bonhomie, then someone had asked the other group the name of their ship. No one could say how it had started – someone had said something, someone else had swung a punch at him. One man, a leading signalman from *Inflexible*, less drunk than the rest, had tried to separate them, but another of *Persephone*'s men had gone to his comrade's aid, knocked the leading hand down and in a moment the whole thing had got out of control. Norton had found himself separated from the rest and edged into a corner by two large stokers from *Persephone*. He'd been carrying the flick knife since he joined the Navy, 'just in case', and had pulled it out in the hope of frightening them off. What happened then he wasn't sure. One minute the stoker had been bearing down on him, the next he was lying on the floor moaning, and the knife in Norton's hand was bloody to the hilt. No, sir, he didn't remember stabbing Cassidy. He remembered Cassidy's shadow over him, the smell of beer on his breath and a sour reek of sweat. Yes, sir, he had been frightened. Cassidy had been on the floor and the bloody knife was in his hand. He hadn't meant to do it, sir. He supposed he must have waved the knife at Cassidy to frighten him off, and Cassidy must have walked into it.

'Stand up straight, Norton!'

Norton's facade had crumpled, his body sagging, as though his legs wouldn't hold him upright.

'I didn't mean it, sir. I swear I didn't!' He snivelled, his hand moving towards his pocket for a handkerchief.

'Norton, stand still!'

'Stand over, Master, and remain handy, please.'

'Sir. Accused and escort, about TURN! Accused and escort, double MARCH!'

Norton and the two Marines moved to the far end of the flat, Norton seeming smaller than ever from behind.

'Do you believe him, Commander?'

'I don't know, sir. It's quite obvious he did it. It may well be that he didn't intend to, but the result is just the same. Grievous bodily harm with intent or plain grievous bodily harm.'

There would have to be a court martial and he, as

Norton's commanding officer, would be required to produce the Circumstantial Letter which set out the Prosecution's case, and one of the other officers from the ship would have to prosecute, a prospect none of them would relish.

'Master-At-Arms, is Norton ready to go on?'

'I will go and find out, sir.'

It was the answer he remembered from his midshipman days. You did not ever say, 'I don't know, sir'. You said, 'I will go and find out, sir', and then you *flew*.

'Yes, sir.'

'Bring him back then.'

Norton was paler than ever, his eyes red-rimmed where he had been blubbering. He stood quite still as the defence witnesses went through their evidence and his divisional officer came forward to say that Norton had been a model rating until now, an excellent signalman who was about to take the exam for leading signalman and who had never been in any trouble before.

But that could make no difference to the end result, which had been clear from the beginning of the investigation.

'Remanded for trial by court martial. Remain in close arrest.'

'Remanded for trial by court martial. Remain in close arrest,' the Master-At-Arms repeated. 'On Cap.' One of the Marines rammed Norton's cap back on to his head. 'Accused and escort, about turn, double march!'

'Keep an eye on him, Master.'

'I will, sir.'

After the investigation was over the urgency seemed to go out of the day. Scott went across to the flagship to discuss the charges against Norton with the Admiral's secretary. Thurston got through the rest of the day's paperwork, decided with the Commander which of the officers would have lunch with him the next day, signed the letters Scott had left in his in-tray, went up on deck. After the bright morning the sky had clouded over by lunchtime. Now it was leaden grey and lowering, already growing dark, rain puddling in the undulations in the metal and concrete. The dockyard hooter had sounded a few minutes before and the workmen were streaming down the gangways at the end of their day's work, leaving the deck as deserted as if it had been midnight. There was something indescribably dreary about a ship in dockyard hands, a dreariness matched by the weather. He looked at his watch; it was still only half-past four. It would not be worth leaving for Jane's place before seven, but once more he was too restless to settle to anything in the interim.

Jane. He was standing at a crossroads in his life. No, not at a crossroads, but on a long straight road with no other roads branching off. He could go on, forward into the unknown, or he could turn back and return to what he knew, treating the night he had spent with Jane as an aberration, an experiment not to be repeated. That was the logical, the proper step to take. It was a stupid thing to have done, especially when he had taken no precautions, not just once, but twice. A cold shiver of apprehension ran through him. She had said it was a safe time, but how safe a time was it? *You bloody fool*. Jane was seventeen years his junior. She was also Alan Roper's wife. A fine way to repay the Ropers' hospitality, seducing their daughter-in-law!

Chapter Twenty-One

Jane arrived home a little later than usual, having stopped on the way to do some shopping, prepared the main course and put it in the oven, then took a bath, dressed and made herself up. She had barely finished, and taken a quick look in the oven, when the doorbell rang.

'Hello. Are you very wet?'

'Not really. It's going off a bit.'

She took his coat and cap, hung them on a peg in the hall. She noticed that his trouser bottoms were damp.

'Put the gas fire on in the sitting room if you want to dry your legs a bit. Dinner won't be long.' She was aware that she must sound hot and a little flustered.

'It smells very interesting, whatever it is.'

'Coq au vin. It's a recipe I got from Mary.'

'You're going to a lot of trouble.'

'Not really. It makes a nice change to actually have to cook something. When you live by yourself it's much too easy not to bother. You live on baked beans or cheese on toast and you get bored to death with it, but you can't work up the energy to do anything more ambitious.'

She had bought a bottle of wine, too, and unearthed some glasses from a set which had been a wedding present. Alan. If she knew with certainty that he was alive she would not be doing this.

Or would she? After three and a half years he was only a memory; she found herself looking at photo-

275

graphs of him and trying to remember whether he had really looked like that. There was one photograph of their wedding, which had been framed to hang on the wall, but she had taken it down because she could no longer bear to look at it. A conventional wartime wedding, Alan in his new second lieutenant's uniform, cap under his arm, the sword borrowed for the occasion at his side, herself in white and orange blossom and looking very young. The honeymoon had been the remainder of Alan's forty-eight hours' leave, spent in a small guest-house a few miles from home. They had gone for walks in the evening and in the early-morning cool Alan had made love to her, shyly and a little clumsily with inexperience. Then on Monday morning they had walked to the station and waited for separate trains, Alan to return to his unit, she to go back to her father's farm.

Thurston was sitting in the armchair nearest the fire, long legs stretched out in front of him, turning the pages of a book he had taken from the shelf. After so long alone, it was a relief to have a man around her again, to have some of the responsibility taken from her shoulders. At the bank she found herself, without intending to, holding aloof from the other girls, partly because she was married and so could not join in their ceaseless quest after young men, partly because her position as the manager's secretary separated her a little from the rest, and partly because she could find little in common with most of them. She did her work efficiently, worked extra hours when required, without complaining, and retired at the end of the day to the private world of her own flat. She was quite aware of the empty space in her life. Alan had gone to Singapore and been taken prisoner, her father had died, her brother Joe was overseas with the army and rarely wrote these days. But she had made this life for herself, and it had been easier not to try to step outside it.

Thurston lifted his head from the book, put it back into its place on the shelf. 'I didn't see you standing there. Bad habit of mine – can't leave a book alone.'

'I'm just the same. The food's just about ready now.' It was easier, somehow, to talk about these practical matters.

Thurston went with her into the kitchen, found a corkscrew and dealt expertly with the wine. Jane gave the baked potatoes another squeeze, satisfying herself once again that they were ready, put the plates into the oven to heat up, thinking she should have done that much earlier. The plates matched, fortunately – another wedding present – though she wished the table was better; like almost all the furniture it had come with the flat.

'You go and sit down. I'll bring it through.'

She felt the blast of heat as she opened the oven door, reached inside for the dish of chicken. Disappointment, at the sight of several blackened strips of onion stuck to the pieces of chicken, themselves charred along one edge because the oven always heated up unevenly. She thought quickly, scraped away the worst of the blackening, gave the sauce a vigorous stir. It smelt as it should, at least. A bead of sweat ran off her forehead, from sudden nervousness as much as the heat in the tiny kitchen.

Here goes. She wondered whether Kate cooked, or whether there were servants to do it. It struck her that she knew very little about Thurston's home life. There was the son who was in submarines, the daughter at medical school, and the twin boys. And there was Kate. Jane had found herself intrigued by Thurston's wife as soon as she felt the pull towards her husband. She would have liked to ask him more about her, but in the circumstances she could not.

They ate sitting at the gate-leg table at one end of the

277

living room, the coq au vin and baked potatoes followed by cheese and biscuits.

'How was your Board of Enquiry? What did they decide?'

'They haven't yet. They won't finish hearing the evidence for a couple more days, and then they'll go away to consider their findings before they actually produce them. That's what normally happens, unless the matter the Board is dealing with is so straightforward that they don't need to.'

'This one won't be like that?'

'No.' He changed the subject. 'How did your day go?'

'Nothing very exciting. I typed a lot of letters for Mr Bush. One of the girls knocked a plant off the shelf while she was watering it and sent soil everywhere. One of the others is about to leave because she's having a baby, but that's old news, and she's married, so there's no scandal about it.' She found herself blushing again, from stepping on to dangerous ground.

Thurston put down his knife and fork, set them parallel to one another as a signal that he had finished eating. 'I'm sorry about last night. I've been meaning to say that to you.'

'It's all right.' She didn't know what else to say.

There was a pause and then he went on. 'Jane, I think it would be better if we didn't see one another again.'

It did not come as a complete surprise. There had been something about his conduct towards her that evening which she could not pin down, and now she knew that this was what he had been meaning to tell her. 'Could I ask why?'

'Jane, I think you know.'

'Because we went to bed together?'

'Yes. I won't be here for very long. Until the repairs are completed, that's all, and I like you too much to want to have my way with you and then throw you aside when we sail as if you were some floozie I'd picked up on the dockside.'

'So you're going to do it now.' She was unable to keep a hard edge of bitterness from her voice.

'I don't make a habit of this, if that's what you mean. Dammit, I've never been unfaithful to my wife before!' Then his voice became steady once more, as he moved back to ground he had rehearsed. 'There's Kate to be considered, and Alan too.'

'Yes there's Kate, but she's ten thousand miles away and she'll never know unless you tell her. And there's Alan, but I don't know if he's alive or dead. And if he's dead, then I've wasted the last three years hoping he'll come back.' She pushed her chair back suddenly, the legs scraping over the worn pile of the carpet, and got to her feet. 'Sometimes I wonder if he ever existed, whether I ever had anything more than a ring on my finger and his name instead of the one I was born with. Three and a half years. Have you any idea what it's been like?

'All right, plenty of girls have husbands overseas and some of them have been away for years. North Africa, New Guinea, Burma, the RAF, but they at least get letters and know he was alive when he wrote the letter, and they know he's alive until they get the telegram to say that he's been killed. I've had nothing since 20th January 1942. That was the date on Alan's last letter. I know it by heart now. He said he was missing me, that it was terribly hot and humid and the insects were a trial, and to give his love to his parents in case he didn't get the chance to write to them straight away. After that I just don't know what happened to him.' The last shreds of her self-control broke, she rushed blindly to the sofa and flung herself on to it, sobbing as she had not done even on the day the telegram arrived to report Alan missing.

She felt Thurston's footfall on the creaking

floorboards, then he lowered himself on to the sofa beside her, reached out to her shoulder.

'Go away. You don't understand. You'll never understand how I feel.' The last came out almost as a scream, and set off another paroxysm of weeping.

But he didn't go. His arm went round her and pulled her up against him, so that her face was jammed up somehow between his lapels, her nose squashed so that she had to wriggle a little before she could breathe properly. He felt big and warm and safe, and relief came, as she remembered from a few occasions when she was very small, just after her mother died and before she went to school and was too old for that sort of thing, when she was upset about something and her father would hold her with his one arm and she would move up against him with that wonderful sense of warmth and safety that flowed from the contact with him.

'I don't know what's the best thing to do, to get used to the idea that he's dead and just get on with my life, or to go on hoping that he's alive somewhere and will be coming home once the war's over.' She lifted her face away. 'Oh Bob, I'm sorry. All over your uniform.'

'It'll be all right. It's used to salt water.'

And then he was telling her that he did know what it was like, because one of his brothers had been posted missing on the Somme and nothing more had ever been heard of him, though it hadn't been quite like it was for her, because he had somehow known from the beginning that George was dead. 'They never found his body; that's all. That's why my son's called George.'

He gave her his handkerchief, and she mopped herself up, insisting that she would be all right in a minute. He shifted a little, settled her against his shoulder, stroked her hair back from her face, kissed her forehead. No lust, only a wave of tenderness for her.

'Are you all right now?'

'Yes, I think so.' She was recovered enough to be

280

embarrassed. 'I don't get like this very often.'

He told her that it didn't matter. They sat in silence for a time, Thurston beginning to think of the plates still on the gate-leg table. But he did not want to move, or to disturb her, huddled against his chest, a vulnerable girl rather than the efficient young woman she was. He kissed her again, his lips barely brushing hers, and the fire began to burn once more in his loins. Her mouth was damp and salty from the crying; the tears had cut two shiny streaks through the light tracing of powder on her cheeks. She uncurled herself from his chest, stretched her arms and legs in the way that Billy Bones did on waking. He kissed her again and felt her hand move to the back of his neck to hold his mouth to hers.

The voice inside his head was telling him to pull away from her, that this was exactly what he had vowed to avoid, but another voice was coming through as well, saying that he had only a short time, that Kate was at the other end of the world and that Alan Roper was probably dead, and then the sudden thought, very sharp and clear, that he might well be dead himself in a few weeks.

'I don't want to leave you with a baby.'

'It'll be all right. Alan knew he was going overseas and he didn't want to leave me with a baby either. I'd almost forgotten I still had the thing.'

He remembered the small drawstring bag on a shelf in the bathroom cupboard, that he had barely noticed that morning. He knew what was in it, because Kate had one too.

'Jane.'

This third time was different again, a slow exploration of each other's bodies in the dim light of Jane's bedroom, reminding him once more of the early days with Kate, the pleasure of new discovery, the delight in teaching her. 'I take it you've had some experience,'

Kate's father, the General, had said a few days before the wedding, standing in his study with his back to the window, then moving to pour them both a glass of whisky from the decanter at his side. 'I don't want to know where. But you look after Katharine, d'ye hear.' Jane was like Kate, the same fair hair, long legs and generous breasts, and yet she was not; there was none of the shared experience of twenty years that he had with Kate, the intimate knowledge of Kate's reaction to every facet of his lovemaking.

'Doesn't anybody call you Robert?' Jane said suddenly out of the darkness.

'Not so many now. My father's always called me Robert, so has my stepmother, but not many other people. Why do you ask?'

'You're really much more a Robert than a Bob. Would you mind if I did?'

'Not at all. But how shall I reciprocate? Is Jane short for something? Or have you an embarrassing middle name I could use?' he asked mischievously.

She giggled. 'Elizabeth.'

'That's not embarrassing at all.' He sighed in mock disappointment. 'I suppose I'll just have to call you Jane.'

'Robert,' she said a few minutes later. 'What happened to your mother?' She hesitated. 'I mean, you've got a stepmother.'

'She died. Pneumonia, when I was six.'

'Do you miss her?'

'Not really. It's too long ago, and I don't really remember her.' It was a subject he found difficult to talk about; it was much easier to throw the question back at her. 'And since we're on the subject, what happened to yours?'

'She died in the Spanish flu epidemic, just after my brother Joe was born.'

'Do you miss her?'

'Yes, I do. I can't really remember her either – I was only two when it happened, but there was always this great gap in my life. My father's sister came to live with us at first and looked after us, but then she got married, and, of course, her husband didn't want to take on two children who weren't even hers. My father did his best, but he had the farm to run, and only one arm, so there was always this gap. And I knew what it was, because there was no one else in the class at school who didn't have a mother, though there were quite a lot who didn't have fathers because of the war. Sometimes I'd go to tea with one of the other girls from school and – it sounds terrible, I know, because my father couldn't do everything – but I could see what it was I didn't have. I sometimes think it would help if I had something to remember,' she said, 'instead of nothing. My father and Aunt Mary would tell me about her, but I can't actually remember anything for myself. I used to think that I could, but of course I was too young, and it was just the things Aunt Mary had told me about.'

He too had had the same sense of incompleteness all his life, pushed to the back of his mind and seldom thought of unless something happened to bring it forward into sharp relief. There had been the ayah in India when he was very small, and then the Crozier aunts before his father got his living, and his stepmother after the old man had remarried, but it was not the same, even though he could not define how.

Perhaps the physical nakedness and closeness after making love encouraged candour, perhaps it was the awareness of shared experience that made him tell her about these things of which he had no memory, how his mother had never got over the trauma of his birth – 'I was born upside down and took two days over it' – how she had refused to have anything to do with him and had left him to the ayah to deal with.

283

' . . . I can remember the ayah telling me the memsahib was dead, and then being on a train with my father when he came for me – my mother died in the hills and my father had stayed behind – but nothing about my mother except that she could sit on her hair and was always ill. Then my father packed me off to prep school in England.'

'That must have been awful.'

'Didn't have much alternative in the circumstances, and I'd have been going there the following year anyway.'

There was one of those brief but complete memories of being on that train, or it might have been the one taking him to Bombay en route to England, but certainly in the aftermath of his mother's death, because of the black bands on his own and his father's arms. He was sitting opposite his father, uncomfortable, because his legs were too short to reach the floor, kicking back against the seat with his heels, and being told firmly to stop it. He had a new white sailor suit with HMS *TERRIBLE* on the cap and a whistle on the end of the lanyard. He pulled out the whistle to look at it, and his father emerged suddenly from behind his newspaper to tell him to put it away and to read his book quietly instead – *The Jungle Book*, also new, the pages fresh and sharp-edged, another sign that one part of his life was over, in a way he did not yet understand. All he did know was about to be taken away.

'We all went to my mother's sisters in Ireland for a couple of years, then my father resigned his commission to go into the church, got a living in Northumberland, right on the edge of the Cheviots. The vicarage was huge, there were at least twenty rooms, and very inconvenient – no electricity and no piped water until after the last war, but the countryside was marvellous. We all had ponies, there were miles of moorland all around, rough shooting, a stream running through the garden – we used to build dams in the shallow bits.'

Externally all had been as it should be after the move to Langdon. The upheaval was over, a few years later his father had married again. But there was still the empty space inside, the sense of insecurity and inability to rely on any other person which Campbell, the psychiatrist in Alexandria, had considered the true cause of his breakdown.

She squeezed his arm and he tightened his hold around her, with the sense once more of shared experience, that she had been through the same thing that he had, though there were other things that would always be outside her knowledge.

'I'll have to go soon.'

'Couldn't you stay?'

'I told MacLeod to be at the ferry landing at eleven if he didn't hear from me earlier, and I don't like to keep him waiting.' He smiled wryly. 'I came to tell you that we shouldn't see each other again, and you weren't supposed to persuade me otherwise.'

'How much longer are you going to be here?'

'About another three weeks, and that's classified, so keep it to yourself. It could be more, it could be less, it depends how long the repairs take. If the dockyard mateys go on strike we could be here for much longer. You look as though you hope that they will.'

'And then?'

'Back to the war.'

'How much longer do you think it'll go on?'

'I don't know. At least another year, if we have to invade the Japanese mainland, and I don't see how it can be avoided. The Japs fight quite literally to the last man and the last round. Iwo Jima's only five miles by two and a half, but the Americans took thirty thousand casualties in capturing it and spent six weeks doing it.

285

Do you know how many Japanese were taken prisoner? Two hundred and sixteen, out of twenty thousand. And that's for a tinpot little island hundreds of miles from Japan. Japan's four large islands and I don't know how many small ones, and bigger than Great Britain. We'll have to fight over every last inch of it, and then go back to mop up anything we've missed.'

'Is it true that they kill themselves rather than be taken prisoner?'

'Yes.'

'And that they deliberately crash their aircraft on ships?'

'One of them hit us. That's why we're here.'

Jane shuddered. 'How could anybody do that?'

He shrugged. 'It's what they believe in. And in any case, if your blood's up enough you can do almost anything. I was going to ram the *Seydlitz* if I got half the chance.'

'I'm glad you didn't.'

Her hand moved over the delicate skin of his inner thigh, upwards to where the hair began.

'You're learning, aren't you. And I thought you were a sweet and innocent girl.'

'Robert, don't.'

But she went on caressing him, her fingertips moving in slow circles, the back of her hand just brushing against his scrotum on each circuit.

'All right, and then I'll have to get back.'

Rain stung the windowpane, a gust rattling some waste paper in the street below. The air in the room had grown cool, but Jane's body was warm beneath the blankets, soft where it should be, her thighs parted slightly in invitation. He rolled over, kissed her, and put his face between her breasts, finding refuge there for a brief time from the war he must go back to.

As he reached the landing he pushed back his raincoat sleeve to look at his watch. Three minutes to eleven; he had timed it nicely.

'Been waiting long?'

'No, sir.' MacLeod moved to his place at the wheel. 'Bear off forrard. Bear off aft. Slow ahead.'

Thurston was standing in the stern sheets, the rain beating on his face.

'Dirty night.'

'Aye, sir.'

MacLeod's cap was pulled well down, his oilskin shiny with water. Thurston could still feel a faint warmth from Jane's body inside his clothes. He wondered how obvious it was to MacLeod what he had been doing that evening. He had checked his face and shirt collar for lipstick; Jane had worn only a faint trace of scent, and the wind and rain would have disposed of that. He could rely on MacLeod to keep the matter to himself, but he felt uncomfortable in front of his coxswain, a Presbyterian who took his religion seriously and read his Bible each day.

'Boat ahoy?'

The watchkeepers were alert, the hail coming out of the darkness when the motor boat was still a cable's length away. MacLeod moved his body against the wheel to hold it steady, cupped his hands and shouted the response – though after sunset there would be no pipe – '*Inflexible!*', a reminder that he was back once more in the real world, taking up the responsibilities he had let go of for the last few hours.

His cabin was in darkness, Spencer still ashore, Billy Bones appearing to rub against his legs in the usual way. Officially he remained Spencer's cat, but it had become obvious now who he preferred, whether or not he was given the slightest encouragement. Thurston put him in the pantry, shut the door quickly as Bones tried to follow him out, and went into his sleeping cabin. Spencer had left a clean pair of pyjamas on his bunk, red silk ones which Kate had bought him in a mad moment.

Damn, Damn, Damn.

Three hours later and at the other end of the ship one of the sentries made the rounds of the dozen cells beneath the ship's bow, thinking somewhat bitterly that if he had been stationed in the UK in a shore job he might well have had his demob date by now. He walked up the passage between the two rows of cells, moving his hand to scratch an itchy place inside his flannel. The lights in the cells themselves were turned off at night, and light came only from the bulbs spaced at equal intervals along the passage. Only three of the cells were occupied, two by drunks thrust in there to sober up, both asleep, curled into awkward attitudes on their hard wooden pallets. He reached the end of the passage, with only the grey steel bulkhead in front, the hemispherical rivet heads casting their own slight shadows on the surface. Go back, write up the book to show that the check had been done. The light in the starboard cell was at its dimmest, the far corners in deep shadow. The pallet was empty - he started, swung his head right and then left, then saw something sagging against the bars, a grey-white loop around his neck. He started to run, his boots echoing all around, reached the telephone at the far end of the flat, wrenched it off its bracket. The switchboard operator took an age to answer. Holed up in his caboose with a cup of tea, the sentry thought bitterly. 'Duty RPO, and hurry up!' He could hear the leads being plugged in, the operator's voice, unconcerned. Hurry up!

'Duty RPO.'

'It's AB Patten. Cell flat. Can you come. It's very important.'

The RPO was very quick; he must have run all the way.

'Got the keys?'

288

Patten handed them over. The key turned in the lock, the RPO pushed the door open. He got out his clasp knife and hacked at the thing around Norton's neck where it was knotted to the bars, cursing under his breath.

A voice came from another cell. 'What's going on?'
'SHUT UP.'

The last few threads parted. Norton's body sagged to the deck. The RPO turned him over, knelt astride him and began to bear down rhythmically on the base of his back. Patten was standing over him, horrified yet fascinated, wondering what he should do.

The RPO looked up, said out of the side of his mouth, 'Get hold of the PMO. Go on – double!'

Patten started to run, was halfway along the passage at the far end of the flat when he remembered the telephone.

'PMO's on his way.'

The body on the deck was moving, and a pool of vomit had appeared beneath his head, beginning to spread over the corticene with his movements. Norton's face was very pale, his eyes screwed tightly shut and a sobbing noise coming from him.

'Why didn't you cut him down?'
'I don't know, RPO. I just didn't think of it.'

He was still shaking, even though the emergency was now almost over, thinking back to the way he had run in panic through the flat, wanting only for someone else to come and take over all responsibility from him.

'Good thing he wasn't much use at bends and hitches.' The RPO used the Navy's traditional term for knots. He got up from his knees, lifted Norton up by the shoulders. 'Up you get. You're not going to cheat a court martial this way.'

Norton was sitting up on the pallet, back against the bulkhead, head slumped forward towards his knees,

289

when the PMO arrived.

'How did he do it?'

'This, sir.' The RPO held up the torn remains of Norton's vest. 'We'd taken his bootlaces and so on away from him as usual. Standing orders,' he said a little defensively. 'He made a noose with it, put a hitch on one of the bars.' He jerked his head upwards, to where some of the bars had been distorted by Norton's weight.

'Fortunately he didn't do it properly.' The PMO was looking at the bars with professional detachment. 'Not enough of a drop. He must have bent his knees, but his feet could still have reached the deck.'

'Yes, sir. His toes were on the deck when we found him.'

'Well, that's what saved him,' Grant said briskly. 'We'll get him to the sick bay and check him over. Aye, but he should be fit for his court martial.'

Chapter Twenty-Two

Norton's court martial was convened for a date ten days hence, just long enough to give the defence time to prepare their case, and for Stoker Cassidy to recover sufficiently to give evidence in person. An officer from the RANVR who was a criminal barrister at the New South Wales Bar in civilian life had been found to defend Norton, and a second was deputed to assist the prosecution. Norton himself was taken ashore to the naval hospital, lodged in a side ward and watched by relays of sick-berth attendants. The Board of Enquiry finished hearing evidence and retired to consider its findings, which were not expected to appear for several weeks. *Inflexible*'s engineers spent five days engaged in boiler cleaning.

Thurston flew to Nowra a couple of times to spend a day with the aircrews, once by himself, once with Commander (Air) dozing in the rear cockpit, and jammed himself into an Avenger turret to try his hand at firing against a drogue target towed by a weary Fulmar.

He gave several more lectures, or, rather, the same lecture to several more audiences. The audiences themselves, whether they were manufacturers of aircraft parts, ball bearings or rubber tyres, or shipyard managers, were basically the same. There were men who had fought in the last war, but were too old now for active service, for whom he felt an affinity as fellow fighting men, and there were younger men, the business whizz kids who were either more valuable in their civilian jobs or had successfully persuaded themselves and other people that they were. They asked the same questions, some in the ten minutes allocated at the end of the lecture, whereas others, the more thoughtful among them, would buttonhole him afterwards with something more specific, or with a point which was a matter for discussion rather than for a straightforward answer. And there were the brash ones, mostly those who could never have worn uniform and perhaps felt a lurking sense of guilt, who wished only to shake hands with a VC. There was the same gulf dividing Thurston from them as had divided him from those newspapermen, both in experience and in outlook on life. Commander Stokes turned up a couple of times and told him he was doing a great job.

'No, honestly, you are. I've sat in on a couple of them, and now you've had some experience they're starting to sound really good. Absolutely sincere, that's the thing. And the reactions have been really good. Some of them are saying that their production figures are going up already.'

Jane gave him a key to her flat, and almost imperceptibly it became a matter of habit to spend a couple of hours with her after dinner on those evenings when his presence was not required at some official function, to talk, listen to the wireless, make love. He found himself juggling his engagements in order to leave the evenings free to see Jane; having more of the officers to lunch instead of dinner; politely declining invitations to meals and drinks from guests at the official functions, with an uneasy sense at the back of his mind that he was fulfilling his duties only in the letter and not in the spirit. But he did not stay the night with her again; somehow it seemed less reprehensible to leave a few minutes before eleven and walk down to the pier to catch the last ferry of the night. He told himself that he was being a fool, it was doing neither of them any good and there was certainly no future in it, that she was another man's wife, and that other man, if still alive, was enduring an unimaginable fate at the hands of the Japanese. But while he was with her it was too good. It was like an alcoholic being faced with a bottle of whisky; ultimately he would come to regret it, but he could not do without; or, to extend the metaphor, while the bottle remained sealed its temptation could be resisted, but now that it had been opened he had to keep going back until it was empty.

He told himself that it would be over soon in any case, for the clock was running and *Inflexible* must shortly leave Sydney, but the knowledge that their time was brief brought its own urgency, heightening the need they each had, so that they began to demand more of one another with every encounter.

There was, too, the thrill of the illicit, something which had long gone out of his marriage, and a certain lurking pleasure at breaking bounds, at taking one step outside the rigid cage of convention and official expectation. And there was, too, the crying need for contact, both physical and mental, with another person, which was always denied him within the service, the need to shed his uniform and rank and forget for those few hours the demands the service made on him.

Sub-Lieutenant Broome stood in the bar of one of Sydney's larger hotels, a pint of beer nursed carefully in one hand, between two other Sub-Lieutenants (A) similarly equipped. The two had just joined the squadron as replacements, and it gave him a pleasant feeling of pride mingled with surprise to find that they regarded him as a veteran, asked his advice, plied him with questions about 'the last show'. He found himself answering in the way the real veterans on the squadron did, understatedly and in a slightly off-hand fashion, thereby conveying the impression he knew more than he really did, which was also gratifying, though he wondered how long he could maintain the illusion.

'Drink up, and let's have another,' he called, slightly unsteady on his feet now.

They finished their drinks, found a flat surface on which to deposit their glasses. 'I'll get these.' Several pints of beer since coming ashore had begun to make him reckless, overriding the question in the back of his mind of whether he had enough money in his wallet to last the evening. He pushed through the throng towards the bar, suddenly found empty space around him and a vaguely familiar form in front.

'Hello. What are you doing here?'

'You haven't seen any of our lot, have you? I'm supposed to be waiting for a couple of my mates, but they haven't turned up yet.'

It was the engineer with the unruly hair, the one he remembered from the day of the kamikaze.

'No, sorry.' The engineer meant other engineers of course, and there were none here he recognised, though several of the arms in the vicinity bore engineers' purple stripes.

'They should have been here by now, if they were going to turn up. I came on ahead to get the beers in.'

'Probably got held up somewhere.'

'Aye, or found another bar on the way.'

Broome managed to attract the barman's attention, ordered and paid for three more pints.

'Tell you what, there's a couple of chaps from our squadron over there. Why don't you come and join us?'

He began to move away from the bar, found the engineer was about to follow and handed him one of the glasses.

'Sorry, forgotten your name.'

'If you ever knew it. Fred Holland.'

'I'm Geoff Broome.' They reached the other two. 'And this is Mike Summers and David Bold. Fred Holland, from our engine room.'

'Pleased to meet you.'

That settled it, Broome thought to himself. Holland was definitely an oik, and that accent of his compounded it, the way he had pronounced his surname almost as two words, Holl-land, with two separate stresses. Well, most engineers were oiks, especially those from the RNR, who came from some machine shop via the engine room of a tramp steamer. But with another couple of pints inside him he decided that Holland wasn't such a bad chap, even though hope still lurked that Holland's 'mates' might yet turn up.

The landlord called time, and all too soon they found themselves outside on the pavement once more.

'What do we do now?' Summers asked.

'Far too early to go back yet.'

'Why do the Aussies have to have such fucking stupid licensing hours?'

'Tell you what,' Broome said. 'There's a club I know. It's only round the corner, and they let you drink there if you're a member.'

'We're not. Are you?' Holland asked.

'Well, no, but one of our chaps signed me in last time and I'll tell them I know him. It should be all right.'

It took a little time to find the club as Broome had some difficulty in remembering the way. 'We approached it from the other direction last time.'

'Should've brought your Bigsworth board.'

'Ah, there it is.'

It was a narrow doorway with a light above it and a large man in a dinner jacket standing outside. There was a brief conversation, and they found themselves paying a pound each for temporary membership, putting their names to a form and being issued with small cardboard rectangles to prove their membership. The interior was smoky and dimly lit, and there was a small dance floor with patrons clustered round, drinks in their hands.

'Some of those bints look a bit of all right,' Summers said eagerly.

'All spoken for, I bet,' cautioned Bold.

'You never know. Worth a try.'

Summers moved towards the bar, weaving between the mass of bodies.

'Doesn't waste any time,' said Holland, as he watched Summers strike up a conversation with two girls who had been talking to a couple of soldiers.

'This is Liz and this is Dawn. They were getting a bit bored with the pongos, so I thought I'd better rescue them.'

They were both heavily made-up, wearing skirts tight enough to accentuate their hips, obviously dressed for a night on the town.

They had noticed the gold wings on Summers' sleeve. 'Are you all pilots?' one of them asked.

'Yes, Corsairs. All except Fred here. He's one of the black gang – need him to keep the engines turning.'

'Aye, you wouldn't get off the deck if it wasn't for us.'

''Course not,' Bold said heartily. 'And time you got us all some drinks. *Seniores priores* as they say.'

'Someone had better come and give me a hand.'

Holland went off to the bar, followed by a slightly reluctant Broome. He didn't want to leave the sprogs to have the best chance with the girls.

They were fairly silly girls, they giggled a lot, and seemed to have nothing between their ears except an interest in clothes and make-up. But they were the first girls Broome had been close to since leaving England; he did not care too much about their brains, and he suspected that the other three felt the same. Summers put his arm round one of them and took her away to dance. Holland followed, leading the other by the hand. They were a couple of tarts really, Broome decided as he watched Dawn – or was it Liz? – with her arms round

296

Holland's neck, reaching up to kiss him. Just a couple of tarts. But he envied Holland all the same, even as he turned to talk to Bold, who despite his name was much the quieter of the young pilots.

It all happened in an instant. Broome had almost forgotten the two soldiers the girls had originally been with. One large khaki figure stepped from the shadows on to the dance floor, wrenched her away from Holland and delivered a stinging slap across her face. Then the man was going down, and he vaguely remembered hearing from somewhere that Holland was a boxer. The soldier was getting up, holding his chin, his friend coming to his aid.

'Come on!'

The band had stopped playing abruptly. Some of the dancers moved hastily away to the side, shepherding their women with them, others turned back to join in, so that suddenly it became blue against khaki, Australia against Britain, the club staff moving in to separate them. It was soon over, in a welter of broken glasses and toppled tables, the floor slick with spilled drinks, the yeasty smell of stale beer rising from it. They were hustled outside, their pieces of cardboard were taken from them and they were told firmly that their presence would not be tolerated again. Broome did not greatly care, full of beer as he was, his blood still up from battle. The two girls had disappeared, which wasn't surprising, and he did not care about that either. It had been a good night anyway.

'Is it true you're a boxer, Fred?'

'Schoolboy champion of the North of England.'

'You'll have to show me that right cross,' Summers said.

So they stopped on the pavement, and Holland demonstrated various moves, manoeuvring adroitly into the road and back again, until a passing policeman began to show rather too much interest. Laughing, they began to walk back towards the docks, steering an erratic course. Summers stopped, opened his trouser fly to piss into the gutter, and seemed to piss for ever, the yellowish stream hosing out at a forty-five-degree angle, steam rising gently from beneath the kerb. 'God, I needed that.' He stepped the wrong way, slipped, and nearly fell into the stuff. Holland pulled him up, they walked on, past groups of ratings who had spilled out of the bars, caps on the backs of their heads, holding one another upright, singing loudly and tunelessly.

'Gawd, it's the pigs! Evening, sirs.' The man drew himself up into a parody of a salute.

'Evening! Good run ashore?'

'Are they from our lot?'

'No idea. Never seen them in my life.'

It was the comradeship of uniform, of strangers in a foreign land, and of drunken men, but Holland was more sober.

'Come on. Let's get back.'

They shambled on, looking forward now to bunks and a night's sleep. On Monday they would go back to Nowra and start flying again. If a hangover lingered, a quick whiff from the oxygen mask would sort that out.

'There's absolutely no excuse for it, and I'm not going to ask you for an explanation. Brawling over a woman like a bunch of street hooligans. I might expect conduct like this from able seamen with a skinful, but not from officers. You all hold the King's Commission, and you're supposed to have some idea how to behave off duty.' The Captain was pacing up and down, the Commander (E) and Commander (Air) standing motionless behind his desk, properly at ease, backs an inch from the bulkhead.

Broome had barely remembered the incident from the night before, but within an hour of breakfast he had been summoned by the Commander (Air), along with

Bold and Summers, and told that they would all be up before the Captain at 1100. He wondered how they had been found out, then remembered the membership cards. They had their names on, and the forms they had filled in had the name of the ship in addition.

'Has any of you anything to say?'

'No, sir.'

'No, sir.'

'No, sir.'

'No, sir.'

'Very well.' The Captain stopped moving and turned towards them, standing directly behind the centre of his desk. 'Had you been able seamen you would not have seen the outside of the cells for fourteen days or more, and had there been any purpose to be served in charging you – all of you – under Article XVIII, I would have done so. But the Navy hasn't the time and resources to waste on court-martialling the likes of you. As you clearly have no idea how to conduct yourselves when ashore, you will not be given the opportunity. Your leave is stopped for thirty days, and, since you all appear to be incapable of holding your liquor, your wine bills are stopped for the same period. In addition, each of you is to carry out any extra duties your respective heads of department require of you. You are each to apologise in person to the owner of the nightclub, and you are to pay for the damage you caused.'

Summers opened his mouth to protest that they couldn't have caused all the damage to the nightclub, but the look on the Captain's face, jaw set, bushy brows drawn together, the white scar above them stark against the red flush of anger, silenced him before he uttered a word.

'And if I hear any of your names again I will not hesitate to deal with you with all the resources at my disposal. Lieutenant Holland, remain behind. The rest of you may go. Thank you, Wings. Carry on.'

Commander (Air) followed the three sub-lieutenants

out. Holland suddenly felt very much alone. He had known this was going to happen when he woke up that morning with a thumping headache and acid in his stomach.

The Captain seated himself at his desk, his forearms with their gold lace resting on the blotter, a precise three-eighths of an inch of white shirt cuff showing at the wrists, and wrote something on a pad with a propelling pencil. Big hands, Holland noticed, square and strong-looking with a coating of black-brown hair on the backs. He finished writing, laid the pencil down parallel with the top edge of the blotter, moved his angular frame to the back of the chair. 'Lieutenant Holland, I have asked the Commander (E) to stay behind to hear what I have to say to you.'

'Yes, sir.'

'By rights I should have torn up your application for a permanent commission as soon as I knew about this. You're a full lieutenant, and you've been in the service a great deal longer than any of those three. There might be some excuse for them – they might claim that they're young lads who can't hold their liquor, and I might even take account of it. There is no such excuse for you. I believe, Holland, that boxing is supposed to teach self-control, to channel your aggression into something more constructive than brawling in a nightclub when drunk.'

'Yes, sir.' It came out as 'sor' once again.

'However, Holland, I have decided, after due reflection, and after discussing the matter with the Commander (E), to treat this as an isolated incident and not to withdraw my recommendation, but for one reason only. When I was a midshipman I hit a sub-lieutenant. The reason I did it doesn't matter, but I might have had a rather better reason for doing it than you. By rights I should have been court-martialled, or logged at least, which would have meant that I'd have been lucky to be commissioned at all, and I'd almost certainly have been quietly shunted out of the service once the war was over. However, someone gave me a second chance, which I probably didn't deserve, and the rest, as they say, is history.' His gaze was fixed on Holland's face, so that the grey eyes seemed to bore into his. 'I am going to give you, Holland, the same chance as I was given. Your application will stand, and whether it has any chance of success depends entirely on your conduct in the future. Do you understand?'

'Yes, sir.'

'Now get out of my sight and convince me I've made the right decision.'

'Aye aye, sir.' Holland hesitated. 'And thank you, sir.'

'Don't thank me, Holland. Just go away and get your nose to the grindstone. And count yourself lucky.'

'It's true I put in a word on your behalf, but it was the Captain's decision.'

They were standing in the Commander (E)'s cramped little office below the water line, Commander Norman shifting out of his best suit preparatory to getting into his overalls once more. He was a quiet, lean man who rarely needed to raise his voice in the engine room, and Holland respected him.

'Thank you, sir.'

'We all do stupid things when we've had a few. Just thank your lucky stars the Captain did hit someone when he was a snotty. But don't go thinking you've got away with it. You're on extra duties until *I'm* satisfied you've learnt your lesson, and by the time I've finished with you you'll probably wish you had been court martialled. Do you still want that permanent commission?'

'Yes, sir.'

'Then you're going to have an uphill job to get it after this. You're damn lucky the Captain didn't tear up your application, and you're also damn lucky he didn't log you, which might well have put paid to your chances. You're being reported on to the Admiralty every six months, and the Captain will take this business into account when he comes to write the report. He wouldn't be human if he didn't.'

'Yes, sir.'

'And it's about time you stopped thinking that all straight-stripers are upper-class nitwits who got where they are because Daddy was an admiral. To take only one example, and there's no shortage of others, the Senior Engineer here started as an ERA and *his* father was a railway porter.'

'I didn't know that, sir.'

'He doesn't exactly shout it around the engine room. He doesn't need to. He's got this far because he's a good officer and a good engineer and for no other reason.'

'Yes, sir.' Holland hesitated, and reddened a little. 'I'm sorry I let you down, sir.'

Norman was sitting on the edge of his chair, pulling one leg of the overalls over his foot and ankle. 'You'll only let me down if you don't learn from this mistake,' he said quietly. 'So you'd better get to work and prove to me and to the Captain that we were right about you.' He stood up, pushed one arm into the overall sleeve. 'And don't forget the boxing championship. As you won't be going ashore you'll have some time to train, so get out there and win.'

They lay together in the hot water, a little sleepy with the steamy warmth, a cold film of condensation covering the window and the tiles around the bath.

'Good idea.'

'Mm.'

Jane leant back languidly, so that her shoulders settled against his chest, and the water reached up to her breasts. The water was faintly green, pine-smelling from the bath essence she had poured in as she turned

302

on the taps. It was Saturday afternoon, another wet day, the blue of the window showing that outside evening was drawing on.

'I'm going to have to have another bath after this. To get rid of the smell.'

'Who's going to notice?'

'Spencer for one. He never misses a trick. He's been feeding me like a fighting cock ever since he met you.'

'Do you mind him knowing?'

'I tell myself that he's in no position to moralise. The smell of cheap scent clings to his tiddley suit, and I've seen lipstick on his face at least twice since we arrived here. I sometimes wonder whether his wife knew what she was letting herself in for.'

'Have you met her?'

'Her name's Rose. Spencer always calls her Rosie, which she doesn't like. She's a widow – was, I should say with two daughters. Rather prim and completely unlike Spencer. But she's been good for him. He's kept his Good Conduct badges since he married her, and writes her enormous letters telling her that she's the best thing that's ever happened to him. It was rather funny really. At first Rosie told him that she wouldn't marry him until he got his leading rate back – he'd just lost it for the umpteenth time – then he promptly got into a fight in a bar when we called at Argentia in Newfoundland, and I took all his badges off to teach him a lesson – nothing else had made much impression. He was far more worried about what Rosie would think than anything else.

'Anyway, he'd have had to wait another eighteen months to get everything back – six months for each badge, and the hook concurrent with that, on the assumption that he could manage to keep his nose clean for as long as that. He's only just got them all back now. But the ship got sunk after four months, Spencer went straight round to Rosie's place, and as far as I can see she fell on his neck and wept tears of gratitude for his safe return. Spencer's not soft, and he took the opportunity to persuade her to marry him straight away, badges or no badges, hook or no hook. He rang me up and asked me to get him a special licence before she had time to change her mind, they were married within the week, and he's been as happy as a sandboy ever since.'

She lifted herself away from him, turned on the hot water once more, let it run for a few minutes, then lay back against him again. He splashed some water over her breasts, weighed them in his hands.

'Comfortable?'

'Mm.' She shifted again, and he realised that she was about to say something more serious. 'But you'll be going soon, and I'll never see you again.'

'You knew that at the beginning.'

'Yes, I know, but I didn't think about it. You know, on the first day you're on holiday the time you have to go back to work is an incredibly long way off, and you don't really think you'll actually have to go back. Then, almost before you know it, it's the last day and you're going back home, and tomorrow you'll be at work again, and it'll be just the same as it was before.'

'Except that you'll be ploughing through all the rubbish that's piled up in your absence, and finding out what everybody hasn't done.'

He was going back to Kate, but that was at some unknown time in the future, months and probably years away. The war loomed nearer, coming back to the forefront of his mind. Not long now; the repairs to the island were virtually complete, and little of the concrete remained to be chipped out of the flight deck.

'Better make a move, I suppose.'

He stood up and reached for a towel, passed a second one to Jane as she followed him out of the bath. She watched as he began to dry himself, droplets of water trapped in the hair on his chest, then escaping to run down his stomach and thighs. She had grown used to his nakedness, a mature man's body, wide-shouldered, slim-waisted, the tattoo of a ship's badge on one arm which he had described as a piece of stupidity in his midshipman's time, the legs a little bowed from riding and well muscled by years of doubling up the near-vertical ladders on board a warship. He was drying his genitals, his penis swinging lazily back and forth as the towel moved around it. She moved towards him, felt his arms swing the towel over her head and pull it close around her. She was standing against him as he dried her back and buttocks, reached out to take hold of him as he kissed her, squeezed his balls gently in the way he liked. His skin was warm from the bath, reddened in places by the heat of the water.

'Ready?'

He took her hand away and rested his arm across her shoulders as they moved towards the bedroom. The curtains were already closed, the room in darkness. They kissed, briefly, hungrily, hands roaming over one another's backs. He twisted a little, so that his thigh pushed between hers. It could not last; he was going back to the war; he might be killed, and in any case he was married and would not come back to her. He moved backwards to the bed, taking her with him, his knowing fingers beginning to work inside her.

'Come on, woman, and I'll give you what you want.'

She knelt astride him, feeling the hard length of him slide inside her as she mounted him. She had never done it like this with Alan; with him it had all been entirely different, shy and tentative but nonetheless fondly remembered. Thurston had been very patient, spending a long time kissing and caressing her and asking what she liked, had told her, when she asked him why, that he didn't much enjoy it unless she did as well, that it was much better for both of them if she didn't just lie back and think of England, 'or Australia in your case'. She began to move in time with his rhythm as he thrust upward, the words beginning to force themselves out as he began to buck beneath her and she came near to her climax.

'Oh, oh, darling, you're filling me up. Oh, I want you, I want you. Oh my darling.'

Chapter Twenty-Three

The Board finds that the damage to His Majesty's Ship Inflexible *on 19th May 1945 was caused by a round fired from Y turret in His Majesty's Ship* Persephone *during an action against Japanese forces. The Board does not consider that disciplinary action against any individual is necessary or appropriate, but recommends that the Officer of the Quarters of Y turret, Lieutenant George Richard Burns, Royal Navy, be advised to exercise greater care in the future.*

He was inside the dream again, the weight of twisted metal on top of him, the fire burning closer, closer. A face turned towards him, the flesh falling away to reveal the bare bone of the skull, the dead eyes accusing.

A voice was shouting his name.

'Robert, ROBERT!'

The talons lunged out of the flames, grasped his shoulder, pulling him into the fire with the rest.

He heard his own scream and awoke, found sudden, cool air, bent forward automatically to get his breath.

'Robert!' It was a woman's voice, anxious, concerned, but he was still disorientated from the dream, and did not know for a moment who it was.

'Robert, it's me, Jane!'

Her hand rested on his shoulder, transformed into a spectre's claws by the dream. She switched on the light. He shut his eyes for a moment against the brightness, felt the sweat run off his face and neck, first hot, then cold.

'What on earth was it?'

He opened his eyes again, edged away from her a little. 'Just a bad dream. I get them sometimes.'

'It sounded as though someone was trying to murder you.'

The bedclothes were bunched on her side of the bed and she pulled them up to conceal her breasts. Her naked shoulders were satin smooth, her face young and suddenly vulnerable.

'Did I frighten you?'

'No, it's all right. Come here.'

But he got out of bed and started towards the bathroom to get a drink of water.

'Tell me about it.'

'Nothing to tell. Just a bad dream.'

He decided that he would feel more dignified with some clothes on, so he reached for his uniform trousers and began to dress.

'Don't go. You shouldn't, not after something like that.'

Like Kate she wanted to kiss him, cuddle him, hold him to her breast like a child, tell him it didn't matter. Logically, of course, it didn't matter, it was just a stupid dream, but there was still the sense of shame and inadequacy which came after, product of the terror and powerlessness in the dream itself. He sat on the end of the bed, began to button his shirt, keeping himself out of her reach.

She got up, padded over the worn carpet in her bare feet to get her dressing gown from the hook on the back of the door, and sat down beside him. 'Tell me about it,' she said again.

'I've told you. Just a bad dream.' He stiffened as she came up against him, looked away from her, towards the photograph of himself that had appeared on top of the chest of drawers. She had got it from one of the newspapers and had it framed. The public image, the square-jawed naval officer on the deck of his ship, the war hero with the VC ribbon on his reefer. The press, the people who read the newspapers, did not know about the other side, the dead men who filed past him shouting their names, the oil-covered wraiths on *Connaught*'s raft, the nightmares.

'You practically kicked me out of bed.' She pulled up one side of the dressing gown to show a couple of whitish marks. 'I'm going to be black and blue in the morning,' she said ruefully.

'I'd better go.'

'No, don't.' The arm round his shoulders gripped tighter. 'Robert, I know about bad dreams. My father used to have them.'

He looked down at his hands, flexed the fingers of the left, felt the familiar pulling of the tendons in the wrist beneath the scar. There was a point where it became painful; he moved beyond it, feeling the pain spread out from the scar as the nails dug into the palm. Jane had asked him about all his scars one night; he had passed that one off as the result of putting his arm through a cold frame on leave, kicking a football with George. There were times now when he could almost believe it.

'You must tell me. You were screaming and shouting and it can't be good for you,' she ended rather lamely. He felt himself begin to weaken. He shouldn't talk about it to anyone outside the service, but he had carried the burden by himself for long enough. Inside the service it could be discussed, with the Admiral, Dent, Scott, and his brother captains, but only in a coldly professional or an offhand, don't-care fashion, so that it was impossible to say honestly what he thought.

'You wouldn't understand.'

She wouldn't understand, because she had not been through it, because her perceptions and ideas had not been shaped as his had been by Osborne and Dartmouth and thirty years in the Navy.

'I won't understand if you don't tell me about it,' she said in a practical tone.

He still said nothing, moved his thumb and watched it working smoothly back and forth. 'If I do tell you, you must keep it to yourself.'

'Of course.'

'It's very highly classified. I shouldn't be telling you about it at all.'

'Of course. I won't breathe a word to anybody.' Her voice showed her intrigue.

'We got hit by a shell during a low-level attack. That's what the Board of Enquiry was about.' Jane looked puzzled, opened her mouth to ask why that should be so secret. 'The shell was fired from one of our cruisers.' He pulled away from her and sat on the corner of the bed nearest the window. 'It wasn't really anybody's fault, before you ask whose it was. We were in the middle of an attack, *Persephone*'s 5.25s were firing at a Jap who was going for us, and they didn't check firing in time. Heat of the moment of course. The Board of Enquiry reported this morning. Didn't blame anybody, quite properly, just told us all to be more careful in future. Just one of those things that happen in a war.' His face lifted and his eyes travelled towards the photograph on the chest of drawers. 'But thirty of my men are dead because of it. The round exploded right inside the island, wrecked the FDR – Fighter Direction Room. None of the chaps in there got out. They wouldn't have known much about it, that's the only consolation.'

'What about you?'

'I was on the bridge. It was just something going off under my feet. I didn't even see the worst of it. I didn't

310

go below until most of it had been cleaned up. Just saw the chaps in the sick bay afterwards. But we couldn't get rid of the smell. Just like rotten meat, only worse, because of what it was. The heat, of course. Even now they've finished putting the island back together you can still catch a whiff of it, or you fancy you can. Imagination probably.'

She got up and moved towards him. Away from the circle of yellow light shed by the lamp on the bedside table it was dark in the room, so that her face and legs appeared very pale against the deep red of her dressing gown. She stopped in front of him, bent to take his face in her hands. 'It's all right, darling, I'm here.'

He was lying in her arms in her bed, his head on her breasts, her fingers running through his hair as he shuddered and trembled, remembering the carnage inside *Inflexible*'s FDR and in *Warrior*'s forward turret long ago. 'It's all right. It's all right.'

'The men know about it, of course. It's all secret but the buzz soon spreads. Our chaps as well as *Persephone*'s. There's been a fair amount of trouble because of it, our chaps taking it out on theirs. One of my signalmen stabbed a stoker from *Persephone*. He's being court-martialled next week for causing grievous bodily harm. He's lucky, I suppose; it was touch and go with the other chap for a couple of days. He's nineteen, five foot three and I could pick him up with one hand; the other chap's twice his size and a bit of a bullyboy by all accounts. Norton got scared and pulled a knife on him. Shouldn't have been carrying the knife, of course.'

'What'll happen to him?' Her hand slid down the back of his shirt, gently massaged the muscles between his shoulder blades where they had knotted up with the tension.

'If he pleads guilty, and his defending officer puts up a good plea in mitigation, he could get away with six months.'

311

'But if he was acting in self-defence?'

'He might plead it, but he's unlikely to get an acquittal on that basis. If he'd simply hit the fellow, or if the other fellow had been holding a broken glass or something, he'd be unlucky not to, but the court is unlikely to regard knifing him with a flick knife as reasonable force in the circumstances. If he had only hit him he wouldn't be facing a court martial in the first place, because I'd have dealt with him summarily and that would have been that.'

'Couldn't you have done that anyway?'

'No, because I don't have sufficient powers of punishment.'

'Can't you do anything to help him?'

'Not all that much. My job is to investigate the incident and to prepare the prosecution's case. Now that I've done that it's more or less out of my hands.'

'But surely if he's one of your men?'

'It doesn't really work like that. My Gunnery Officer has been told off to prosecute – someone from the Accused's ship usually prosecutes – and Norton's Divisional Officer will appear as a character witness on his behalf, and then it's up to the court.' He went on more quietly, almost to himself. 'I don't know how he'll stand up to it. He's already tried to hang himself in his cell and they're keeping him under twenty-four-hour guard in hospital until the court martial to stop him from doing it again. The sentries check the cells every fifteen minutes for just that reason, also to make sure the drunks don't choke themselves, and one of them found him. He might not have done it if I hadn't kept him in close arrest, but there wouldn't have been anyone to find him on his mess deck if he had. All in their hammocks and sound asleep at that time of night.' He was drawn back inexorably into memory, shuddered again at the thought of waking up in that room with barred windows and a wire cage around the light bulb, with his arm in plaster and a sick-berth attendant watching at the foot of the bed.

She said nothing, but went on massaging his back, her touch cool against his overheated flesh. She was like Kate, wordlessly giving him what he wanted at these times, but could not ask for, what he instinctively pulled away from and tried to resist because he should not need it.

'Feel better now, darling?'

Her hand continued to move over his back, finding the depression which *Seydlitz*'s splinter had left, and the knot of pain beneath.

'Go on. You're not doing it hard enough.' The fingers paused for a second, then dug deeper, seeking the source of the pain.

'Ah, that's more like it.'

She giggled. 'You sound like I do when you're in me.'

For a moment he was silent, then he raised his head and let out a roar of laughter. 'Woman, you're insatiable.'

'Do you mind?'

'No.' He moved up the bed until his face was level with hers and began to kiss her, feeling himself harden against her thigh. There had been two letters from Kate in the morning's post, and one from Helen who was about to face her first-year medical exams, bringing another rush of guilt about his affair with Jane, but all that was forgotten when he was with her.

Jane awoke first. Thurston lay half across her, relaxed in sleep. The curtain had pulled away from the window at the end nearest the head of the bed, so that the light from the streetlamp outside shone through a chink and fell on the side of his face which was uppermost, deepening the shadows and leaving the angles more sharply defined than usual. A few more days, and then he would be gone. She knew he liked her, and he liked

313

her body sufficiently to overcome his scruples about making love to her. But he did not love her in the way that she had come to love him. For him she was a pleasant distraction, to be forgotten when he went back to his ship and his war, leaving her more alone still after the brief taste of love and companionship. It was different for a man, of course, they did not think in the same way. He would forget her, but she could not forget him.

Her fingertips traced his divided eyebrow, very gently, so as not to wake him. The drawn look he had had when she first knew him had disappeared; in his sleep he looked younger, almost like a boy, despite the hawkish adult features and broken nose, the faint bluish beard shadow beneath the skin. Asleep, with his head pillowed on her breasts, his hair tousled by her fingers, his mouth a few inches from her nipple as if he had been sucking it, he was hers, more truly than when he had been making love to her.

She thought of the things he had told her about, wondered again about what he was going back to, the fighting which he had been through and she had not, the differing experience of war which would always separate them. He had been sunk three times; the first almost didn't count, he said, because he hadn't even got his feet wet; the second had been the bad one, something she instinctively knew not to ask about. She felt a great surge of love and fear for him, tightened her arms around his sleeping form. *Oh God, please keep him safe. Even if I never see him again, keep him safe.*

Thurston went out to Nowra again the next day. He admitted privately that though it was proper and desirable that he should visit the aircrews and see for himself the training they were now doing, it was not essential that he go as frequently as he had begun to do, and that it was in part the lure of flying himself there and back which took him. Since leaving Tern Hill he had notched up another twenty-odd hours on Tiger Moths and Harvards, enough to make him regret more keenly that he had not begun to fly earlier, at a time when he could have qualified as a pilot and done it properly. He began to cast covetous eyes on the operational aircraft, the Corsairs and Seafires the young pilots climbed so casually into, flew and then walked away from, hands in pockets, talking noisily about what they would be doing that night. There was an old Sea Hurricane at Jervis Bay, left behind as unserviceable by some carrier which had passed through Sydney three years ago, and now used as a hack. To fly a Corsair was an impossible dream, a Seafire perhaps also, but a Hurricane?

'I can see you're itching to get your hands on that thing,' the Australian Commander (Air) remarked as they were walking back from the hangar.

'Is it that obvious?'

'I know the signs, sir. Most of the young lads passing through want to go up in her, just so they can put another type in their logbooks and say they've flown a Hurricane. I think you're probably just about ready, but we'd really be stretching a point by letting you fly it. Their Lordships might be happy to let you carry on flying Harvards and the like, but they could well start asking awkward questions if you were to have a prang. Still, she's not actually a difficult aircraft to fly, and Saturday's a make-and-mend, so there won't be anything much going on round the place.' The Commander gave a conspiratorial grin almost like Spencer's. 'If you were to come over then, sir, you might just find that I've got something organised.'

There was an official reception that night, held in one of the Australian Government buildings ashore, in a long narrow room upstairs with three polished chandeliers spaced along its length. There was a cold buffet at one end, stewards in white jackets moving about with silver trays of drinks, the usual assortment of invited guests, a couple of Australian MPs, businessmen, lawyers, senior civil servants, their wives and daughters, various quietly spoken men in immaculately tailored suits from the British High Commission, and everywhere the blue uniforms of the Royal Navy and Royal Australian Navy. Receptions like this could be quite enjoyable, but more often they were simply a duty, a couple of hours of polite small talk, introductions to the great and the good of Sydney – 'Captain Thurston, you must come and meet the Deputy Chairman of the Harbour Board,' and the Deputy Chairman would reminisce about his days before the mast, or speak proudly of his son who was in the RAN – and evading the attentions of middle-aged Australian matrons to whom gold lace was an aphrodisiac. Standing with a barely sipped glass of gin and tonic in his hand, answering the usual questions from the wife of the Managing Director of one of the shipyards, he wished he could simply turn on his heel and walk away, go and surprise Jane.

He had been surprised at the strength of his feelings for Jane, that they could coexist with the quiet certainty of his love for Kate. At the beginning, that weekend at the Ropers' farm, he had liked her, felt a pull of desire for her, and had been confident that he could keep his relationship with her on the level of simple friendship. But since they had begun sleeping together he had found himself being drawn to her more and more, thinking about her when he should be concentrating on his work, remembering the feel of her body against his, her lush breasts in his hands, a crowding coming in his groin as he recalled her and the time spent in her bed or on the sagging sofa. The Captain of the destroyer he had been in as a sub-lieutenant was in the habit of saying that you were only truly alive when you were fighting or fucking. But it wasn't just the physical thing. Jane affected him as no other woman had apart from

316

Kate. With Jane he was free for a few hours from the demands of the service; he could talk to her in a way he could to no one else except for Kate, and Kate was far away. Like Kate she had looked after him at a time when he had needed it but could not simply say 'Hold me, I'm frightened', had made him feel safe again after the primeval terror of his nightmares. She reminded him very much of Kate, both as she was now and as he had first known her, laughing and serious by turns, and making him laugh, sensuous in a way which was also completely innocent.

Mrs Managing Director continued to talk to him; he continued to answer her questions, laughed politely as she flirted with him. She was pleasant enough, not one of the more obvious or demanding ones, but his thoughts were far away. Soon the fleet would be leaving Sydney, and then the affair with Jane must end. He had allowed himself to wonder at times, usually when they were lying entwined after making love, whether it had to end. Alan Roper was probably dead, and so Jane would be free; he would be in Sydney again in a few months' time. But there was Kate, and there were his children, and the ties of twenty shared years which could not be sundered.

'Captain Thurston,' the Managing Director's wife said gently, jerking him back to the present. The room was emptying, the great and the good saying their goodnights and moving towards the doors. 'Here's my husband. We must be going.'

He talked for a few minutes to the Managing Director, declined an invitation to dinner with them one night before he left, because it would be one night less that he could spend with Jane.

The Flag Captain came over from the other side of the room. 'That's just about it for tonight.' There was a glass in his hand, and a waft of gin fumes on his breath. 'Hate these things. Stand about trying to talk to people

317

you'd run a mile to avoid if you had any choice in the matter.'

'Women who talk too much.'

'You got the one I did, I suppose? She told me I must spend the weekend with her. "You poor boy. You need to relax after all you've been through."'

'And me.' Thurston looked across the room. 'She seems to have inflicted herself on one of my engineers now.'

He had asked Commander Norman earlier what Holland was doing there. 'It's part of his extra duties, sir. I don't think we need worry about him. He's taking life very seriously at the moment.'

'Mind you,' Strickland mused. 'If that's her daughter it might even be worth a weekend with the mother.'

'Are you sure?'

They both laughed.

Strickland looked at his watch. 'Fancy some supper? Always get hungry at these things.'

It was too late to be worth going to see Jane. 'Why not?'

They filed out, collected their coats and caps from a porter who appeared with them. Outside it was raining again.

'Filthy climate. Never stopped raining since we got here,' Strickland said disgustedly.

Strickland was angry and disillusioned, and once in the restaurant it soon became clear what he was angry about.

'The Windbag and I are about to part company. He's been trying to run my ship and I've told him once too often that I won't have it. He'd have me relieved, I suppose, if there was anyone available to relieve me, and I suppose he might do that yet, but my guess is he'll shift his flag and start trying to run someone else's ship for him.' Strickland's fork stabbed savagely into the steak in front of him, and the point of his knife scraped on the plate audibly as it cut in. 'You're junior to the rest of us, so I expect you'll be the next in line. He'll probably think he can walk over you more easily, gong or no gong.' The fork pointed at Thurston's red ribbon.

'So you're giving me a bit of advance warning?'

'More or less. My guess is that if he does shift his flag he'll do it before we leave this place. Be too much of an upheaval if he leaves it until later, when we're all back up at the sharp end.' Strickland picked up the bottle of wine and sloshed some of its contents into both their glasses. Thurston had paced himself through the reception, but it was clear that Strickland simply hadn't bothered; a bad sign.

'It's not that he doesn't know what he's talking about. I have to admit that he makes a pretty good job of what he's supposed to do. But he just won't let me run my ship the way I want to. He's looking over my shoulder all the time. "Edward, I don't agree with that. If I were you I'd do it this way", and so on. Twice now he hasn't confirmed my punishments, and it's never happened to me before. With every other admiral I've ever served under I've just given him the warrant and he's put his moniker on it. Not this one. He always insists on telling me what he thinks. The first time I'd actually told the chap he was going to get ninety days, and still the Windbag wouldn't confirm it. Made me look a bloody fool, of course. The chap was grinning all over his face when the thing was read out and all he got was sixty. Of course, as soon as he got out of DQs he did the same thing again and I gave him another ninety days. The Windbag had the grace to confirm it the second time. But did he admit he was wrong? Oh no.' Strickland gulped down some of his wine. 'Do you know how he managed to get where he is? Invergordon. Were you involved in that at all?'

'No, I was in China.'

'Lucky for you. You have to feel some sympathy for the troops – the sheer scale of the pay cuts – though the mutiny, or strike as they called it, could never be justified. The Windbag was a commander then. I forget which ship it was, but the Captain had gone sick with something fairly unpleasant – ulcers or whatever – so the Windbag was temporarily in command. Anyway, he managed to get the ship to sea with the chief POs and petty officers only, which completely scotched the protest, got him a reputation as a ball of fire and he's never looked back since.' Strickland paused. 'Yes, I've had one over the eight and it's the wine talking, but I've had as much as I can stand of the bloody man. So I'm warning you, Bob, watch your back. If he's anything like he was with me, he'll be very nice, very matey to begin with. "Edward, we must work together." But he'll soon try to take over from you, and start trying to treat *Inflexible* as his private bloody yacht.'

A waiter hovered nearby. 'Is everything satisfactory, sirs?'

'Yes, thank you,' Thurston said.

The waiter moved away and Strickland continued his diatribe.

'And his staff are a bunch of sycophants. You want to watch the Flag Lieutenant; I wouldn't trust him an inch. I've been having breakfast in my cabin, of course, and lunch as well recently, but I'm still expected to have dinner with him, and dinner is sheer bloody purgatory with that lot sucking up to him.' He finished the last of the steak and put his knife and fork together on the plate. Thurston had already finished.

'In a way I wouldn't mind if he did have me relieved. Scupper my chances of a flag, of course, but after all this they're not looking all that hot anyway.' He lowered his voice. 'Wife's kicking over the traces again, and there's not much I can do about it from this distance.'

Thurston offered his sympathies. The waiter returned with the menu.

'Are we going to bother with a pudding?'

320

'Just cheese and biscuits for me.'

'And I'll have the same.'

'There's an RNVR Commander in a shore job sniffing around her. Doing more than sniffing by now. He's where he wants to be, some sort of non-job on the staff of C in C Plymouth, all winding down nicely now the war in Europe's over. She's done it before – it was a Royal Marine major then. I found out about it, she said it wouldn't happen again and I was fool enough to believe her. He was killed in the Salerno landings – the Marine I mean; the other fellow doesn't even have the guts to get himself killed. This was after she was supposed to have broken it off with him. Came home one day and found her in floods because the fellow was dead, even though it was all supposed to be finished. She's fifteen years younger than I am, and between you and me she's always been a bit of a goer. Can't get enough of it. I've been glad to get back to sea to recover before now, if the truth be known. Since the younger boy's been at prep school she's given up trying to hide what's going on. A Bloody Wavy Navy desk wallah, I ask you!'

Strickland went silent for a time and concentrated on his cheese and biscuits. By now he was clearly drunk, and Thurston quietly took the wine bottle from beside him, and finished what was left.

They paid the bill, left the restaurant and began to walk back towards the harbour. It had stopped raining during the meal, but started again before they had gone more than a few yards.

'Filthy bloody climate. Tell you what, Bob, do you fancy a woman? Always hunt better in pairs.' Strickland was unsteady on his feet, and having difficulty in steering a straight course.

'I think I'd better get you back.'

A few yards further on Strickland tripped on a raised paving stone, lurched and fell against him. Thurston pushed him upright again, grasped him around the

321

elbow. The alcohol fumes were much stronger now. Of course, Strickland had had most of the wine, and had hardly been sober before that.

'S'pose you're right. Probably wouldn't get it up properly anyway now. What's it they say? Increases the desire but takes away the performance.'

The clubs and after-hours bars were emptying, so that the pavements were full of sailors and scantily dressed girls who shivered as the rain struck their bare shoulders. The air was filled with shouts and wolf whistles. A group of chief petty officers appeared, going in the other direction. Thurston recognised the Chief Air Fitter from one of *Inflexible*'s Corsair squadrons and a couple of the others, straggling across the pavement with their arms around each other's shoulders, noisily singing 'Bless 'em All' and swinging their legs in what was meant to be a cancan. One of them had his trouser buttons undone and his member jerked from side to side in time with his movements.

For a moment discipline asserted itself. The line disentangled itself, caps were hastily straightened. 'Hey, Charlie, do yourself up!' There were salutes and cheerful 'Good evening, sirs!' all of them swaying a little as they stood still, then the line reassembled, and they managed a jerky mock bow before moving on. They were good men, regulars all, none of them with less than ten years' service, and, hungover or not, they would be sober and on duty in the morning, and no doubt giving a hard time to any ratings in a similar condition.

'Bloody woman,' Strickland said, almost to himself. 'Should never have agreed to marry her. Should have had more bloody sense.' He tripped again, and would have gone down on to the wet pavement had Thurston not been gripping his elbow. 'Told my coxswain to wait. He should be there.' A taxi moved slowly along the street, stopping frequently to avoid the revellers who staggered without warning into its path. Its sign was lit.

Thurston put his arm out and the taxi stopped.

'Garden Island?' the driver asked.

Garden Island was the naval base. He nodded, pushed Strickland into the back and picked up Strickland's cap where it had fallen into the gutter.

'Hey, your mate's had a few.'

'Bad oyster.' He didn't think the driver would fall for that one. He was obscurely glad that they were both wearing raincoats so that their rank badges were covered up, though the brass hats would inevitably give them away. Strickland seemed to have gone to sleep, head lolling backwards over the top of the seat and rolling about with the taxi's motion.

'Doing wonders for business, your people. They get sloshed, and can't manage to walk back, so they stop me. 'Course, it's all short trips down to Garden Island, but I hardly stop all night. Your lot can stay here and forget about the war as far as I'm concerned.' The driver glanced at Strickland in his driving mirror. ''Course, I've been a merchant seaman so I know what it's like when you get ashore. 'Specially after a long trip.'

The taxi stopped on the dockside. Thurston was relieved to see Strickland's boat waiting, a man in oilskins and a petty officer's cap appearing from its cabin.

'I'll look after him now, sir,' the Petty Officer said, in a tone which suggested that this was something he was used to. He had put his arm round Strickland's shoulders and was assisting him towards the boat. 'It's his bloody wife, sir . . . Come on, Captain, sir. Nearly there. Just lift your foot up a bit. That's better, sir.'

Strickland turned his head back towards Thurston.

'Thanksh, old boy.'

Chapter Twenty-Four

Thurston was going through the papers for Norton's court martial with Scott the following afternoon when the Midshipman of the Watch came in with a signal.

'*Repair on board forthwith*. Sounds like a best uniform and medals job.'

'Have you any idea what it's about, sir?'

'None at all. We'll have to finish this off when I get back. Ask the Officer of the Watch to call away my boat.'

'Aye aye, sir.'

He shifted rapidly into his best uniform. Spencer came from the pantry, went over him with a clothes brush, then brought the medals out of their box, pushed the pin on the bar through the thread loops on the left breast of his reefer. 'That all right, sir?'

Billy Bones appeared and tried to rub himself against his legs. Thurston pushed him away with his toe. 'Not now, Billy.'

'He's getting big, isn't he, sir.'

'It's all the titbits you give him.'

'He needs 'em to keep his strength up, sir.'

There was a knock on the bulkhead. 'Boat's alongside, sir.'

'Thank you.'

Spencer got down on his knees, passed a duster over Thurston's toecaps. 'There you are, sir.'

'Captain Thurston, sir,' the Flag Lieutenant announced.

'Thank you, Flags. Have you seen this?' he demanded, without preamble.

The Admiral handed him the sheet of paper. It was a carbon copy, with a streak of blue at the bottom where the carbon paper had turned back on itself inside the typewriter.

'No, sir.'

'Do you know anything about it?'

He kept the Admiral waiting while he read it, aware of eyes upon him. The Flag Captain was there, looking rather pale, the Admiral's Staff Officer (Operations), a lieutenant-commander, the Flag Lieutenant, and, unexpectedly, Commander Stokes. Thurston wondered where Stokes had managed to get his MBE (Military Division).

ARE OUR WARSHIPS SAFE FROM THEIR OWN GUNS?

Did shells from a Royal Navy warship seriously damage another British warship during operations off Okinawa? Twenty-nine sailors died when shells exploded beneath the bridge of one of the aircraft carriers now under repair in Sydney Harbour. Many more were seriously injured. Royal Navy sources have declined to comment on speculation that the rounds were fired from the guns of another British ship. An internal enquiry is believed to have been held, but it is understood that no action will be taken against those responsible, and the findings of the enquiry will not be made public.

Thurston did not bother to read any further. 'No, sir.'

'It's typical bloody newspaper claptrap, of course. The censor's put a stop on it, and rounded up all the copies, and we're trying to track down who it was who wrote it. But what I want to know *now* is how he got hold of the information in the first place. Do you have any ideas?' The question was almost a sneer.

'Sir, with two thousand men aboard *Inflexible* and another five hundred-odd in *Persephone*, to say nothing of the rest of the Fleet, it was never going to be possible to keep this absolutely quiet.'

'I don't see why it shouldn't have been,' the Admiral snapped.

Winthrop had not asked Thurston to sit down. He was standing in front of the Admiral's desk, cap under his arm. The Admiral was pacing up and down behind the desk, stabbing the air with his cigarette butt.

'Did you impress on them the need for silence about this?'

'Yes, sir.'

'Did you make it clear that there would be the strictest penalties for anyone who talked to anybody whatsoever about this matter?'

'Yes, sir.' Thurston found himself speaking defensively. 'I cleared lower deck before we arrived in Sydney and made it clear to the men then. With respect, sir, all it needed was one man to have a drink too many and say too much in a bar when he got ashore.'

'Has it not occurred to you, Thurston, that this could have been a deliberate breach of security? Some rating, or officer for that matter, with a grudge. Brassed off because he isn't getting his demob number through as soon as he thinks he should.'

'I think that's most unlikely, sir.'

'You seem very confident in your men.' The Admiral's eyes rolled towards the deckhead.

'I am, sir, and with good reason.'

'The sentiment does you credit.' The Admiral was moving up and down the same strip of carpet, throwing the words over his left shoulder. 'However, you are to find the man, or men, responsible so that he can be dealt with. How many among your ship's company know about the Board of Enquiry findings?'

'Officially, sir, my Commander and heads of department, and my secretary. But I've no doubt that the buzz will have got around. Sir, with respect, I doubt if these enquiries will achieve anything, certainly not in proportion to the effort involved.'

'Nevertheless, you are to take immediate steps to find the culprit, so that he can be properly dealt with by a court martial. That will be all, gentlemen.'

Thurston prepared to follow Strickland out.

'Thurston, would you remain behind?'

It was an order, not a request. Stokes, the SOO and flag lieutenant filed out of the cabin. Thurston waited, his eyes wandering around the bulkheads, taking in the royal portrait that was twin to the one above his own desk, a photograph of the Admiral as a midshipman with his boat's crew, and grey representations of the battleships the Admiral had served in, arranged in order of date.

The Admiral motioned him towards a chair. 'Sit yourself down,' he said in genial tones. 'What would you like to drink?'

Thurston told him and the Admiral's Chief Steward busied himself with glasses and then withdrew. 'You've probably realised why I've asked you to stay behind instead of letting you get back to your ship, what?'

'I think I have some idea, sir.'

'I had already made up my mind to shift my flag, but I had not intended to do so until the Fleet left Sydney. I've decided to move over to *Inflexible* without any further delay. I would like you to make the necessary arrangements.'

'Sir.'

'It'll give us all a bit of time to shake down before we get back to sea. I trust you approve of that?'

'Yes, sir.'

'Of course, it'll come as a bit of a shock after you've

327

been running your own show for so long. I've been taking another look at your record. Really very impressive.'

'Thank you, sir.' The Admiral's outward mood had changed entirely. He might have been a different man from the one who had been shouting and glowering only a few minutes before.

'And don't try to tell me it was all a matter of being in the right place at the right time. That business with the *Seydlitz*, pure Grenville. And just the sort of thing we needed at that stage in the war.' The Admiral took a sip of his drink. 'It's really time I made a move. Been in this ship a bit too long, and about time I inflicted myself on the rest of you. I'll admit that things haven't been all that easy with Strickland. Of course, he's got problems of his own, and they're distracting him from the job in hand. Anyway, let's drink to a fresh start.'

The Admiral drained what was left in his glass, put it down decisively on the table at his elbow. Thurston followed suit, remembering with a vague sense of disquiet Strickland's warning of two nights' earlier even as he did so. Perhaps the Admiral was buttering him up, trying to bring him round to his way of thinking. Or perhaps Strickland had been mistaken, his words those of an embittered and unhappy man.

'You certainly seem to have taken to carriers. No thoughts of going back to cruisers?'

'Not now, sir.'

'Well, I suppose a cruiser would be a bit of a comedown after something like *Inflexible*. You're pretty junior to get command of a ship this size. But you had carrier experience already, of course, and not so many have. Is it true that you've been doing a spot of illicit flying yourself?'

'Yes, sir, but most of my flying time has been quite legitimate. I did some flying at Abbotsinch when I was in *Crusader*, and went solo in Tiger Moths, all on the quiet. Then when I was between ships, before I took over *Inflexible*, I was able to do some more advanced training on Harvards, officially.'

'For what reason?'

'I found when I was commanding *Crusader* that I was at a tremendous disadvantage by not being a flyer and really knowing almost nothing about flying. When you come to command a conventional warship you at least have some experience of gunnery, torpedoes and the rest, but in a carrier the aircraft themselves are really the main weapons, and the only way to find out what was going on was to learn to fly myself.'

'Mm.' The Admiral thought for a moment. 'I suppose that's one way of looking at it. Shouldn't expect your subordinates to do things you won't do yourself, but I'm not sure you really need to. The rest of the chaps seem to manage well enough.'

'Yes, sir, but that does depend very much on having a good Commander (Air) and having the confidence to let him get on with it. It also means that the division you tend to get between the flyers and the non-flyers on board is perpetuated at the highest level. And quite simply, sir, my having done some flying gives me a much better idea of what's going on, and it would make it more difficult for my Commander (Air) to pull the wool over my eyes if he should think of doing so.'

'Quite so. And are you still flying?'

There was a harder edge beneath the question, and Thurston, remembering the Admiral's earlier display of anger, wondered again whether Strickland had been right in his assessment. 'Yes, sir. The Fifth Sea Lord authorised me to go on the Harvard course originally and then to keep in practice.'

'I see. But I presume that you're not spending so much time flying that you're neglecting your ship.'

Again that hard edge, and the sense of unease. 'No, sir. Of course not.'

'I'm pleased to hear it. But as this is the first I've heard of it, I'd prefer you not to fly, except as a passenger, of course, until I've signalled the Fifth Sea Lord and seen exactly what you're authorised to do.'

The Admiral's manner had not changed, but it was quite clear that this was an order.

'Aye aye, sir.'

'That'll be all for the time being. I'm looking forward to flying my flag aboard *Inflexible*.'

Strickland emerged from his own cabin as Thurston came out. 'I'll see you over the side. I'm still in command of this ship, whatever the Windbag thinks.'

They were walking along the passage which led towards the quarterdeck, the mirror image of the same passage in *Inflexible*, grey paint, electrical wiring running along the deckhead, .303 Lee Enfields chained into racks on either side. It was quite easy to see how someone could go aboard the wrong ship, drunk or even sober, go below to his cabin, and only realise his mistake when he discovered someone else in 'his' bunk.

'You'll never find him. The chap who spilled the beans.'

Thurston had temporarily forgotten the original reason for his summons. 'I know that, and you know it. All I can do is go through the motions.'

'Well, if it keeps the bugger happy . . . but watch your back, Bob. Sorry he's inflicted himself on you.'

'He kept me standing in front of him in my best uniform and medals like a naughty schoolboy while he held forth at me, in front of the Fleet PRO and a couple of his staff to boot.' Meeting with the Admiral in private had lulled him for a while, but since then, as he put the investigation in train, he had had time to grow angry again.

'You haven't really told me what it was all about.'

'Some newspaper reporter has managed to get hold of something about the business with *Persephone*. It won't be printed, of course, the censor's seen to that, but Winthrop's out for blood.'

'He doesn't think you went to the press about it?' Jane pressed a mug of tea into his hand.

'No, of course not, but he's decided that someone let the cat out of the bag deliberately and expects me to turn my ship upside down to find him. I told him that it was almost certainly someone talking out of turn in a bar, but he wouldn't have it. I've got two thousand men aboard *Inflexible*, it's going to mean questioning the whole lot of them, and none of them is likely to admit to anything, even if he wasn't too drunk to remember doing it. Just the sort of thing we don't need when we're sailing in a few days.' He sipped at the tea, found it was still too hot and put it down again beside him.

'Could he be right?'

'It's possible, but I doubt it. There's no need for anyone to do it deliberately. My guess is that one of our chaps, or one of *Persephone*'s for that matter, said one thing too many over the bar when he'd had a few. Some reporter, on or off duty, heard him, possibly bought him another drink and pumped him a bit, and that's what happened. That sort of thing's always going to happen. There are plenty of things that are supposed to be restricted to only a few, but they become general knowledge within the service all the same, and then it only needs one man to speak out of turn and it goes outside as well. There is just one thing.' He swivelled on the sofa to face her, found himself choosing his words carefully once again. 'Whoever it was evidently knew the Board of Enquiry's findings, so it could only have happened in the last few days.'

Jane's body jerked suddenly beside him, so that the sofa vibrated. 'You don't mean that you think I went to the newspapers?'

'I'm sorry, Jane, I have to know.'

'Robert, of course I didn't! It never even occurred to me to talk to the newspapers about it. Anyway, what would it have achieved? You said yourself that the censor wouldn't let them print anything.'

'I don't mean that you could have done it deliberately. But could you possibly have let something slip? By accident, I mean.'

'In the bar when I'd had too much to drink, I suppose! Robert, I'm quite sure I didn't. I haven't even mentioned it to anyone. It's not the kind of thing I would want to talk about. You told me about it, but I could see it was something very private. Even if it hadn't been secret I wouldn't have told anyone.' She was on the verge of tears. 'Are you satisfied?'

'Yes.'

'So now you can report back to your Admiral that it wasn't your floozie ashore who spilled the beans.'

'Jane, it's not like that!'

There was a long tense pause, while he wondered what more he could say.

She sighed at last, and ran her fingers through her hair to take it back off her face. 'Will it ever come out?'

'Not officially. Someone will write a sensational newspaper article in ten or fifteen years' time, saying what a scandal this was, that the Navy can't even be trusted to shoot at the enemy instead of their own people, and how much more of a scandal it is that it has all been covered up all this time. And some socialist MP will start asking questions in the House, and demand an enquiry. Then some bright spark who's never got nearer the front line than Whitehall will decide that heads should roll. But all that won't bring any of them back, and it'll only upset their families all over again.'

'But shouldn't the families be allowed to know what really happened, once the war's over?'

'It'll only make things worse for them. It's quite bad enough having someone killed without having him killed by his own side.'

'But surely they're entitled to know? Didn't you want

to know how your brother died?'

'It's not the same.' He reddened, aware that he was moving on to still more dangerous ground, that a whole section of the ethos he had grown up with was being challenged.

'No, because it doesn't embarrass the Navy,' she mocked.

'So you'd be happy to let some pipsqueak who's never seen action, who's very conveniently got flat feet and stayed out of uniform, and has nothing better to do than write sensational and one-sided rubbish for the *News of the World*, splash some poor devil's error of judgement all over the front pages, with no idea what you're up against when you're under fire, and prattling on about doing justice to the dead, when all he's really concerned about is selling more copies of his rag?'

'No, I didn't mean that.'

'But that's the way it happens. Some reporter gets hold of something; he doesn't even bother to find out what really happened, or the circumstances in which it occurred. He's not concerned about the damage he causes; all he's interested in is getting a story, no matter how inaccurate or one-sided it is.' He stopped himself from saying any more. He had deliberately gone to Jane's flat a little earlier than usual in order to get away from the service, but tonight, even more than usual, the service had been ever present, pressing in on them from outside, and they seemed to have done nothing but argue.

'Sorry, Jane, I'm not being very good company tonight.'

She smiled. 'That Admiral of yours must really have got up your nose. I wish I could have been a fly on the wall!' She glanced at the mug beside him. 'Don't forget about your tea.'

'I hadn't.'

As on other occasions her outsider's view helped to put matters into perspective, stopped him from dwelling on what had gone before and on what was to come, encouraging him, for once, to live in the present. He realised suddenly that he had barely thought of Kate for days. Her letters arrived, his conscience prickled for a time at the reminder of his betrayal, then she faded into the background once more. But there were only a few days left. *Inflexible*'s repairs were complete and she had moved out to anchor in the stream. He felt a shiver of apprehension, quickly suppressed.

'You still haven't drunk that tea,' she chided him.

'And I still haven't made love to you this evening.' He pulled her towards him, began to kiss her. 'God, I wish I'd known you when I was thirty.'

'But wouldn't that be cradle-snatching?' she said practically. 'When you were thirty I was thirteen, all pigtails and horrible school gymslip.'

'And I'd have finished up in jail for corrupting the young and innocent.'

'I'm afraid we weren't all that innocent. We were always combing through the medical articles in women's magazines trying to find out what it was all about, and wondering how on earth we could get hold of *Lady Chatterley's Lover*. What were you doing when you were thirteen?'

'Concentrating on weightier matters like boxing the compass and learning to tie sixteen different bends and hitches and holding my place as full back on the rugby fifteen in the face of competition from a chap named Scott-Campbell who was killed at Coronel. Though when my father married my stepmother, my brother George and I spent most of Easter leave trying to decide whether Father actually did it to her.'

'And did he?'

'George and I thought he must be past it.'

'You're not.'

'I know.'

He was forty-five, but as he thrust into her he was thirty again.

The court martial was held in the same classroom as the Board of Enquiry, and the same atmosphere of secrecy prevailed. Half a dozen junior officers under instruction settled themselves on to chairs at the rear of the classroom; the rest of the seating remained empty. A minute before 1000 the president and members of the court martial – the Captain of one of the battleships and four commanders – filed in. On the stroke of 1000 the Accused was marched in, pale-faced and smaller than ever between his escorts. Outside a puff of greyish smoke rose from the breech of an aged saluting gun, the spent case clattered on the gravel beneath, and a second later the sound of the shot reached the classroom.

'You are Signalman Robert James Norton, Official Number P/JX 485106, of His Majesty's Ship *Inflexible*.'

The shorthand writer's pencil moved over the page of his notebook to record that the Accused had made no reply.

'You are charged under Section 18 of the Offences Against the Person Act 1861 and Article XVIII of the Articles of War in that you, a person subject to the Naval Discipline Act, did cause grievous bodily harm to Stoker First Class William Cassidy, Official Number C/KX 377971, of His Majesty's Ship *Persephone*, with intent to cause him grievous bodily harm, in the Southern Cross bar, Milton Street, Sydney, Australia, on 2nd June 1945. Do you plead Guilty or Not Guilty to the charge?'

The Judge Advocate finished speaking. For a long moment there was only silence, the shorthand writer's pencil poised half an inch above his page, the President moving his half-moon spectacles up towards the bridge of his nose. Thurston looked across the room towards the Gunnery Officer, who was studying the pile of papers in front of him. Norton was standing quite still, eyes fixed on the wall above the President's head. He was paler than ever, an unhealthy greyish colour from being indoors too long.

'Guilty, sir,' he said at last, in a barely audible voice.

The rest of the proceedings were dealt with quickly, and almost anticlimactically. The necessary speeches were made, the court retired, and returned within a few minutes to sentence the Accused to nine months' detention, subject to confirmation.

'I did try to persuade him to plead Not Guilty. Make you prove that Cassidy hadn't walked into the knife. But he was adamant that he'd done it and would rather take what was coming to him.'

Norton's Defending Officer was an Australian in his mid-thirties, with a beard which Thurston strongly suspected had been grown to give him a nautical appearance to go with the uniform and lieutenant-commander's rank.

'Thought I might even have got him off, but he wasn't having it. Still, I thought the sentence was about right in the circumstances. He'd have been lucky to get away with anything less.'

With the court martial over so quickly, the mood of the day had suddenly lightened. Thurston had spoken to Norton briefly, before he was taken to the Detention Quarters to begin his sentence.

'I'm sorry, sir.'

'I'm sorry too, Norton. Just get through your sentence and then put all this behind you. Keep your nose clean and you may not have to do the full nine months.'

The cell was small and bare, partly below ground level so that Thurston could see long grass between the bars on the window and then a flat shaved expanse running down towards the road. A large regulating petty officer stood in the corner nearest the door, his presence preventing further conversation.

'Well, goodbye, Norton, and good luck.'

'Goodbye, sir.'

Nothing more to be said. DQs would have to be warned that Norton was a suicide risk, but that was all that he could do. His part in the affair was over; Norton was out of his hands. He would almost certainly not go back to *Inflexible* when his sentence was complete, but be drafted to some other ship or shore establishment. The scar on his wrist began to itch as his mind was drawn to it; he slid his little finger beneath his watch strap and scratched gently. It was still only half-past eleven; the rest of the day, suddenly empty, stretched before him.

'You're back quicker than I thought, sir. Pleaded guilty, did he?'

Thurston told Spencer briefly what had happened.

'Could have been a lot worse, sir, 'specially if the bloke 'e stabbed had gone and died.'

Spencer bustled around, produced coffee and chocolate biscuits. Billy Bones tried to climb on to Thurston's shoulder and had to be put back on to the carpet.

Chapter Twenty-Five

NAVAL MESSAGE

   CONFIDENTIAL

To: *From:*
RAA British Pacific Fleet   Admiralty
(reptd) Commanding
Officer, Inflexible
Personal from 5th Sea Lord

Your 201615 June

*US practice is to appoint senior officers qual-
ified as pilots or observers to command carriers. Admiralty considering adopting similar
policy, but currently there are few post captains suitably qualified in all respects. Inten-
tion in due course is to give selected officers
some pilot training prior to taking up carrier
command appointment. Captain Thurston is
guinea pig. RAF report Thurston high average
as pilot despite limited training and strongly
recommend that he take every opportunity to
keep in practice and to gain further experience
on suitable aircraft. Admiralty concurs. Thurston is to be allowed to continue flying as pilot
provided suitable aircraft are available and
flying can be accomplished without conflicting
with primary duties.*

'Do you want an early lunch, sir, if you're going flying?'

'How did you know?'

'Ear to the ground, sir.'

The Commander (Air) at Blacktown was as good as his word. At 1400 on Saturday the air station was virtually empty, except for the few who found themselves on duty instead of catching the train into Sydney proper. The Commander sat in the rear cockpit of the Harvard in silence while Thurston performed half a dozen circuits and bumps, concentrating hard on making them as precise as possible. Finally he said, 'All right, sir, I think you'll do.'

The Hurricane was a single-seater, so there was no possibility of being broken in gently by flying it dual.

'No room for mistakes, sir. She's actually very sweet to fly, but you do need to know what you're doing.'

The Commander (Air) made Thurston sit in the Hurricane's cockpit while he squatted on the wing and took him through the instrument panel, then made him go through everything himself, again and again, and then again blindfolded.

'All right, sir. Don't break anything.' He jumped down from the wing and began to walk away towards the hangar.

The Hurricane's cockpit was narrower and more enclosed than any Thurston had been in before, with a solid metal bulkhead behind his head instead of the familiar glass canopy and instructor's cockpit of the Harvard. Around him was armour plate, and on the spade grip of the stick a red gun button, reminding him that the Hurricane had once been the RAF's main fighter aircraft, more numerous than the Spitfire. He checked his straps, started the engine, let off the brakes and began to taxi forward. The Hurricane's brakes were hand-operated, unlike the foot brakes he had painfully got used to in the Harvard; the long nose cut out all forward vision. He zigzagged carefully using the rudder, looking out through the sides of the open canopy. Reaching the foot of the runway, he called up the tower and got clearance to take off.

H – Hydraulic lever; set forward.
T – Trim; set forward for take off.
M – Mixture; set fully rich.
P – Pitch; set fully fine. ('Try to take off in coarse pitch and you'll end up on the operating table, if not the coffin table,' he heard Lines' voice say. Where was Lines now, he wondered. Concentrate.)
F – Flaps up.
F – Fuel; cocks on, check the gauge, enough in the tanks.
S – Ignition switches on. Mag drop on run-up not over one hundred.

The familiar routine of checks was unexpectedly calming. He pulled his shoulder straps a hole tighter, took a deep breath in, and then out again. *Look round once more, then let the brakes off, taxi forward, move the nose to port and starboard with the rudder for a final check that the runway ahead is clear. Straighten the aircraft up and open the throttle. The speed builds up quicker than in the Harvard. Stick forward to bring the tail off the ground, see the dark green of the hedge at the far end of the field and the nondescript suburban houses beyond. Ease the stick back a little and feel the Hurricane lift herself clear of the tarmac. Undercarriage up; look all around.*

The Commander had been right. There was nothing else in the sky, only some white puffs of cumulus on the horizon to seaward. At a thousand feet the landscape had opened out beneath, the huge blue expanse of the harbour, the steel structure of the bridge shining in the sun, the city and its suburbs spread out on either side, the distant slopes of the Blue Mountains thirty miles or more to the west. He tried some turns, cautiously at first, then with growing confidence as he got used to handling the aircraft. He moved out over the harbour itself, dipped one wing to look down on the warships lying offshore, picked out *Inflexible* among them, bows pointed seawards, the anchor cable just visible above the water, dark shadow to her port side. Aboard the warships it was also a make-and-mend, the decks empty except for a scatter of men walking the length of them for exercise, and a deck hockey game going on aboard *Irresistible*.

He straightened the Hurricane up, brought her round in a hundred-and-eighty-degree turn to starboard over the North Shore to take him back across the harbour. The Hurricane, old and clapped out as she was, responded at once to the movements of stick and rudder, the Merlin engine giving out its instantly recognisable note. He worked a couple of fingers beneath one of the straps of his parachute harness where it had begun to cut into his thigh, eased the stick forward to put the aircraft into a shallow dive. There was a fresh wind blowing, humping the harbour waters into white-capped waves which broke into spray as they met the shore. Closer to the water the sensation of speed was greater, tempting him to go lower still, to flash over the sea only feet above those white-capped waves. *Don't go mad.*

He eased the stick back into level flight, brought the Hurricane round a few degrees to port to take her directly over *Inflexible*'s flight deck from stern to bow, thinking of what it must be like to land on that with the ship rolling and pitching and vibrating as she steamed into wind at thirty knots. G-forces pressed him down into the seat as he moved the stick back and began to climb away. He grinned to himself. *Thurston, you're just like a boy with a new toy.* He looked down once more at the anchorage, noticed a white gush of propeller wash at *Inflexible*'s gangway as one of her boats moved away from beneath the overhang of the ship's side, turned and set course towards the shore. There was no mistaking which boat it was; it was the Admiral's barge, and the flash of the sun off the gold oak leaves on the cap peak told him that the Admiral himself was on board.

He looked at his watch, found to his surprise that he had been up for almost an hour. He had been entirely absorbed in the pleasure of flying, the time had passed without his noticing where it had gone. It was after half-past three, the evening was beginning to draw in. Regretfully, he set course back to the airfield.

Landing the Hurricane brought back the early days at Abbotsinch and Tern Hill. As the nose came up the runway disappeared, the crosswind which had strengthened while he was airborne caught him and swayed him out to starboard. The main wheels touched down before he expected, when he was still going far too fast. The Hurricane bounced, he pulled the stick back hard, so that the aircraft slammed back on to the tarmac, bounced again. He was on the extreme edge of the runway, still moving diagonally to starboard. He jabbed on left rudder, slewed round to port once more, back towards the centre of the runway. He let his breath out once more, straightened up, applied the brakes and brought her to a halt, then turned and taxied back soberly towards the hangar.

'Enjoy it, sir?'
    'All except the landing. Never been my strong point.'
    'She's a lot taller off the ground than the Harvard. Bit disconcerting until you get used to it. You have to look much further ahead when you start your approach and then feel her down. You soon get used to it and the Seafire's just the same. Anyway, sir, we always say it's a good landing if you walk away from it.'

The Australian Commander suggested a cup of tea, and they sat in his office and talked about flying for a time, until the telephone rang.

'I'll just go next door and deal with this, sir.'

The Commander was away for several minutes, and returned looking very serious.

'You didn't make any low passes over the Fleet anchorage while you were up, sir? That was RAA's Flag Lieutenant, wanting to know who'd been flying from here this afternoon. It didn't hit me that there was anything in it, so I told him you'd been doing a bit of type familiarisation in a Hurricane. Seems the Admiral's got his knickers in a knot about someone buzzing his barge practically on the deck. I'm sure that's an exaggeration, sir, but how low did you get?'

'Two-fifty feet, according to the altimeter. I was simply taking a good look at my ship, getting a pilot's eye view of her from low level. I certainly didn't go buzzing any barges.'

'I told the Flag Lieutenant that I'd be extremely surprised if you had, and he seemed satisfied with that. But I thought I should warn you.'

'There are wheels within wheels.' Thurston left anything more unsaid, and stood up. 'I'd better be getting back.'

It was Saturday evening, a few minutes after 2000. Holland had weighed in an hour earlier, the scales settling exactly on eleven stone six. A few minutes ago one of the sick-berth attendants had wrapped his hands in gauze, then wound a layer of tape over the gauze, and laced the leather gloves over them.

'Ready, sir?'

'Ready.'

'Good luck, sir.'

The SBA would have said that to everybody, including the Stoker Petty Officer sitting on the bench opposite, who would be in the ring with him in a few

343

minutes. At the other end of the hangar the welter-weight final was reaching its climax, the shouts and yells of the audience echoing off the bulkheads. Then the bell went, there was a brief silence, then more shouting, and a burst of clapping.

'Right, sir, this is you.' The Petty Officer PTI had come back from the ring, his face sweaty as if he himself had been fighting.

'Who won?'

'Pettifer. Just. Bloody lucky. It might easily have gone the other way.'

The forward lift, newly repaired, had been lowered to a few feet off the deck and locked down, the posts and ropes erected on top of it. Benches had been brought up from the mess decks to fill most of the hangar, leaving a central aisle down which Holland and his opponent walked, a few feet apart, not looking at one another. Holland knew him fairly well, they had stood the same watches, had often sparred together in the past, which meant they knew each other's style and likely moves, but it would also make them reluctant to hit hard. The men squeezed together on the benches were shouting good-humoured jests, their cigarettes sending greyish wisps of smoke curling up towards the deckhead. A clutch of the boy seamen Holland had been coaching gave him the thumbs up sign. 'Come on, sir. Knock his head in.' At the front, three rows of wardroom chairs had been set up, occupied by officers in bow ties and mess wellingtons, the most senior nearest the ring, a reminder to Holland of his boyhood fights at home, the sleek men in dinner jackets who looked for blood, with their overdressed wives or mistresses beside them. The Admiral was saying something to the Captain; a couple of places further on the Commander (E) was sitting poker-faced. Holland climbed up the ladder behind the Stoker PO, ducked under the ropes. Something made him look back for a moment;

his eyes met the Commander (E)'s, and the Commander (E)'s face relaxed into a small smile.

He waited, quite calm now, wanting only to get on with it, while the referee announced their names and what everyone watching already knew, that this was the middleweight final and would consist of three rounds of three minutes each. The referee finished speaking, stepped back to the ropes. Holland and the Petty Officer came out of their corners, circled warily for a time, waiting for an opening. The audience was quiet, waiting for the fight to start in earnest. The Petty Officer's left hand came out, caught Holland on the taut muscles of his belly, hardened by hundreds and hundreds of sit-ups over the last few weeks. That was the start, he was in there now, punching, ducking, weaving, oblivious now to the shouting which echoed all around, feeling only the impact of the other man's punches, and of his own on his opponent's head and torso. He smelt sweat, old leather and liniment, tobacco and rum on the other man's breath. The Petty Officer smoked, and that would spoil his wind, so that in the third round he would tire more quickly, and Holland could seize his chance then and finish him off.

He didn't see the punch coming. It landed on the left side of his jaw, jerking his head back so that his vision swam and it was only some hasty slithering of his feet on the canvas which made him retain his balance and stay upright. The Petty Officer was straight in, exploiting the sudden weakness, both fists slamming into Holland's midriff and forcing him back towards the ropes. He sidestepped, managed as his eyes cleared to land a few punches on the other man's biceps, breaking his rhythm, kept on moving sideways, inch by inch away from the corner and back towards the centre of the ring. Sweat beaded the Petty Officer's upper lip; there were twin copses of black hair growing out of his nostrils.

The bell was unexpected. Someone steered him back to his corner, wiped a cold sponge over his face, icy against the overheated flesh. Another man put an old beer bottle to his lips, allowed a little of the water to trickle inside.

'Spit it out. Don't swallow any of it.'

That too was familiar – back to when he was eleven and had his first fight in the boys' club at home – and therefore comforting.

'Just get out there and keep hitting him. And concentrate on what you're doing this time. You let your attention go for a second just then, and he nearly had you.'

The bell rang again. The PTI patted him on the shoulder and he was up and trading punches once more. Three minutes, only three minutes, but always the longest three minutes there could ever be. The Petty Officer had made good use of the brief respite, and was coming at him hard again, more punches landing on the parts which already hurt from the first round. But he was hitting back, automatically, oblivious once again to anything but the man he was fighting. Another punch came at his jaw, he dodged away to the left, twisted back to land a short jab beneath the Petty Officer's ribs. It was a good punch, the man went back a pace, and before he could recover Holland's right fist had shot out to his nose. There was a bright gush of blood on to the upper lip, tears glistening at the corners of his eyes. Holland thought for a second that he was going down, but then he recovered and was coming back at him.

'Pretty close so far, but you've just got the edge. And he smokes, so he'll be getting tired now. Keep hitting him and you'll have him on the run.'

Out again for the final round. Two plugs of cotton wool protruded from the Petty Officer's nostrils, and his

346

mouth was open slightly so that he could breathe, the upper teeth showing very white and glistening with saliva. He might be tiring, but had come out intent on a final effort, charging at Holland and trying to force him back to the ropes. Holland feinted, dropped back to ugly shouts from the crowd, then twisted to one side, bounced back from the ropes to take his opponent by surprise. He was hammering away at him, feeling the other man's arms all around, trying unsuccessfully to land a punch and bring a respite, forcing him back, step by step to the other side of the ring. The crowd were on their feet, roaring their delight, the noise breaking into Holland's concentration. The cotton-wool plugs, bloody now, had dropped on to the canvas and blood was coursing in twin streams down the Petty Officer's upper lip. He had him now. His fist shot out, took the other man on the point of his chin. He crumpled slowly, and lay still.

It was hardly necessary to count the other man out. His handlers came out from the corner, got him upright, his body hanging between theirs, the blood from his nose running down his chin and falling in bright droplets on to the white canvas.

'Is he all right?'

'Should be, sir. Just gave his head a thump on the canvas.' The man slapped his cheek. 'Hey, Jim, who's the Prime Minister?'

'Churchill,' the Petty Officer slurred.

'*Mr* Churchill. Haven't you got any respect? There you see, sir. He's all right. But we'll just get him over to the sick bay and have the doc look him over.'

It was strange how quickly the triumph evaporated. Someone draped his dressing gown around his shoulders, someone else pulled his gloves off and began cutting away the gauze and tape. He found a place on a bench, watched the last two fights with the rest of the men who had already had their bouts. He went up and got his prize, shook hands with the Captain for a second time, listened without paying much attention to a lengthy speech by the Admiral on how they needed to hit the Japanese and keep hitting them, just as you chaps have been hitting each other all evening. He went below, had a shower and shifted back into his uniform.

'Coming for a drink, Fred?'

'Orange juice!' someone else shouted.

'In a minute.'

He always wanted to be by himself for a time after a successful fight, even more than after a defeat, away from the people who slapped him on the back, wanted him to go through every punch, every manoeuvre once again. He went across the open flight deck, feeling the cool night air on his bruised face, looking for a time at the lights of the city half a mile away. It would be nice to have a girl ashore, someone to write to when the ship was back at sea, someone who would write to him, but he hadn't met anyone like that, and now his leave was stopped he would not. He had almost given up writing to his parents because he and they had nothing in common any more except the accident of blood. He remembered the Petty Officer, and went up to the sick bay, to be told that he was all right, that he was sleeping it off, and would have a hell of a headache in the morning.

He was crossing the flight deck when he heard footsteps, saw a tall figure emerging from the shadow of the island, stiffened as he heard the Captain's voice.

'Good evening, Holland.'

'Good evening, sir.' The Captain was bareheaded, brass hat in his hand, so no salute. 'I just came up here for some air, sir.' He wondered why he felt the need to excuse his presence, wished suddenly that he could go back to being just another of the anonymous junior officers aboard the carrier, instead of the marked man he had made himself by applying for a permanent commission.

He answered the Captain's brief questions. Yes, it had been a good fight, and Hodges had given him a few nasty moments, but he wouldn't have wanted a walkover, he'd just been up to the sick bay and Hodges was all right. He said goodnight, and walked away towards the ladder, looked back to see the Captain standing by himself at the edge of the flight deck, his back towards him, looking out across the water to the lights of the North Shore, and it suddenly struck him what a lonely business it must be, to be forever a demigod on a pedestal, with two thousand men under his command but none with whom he could claim friendship, isolated in his solitary splendour aft instead of being part of the noisy and cheerful society of the wardroom, denied also the camaraderie of working in a close-knit team like that of the engine room, which had given Holland the sense of belonging he had failed to find elsewhere.

Chapter Twenty-Six

Sunday began and for most of the forenoon continued as did all Sundays in harbour. Hands were called half an hour later than usual, breakfast was eaten in a fashion that was almost leisurely. The Roman Catholics went to church ashore at 0930 and for the remainder there was Sunday Divisions on the flight deck. Thurston would have lunch in the wardroom by invitation and then cross to the North Shore to spend the rest of the day with Jane. The storm broke just before lunch.

'I understand you went flying again yesterday.'
   'Yes, sir, I did.'
   'Against my express orders.'
   'No, sir, I understood that your orders were that I was not to fly until you received the Fifth Sea Lord's reply to your signal. The reply arrived before I went.'
   The Admiral's anger was unmistakable. 'You might have had the manners to wait to hear my reaction to that signal. I'm quite sure that the Fifth Sea Lord did not intend you to go joyriding all over the sky in an aircraft you're not even qualified to fly. I don't suppose the Fifth Sea Lord or anybody else authorised you to break your bloody neck in an aircraft you haven't the experience to fly. The service is short enough of experienced officers to begin with.'
   'I have over seventy hours in Harvards, sir, and am at the stage where pilots convert on to the Hurricane as part of their normal training. Not all that long ago there were pilots flying them on operations with very few

more hours. I was permitted by the Admiralty to learn to fly to give me some insight into the conditions my pilots face, and there's not much point in my flying in the first place unless I fly operational aircraft as well as trainers.'

'Which the Hurricane is not,' the Admiral snapped in the way which had begun to be familiar.

'Not now, sir, but it is the final stepping stone to aircraft like the Seafire and from the Seafire to the Corsair, which my pilots *are* flying in operations.'

The Admiral was marshalling his thoughts for a further assault. Thurston looked round the cabin, at the Admiral's pictures on the bulkheads and his books in the bookcase. Since he had arrived on board *Inflexible*, and the Rear Admiral's flag had been hoisted, the Admiral had been pleasant enough, dined with him in private one night and discussed the squadron and the forthcoming operations at length, canvassed his opinion on service matters, and appeared intent upon avoiding any repetition of the clash which had developed between himself and the previous flag captain.

'Captain Thurston, it is quite obvious to me that you've been running a private ship for far too long. You've had a good war, and generally succeeded in covering yourself with glory. You've got a good VC, I can hardly deny that, but it's becoming all too clear that all that has gone to your head. As my flag captain I expect some co-operation from you. I do not expect, neither will I tolerate, the kind of bolshiness that I had to put up with from your friend Strickland.'

The Admiral had been standing on the far side of his desk. He now moved close to Thurston, fixed his eyes on the red ribbon. The top of his head barely reached Thurston's chin; Thurston could smell his hair oil a few inches beneath his nostrils. It was a piece of psychological warfare that might be expected of a Whale Island drill instructor, but unusual, to say the least, from a flag officer to his flag captain. 'Is that understood?'

Thurston concentrated his attention on a patch of bulkhead opposite, where a hairline crack ran diagonally across the pale green paintwork. He was surprised at the extent of the Admiral's fury. Winthrop had a temper, he had seen that before, and perhaps he should have waited to hear the Admiral's views before flying again, but the Admiral's anger and sheer venom was completely out of proportion to the circumstances. He could feel his jaw muscles tightening, the red flush of anger spreading across his face, kept his voice level with an effort. 'You've made your meaning quite clear, sir.'

'Thank you. I'm pleased to hear it.' The Admiral stepped one pace back, turned abruptly and went back to the desk, picked up the half-smoked cigar which rested in the ashtray. 'Thurston, I am not prepared to have you gallivanting about the sky when you should be concentrating your attentions upon this ship. Quite apart from anything else, you have so far failed to produce the man responsible for splashing the *Persephone* business all over the Aussie press.'

'Every officer and man on board has been interviewed, or will be interviewed. No one has admitted anything as yet.'

For the last few days men had been summoned to their divisional officers at odd times in between their normal duties, and formally asked the same brief questions. So far, every answer had been in the negative, and few expected any other result.

'Thurston, you have failed to advance any compelling reason why you should be flying at all, and certainly no reason which could justify your neglecting your ship in the way you obviously have been. It is my view that it is neither necessary nor even advantageous for you to fly, whatever Their Lordships' view of the matter. The Fifth Sea Lord's polishing the seat of his trousers in Whitehall. I'm here, and I'm not prepared to have you neglect your ship in order to fly.'

Thurston felt a hot rush of rage, his fists clenching by his sides. 'If my flying meant that I was neglecting my ship, sir, I would not be doing it. My flying is done in such time as I can legitimately spare from my duties as Captain, and if I prefer to use this time to fly rather than to go ashore and play golf, then I believe it is my own affair.'

'Captain Thurston, I am warning you that you are treading on very thin ice. I am not prepared to tolerate insubordination from you or from anyone else. This discussion has gone on long enough. I have made my position quite clear, and in case you cannot understand plain words, I am now giving you a direct order, which I expect to be obeyed. As of this moment, and until further notice, you will not fly other than as a passenger without my express authority. And if you are foolish enough to flout my orders, I will not hesitate to have you court-martialled. Is that clear?'

'Quite clear, sir.'

'I am pleased to hear it.' The Admiral picked up a pen from his desk.

'Is that all, sir?'

'There is one other thing, Thurston.' The Admiral laid the pen down on the blotter. 'You're not a mid-shipman any longer, and it's no business of mine what you do with yourself ashore, *provided it doesn't show up the service in a bad light.*'

How had the Admiral found out about Jane? Perhaps he hadn't, perhaps this was no more than a ranging shot. So Thurston said nothing, stood quite still, determined that his face would give nothing away. The silence seemed to stretch into minutes, the Admiral waiting for him to respond. But an indignant denial of any impropriety would only act as an admission, so he continued to say nothing.

'You may go,' the Admiral eventually said in dismissal, almost as an afterthought.

Back in his own cabin, Thurston went into the bathroom and swore at the bulkhead for several minutes.

As he had expected, the honeymoon period after the Admiral's arrival was over. There was no repetition of the confrontation which had occurred on the Sunday morning, but in the last days before the Fleet left Sydney it was as if the Admiral was going out of his way to find fault with *Inflexible*, with her officers and with her ship's company, so that time spent with Jane became more precious than ever. If the Admiral did indeed know about his association with Jane, and he doubted that he had done more than draw the obvious conclusion from his regular evening visits to the North Shore, he was angry enough not to care. Adultery, provided, of course, that it was discreet, was tacitly accepted by the service; indeed some cynics might claim that it was almost expected of red-blooded naval officers who spent months and years apart from their wives.

'He sounds an absolute beast,' Jane told him. 'Isn't there anything you can do about it?'

'He's an admiral and I'm not. He may simmer down when he decides that he's thrown his weight about enough. He's being a typical new broom. They come on board determined to make their mark, they turn everything upside down for the first six weeks, and then they suddenly realise that perhaps things weren't quite as sloppy and inefficient under their predecessor as they thought, and so they settle down and like as not finish up running things in much the same way as he did.' He was making light of it all in front of Jane, and wondered if he too had been overreacting, seeing personal antagonism where there was only a desire to run a tight ship.

'Are you going to be an admiral?'

'Not for a few years yet. I'm not senior enough. And

354

certainly not if Winthrop were to write my next confidential report now.' Jane's hand squeezed his. 'In any
case, I might not stay in the service after this lot's over.'
It was the first time he had voiced this to anyone apart
from Kate and his father. 'By the time I leave *Inflexible*
I'll have had all the sea time I'm due as a captain, and
more. It's been made quite clear to me that it's time I
was reminded what a desk looks like and that I can expect nothing but shore jobs from now on.'

'But surely they must realise that you're good at what
you're doing now?'

'Yes, but there are only so many ships to go round,
and a lot of other chaps champing at the bit to get their
hands on them. And before they promote me, Their
Lordships will want to satisfy themselves that I can
function behind a desk as well as on a bridge.'

'If you did leave the Navy, what would you do? I
can't really imagine you doing anything else.'

'I know a chap who has a place in Northumberland,
not very far from where my father lives, about four
thousand acres of farmland, mainly grazing, in seven or
eight farms, plus some forestry and shooting. Known
him a long time, in fact since I was a boy. He's asked
me to run it for him once the war's over. His agent's
getting on and the place has been allowed to get very
run down; he wants a new broom to put some effort
into sorting it out.'

'Are you going to?'

'I don't know.' Masters' offer had lain in the back of
his mind for a full year now, but it was many weeks
since he had consciously thought about it, and the first
time he had spoken of it other than to Kate and his
father. 'It would please Kate; she'd like to settle down
somewhere instead of having to uproot every couple of
years. She doesn't say very much about it, but she's had
a bellyful of it all.'

'But you wouldn't give up the Navy just for Kate?'

'No, of course not. But I've been in the Navy since I

was twelve. Perhaps it's about time I did something else.' He stretched his arms above his head and laughed. 'The eternal sailor's dream. The matelot dreams dreams of a whitewashed cottage with roses round the door, the admiral of buying a country seat with his prize money. But all that's academic at the moment. We've got to finish the war first. And I'll manage with Winthrop. Once we're back at sea he'll have a bit more to occupy himself with than chasing us.'

Jane's face fell at the reminder. As the time of his departure drew nearer she grew hungry for contact with him, moving up against him on the sofa where earlier she had been content to sit opposite, her hand sooner or later beginning to wander over his thigh as a signal that she wanted him inside her again. She had grown bolder, too, more ready to take the initiative, surprising him with her inventiveness, so that he found himself spurred on to experiment with ways of lovemaking he had left unpractised since the early days of his marriage, the few heady weeks when he and Kate were still discovering each other, and which had ended when Kate found that she was expecting George.

He found himself wrestling with her in front of the sitting-room fire, the light of the flames playing over their entwined bodies. But though in the recesses of his mind he knew he was doing wrong, that he was betraying Kate and his marriage, there was a curious sense of innocence about it, as though Jane were Kate and the journey of discovery was being made anew. He had Jane, sometimes with gentleness, at other times made fierce by urgency and the short time they had left, but always with delight and a melting tenderness for her which was as powerful as the lust.

'There's something I've been meaning to ask you. We're having a cocktail party on board before we sail. I'm asking Jack and Mary anyway, but would you like to come as well?'

356

'Are you sure?'

She meant was it safe? 'I'll be on parade, so I won't be able to see much of you. You've always said you'd like to see the ship. I thought you might enjoy it.'

She thought for a moment. 'Yes, I would like to.' She sounded unsure of herself.

'MacLeod will pick you all up from the ferry landing at 1845, and we can have some supper in my cabin afterwards. Do you like curry? My PO Cook's good with curry.' He noticed her expression. 'You don't have to come if you don't want to.'

'No, I would like to. After all, it's the only chance I'm going to get to see your ship, and I suppose it'll be the last chance I'll have to see you.' She gave a deep sigh which was almost a gasp, and looked away from him. 'Oh, I'm sorry, Robert, it was stupid of me to think that it would be any different. You're going back to sea, and heaven knows where you'll go after that, and you've got Kate and of course you're going back to her.'

Yes, he was going back to Kate – if Kate was prepared to have him after this – but he knew that it was going to be a wrench to leave Jane.

'Jane, you knew this was going to happen.' In the confusion of his feelings for Jane, overlying and coexisting with the permanency of his ties to Kate, he was finding it more and more difficult to put into words what he felt, so that the statement came out more harshly than he intended.

'Yes, and at least you've never tried to fool me into thinking it wouldn't. I suppose I should be grateful to you for that.'

'Look, Jane, it's never been like this with anyone else except for Kate. Dammit, if it hadn't been I'd never have laid a finger on you. There are plenty of chaps who might but I happen not to be one of them.' It was coming out all wrong; instead of trying calmly to tell her that she did mean a great deal to him and he was

357

sorry to be leaving her and all that, he had found himself pushed on to the defensive, his cheeks reddening in the embarrassment and uncertainty.

She snivelled and buried her face in his shoulder, her forehead resting beneath his neck, both her arms around him. He stroked the wisps of hair flying away from the main body at collar level, smelt the slightly antiseptic smell of shampoo which clung to her scalp, felt, more embarrassingly still in the circumstances, the beginnings of an erection.

She raised her head after a moment, sighed deeply once more. 'I love you, you bastard.'

'Jane, it would never have been any good. You're twenty-eight, I'm forty-five, you're married and I'm married. You wouldn't want it to drag on, being my bit on the side. You deserve better than that.'

'I know, I shouldn't blame you for it. I knew you were here today and gone tomorrow, and I can't expect you to throw over your wife for me, but I can't help it.' She sat upright, his arm still around her, looked at him with what was almost defiance. 'I know. It's the war. We met. You gave me something I needed and I gave you something as well.' She rested a hand lightly on his trouser buttons. 'Not just that.' Her thumb and fingers traced the outline of his erection.

'You made me feel wanted, that I had someone who belonged to me again. I don't think I realised just how alone I was until you came along. There were the people at the bank, and Alan's parents of course, but nobody that I could be close to, tell them what was really happening. When Alan was first missing everyone was terribly kind, and even more when my father died almost immediately after, but it wasn't really what I needed. So I came here, and got a job, and that helped, but I couldn't bear people to get too near me for a long time. The girls in the bank had their boyfriends and they'd ask me to join in a foursome, and the boyfriend's friend would be my chap for the night, but it was always as if I was betraying Alan. I didn't want him to come back and I'd been having a good time with other men. It was different with you. You were older than me, and too much of a gentleman, so that was all right. And then I didn't care any more. All I wanted was to have you with me.

'I'll come to your cocktail party. I won't make a scene and embarrass you, and then I'll go back to being the bank manager's secretary, waiting for my husband to come back. But I'll look for your name or your ship's name in the newspapers, and I'll think about you at night, and wonder whether you're all right. But no one will know, not Jack or Mary, not Alan, nor anyone else.'

While she had been speaking her hand had been running almost absent-mindedly over his trouser fly. He kissed her, lifted her skirt and moved his hand over the soft skin of her stomach, then stood up, pulling her upright with him, wrapped one arm round her while the other hand crept downwards into the most secret parts of her. 'Not just this.'

Chapter Twenty-Seven

There was complete but unobtrusive efficiency about the cocktail party, from the moment Jane was handed aboard the Captain's motorboat by Petty Officer MacLeod. Someone told them to watch their step on the ship's accommodation ladder ('Gets slippery when it's wet'), a petty officer with a clipboard glanced at her invitation and ticked her name off on his list. 'If you follow that passage aft, ma'am, someone will show you the way to the wardroom.' Jack and Mary caught up with her, and they walked three abreast along the long grey corridor. Men in uniform stood at every junction, quietly directing them further towards the ship's stern, offered a hand to Mary and herself on the ladders which seemed to appear with increasing frequency. She wished she had thought of this and not worn high heels. 'Just take it slowly, ma'am, and watch where you're putting your feet.'

Picking her way uncertainly on to each rung she felt a rush of envy for a baby-faced sailor who casually put his clipboard between his teeth, put both hands on the metal rails on either side of the ladder, lifted his feet and slid down on his hands as if it was the most natural thing in the world. She thought of the newsreel films she had seen before the war, with film stars dancing and drinking cocktails in huge elegant ballrooms aboard ocean liners. Only this was not a pleasure ship but a machine built for war, as she was reminded by the rifles in their racks, narrow polished lengths of chain through the trigger guards, the barrels blue and dully gleaming, the curt notices on the grey bulkheads, red lettering on white: WATERTIGHT DOOR KEEP SHUT. The doors themselves were open now and fastened back, solid steel inches thick, with eight heavy steel clips around the frames. She imagined them slamming shut, converting the passage into narrow cells a few yards in length, imagined what it would be like to be down here alone, with the ship rolling in a heavy sea and enemy bombs coming down on the vast expanse of flight deck above. Jack noticed her shiver.

'Not cold, are you?'

'No, just thinking.'

It was a relief from her thoughts to see Spencer's familiar form emerge from a knot of blue-clad men in front. 'Hello, ma'am. Nice to see you again. Can I take your coat?'

She had wondered whether she would give herself away by some word or gesture, but she found herself saying quite casually that Captain Thurston had taken her sailing one day and that she had met Spencer then. Spencer was taking the coats, stowing them beneath his arm. 'I'll stick them in the Captain's cabin for now. They'll be all right there. Hope you all like curry. Cookie's got some powerful stuff on the go.' He grinned mischievously.

In the wardroom the same efficiency prevailed. A white-jacketed steward brought a tray of drinks, a young officer with a line of white between the gold lace on his arm introduced himself as John Scott and engaged her in quiet conversation, separating her from Jack and Mary almost without her noticing. He was discreetly attentive, got her another drink when she finished the first, chatted generally about the ship and the time he had spent in Sydney. Jane looked round for Jack and Mary, saw them safely occupied with two other young officers, drinks in their hands, laughing at some story one of them was telling. The young man was the Captain's secretary, and she realised with a flash of annoyance that Thurston must have told him to look after her. She found Thurston with her eyes on the other side of the wardroom, in conversation with a middle-aged man whose face she could vaguely recall from the newspapers.

'Would you like to meet some of our flyers?'

The secretary had used up his flow of small talk. He led her to one of the knots of young men, made introductions and then stepped back a little. The aircrew officers seemed very young, little more than schoolboys, talking only of flying.

'The Yanks told us you can't pull a Corsair out of a spin and he proved it. He got just a bit slow on his final turn and flipped straight in. Not a hope. They had to dig the engine out of the ground, he'd gone in that hard. Not much left of him, of course. First chap we lost from the squadron. Sorry, love, you don't want to be hearing about that sort of thing.'

'Pity we can't get you into a Corsair. You'd make a nice change from ugly mugs like Dave here.' The pilot put his arm around her. She stiffened, and the arm dropped swiftly back to the man's side.

'Would you like a drink?'

'Not just yet. I think I've had enough.'

'No one's ever had enough to drink.'

'You haven't, anyway. What about the time in Greenock?'

'We went on a run ashore in Greenock after we got back from forming in the US and Frankie got through four gallons of beer in one night. Four gallons! You should have seen the state he was in.'

'I don't think she'd have wanted to.'

'And he had to fly the next day.'

'Quick whiff from the oxygen shifts any hangover.'

They all laughed.

'Why don't you come ashore with us once we've got rid of this lot?'

362

'Careful, she's a married woman.'

'Have you got rid of your husband?'

The secretary was trying to ease her away. She shrugged him off. 'My husband was posted missing in Singapore.'

There was a stunned silence, and then a rush of embarrassed apologies. She let the secretary guide her away.

'I'm sorry about that. They've had a bit too much to drink.'

Her annoyance was unworthy. The secretary was pleasant enough, and an undemanding companion. He opened up a little, told her about his home in Scotland and the Wren officer he was engaged to. She wondered how much he knew, what he would say if she told him she was his Captain's mistress. Perhaps he did know; Thurston had mentioned once that he'd had to leave her address with his secretary 'in case something comes up'. Just the address, not her name, but it wouldn't be difficult to work it out. But she supposed that discretion was part of his job.

She noticed that the compartment was beginning to empty. 'The band are going to beat Retreat.' The secretary guided her up to the flight deck, found her a place to watch as music began to drift over the deck, faintly at first and then becoming louder.

'Where are they?'

The secretary grinned. 'Watch.'

She noticed a black hole in the deck near the bows, realised that that was where the music was coming from, just as the forward lift came up from the hangar. A spotlight flashed on, reflected off the white sun helmets of the Marine bandsmen and the polished brass of their instruments, their feet lifting off the deck as they marked time.

'Band and Drums, slo-ow MARCH.'

The cadence and the music changed, the band marched and counter-marched over the deck, one march seamlessly succeeding another. 'Good, aren't they,' the secretary said with understated pride. She watched as the drummers separated from the rest and formed up in a single line as the remainder continued to play. The music stopped, and the drums began to beat alone, the drumsticks moving up and down in perfect unison, all the right hands together, all the left hands together, the sound reaching a climax, and then gradually made to fade away into the darkness.

Then the spotlight flashed on the bugles as they sounded a long call which searched the heart, and carried with it three hundred years of glory, and another searchlight rested on the white ensign as it came slowly down from the masthead. 'That's Sunset,' the secretary whispered. A woman snivelled nearby, then looked away to hide her embarrassment. The Drum Major came forward and saluted; she could see Thurston standing on a low platform by himself and saying something as he returned the salute. The band played 'God Save the King'; the civilians straightened up and pushed out their chests, the officers saluted. Then other familiar tunes, 'A Life on the Ocean Wave', 'Hearts of Oak', and finally 'Waltzing Matilda' as they marched away, fading into the darkness as the lift went down into the hangar once more. Jane sniffed, groped for her handkerchief.

'Are you all right?'

'Yes, I think so. Sorry, it's silly of me.'

'I know. It gets to all of us sometimes.' He smiled in knowledge of shared experience.

She wondered just how many of these young men would be part of this again; remembered that the brash schoolboy pilots would be taking off from this deck against the Japanese in a few more days.

'Shall I get you a drink?' the secretary asked politely.

Back down to the wardroom to be reunited with Jack and Mary, and then to the Captain's cabin to be faced with a sideboard spread with bowls of rice, two different curries and various side dishes. They served themselves, sat down at the dining table, ate and talked, of ordinary things, divorced from the war, the farm, the weather, the prospects for the British general election. She was conscious of the resentment again. *He's been in my bed every night for weeks, and he acts as though he hardly knows me.* But, of course, he was covering his tracks, making sure that he did not betray anything in front of her husband's parents. She wondered once more where Alan was, what he was doing, somewhere deep in the Malayan jungle, half starved and beaten by his Japanese guards, while she loved another man.

She asked where the bathroom was and went through into Thurston's sleeping cabin. It was in near-darkness, lit only by the light above the bed, spartan and ordered, a telephone at the head of the bed in case he had to be called at night, no curtains, only a raised steel deadlight over the scuttle. She had expected a bunk, but instead there was a brass bed which filled half the width of the cabin. It might have been unoccupied; the sheets on the bed were unused, pressed into knife-edged creases ('I know why that is,' she thought to herself), the waste-paper basket empty, clothes and shoes put away. The only softening touches were photographs, one on the locker top next to the bed which could only be Kate, and a young man in midshipman's uniform who must be George. Kate, who had shared his life for twenty years; Kate who was the mother of his children; Kate, the good naval wife who had been to see all the widows after *Connaught* was sunk, and still wrote to some of them. ('Most of the men were reservists and didn't live very far away, but it took Kate about three months to get round them all.') The quiet cabin with its austere service pattern furnishings brought home even more forcefully than the beating of Retreat that she was only a peripheral part of his life, that this was his world, which she could never be part of. She went into the bathroom, splashed her face with water, dealt with the damage to her make-up, determined to face up to things as they really were.

'You were a long time,' Jack said. 'Did you get lost?'

'Well, thanks for a great evening, Bob, but I think we'll have to be going. Cows will still want milking tomorrow, no matter what time we've got back the night before. We've left the car at Jane's so we can see her back.'

There was a brief few minutes after Jack and Mary had both decided to use the bathroom when she found herself alone with Thurston for the first time that evening.

'I hope Scott looked after you properly.'

'Yes, he was very good.'

Thurston's voice dropped lower, almost to a whisper, for the sleeping cabin was separated from the main one by only a curtain. 'I can come across later on, if you want me to.'

She found herself saying yes, even though it would only prolong the parting. All over Sydney there would be the same partings tonight, the sailor and his girl saying goodbye, the promises which would not be kept.

'I'll come across in about an hour then. That should give you time to get rid of Jack and Mary.'

They heard footsteps, a rustling as the curtain was drawn back, and Jack Roper emerged. Jane wondered whether he had heard anything, but he gave no sign.

Thurston put on his raincoat, pushed his razor, soap and brush into one of the pockets, went up on deck to await the return of MacLeod with the Captain's boat. The sky which had been clear earlier was ragged now with broken cloud, promising rain before the morning, the moon shining through one of the gaps, faintly luminous, a few points of starlight around it. After tonight it would be over, and mingled with the regret there was relief too that the deceit was ended and with it his betrayal of his marriage. He wondered whether he had been using Jane all this time; he had slept with her, allowed her to fall in love with him, and now he was about to cast her aside, to go back to his war, to try to forget her.

She was sitting in her window as he walked up the street, fair hair outlined in the light from inside the room.

'You looked like the Lady of Shalott just now.'

As he stepped over the threshold she came towards him, rested her head on his chest. His arms went around her; he stroked her hair, kissed the top of her head.

'I'm going to miss you.'

'I'm going to miss you too.'

'Really?' she said, as if she was uncertain of the truth of his words.

'Yes.' He stepped back a little, bent to kiss her mouth. Her face turned upwards to meet his, one of her hands smoothed the medal ribbons. 'Do you want to? I mean, I'm going off tomorrow.'

She did not speak, returning the kiss in silence, her hand moving to caress the nape of his neck, to hold his mouth to hers. He steered her towards the bedroom, undressed her, continuing all the time to kiss her, found her nipples with his tongue and explored her with his fingers. The act was both fierce and tender at the same time, their mouths locked together, her hands bearing down on his buttocks as if she was trying to force more of him inside her, then wandering over his back as they came down from the summit. They lay together for a time, quietly, without speaking more than a few words,

367

then her hands began to move on him, rousing him again. She mounted him, and they rode on together until both were sated, then she came to rest gently on his chest, he put his arms around her, and they slept.

He awoke early from force of habit, propped himself on one elbow to look at Jane as she lay curled against him, reminded irresistibly of his many partings from Kate. There were the same ingredients, the final love-making which was tinged with desperation as well as tenderness, the apprehension of what was to come, the unanswered question of when, and even if they might meet again. She stirred, half awake, her hand stealing down into his groin once more.

'Leave me alone,' he chaffed her, lifting the hand away. 'You've worn him out and he's got to go on a long sea voyage to recover.' He lay back on the pillows, put his arms round her and pulled her over on top of him.

'You will be careful.'

'I'll be all right. I'm a professional survivor.'

He had said the same words to Kate, a year and a half ago, and in the same circumstances. Bare weeks after that, a U-boat had got *Crusader* and he had been struggling in a below-freezing sea, resigning himself to death alone in the Arctic darkness. Out here there were no U-boats, but there were the kamikazes, prepared to press home their attacks to the ultimate, smashing their bomb-laden aircraft on the carriers' vulnerable parts for the glory of their Emperor.

'Would you like me to make you some breakfast?'

'Cornflakes again?'

'I can do better than that. Steak and eggs.'

'Australia's contribution to civilisation.'

'And toast and two kinds of marmalade.'

'Done.'

She lifted herself away from him, and there was a faint stirring of desire at the sight of her breasts, and

368

the bush of pubic hair slick with his seed. Forget it. *Shagged out*, Spencer would have said.

'Well, we've sure left some broken hearts behind us,' Murillo remarked.

Every space on the waterfront was occupied, people sitting on the tops of walls, children being held up to watch, an assemblage of harbour tugs and small boats following the Fleet as the warships left Sydney. Thurston found himself wondering whether Jane was somewhere out there; resisted the temptation to look for her through his binoculars.

'Look at all those lovelies. Why didn't I meet any of them?' sighed Midshipman Jacobs.

'Because they've got more taste and discrimination than to go for a pipsqueak like you.'

'Your problem is that the rabbi cut off the wrong bit,' said Bingham.

Jacobs had heard it all before and merely grinned.

'Lots of broken hearts, and angry fathers, and nasty surprises in nine months' time,' mused the Navigator.

'Didn't you have the sense to take proper seamanlike precautions like you guys are always talking about?' enquired Murillo.

There was the familiar banter, but with an unspoken edge beneath. The padre had been asked to hold a church service before leaving, and the men had roared out 'I Vow to Thee, My Country' and 'Lead Us, Heavenly Father, Lead Us', and Thurston had gone up to the lectern to read the first lesson.

> . . . *Only be thou strong and very courageous, that thou mayest observe to do according to all the law, which Moses my servant commanded thee: turn not from it to the right hand or the left, that thou mayest prosper whithersoever thou goest . . . for then thou shalt have good*

369

success. Have I not commanded thee? Be
strong and of a good courage; be not afraid,
neither be thou dismayed: for the Lord thy
God is with thee whithersoever thou goest.

Jane had been dignified at the end, in the same way that
Kate always was when he left her to go back to sea. She
had watched him as he shaved, dressed for work, had
cooked him a plate of steak and eggs and watched him
eat, and finally had said goodbye as though he was only
leaving for another day in some office ashore. He had
said goodbye in the same way; then the effort had been
too much for both of them. They had kissed for the last
time, half inside her flat and half out of her front door,
hearing the footsteps of another tenant as he went
down the stairs on his way to work, but absorbed in
themselves. The usual inadequate words. 'I've got to
go.' 'Look after yourself.' 'I'll be all right.' He had
squeezed her against his chest, then let her go, had
pulled away from her and gone down the stairs, forcing
himself not to look back.

'Steer oh-seven-two. Nothing to port.'
    'Course oh-seven-two, sir. Nothing to port, sir.'
He concentrated on manoeuvring *Inflexible* away
from her anchorage, aware that the Admiral would be
watching for the slightest misjudgement, as would the
captains of the other ships in the squadron. A sharp
crosswind was blowing, and *Inflexible*'s high sides acted
as a sail so that the wind tended to push her from her
course, leaving little room for error. Leaving harbour
had its own ceremonial, the ratings lining the flight-
deck edges, collars flapping in the windstream, bands
playing aboard all of the larger ships. The destroyers,
not to be outdone, were broadcasting records over their
broadcast systems, a noisy medley of sound, mingled
with bugle calls as salutes were made and returned, and
then the sirens of the harbour tugs and shouting from

the small boats keeping pace with the warships. A blue-painted yacht with red sails approached, knifing in towards the carrier's side, two young girls in bathing costumes waving from the deck and blowing kisses.

'Can't we press gang them for one of our boat's crews?'

'Yeoman, signal those idiots to keep clear,' Thurston said irritably.

The Aldis lamp flashed, the boat curved away with a final rueful wave. The band paused for a moment, and then began to play again, the familiar tune cutting into his consciousness, the trite sentimental words that went with it hitting home more than ever before, the final drum rattle beating its way inside his skull.

> *I'm lonesome since I crossed the hill,*
> *Went over moor and valley,*
> *Such heavy thoughts my heart do fill*
> *Since parting from my Sally.*

> *And now I'm bound for Brighton Camp,*
> *Kind heaven then pray guide me,*
> *And bring me safely back again*
> *To the girl I left behind me.*

Chapter Twenty-Eight

Almost as soon as the Fleet was clear of the harbour and the last of the small boats had been left behind, a heavy programme of exercises began. Commander (Air) worked the aircrews hard, and for the gunnery department there were shoots on full and reduced charge by day and night, damage control exercises, and then squadron and Fleet manoeuvres. Bugle calls at unpredictable intervals summoned men to Action Stations, broadcasts clicked on. 'D'ye hear there? For exercise, fire in the canteen flat. For exercise, fire in the canteen flat.' 'D'ye hear there? Hands to Emergency Stations. Hands to Emergency Stations.'

It was a busy and strenuous period, but in a sense it was a relief to shake off the dust of the land after the long period in harbour, to turn again to the work they were trained for, and to prepare for the action that lay ahead. One of *Inflexible*'s Corsair squadrons had been pulled out of line and replaced by another, most of whose pilots had not served aboard a carrier before and had done only the basic quota of deck landings which were part of their training. They could be seen approaching warily, wings rocking a little from side to side as the pilots studied the deck on which they were to land, or coming in fast, eager to get the business over. One, coming in a little too fast and a little too high, ignored the batsman's signals to go round again and overcorrected as he tried to get in the right position for landing at the last moment. The Corsair bounced hard

372

on the deck between two of the wires and slithered out to port before the pilot could catch it. The flight-deck party began to run from the base of the island, hoses unreeling behind them. The Corsair's nose went down into the catwalk below deck level, the tail slowly rising towards the vertical. The pilot had locked his canopy back in accordance with standing orders; the men on deck could see him scrabbling frantically at his straps. One of the flight-deck party reached the aircraft, close enough to put his hand out to the wing tip, then the tail stood straight against the sky for a second, and began to go over. The man turned away and started to walk back, aware that there was nothing more he could do.

The pilot jumped clear, a black shape dropping into the water forty feet below, the aircraft following him, turning over once more so that the nose hit the water first. They saw the pilot's head above the white foam at the ship's side, then he disappeared. One of the destroyers hustled up, lowered a boat and made a slow and painstaking search, but everyone knew it was for form only. The usual letters were written, one by his squadron commander, one by the Captain and one by Commander (Air), an accident report completed, a memorial service held in the ship's chapel, the pilot's effects sorted and parcelled up to be sent to his parents.

The accident signalled the beginning of a lean period, just at a time when it was most necessary for *Inflexible* to show her efficient face. Small defects, not of much consequence in themselves, emerged to slow down or interrupt flying operations, and six weeks in harbour had taken the edge off the men's preparedness for battle. The Admiral made it clear that he was not satisfied with the flagship's performance, a view with which Thurston concurred. But where Thurston knew that the problems would right themselves in a few more days of steady training, as the men got back into seagoing routine once more, the Admiral seemed convinced that the malaise went deeper, made his opinion clear that the officers should get a grip, that there were too many inexperienced petty officers who did not know what they were doing and did not exert their authority sufficiently.

But it was not only *Inflexible* which had difficulties. *Irresistible*'s anti-aircraft crews failed to score a single hit on the towed target in the first full-calibre shoot, and within twenty-four hours of leaving Sydney Strickland had signalled that his ship must return to harbour as defective air compressors prevented her from operating aircraft at all.

'Air compressors. I'll give him air compressors! He's had a month in harbour to put his fucking ship to rights!' the Admiral stormed.

But there was nothing to be done. The former flagship turned and steamed away into the dusk, a destroyer on either bow.

The Fleet called at Manus a week later, a Manus quite unchanged, still, hot, but seemingly more humid than ever. Explosives were dropped over the ships' sides to deter the sharks, and 'Hands to bathe' piped, a guard boat prowling round with an armed sentry on board; but the water in the lagoon was too warm to be refreshing, and few bothered to swim a second time.

Two days out from Manus, just as the setting sun touched the sea to the west, the Commander (E) suddenly telephoned the bridge. 'We've got a problem with the port outer shaft, sir. Have I your permission to stop the shaft while we check it?'

The request was couched in the usual unemotional terms, but there was a worried undertone in the Chief's voice, and Thurston could hear someone else shouting in the background, too far away for his words to be distinguished.

'All right, Chief. Keep me informed.'

The ship slowed and began to lose her station on the rest of the task force, then regained it as the revolutions on the other two shafts increased to take her back up to twenty knots. The entire after part began to vibrate. Pencils fell from the chart table, and it became difficult to remain upright on the bridge.

'What can they be doing down there?' muttered Bingham.

'We don't know how long this is going to last, so pipe everything breakable to be secured,' Thurston told the Officer of the Watch.

Fifteen minutes later Commander Norman came up to the bridge with a worried expression on his usually impassive face. Thurston ushered him into his sea cabin.

'I'm afraid it looks as though we've a run shaft bearing, sir. The port outer shaft suddenly started to run hot and we were just getting hoses on it to try to cool it down when the temperature literally went off the gauge and we couldn't get the shaft stopped in time. I can't be absolutely certain until we've got the covers up and had a look, but it really couldn't be anything else.'

A run bearing was normally a dockyard job, but the task force was one carrier short already. 'Can you deal with it at sea?'

'I think so, sir.' The Chief sounded quietly confident. 'We've got the spares on board, and we can keep going on two shafts for as long as it takes.'

Thurston remembered that the Admiral would have to be told.

'You'd better come with me to see the Admiral, Chief.'

'Yes, sir.'

It was quite dark now, and the Admiral's sea cabin, like his own, was suffocatingly hot, the deadlight clipped down, the fan in the corner merely stirring the humid air. The Admiral was sitting at the desk writing a letter,

375

the ink smearing in the heat, his shirt unbuttoned, his belly hanging flabby and greyish over the waistband of his shorts.

'Yes, what is it?'

Thurston told him in a few brief words.

The Admiral put down his pen, swivelled round on his chair. 'Dammit, you've only just had a refit! What the hell caused it?'

Thurston looked at Norman.

'Something has blocked off the oil supply to the bearing, sir, and caused it to overheat so that the white metal layer inside has melted. What it is I don't yet know.' Norman was still in his overalls, a long streak of oil running down his right sleeve, meeting with another which glistened blackly on the back of his hand.

'And I suppose you're going to say that it's a dock-yard job and we'll have to go back to Sydney! Well, I'm telling you that I can't afford to lose another carrier.'

'The Commander (E) believes he and his staff can deal with it, sir.'

'I should hope so, since they let it happen in the first place.' Norman's jaw tightened, the muscles in his cheeks standing out in hard ridges. 'And is that what's causing this bloody vibration?'

'Yes, sir, because of the shaft being stopped. Because it's one of the outer shafts, we're getting an uneven thrust from the other two, and at these speeds the stationary screw is being dragged through the water sideways. Slowing down would lessen the vibration and eventually stop it altogether.'

'We can't afford to slow down. We've got a rendez-vous to make. How long will it take?'

'I don't know, sir.'

'What do you mean, you don't know? Dammit, it's your job to know! You're supposed to be an engineer!'

'Replacing a run bearing is a very big job, sir, and one that isn't usually attempted at sea. We do have the spares on board, but before we do anything we'll have to give the shaft time to cool down, then get the bearing shells off and the run metal cleaned off. Then the new bearing pads will have to be scraped down to fit. That can be a very slow job, sir. We'll be working to very precise tolerances and we can't afford to rush it. At the same time we'll also need to overhaul the lubricating system for that shaft, and for the other two as well, in case the same sort of trouble is brewing up there.'

'I don't want to hear what you're going to do. I expect you to get on and do it!' The Admiral thumped his fist on the desk top. Thurston found himself looking into the heavy, sensual face, thinking almost inconsequentially that the Admiral's eyebrows met in the middle, and possessed by an insane desire to take a razor to the hair on the Admiral's cheeks.

'Yes, sir,' Norman said evenly.

'Now listen to me, both of you. We've a rendezvous to make with the Americans, and I am not prepared to miss it because my flagship's engineers are incapable of doing the job they're paid to do. I can't afford to lose another carrier, or to have this ship operating at anything other than peak efficiency. There's far too much slackness in this ship, and I want to see an end to it.'

'Yes, sir.'

'Thurston, will you stop saying "Yes sir" to me when I know damn well you mean nothing of the sort. Now, Commander Newman, or whatever your name is, I want you to go away and get those repairs done, and you can report to me when they're completed.'

'The Commander (E) will inform *me* when the repairs are completed, sir, and I will report to you myself.'

'Thank you, Captain Thurston,' the Admiral said in heavily sarcastic tones. 'And I won't listen to any excuses.' The Admiral turned in his chair, the back of his shirt dark with sweat, picked up his pen to go back to his letter. 'That will be all.'

Thurston and Norman left. The Commander (E)

pulled a handkerchief from his pocket and mopped the back of his neck. He managed a weary grin. 'Well, sir, I'd better get started.'

Thurston went back to his sea cabin, took off his sodden shirt and sat at the desk. Two letters from Kate had been in the mail at Manus. He read them both once more, inconsequential stuff about the latest doings of the twins – Thomas, always the bolder of the two, had walked into a deck chair in the garden and given himself a black eye *and yelled so much that I half expected the neighbours to come rushing round to stop me from murdering him.*

Kate. The pricklings of conscience he had felt and ignored in Sydney had intensified since his departure. While he had been with Jane his need for her had overcome everything else, but now there was only remembrance and guilt. He wondered whether Kate would realise what had been going on in Sydney. His letters to her had been briefer and less frequent than usual; there had seemed so little he could actually say to her. Twenty years of marriage, just thrown aside. And the Ropers. Mary had remarked on the night of the cocktail party that Jane was rather taken with him, poor girl. Surely she wouldn't have said that if she had known? But even so he had found himself blushing a little, taking a too-hasty drink from his glass. It had been a near thing. Their son's wife. And what could he say to Kate? *The woman tempted me, and I did eat.* Be your age, Thurston. You seduced her, you used her and then you cast her aside like some tart you'd picked up on the dockside. She was in love with you, dammit, and you took advantage of her.

He added a few lines to the letter he had already started, some silly story Spencer had told him about Billy Bones being found by the Admiral asleep on the bunk in the Admiral's sea cabin and being returned to his master by one of Winthrop's Marine orderlies, who had found it extremely difficult to keep a straight face. Billy was another who didn't think all that much of the new regime. He was curled up at the foot of Thurston's own bunk now, head turned half upwards, front teeth slightly bared, black sides gently rising and falling as he breathed. Officially he remained Spencer's kitten, but more and more he seemed to have attached himself to Thurston, and Spencer had done nothing to stop this. It was all too typical of Spencer. The thought made him smile, and it became easier to get on with the letter, though the underlying thoughts of his betrayal and hypocrisy remained.

The damaged bearing curtailed the flying programme. Each time aircraft flew off or landed on, the carriers had to turn into wind, and with her maximum speed reduced to twenty-four knots it became difficult to overhaul the rest of the Fleet after the evolution had been completed. Flying had to be concentrated into shorter periods in the morning and afternoon watches, the long hours between occupied with more training for the other departments and endless dry training for the flight-deck party, raising and lowering the wires and barriers, trundling aircraft over the deck, trying to shave tenths of seconds off the time it took to range aircraft on the flight deck, or to strike them down in the hangar, or to get a particular aircraft, inevitably the one in the most inaccessible place in the hangar, in position ready for take-off. The dry training, though vital, lacked the realism which flying brought, and there was the danger that the men would be pushed over the hard edge of efficiency and grow bored and stale if the pressure of training was kept up for too long.

It remained suffocatingly hot, the smoke from the carrier's funnel seeming to settle over the deck in an acrid brown cloud, hotter than ever. Water had to be rationed again, turned off for all but a couple of hours in the morning and again in the evening. Men doused themselves with water from the wash-deck salt-water mains in search of momentary relief, but the water dried on the skin in an instant, leaving a whitish deposit which irritated the prickly heat almost beyond endurance. The vibration made life still more uncomfortable. It was impossible to sleep soundly, even though the effort of working in the vibration made men more tired than ever, and everything had to be wedged into place and secured there before it could be worked on.

During the afternoon watch on the third day of the vibration, Thurston went down the long series of ladders to the engine room, Boy Maxwell following at his heels. A wall of heat, damp and almost solid, hit him as the door was opened, making him reach instinctively for a handkerchief to mop his brow, but the sweat was there again in a second, running into his eyes and irritating the lids.

'Bit hot in here, Chief.'

Norman grinned, and indicated the thermometer on the bulkhead, the column of red liquid standing steady at one hundred and forty-two degrees. 'It's been worse, sir. Up to a hundred and seventy before now.' He picked up an enamel mug from a shelf, and dipped it into the bucket beneath. 'Salted water, sir. Better have some before we start.'

Norman led them to the far end of the engine room. 'Watch your heads.'

The shaft tunnel was a long low claustrophobic tube, little more than four feet high, and completely circular. It was damp with water and oil, separated from the bilge beneath by a metal grating which was slightly slippery underfoot, making it difficult at first for Thurston to stay on his feet, and unlit except by Norman's torch and another light far ahead. 'We've normally got electric light in here, but the bulbs keep going and we're not going to bother replacing them at the moment.'

The vibration here, only feet away from the twenty-foot-diameter phosphor-bronze screws, was more marked than ever, rattling Thurston's teeth and shaking him from side to side. The shaft ran a few inches above the floor, static now and discoloured with oil smears, stretching away into the darkness. With the shaft stopped it was very quiet, except for the noise of the vibration, a faint echoing of voices coming from further on, a sudden dull impact of metal against metal, and then more talking. They were far below the water line now; the bilge beneath their feet was the deepest part of the ship, cut off from the engine room by two watertight doors. Oily water gleamed in the bilge, and where the shaft went out into the water there was only a layer of the oil-bearing wood, lignum vitae, to keep the sea from flooding in through the breach in the ship's plates. It was cooler in the shaft tunnel than in the engine room itself, but Thurston knew it was not the change in temperature which made him shiver and made his flesh creep a little inside the overalls he was wearing. He glanced back, saw Maxwell's face looking pale through the dimness, and found himself obscurely relieved that he was not the only one who found the place unpleasant.

There was a sudden blaze of light from a lamp hung up on a bracket, and the crouched shapes of men ahead, three dark silhouettes against the light.

'This is it, sir.' Norman dropped into a squat as one of the men moved aside to make a space for him. Thurston followed suit, wincing as his back straightened from its crouch. 'How's it going?'

'Not too bad, sir. We're getting nearer.' The man patted the lower half of the bearing shell which lay on the floor of the tunnel next to him. 'All right to take a breather, sir?'

'Of course. We've just come to see what you're up to.'

There was another bucket of water to hand. More mugs were dipped into it, and handed round, backs settled against the sides of the tunnel, one man's face relaxing into a smile of relief as he took a long swig of the salty water.

'As you see, sir, we've now got the covers off the bearing, and cleaned off the muck that was left by the white metal running. That took us longer than we'd hoped; it's just the sort of place where you'd rather not have to use lifting tackle, and a couple of the bolts had rusted in so that we had a job to get them out. It took the better part of a day, all told, because after we stopped the shaft it had to be allowed to cool down before we could touch anything on it.' The Chief grinned. 'Actually, the shaft isn't quite stopped, though you can't see it moving, because we've had to put turning gear on it.'

Thurston looked puzzled, and Norman explained. 'The shaft is very heavy, and unsupported for most of its length. If we stopped the shaft completely, and left it stopped, it would start to distort under its own weight, which would create all sorts of problems later on. If you remember, sir, *Illustrious* had a distorted centre shaft a few months ago, and they had so much trouble with it that they had to take it right out in the end, and operate on the two outer shafts. Fortunately for them, with it being the centre shaft they wouldn't have had the vibration we've been getting. So, what we've had to do is connect a little electric motor up, which keeps the shaft turning very slowly, something like one revolution in twenty minutes, which is just enough to stop it from distorting, but doesn't stop us from working on it.'

One of the ERAs smiled. 'Learn something new every day, sir.' At some time he had taken off his overalls in the heat and was wearing only his underpants, which, like his body and legs, were damp with sweat and streaked black with oil, and he had a strip of rag tied round his head to keep the sweat from running into his eyes. Resting against the bare metal behind, legs drawn up in front, he managed to appear a picture of contentment, even in these surroundings.

'Where have you got to now, Chief?'

'We're now scraping down the new bearing shells to fit the shaft. What we do is put a layer of blue stuff on the inside, try it against the shaft, and where the blue's come off that's a high spot and we file it down. Then we try it again, and we'll keep on doing it until we've got rid of all the high spots. Once that's done, and you'll appreciate, sir, that it's a slow business and we can't afford to take short cuts, we carry on scraping until we've got the bearing shells to the correct tolerances.

'What we do is put little strips of lead between the bearing shell and the shaft. They get squashed flat, of course, and then we measure the thickness of the strips with a micrometer gauge. And we carry on scraping the shells until the lead strips are squashed to the correct thickness all round the bearing. Primitive, but it works. Unfortunately, it tends to take a long time, unless you're very lucky and the new bearing shell happens to be a fairly good fit to begin with. This one wasn't, unfortunately.'

'Can you say yet when you're likely to be finished?'

'I'm afraid not, sir.' Norman looked uncomfortable.

'It's all right, Chief. I can see you're all working like blacks on it, and I don't suppose this vibration will help.' The salted water was slopping over the rim of the mug in his hand.

'Thank you, sir.'

Thurston put down the mug, creating a small echo which ran up and down the tunnel. 'I'd better leave you to get on with it.'

'It's good of you to come and see us, sir.'

Thurston brushed it aside. 'Oh, I just thought I'd

better see what was happening,' but he knew that even a brief visit to the site of the problem would have given the engine-room staff a boost. Too often they felt they were ignored by the executive branch when things went well, lambasted when they did not, and given scant recognition for their efforts at any time.

Out into the brightness of the engine room again, the second of the watertight doors shutting reassuringly behind them. Maxwell's breath came out in an audible sigh.

'Glad to be out of there, Maxwell?'

A blush coloured Maxwell's pallor. 'Yes, sir.'

'It's all right, Maxwell. I didn't enjoy it very much myself.'

'While we're working on the bearing itself, I've also got a party overhauling the lubricating system for all three shafts. Do you have time for a quick look, sir?'

Thurston glanced at his watch. 'Yes, but it had better be fairly quick.' The Avenger squadron was due to begin landing on in half an hour.

'If you come this way, sir.'

In another part of the engine room a lubricating oil pump had been dismantled and its parts spread out on an old piece of tarpaulin. Two more ERAs were at work with wire wool and bits of oily rag, one in gaudily striped swimming trunks, the other with the top half of his overalls pushed down and the sleeves knotted round his waist. They were under the supervision of a young officer whose eyes, like the ERAs', were red-rimmed with fatigue, and who swayed gently on his feet in time with the vibration. 'I've put young Holland in charge of this, sir, since he worked at Parsons and knows his way round the system better than most of us.'

Holland woke from his daze, realised who it was standing in front of him and stiffened to attention, looking rigidly past Thurston's shoulder.

'How are you getting on, Holland?'

'All right, sir. We've nearly finished with this pump and we'll start putting it back together once ERA Fife here has finished what he's doing.' The man in swimming trunks looked up briefly, and then went back to the piece of metal he was working on. 'We can't do such a complete job on the others while the shafts are turning, but we've been over them now and they look all right.' There was a hint of pride coming into Holland's voice at a job well done. 'And we've found what was blocking the oil feed, sir.' Holland fished in the pocket of his overalls, held a fragment of oil-filmed metal up to the light. 'It looks like it's broken off the thrust and adjusting block. It was jammed up inside the pipe, sir, face on, so there was only a trickle getting past it. We had to cut the pipe up to get it out, and then braze it back together again.'

'Rotten job in this heat.'

'Yes, sir.' Holland seemed about to say more, then he remembered who he was speaking to, and stopped abruptly.

'Good lad, Holland,' Chief said after they had moved away. 'He's doing all that in addition to his normal watches and I've had to order him out a couple of times to make sure he gets some rest.'

'It looks as though I might have to do the same with you, Chief.'

'Oh, I'm all right, sir. I've got a camp bed rigged and I get my head down for a couple of hours when I feel like it. And Pay's keeping us supplied with soup and sandwiches so we don't have to keep breaking off for meals.'

'Is there anything else you need?'

'I don't think so, sir.' The Chief looked at another of the buckets of salted water that lay in various corners of the engine room. 'The chaps are all saying that they

385

wish they could have beer instead, but if that's the only thing they're grumbling about I think they're happy enough.'

It was another of those strange phenomena Thurston had often noticed in the past. The British matelot grumbled when things were going well and his life was comparatively easy, but when things became difficult, he was at Action Stations twenty hours a day in the worst of weather conditions, and not only did the grumbling cease, but a kind of defiant cheerfulness would supersede it.

'How much longer is he going to be?'

'I don't know, sir.'

'What are they doing down there? You'd think they could have finished the job by now.'

'Replacing a run bearing is normally a dockyard job, sir, and my Commander (E) and his staff are doing all they can. They're working twenty-four hours a day on it, in addition to their normal steaming watches and the conditions they're working in are absolutely hellish.'

Thurston was angry on behalf of the men toiling in the heat and darkness of the shaft tunnel, wondered again whether the Admiral was deliberately trying to provoke him. Probably not, he told himself. The Admiral was worried about making the rendezvous with the Americans. It had taken a long time and considerable efforts at the highest level to persuade the Americans that the British Pacific Fleet was battle-ready enough to fight alongside them, and no one wanted the Fleet to show anything but its most efficient face to its allies. The American Navy regarded the Pacific war as theirs, had been developing and prosecuting carrier warfare against the Japanese for the past three years, while the British had been occupied in a very different kind of war in other oceans. The Americans, some with a wariness about the British which went back to the Revolution and the War of 1812, regarded the Royal Navy as interlopers, and were sceptical about the contribution their three carriers could make to the final assault on Japan. The Americans had thirteen carriers, each with nearly a hundred aircraft on board, compared with the forty or fifty the British could carry.

'But we've got armoured decks, and they haven't,' the British always reminded themselves. 'Their carriers may have more aircraft, but they're not much bloody use when a kamikaze hits them and they have to stagger back to Pearl for six months.'

Evening came once more, and flying finished for the day, the last Corsair landing on in a screech of wheels, and then being trundled forward to the lift and taken below to the hangar where the nightly servicing routine was already in progress. The weather had been worsening all day, the wind and sea rising and grey cloud thickening over the sky. In the hangar double lashings had been put on all the aircraft, and a party was checking and rechecking the lashings on the dozen Corsairs parked on the flight deck abreast the island.

'Looks as though we're in for a blow, sir,' the Instructor Lieutenant commented as he came up with the met an hour later.

He spread his chart out on the hooded table to the rear of the bridge, waited until Thurston had moved in alongside him. 'You see that low coming in, sir?' The isobars were packed together, circling an irregularly shaped core. 'And all the Yank met stations are reporting high winds – over thirty knots in places. I've just had another look at our glass, and it's gone down over five millibars in the last hour.'

Thurston thought for a moment. 'This is the typhoon belt, isn't it, and the season.'

'Yes, sir. They can happen at any time, but you get most of them at this time of year, especially the big 'uns, and anywhere between about seven and fifteen degrees north.'

'And on this course we're going to run straight into it.'

'I think we'll miss the centre, sir, if it sticks to the usual pattern and keeps moving west-nor'-west as it is at the moment, assuming that this low is going to be the storm centre in a few hours' time, when the typhoon's had time to build up properly.'

'You sound as though you're looking forward to it.'

'As a matter of professional interest, sir,' Schooly said in the dry manner of the traditional pedagogue, looking over spectacles that were misted in rain from the sudden squall which was sweeping over their heads.

'So in order to satisfy your professional curiosity, we've got to weather a full-scale typhoon just to prove that the textbooks are correct.'

'If we keep to our present course and speed I think we have little choice, sir. As I've already said, the centre should miss us by a fair margin if the typhoon behaves according to type, but we're in for a very rough ride whatever happens. And if the storm does a kind of dogleg east-nor'-east, as they quite often do, we could find it hitting us.'

'We've all got to fuel tomorrow. *We'll* manage for another day or two on the fuel we've got, but if we're going into a typhoon I'd like a bit more fuel in the bunkers. And the destroyers are riding very light now. They'll be in real trouble if they don't get some more weight below the water line.' He was speaking almost to himself, the Instructor Lieutenant peering at him upwards over the wet lenses. 'Thank you, Schooly. Keep me informed.'

Through the darkness it was possible to see the white foam which streaked the dark waves as they moved inexorably onwards. The wind and sea were coming from the same direction, *Inflexible* lifting herself ponderously over each wave and sliding down the far side of the crest and into the trough.

'Going to be some full buckets below tonight,' someone said.

'And tomorrow. Be ready with the lashings when you get to your bunk.'

'I prefer a different kind of lashing,' said Bingham in unmistakably camp tones.

Even if Schooly's met report had been for the ears of Captain and Officer of the Watch only, the significance of the rising wind and sea had not been lost on the rest.

Chapter Twenty-Nine

The next morning the situation was no longer in doubt. The waves were larger than Thurston and most of those around him had ever experienced, so large that as the destroyers went into the troughs between they disappeared from view for long minutes, until they could once more be seen dragging themselves up towards the crest.

'And we've got to fuel in this?' one of the signalmen said, wide-eyed.

'Got no choice,' the Yeoman said brusquely. 'And instead of standing there gawping, you can go and straighten up the flag locker.'

'In this, Yeoman?'

'You heard me. And use what little common sense you've got and make sure you don't end up with half the stuff flying about like mummy's wet washing on a Monday morning.'

The Signalman went away, glancing back at his superior in wonderment.

'Give the little blighter something to do, sir,' the Yeoman remarked to Carstairs, who had the watch.

Thurston had forced himself to go below at midnight for a few hours in his bunk, knowing that it was vital he be alert for the fuelling, which in the present conditions was certain to take most of the day. But he had slept little, and it had been a relief to get back into his oilskins and go up to the bridge once more. Despite the wind, strong enough now to howl and occasionally

scream as it eddied about the island, it was still uncomfortably hot, so that he was as wet with sweat as with
rain which forced its way down his neck and up his
sleeves, and the spray which had begun to reach even
the bridge, seventy feet above the water line. All those
not actually required on watch had been told to get into
their hammocks and to stay there, so that the ship
seemed more empty than usual, strangely ghost-like in
the gloom.

'Fuelling group in sight, sir,' the port lookout reported.
  'Challenge them.'
This was the correct rendezvous, and the fuelling
group was expected, but you could never be certain. In
all the greyness the distant shapes looked strangely
sinister, as though they might indeed be Japanese warships instead of a motley assortment of tankers with
their escorts. The Aldis lamp flashed into the grey
murk, and a moment later there was an answering
flash, unexpectedly dim through the gloom.
  'Weather's clamping in,' someone said unnecessarily.
  'Correct, sir,' the Yeoman reported.

The fuelling group split up, and the tankers moved out
to meet the individual warships.
  'Tell him I want him to come up on my port side.'
  'Aye aye, sir.'
The wind and sea were on the starboard bow, and
would tend to carry *Inflexible* down on to the tanker,
but *Inflexible* was a much larger ship and might offer
her some shelter. The Chief Quartermaster was on the
wheel, working turn about with his most experienced
quartermaster, and the Commander had personally
picked a good man with the Coston gun to shoot the
line across to the tanker.

The tanker came up on *Inflexible*'s port side, her tattered red ensign streaming back in the wind, and rolled

wickedly to port so that red lead showed all along her water line. The first three lines were whipped away aft in the seventy-mile-an-hour wind.

'Have to go round again,' someone muttered.

In a sudden lull they heard the high crack as the gun went off, saw the metal rod flying across the gap.

'Nice shot.'

Another gust, and the line was flying away towards the tanker's stern. A clang as the rod hit one of the upright iron stanchions, and someone was running across the deck, bundled up in oilskins that were shiny with water. The tanker rolled to starboard, her rails dipping below the water so that the man was suddenly waist-deep in the sea.

'Hope he's got a bloody lifeline.'

The man was up against the tanker's rails, scrabbling under the water.

'Come on!'

Suddenly a hand went up, waving above the man's head, the other hand grasping the rail.

'He's got it!'

Then other men were joining him, hauling the line in, and the heavier messenger attached to it, then finally the hose itself, a huge black snake dipping into the water between the two ships and rising out of it, 'like the Loch Ness monster' as some wag had once said, a simile which had remained in Thurston's mind ever since. Men were at work on the tanker's deck, some getting the open end of the hose into position and holding it there, others working on either side with spanners to anchor it so that the fuelling could begin. The deck was thirty or more feet above the water line, but with each roll to port they were half-buried in tons of water, saved only by their lifelines from going over the side as the water fell away.

Quite suddenly the job was done. A green flag appeared on the tanker's bridge and the black hose began to pulsate as the tanker's pumps forced the fuel oil through it. All the time that the hose was being connected Thurston had been holding *Inflexible* on her course, keeping her in the same position relative to the tanker with small alterations of course and one and two revolution increases and decreases on the engines, and this would have to be kept up all the time they were fuelling. The stopped shaft was making the task still more difficult, the thrust of the other two engines continually moving the ship's head to starboard, something else which had to be allowed for as he gave his wheel and engine orders, tried to anticipate the next requirement.

The rain was falling harder, surging in triumph through the gap between collar and neck, soaking the towel he had put there and running down in a small river inside his shirt to create a spreading patch of sodden cloth against his stomach. It was uncomfortable, but the water was sufficiently warm for it not to matter, except as a distraction. The murk, too, had clamped in on them, so that apart from the greyhound shape of a destroyer over to starboard, flung on to her beam ends at times like a child's toy, the ocean could have been empty except for *Inflexible* and the tanker, and the hose which connected them, one second taut, the next dipping in a huge semicircle into the foaming grey water between.

Spencer arrived on the bridge in oilskins and sou'wester, managing to grin despite the effort needed to keep himself upright. 'Cup o' tea, sir. Thought you could do with something.'

It was well meant, but he was concentrating too hard on the job he was doing to shift his mind to the drinking of tea. He held the mug in his hand for a moment, then another wave threw him over to starboard and the contents were lost in the water flowing out of the outlet holes at the base of the bridge screen.

'Do you another one, sir.'

'It's all right, Spencer. Later on.' He wondered how Spencer had avoided losing the tea on the long journey up from the galley.

'Just like old times, sir,' Spencer said, water streaming down his face beneath the sou'wester.

Spencer meant the Stonehenge convoy, the six days on tow after *Marathon* had been torpedoed. She was out there now, refuelling somewhere in the murk, with the Fleet once more after a year of repairs in an American dockyard. A new captain and a new ship's company, of course, who would wonder a little about those who had gone before them, those who had been through the two years in the North Atlantic and Mediterranean, the *Seydlitz* action, the strikes from Malta against the Axis convoys between Italy and North Africa before the island finally became untenable for surface ships, and the fight to get her back to Alexandria after the torpedoing.

The men who had shared those two years with him were scattered now. Some of the regular petty officers might find themselves serving together again in years to come, but most of them would go back to their civilian lives, perhaps meeting occasionally with two or three other ex-*Marathon*s who lived nearby to drink beer and talk of past glories, rekindling the sense of purpose, the feeling of belonging to something greater than themselves, which they had lost in the civilian world and now tried to regain, if only for a brief time.

But Spencer was right in a way. There was once more the struggle, not against a human enemy, but against the sea itself, and the wind which now whipped the sea into a frenzy, stronger even than the gales which had lashed *Marathon* all through those six days. And there was the effort to remain alert, to keep on anticipating the next combination of wind and sea and what it would do to *Inflexible*, to the tanker and to the hose which joined them like an umbilical cord, bringing to the carrier the oil without which she could not operate, could not survive these conditions.

In the same way, too, there was detachment from it all, his eyes constantly watching the hose and the motion of the other ship, his ears absorbing the reports which came from the watchkeepers, his brain making its calculations and his voice speaking the necessary orders, but another part of his brain floating free, so it did not seem that it was himself who was standing at one side of *Inflexible*'s bridge, gripping the bridge screen with both hands to keep himself upright, wet khaki drill moulded to his body. His cap had long gone, lifted off his head and whirled away by an earlier gust, so that his hair hung in damp tendrils over his forehead and more water streamed into his eyes.

Inflexible was no longer riding over the waves, but burrowing her way through them, tossed violently from side to side so that at times her flat expanse of flight deck seemed almost vertical against the sky, blotting the tanker from view for long seconds, and bringing a certainty that the fuelling hose must have given way. Yet each time, as the ship righted itself, the hose was miraculously still there, and another brief profane prayer of thanks went up. Tons of grey water came up over the ship's bow as she hit each oncoming wave, running back almost as far as the island before flowing away.

'Well, Schooly, is your professional curiosity satisfied?'

'Yes, sir.' The Instructor Lieutenant's sharp-featured face was very white, the pallor tinged faintly green with seasickness.

'And is this the typhoon itself?'

'Yes, sir. As you have no doubt gathered, the typhoon struck us on our starboard bow, much as the forecast suggested it would. We are still on the edges of it, sir.' Schooly was maintaining his professional detachment with an effort.

'If this is only the edge, what must it be like nearer the centre?' breathed Carstairs.

'Worse,' Thurston said laconically.

Carstairs raised his eyes to the blackening sky in an expression which meant, 'Can it get worse?'

'Whereabouts is the centre now?'

'We've just managed to pick it up on radar, sir. Almost due south-east of us, and it seems to be heading west, so unless it decides to dog-leg it should pass safely astern of us.' Schooly stopped speaking abruptly, and made a dash for the bucket which was bracketed in one corner of the bridge, already three parts full of water, with a scum of vomit floating on top.

'Wonder how the Yanks are getting on, sir?' said the Torpedo Officer, who was PCO.

'Oh they'll be complaining that they can't have their ice cream and movies today.'

'Oh Ah do feel sorry for those poor bo-oys,' said Carstairs in a very fair Southern drawl.

The Instructor Lieutenant straightened from the bucket, and wiped his mouth with a sodden handkerchief. He looked worse than ever, the pallor now grey rather than white, his long bony nose jutting out of a face which seemed to have lost all its flesh. He grasped the top of the bridge screen, gulped air in several large breaths, then dropped once more to the bucket, doubled over and gasping as he threw up the last of the contents of his stomach. He went on retching for a long time, in painful dry heaves, then finally shuffled away towards the ladder, insisting in a faint voice that he was all right.

It was not yet noon, but in all the mist and water it could have been the dusk of a wet English winter day. A wave smashed into *Inflexible*'s starboard side, spray

396

shot up in a column higher than the mast, and crashed down on the island.

'Ask Commander (E) how much longer the fuelling will take.'

A destroyer emerged from the mist, half a mile away on *Inflexible*'s starboard beam. She rose up over a wave, seemed to balance endlessly on the crest before plunging down into the trough, her screws turning uselessly in air instead of water. For a moment the wave blotted her out, then she reappeared, pushed right over on to her beam ends by another wave, lying there for so long that it seemed impossible that she could ever right herself. The same wave hit *Inflexible*, rolling her over to port so that the edge of the flight deck seemed about to dip into the water.

The Midshipman of the Watch shouted above the storm, 'Commander (E) says the pumping rate is very slow, sir. At least another two hours at this rate.'

'Thank you.'

Inflexible slowly moved upright again, the fuelling hose tautening into a horizontal bar once more. Thurston rapped out another helm order; the ship's bow shifted to port, and he breathed again as the tension came off the hose.

The telephone buzzed. 'The Admiral wants to know how much longer we'll take to complete fuelling, sir.'

'Tell him another two hours.'

'Aye aye, sir.'

The weather had grown perceptibly worse since the fuelling began, each of the great waves a little higher, the wind stronger still. Thurston glanced at the anemometer, its metal cups whirling so fast that they merged into one. Eighty-five knots, direction three-five-five degrees. An object appeared on the carrier's starboard side, half full of water, carried past her by another wave.

'Someone's losing their boats.'

The waterlogged boat, white upperworks still a foot above the surface, kept pace with *Inflexible* for a time, rolling drunkenly a few yards from her starboard side abreast the island before being carried away astern by another great wave.

The TBS speaker crackled and a disembodied voice came from it. 'Task Force three-seven, this is CTF three-seven. Formation Shrapnel, execute. Point option Queenie zero-one-one, Roger five knots, over.'

'Acknowledge.' Translated, it was the order to scatter, for the ships to make their way independently towards the rendezvous at five knots. It showed the seriousness of the situation, but it also came as a relief that there was no longer any question of trying to maintain formation with the rest of the task force in these conditions. The danger of collisions as the warships were flung about in the near-zero visibility was ended, but it also meant that they were on their own for as long as the typhoon lasted.

The Admiral appeared from the Admiral's bridge on the deck below, almost unrecognisable in oilskins, sou'wester concealing most of his face. 'Well, that's really the only thing to do in the circumstances.'

He took off his sou'wester, shook it so that water streamed away. He grinned, teeth showing very white in his brown face. He seemed actually to be enjoying himself as the sea and wind raged all around him. 'How's the fuelling going?'

'Slowly, sir.' Thurston gave him a tired smile.

'You may not manage to fill the tanks, but try to get as much as you can.'

The Admiral moved away, settled himself into a corner at the rear of the bridge, and fell silent.

Another wave hit *Inflexible* head-on, so that her bows

were buried in tons of water which came sweeping back as far as the island, smashing away the lashings on one of the Corsairs, spinning the aircraft round on its wheels and slamming it against one of its neighbours. There was a flash, a small explosion, its sound unnoticed above the roaring of the storm, and both Corsairs were burning. The carrier rolled again to starboard and both the loose aircraft were carried into the main mass of the deck park, breaking the double lashings as though they were no more than wet string, igniting the petrol in their tanks so that within minutes the entire dozen were on fire.

'Shall I pipe for the fire party, sir?' asked Carstairs.

'No, don't bother.' Thurston knew even as he spoke that no one could move on that flight deck without being swept over the side. Lifelines would make no difference in this sea.

Another wave, and the ship gave a violent lurch to port. Two of the Corsairs began to slide, spun round on their wheels, and, still locked together, they slithered across the width of the deck and over the side. More followed them, one knocked off its wheels and resting on a folded wing, making a deep score mark on the steel deck, the screech of metal on metal audible even over the noise of the storm. Another hung over the catwalk on its side, the tailplane and rear fuselage settling against the edge of the deck as the ship came back upright.

A cruiser appeared briefly ahead of them, a great grey wave building above it. She was moving to port; her Captain must have seen the wave coming and altered course so as to take the wave head on. On *Inflexible*'s bridge they watched as she began to turn, agonisingly slowly, the wave growing all the time above her. The wave hit her forty-five degrees on, smashing her on to her port side so that the tops of her funnels were almost horizontal, great black holes with wisps of brownish smoke coming from them.

The same wave hit *Inflexible* and her tanker, untold tons of water forcing its way between them, crashing down on the tanker's decks and forcing the two ships apart. The Corsair which had stuck in the catwalk disappeared below the water, the fuelling hose jerked taut, seemed to stretch, and then the coupling gave way, black fuel oil falling in great globules on to the tanker's deck to mingle with the water before the hose fell away into the sea. *Inflexible*'s bows came up out of the sea, water and white foam streaming away on both sides. The last Corsair had gone, floating just long enough to remain in sight as the sea carried her past the ship's stern.

'Ask Commander (E) how much fuel he's got and tell him that's his lot.' The tanker was already shearing away to port, showing her red lead once more as she rolled. 'Pass the word to the Commander to secure all fuelling gear and fuelling parties. Yeoman, thank the tanker and tell him we'll manage on what we've got.'

'Commander (E) says about eighty-five per cent, sir.' The Midshipman grinned. 'And there's something else he wants to tell you himself.'

'Yes, Chief, what is it?'

'We've got the bearing fitted, sir, and we're just getting the covers back on.'

It took a moment for Thurston to shift his mind and appreciate the significance of the words. 'Well done Chief, very well done. I never thought you'd be working on it in these conditions.'

Chief sounded both proud and pleased. 'We wanted to get it finished, sir, and it gave the chaps something to take their minds off the weather. We should be able to give the shaft a trial run in a couple of hours or so, all being well.'

Thurston thought of the shaft tunnel and the hell it must be with the ship's motion as violent as this;

pictured the bearing covers, weighing more than a hundredweight each, suspended on chains from the tunnel roof and swinging out of control as the ship rolled. 'If you're using lifting tackle, don't take too many risks. It might be better to leave it until the weather moderates.'

'I've thought of that, sir, and we should be all right.'

'I'll leave it to you then, Chief.' He remembered something the Chief had said to him when he visited the engine room. 'It was beer your chaps were pining for, wasn't it.'

'Yes, sir.'

'Then I think we might relax the rule for once. Get a crate from the wardroom and put it on my bill.'

'*Aye aye*, sir.'

Thurston realised with a jerk that he had entirely forgotten the Admiral's presence on the bridge. He looked round. The Admiral had not moved, wedged into his corner with one arm over the bridge screen to save himself from being flung about.

'You've decided to discontinue fuelling?'

'Yes, sir, I have.' He found himself instantly on the defensive once again, and felt a rush of annoyance with himself.

There was a long pause, his eyes and the Admiral's meeting. 'I think you're quite right. We've got enough to manage on for the time being, and we've done pretty well to get as much as that in these conditions. We'd be lucky if we managed to get the hose connected again, let alone keep it connected for long enough to make it worthwhile. Anyway, it looks as though our friends of the red duster have seen quite enough.'

As he half turned and looked out over the bridge screen to port, Thurston could see that the tanker had already withdrawn a full half-mile away, and he doubted whether her master would be prepared to get close to *Inflexible* a second time before the weather moderated.

'Cuppa tea, sir?' Spencer said at his elbow.

The tea was strong and hot, its warmth stealing from his stomach and pervading his entire body. He had barely noticed it before, but in the last hour he had grown cold inside his sodden clothing, though the air temperature remained in the high seventies.

'Got you some ginger nuts as well, sir, and I'll have your lunch done when you want it.'

Spencer's priorities had not changed. Food and drink remained his solace for all ills. 'How are things below, Spencer?'

'Regular potmess, sir. All the blokes who say they've got gyroscopic guts and don't get sick are throwing up all over the place, and so's everybody else.'

'How about you?'

'Oh, I'm all right, sir. I really 'ave got gyroscopic guts!' Spencer said with a wide grin.

Noon came and the watches changed. Almost imperceptibly at first, the weather began to moderate as the storm centre of the typhoon fell away astern. The waves were still huge, but they were no longer whipped into a frenzy by the wind, and the fury had gone out of them. The ghost-like quality disappeared as men off watch tottered from their hammocks and came alive again.

'Now I s'pose we've got to start cleaning the mess up,' said Spencer, speaking for every man on board.

The casualties proved surprisingly light: the usual assortment of broken bones as men had lost their footing or been thrown from their bunks, a number totally prostrated by seasickness, all the Corsairs on the deck park lost overboard, and, to the wicked delight of the ship's company, the Admiral's barge lifted off its crutches on the boat deck to splinter its bows to matchwood against a neighbouring bulkhead.

At first *Inflexible* was quite alone as she moved north-

wards, although other ships showed as small bright
blips on the radar. Gradually, others were sighted and
given instructions by lamp to join; first a destroyer,
then two more, then *Irresistible* and the flock she herself had rounded up. The mist had cleared, but black
cloud still hung over the sky, so that by mid-afternoon
it was already near dusk, and long after the hour the
Americans had appointed for the rendezvous.

'Ship bearing red one-oh, sir!'

A squally rain had begun to fall once more, reducing
the visibility again, so that the other ship was no more
than a dark angular shadow against the lesser dark, the
anvil-like shape betraying her as another carrier.

'Challenge.'

'Aye aye, sir.' The lamp blinked its message.

There was a tense moment of waiting. According to
intelligence reports the Japanese had no carriers left
which were fit for sea, but there was always a chance.

'It's the Yanks, sir.'

'Ask them which ship.'

There was another burst and dots and dashes from
the strange ship. '*Lexington*, sir.'

That would be the new *Lexington*, not the one which
had been sunk in the Battle of the Coral Sea three years
earlier.

'She's signalling, sir. *Good to see you at last. How did
you weather the typhoon?*'

Thurston thought for a moment. *Lexington* was a
brand-new ship, with, no doubt, a cocky young complement bursting to prove that they and their ship were
about to win the war single-handed.

'Oh, ask them what typhoon.'

There were smiles all round, and an eager wait for
the Americans' response, but there was no reply.

Chapter Thirty

The American Fleet was itself scattered over two hundred square miles of ocean, and it took most of the next two days to round up all the strays and to take stock of the damage. Two American destroyers had been lost after water pouring down their funnels had extinguished the fires in their boiler rooms, causing them to drift helplessly, broach to, and then founder. Only three survivors had been picked up, two of them after a fortunate wave had flung them on to the deck of another ship. One of the American carriers had lost nearly half her aircraft after one had broken loose from its lashings and set off a fire in the hangar, and there were no ships which did not show some damage.

But operations began again almost at once, directed for the first time against the main Japanese islands themselves. Several times the British had seen the huge silver-painted Superfortresses flying from their island bases to bomb the Japanese mainland, leaving white vapour trails as they flew at thirty thousand feet, out of reach of anti-aircraft fire and endangered only by the few fighter aircraft the Japanese had left. The Superfortresses attacked area targets, the Japanese cities themselves. As before, the aircraft of the British and American navies were ranged against airfields, some of them far inland, so there was a new kind of strain on the aircrews in the long run in over enemy territory before reaching the target. Each island was ringed by clusters of anti-aircraft guns putting up a barrage of lethally accurate flak which began as soon as the Corsairs and Avengers approached, grew in intensity as they closed in on the target, and followed hard on their heels as they ran for home. As the war reached their own islands the Japanese seemed to be fighting with more of their ruthless determination than ever. If they could not defeat the high-level bombers, they could concentrate all their attentions on those aircraft which came within range of their guns. *Inflexible* lost two Corsairs in the first day's operations, and one of the Avengers limped back with the gunner dead in his turret and the observer badly wounded.

The second Corsair squadron was untried, most of its pilots having yet to see action. There were newcomers in the other squadrons, too, replacing those who had been left behind in Australia as the tour expired. The RAF expected its fighter pilots to fly two hundred operational hours, its bomber aircrew thirty operations before being automatically posted to training duties for six months. The Americans took their men off operations permanently at the end of their tour. But the Fleet Air Arm expected its aircrew, pilots, observers and gunners to go on flying until they were dead, medically unfit through wounds or sickness, someone in authority had taken the decision to ground them, or they themselves had asked to be taken off operations. A very few had been flying, on and off, since the first days of the war, when the Fleet Air Arm, under the joint authority of the Navy and the RAF until 1938, was the Cinderella of the service: only two of the seven carriers had been built as such, four had been converted from battle cruisers, the other built on the hull of a battleship originally destined for the Chilean Navy. They had had to make do with obsolete and hopelessly outclassed aircraft, the Gladiator, Skua, Roc and Swordfish – it was believed that the modern high-performance fighters which had reached the RAF were too fast and too fragile to be operated from aircraft carriers. Rather more survived from the middle years, when first the Hurricane and then the Spitfire were adapted for carrier flying, and American-built aircraft designed specifically for the job had reached the squadrons, but they too had mostly been grounded, worn out by operations and the strain of landing over and over again on a rolling ship at the end of each sortie.

Now, at last, with Germany defeated and the Japanese in retreat, the Fleet Air Arm had the ships and aircraft it needed, as well as eager young pilots and observers pouring out of the training schools in Canada and America. They approached their first sorties warily, like their first 'real' deck landings, but a few days of operational flying turned them into veterans. Flying two and three sorties a day they soon learned to keep low, to keep watching all the time for the thing which might be simply a speck on the cockpit canopy, or even a bird, but which might also be an enemy fighter. Over Japan, as earlier over the islands, they learned fast, or they did not come back.

For all the long period *Inflexible* had spent away from the front line, more than two months when the four-thousand-mile passages to and from Sydney were included, it seemed to take no time at all to fall back into the routine of operations, and after the first days it was as if the time in Sydney had never been. Again there was the intense heat and the heavy humidity which lay over everything and made it impossible ever to be cool, the long hot days closed up at Action Stations, running with sweat inside the heavy anti-flash gear, a return to the monotony of action messing, soup, sandwiches and overstrong, oversweetened tea. For the aircrews, life was reduced to a round of brief, sortie, debrief, eat, brief, sortie, debrief, eat again, through the day and then fitful sleep in an overheated cabin at night, reliving in dreams the excitements and moments of stark terror of the days. While they slept and in between the sorties, the ground crews worked on, fuelling and arming the aircraft, dealing with action damage that could be repaired on the spot, occasionally taking parts from one for use on another, so that the squadron would have sufficient aircraft available for the next day's operations. Sometimes it was after midnight before all the work was completed, and then a quiet would descend on the ship for a few hours, with only the duty watch still awake and at their posts.

For Thurston life became restricted to the bridge and his sea cabin a few seconds away from it. Spencer shook him before the first sortie went off at dawn; from then until dark he left the bridge only fleetingly, to go into the Ops Room or the FDR, or into his sea cabin to hear the post-sortie reports from the squadron commanders. After the dusk stand-down, he had a session with Scott to deal with the day's paperwork, though even that was now reduced to the bare essentials and Scott spent his days on the bridge keeping the ship's action diary. At some time there would be a meeting with the Admiral, going over the day's events and the plans for the morrow.

Since the typhoon his relations with the Admiral had undergone a change. Winthrop might have little time for flyers – they were tolerated only because they were on board to do a job and only as long as they did that job – but he respected seamanship. Nothing had been said, but it was as if in taking *Inflexible* through the storm and fuelling in conditions which were on the limit Thurston had won his confidence, and the Admiral was now prepared to leave the running of the ship to him. Perhaps Strickland, preoccupied by his domestic problems and wearied by a long period of active service, had let things slide, so that the Admiral had felt it necessary to intervene, causing Strickland to stand on his dignity and a vicious circle of mutual antagonism to develop.

On his arrival on board *Inflexible* the Admiral, smarting from what he must have seen as defeat in being forced out of his previous flagship, had instituted a drive for efficiency, sought to shock her officers and men out of what he saw as the inevitable slackness of a private ship, and had made himself thoroughly unpopular in the process. He and his staff were still regarded with a certain wariness, the attitude still pertained that 'We've got on perfectly well without that lot all this time'; they were regarded, like the aircrew in some quarters, as 'not really belonging to us'. The Admiral was a bachelor, and the cynics who considered that any man who remained unmarried beyond the age of forty must automatically be suspect, indulged in ribald speculation about the precise relationship between the Admiral and his flag lieutenant, a blond Adonis who had, however, been seen decorating various Sydney nightclubs with a succession of attractive young women.

There was a change, too, in the nature of operations. The task force had previously operated by itself, co-operating with the American fleets but separate from them and at a distance. Now they were working directly with the Americans, on the right flank of the huge American Fleet, and in the position of most honour, a generous gesture by the American Commander in Chief.

Where the squadrons had been accustomed to operating as single units, bound together only by the accident of flying from the same carrier, more and more *Inflexible*'s Corsair squadrons operated together and formed a wing with the fighter squadrons from other ships under the overall command of a youthful lieutenant-colonel of the Royal Marines. In the same way the Avengers now worked in co-operation with squadrons from the other ships. And now the whole of the task force's airborne strength were working in conjunction

408

with the Americans, allotted their own targets and area of operations by the Americans, occasionally following up an American sortie against the same airfield. It meant much more work for Lieutenant-Commander Murillo and his small signals staff, and more still for the already heavily burdened FDR and Ops Room staff, who now had to keep track of American aircraft movements as well as their own.

'There it is.'

The airfield was an open area of brown standing out among the small square fields, crossed by a single grey ribbon of runway, another runway lying at thirty degrees to it, with a grey perimeter track running round. It seemed strangely deserted, without an aircraft or even a vehicle in sight. Perhaps this wasn't going to be too bad. The altimeter needle reached six thousand feet, the pilot pushed the stick forward and levelled the Avenger out of the climb. In the observer's cockpit behind him, Sub-Lieutenant Bennett glanced round almost guiltily to satisfy himself that his parachute was safely in its rack, the rear side with the D-rings uppermost so that it was ready to be clipped on to the hooks on his chest as soon as it was needed. The CO was signalling, the twelve Avengers spread out into echelon, ready to go in. There was a sudden jolt underneath them, and Bennett barely had time to realise what it was when the air suddenly came alive with puffs of grey smoke, so dark as to be almost black, each explosion sending a shower of hot steel fragments in every direction.

'Right, we're going in. Bomb doors open.'

The shallow dive on to the target was the worst part. The pilot could concentrate on flying the aircraft, keeping it lined up with the runway that was their target, and dropping the bombs accurately; Leading Airman Collis could at least traverse his turret in each direction and keep watch for the Japanese fighters which might be defending their field; but the observer could do nothing except watch and wait until the bombing run was over and he could lay off a course home. Instinctively Bennett dropped his head down towards his chest, as far down inside the cockpit as he could get it, but not being able to see what was happening around him was almost worse than seeing it, so he kept jerking back upright, swivelling his head rapidly in both directions, then dropping it again.

As they went down the flak seemed to get heavier. The Corsairs were supposed to have been strafing the flak positions, keeping the gunners occupied as the Avengers made their bombing run. Where were they? Bennett jerked upright again, to see another explosion rock another Avenger on its starboard side, a thin line of orange flame begin to travel along the fuselage. He could see the crew in their positions, the gunner working his turret back and forth, the guns pointing towards Bennett for a moment in a way that seemed peculiarly threatening. The thin line travelled on, there was a brief flash of orange light, and the entire tail assembly broke away. The remainder of the aircraft fell vertically towards the earth.

'Would you look at that!' the pilot shouted over the intercom. He was a Canadian from Vancouver, nicknamed 'Moose' from his nationality and prominent nose, and in the tension of the moment his accent seemed more noticeable than usual.

Sub-Lieutenant Macpherson did not see, but Bennett did, a small dark object falling away from the stricken aircraft, the white canopy and rigging lines streaming out behind him, orange flames already eating up them, so that before it was fully deployed the canopy had been burnt to nothing. Bennett dropped down once more, shut his eyes, listening to Macpherson's voice over the intercom. 'Eighteen hundred, seventeen hundred, sixteen hundred, fifteen hundred, NOW!'

Suddenly freed of the thousand-pound bomb load the Avenger gave a jolt upwards.

'Bombs gone.'

Bombs were exploding along the length of the runway, sending up grey dust which made it difficult to see what damage was being caused.

'Bomb doors closed.' Macpherson kept the aircraft in her dive, trying to get below the flak. Ahead of them another Avenger disappeared, leaving only a few shreds of metal and part of a wing, which for some reason maintained its aerodynamic qualities and flew itself gently towards the earth.

Seven hundred feet and suddenly the airfield was behind them, the last of the flak falling harmlessly short. Macpherson took the aircraft round in a wide turn to starboard, back towards the coast but not over the flak positions a second time.

'Let's get out of here.'

Bennett looked around him, counting the other Avengers. Five, six, seven. Two had gone down, he remembered, but where were the rest? He counted again. Still only seven.

'How many do you make?' he asked the gunner.

Collis's voice came back through the wad of gum he always chewed when flying, claiming that it helped his ears with all the pressure changes. 'Seven.'

Seven, and themselves, which meant four shot down. He noticed the large letter Q on the fuselage of the nearest Avenger, which meant the Senior Pilot's aircraft. The Senior Pilot was signalling, which meant that the CO must have bought it. Bennett found that both his hands were gripping the edges of his Bigsworth board; he let one go, and found that it was shaking. The squadron had formed up again on the Senior Pilot. Bennett concentrated on the Bigsworth board, sorted out their position and laid off a course back towards the coast. The lead aircraft would navigate the squadron, but the rest had to be ready to take over in case they became separated.

Four aircraft gone, and twelve men with them. At least six of them were dead, in the Avenger whose tail had broken off and the one blown to pieces by a direct hit. The flak was still coming up, only gradually falling behind them as they moved beyond the gunners' range. Collis was saying something into the intercom, gesticulating at the large jagged hole which had appeared in the smooth metal skin of the starboard wing, almost exactly at the mid-point. The hole was disturbing, the final proof of their own vulnerability. Bennett found himself shivering again, though the sun beat down on the cockpit canopy. His mouth was very dry, and he knew that it was only partly because of the heat.

The flight back to the ship seemed to go on for ever, going as close to the ground as they dared, tensed at every moment for the appearance of a Japanese fighter, or another burst of flak. Relief finally hit when they crossed a line of low cliffs with a narrow strip of sand beyond and were out over the sea once more. They climbed to five thousand feet in order to pick up the task force on ASV, and there was another surge of relief when the pattern of echoes appeared on the radar display and the dots and dashes of *Inflexible*'s beacon could be picked out from those of the other carriers. Not long now, and the tension began to fade, leaving a swathe of weariness in its wake. The others must have been affected in the same way, for the intercom had remained silent for a long time, the only sound being the droning of the Avenger's engine, and an occasional brief instruction from the Senior Pilot.

There was the task force, spread out over several square miles of ocean like chessmen, each ship in the position allotted to her, the Americans further off, their huge fleet stretching away to the horizon. Not long now. A cold drink, and then a late lunch in the ready room. In his weariness the losses had become remote; now it struck him forcibly that some of the men he had breakfasted with a few hours before would not sit down to lunch on this or any other day.

They watched the first four Avengers land on, then the Senior Pilot signalled them to go in. Down *Inflexible*'s port side, the ship looking reassuringly large and solid, the red cross on her ensign standing out against the prevailing grey, the batsman on his platform amidships, Moose going through the pre-landing sequence. Hood back. Full flap. Down undercarriage. Down hook. Fine pitch. The final turn in, the orange bats making their signals for Moose alone; he and Collis must put their trust in pilot and batsman. *A little to starboard, straighten up, the first four Avengers clustered on the deck beyond the barrier, wings already folded. CUT.* The throttle closed, and the aircraft dropped towards the deck. A jerk as the hook picked up a wire, then a bump as the main wheels found the deck. Moose opened the throttle again and the Avenger taxied forward. *Hook clear. Select wing folding lever, over the barrier as it comes down.* The next Avenger was already on its approach. Bennett released his straps, put his hands out to the cockpit sides and levered himself out of his seat. *Follow Moose out on to the wing root, drop down the three feet or so to the deck.* The ground crew were already there, manoeuvring the Avenger towards the four already parked. The next aircraft was down, taxying over the barrier, wings rising towards the vertical.

Someone shouted in his ear – 'What happened?' – and the numb weariness lifted suddenly so that the reality of the losses hit him again, and a wave of bitterness came with it. 'Fucking Corsairs weren't there when they should have been!' He swayed on his feet, and someone steered him into the shade beneath the island. He released his parachute harness, let it fall away to the deck without bothering to pick it up. Someone else came up beside him; he saw that it was Moose but neither of them spoke. The Senior Pilot's aircraft had landed on, the last of the eight, they watched him climb out and stride purposefully towards the ladder which led up from the base of the island, and a few minutes later heard his voice raised in anger, then the measured Dartmouth tones of the Captain and Commander (Air) telling him quietly but firmly to calm down. But the Senior Pilot was shouting again, for all the survivors of the squadron. 'Where were those fucking Corsairs?'

Moose was the first to recover.

'We-ell, I suppose we'd better go get some lunch.'

Night came after another day of flying. Thurston ate his supper, curry made with the last of the fresh meat from Sydney, followed by the tinned orange segments which had begun to be familiar once more. He had barely finished when there was a knock on the bulkhead and the Admiral's messenger pushed aside the curtain.

'Captain, sir, the Admiral would like to see you in his sea cabin.'

It was like Winthrop. The Admiral's and Captain's sea cabins faced one another across the passage, but it was only on rare occasions that the Admiral would put his head through the doorway or even summon him by telephone.

Winthrop was sitting on his desk chair, shirt unbuttoned in the heat, a blue signal form lying on the desk in front of him.

'Oh, hello, Thurston. Sorry to disturb you.'

'That's all right, sir.'

The Admiral hesitated, as if unsure of what he was to say. 'Look, you'd better sit down. I've got some bad news for you.'

Kate? George, or one of the others? *Jane* pregnant?

The Admiral picked up the signal form. 'You'd better read this.'

Thurston picked up the form, took in the words hastily printed across it: DEEPLY REGRET TO INFORM CAPTAIN THURSTON THAT HIS FATHER REVEREND HENRY MAITLAND THURSTON DSO DIED . . . There was the date, the brief conventional expression of Their Lordships' condolences and a string of letters and figures giving time of origin, signal strength and other details required by the wireless office.

'I'm very sorry.'

'Yes, sir.'

It was in a way a replay of a similar awkward interview twenty-nine years ago when George had been posted missing and *Oudenarde*'s Captain had broken the news; Thurston had only been on board two weeks and had barely set eyes on the Captain before.

'Was it sudden?'

'I think so, sir. I had a letter from him in the last mail and he was all right when he wrote it.'

'Probably a heart attack then. It's not such a bad way to go, and he can't have been a young man.' ('It doesn't necessarily mean that he's been killed, you know. There's a pretty good chance that he's been taken prisoner.')

'Eighty-six or eighty-seven, I'm not sure.'

'Well, that's not a bad innings.' The Admiral was trying to be kind, to lessen the impact of the news.

'Mother still alive?'

'No, sir.' ('Go home and look after your mother.' 'My mother's dead, sir, and I'd rather not leave.')

'That's a pity. Were you close, you and your father?'

How long is a piece of string? His relations with the old man had been too complicated to sum up in a few words. 'Not really, sir.'

415

Thurston had put the signal down; the Admiral picked it up and squinted at it once again. 'Padre with a DSO? That's a bit unusual.'

'He got it in the Tirah, before he took orders. Indian Army, the Guides Cavalry.'

'If there's anything you need . . . '

The meeting was at an end. 'Yes, sir.'

'See you tomorrow at the usual ungodly hour.' The Admiral yawned. 'I think I'm going to get my head down. All these pre-dawn starts are catching up with me.'

His father was dead, four days ago, and it was only now that the news had reached him. How he had died he did not know, and would not know until a letter reached him from his stepmother or sister, ten days away at least. His father was dead, but so too were a dozen of his men. Four aircraft had gone down, only one parachute had been seen and even that had been devoured by the fire when still hundreds of feet above the ground. He sat at his desk, poured himself a glass of lime juice from the jug which Spencer had left there earlier, drank it, then took out his pen and writing pad.

Dear Mr and Mrs Faulkner. The Avenger squadron's Senior Pilot had been an angry man, and justifiably so. The attack on the Japanese airfield had been planned so that a Corsair squadron from *Imperious* would come in at low level – at ninety degrees to the Avengers as they made their bombing run – to draw the flak and use their guns on the Japanese positions. The planning had been precise, but something had gone wrong with the execution. The Corsairs had been late in taking off – something had needed to be done on one of the aircraft at the last minute – a decision had been taken that the attack should be put back ten minutes to give the Corsairs time to reach the target, but the information had for some reason not reached the Avengers and they had gone in unsupported. The Japanese radar had picked them up as soon as they had climbed up from deck level to begin their bombing run, and the guns had been ready for them. The Senior Pilot had stormed at Commander (Air) and then at Thurston himself, until the flight-deck doctor had come up on to the bridge and quietly led him away. He had come up again an hour later, still looking white and shaken, and apologised. He was acting CO of the Avenger squadron now, and would be unless and until a replacement arrived via the Fleet Train; there was nobody else.

Thurston wrote a few lines, then read them through, and tore the sheet off in frustration. He started again, wrote his stepmother's name on the paper. *My dear Maud.* The fan in the corner blew hot air over him, continuing to make its annoying click as it turned on its bracket. Father. But what was one old man, come to the end of his life and dying by natural causes, against twelve of the men under his command — the youngest nineteen, the oldest twenty-four — who had been alive and in their prime nine hours ago, and had met death by fire and bullet?

Scott's familiar double knock on the bulkhead. Thurston pushed the pad aside, swivelled round on the chair.

'Not much tonight, sir.' Scott put a wire basket down on the cleared surface, lifted out a pile of typed correspondence. There was a little less than usual, and it did not take long to sign his name at the bottom of each sheet: simply *R. H. M. Thurston* on most of them; *Yours sincerely, Robert Thurston* (to the Captain of the dockyard in Sydney whom he knew sufficiently well to address less formally), *I have the honour to remain, Sir, your obedient servant, R. H. M. Thurston, Captain RN*, on a recommendation addressed to the Commander in Chief.

'I'm sorry to hear about your father, sir.'

'Thank you, Scratch. How did you know?'

'One of the telegraphists told me, sir.'

'Then it'll be all round the ship by tomorrow.'

'I'm afraid so.'

'I've been trying to write to my stepmother.' He indicated the writing pad. 'I'm not doing very well.'

'It's something I find terribly difficult too, sir. I suppose it must have come as quite a shock.'

'Yes, but he'd had a good innings, and we none of us can live for ever,' he said almost savagely, echoing the Admiral's words and conscious of this as he did so.

'No sir, but all the same . . . Goodnight, sir.' Scott picked up the basket of correspondence and stepped over the coaming.

Chapter Thirty-One

A Seafire from *Irresistible* took off before first light, climbed to thirty thousand feet and reached the Japanese airfield just after dawn. As it began its pass the cameras in its belly clicked on, taking a series of pictures of the target. The Japanese picked it up on radar as soon as it came within range, but the Seafire flew too fast and too high for interception, and remained unmolested. As soon as it landed the film was unloaded and taken to the cramped little darkroom in the island. Half an hour later *Irresistible*'s Commander (Air) was talking on the TBS to his opposite number in *Inflexible*, the prints pinned to the bulkhead next to him, still wet from developing.

'Yes, no doubt about it. Half a dozen aircraft on the tarmac and probably more in the hangars. It looks as though they were fuelling when the PR Seafire went over; couple of petrol bowsers there as well.'

The Avenger squadron had not been rostered for the dawn operation that morning. They had had to get up and clear out of their cabins when the call sounded for Action Stations, of course, in one or two cases still in pyjamas, taking their washing and shaving tackle with them, but it meant a relatively leisurely start to the day, eating breakfast in the ready room and leafing idly through the magazines and old newspapers that always found their way there eventually. Nobody ever had much to say at these times, and it was easier not to make any attempt at conversation. One of the Corsair

419

squadrons returned from a Ramrod, and the quietness was briefly disturbed as the pilots trooped in demanding breakfast and slumped into the few empty chairs. There were the usual good mornings, questions on how the Ramrod had gone, and then silence once more. The Corsair pilots tended to stick together, and there was an unspoken division between them and the Avenger aircrew, just as there was another and more noticeable division on board the carrier itself between the flyers and their associated ground crews and the rest of the officers and men. A messenger came in, spoke in an undertone to the acting CO, who got up and went out, the heavy steel door shutting behind them.

'Here comes trouble,' said Moose.

Bennett gave him a weak grin in return.

The CO came back. 'Right, briefing room in five minutes. We've got to go again.'

The day was already hot, but Bennett felt a cold hand of fear grasp at his windpipe, and, looking at Moose, he was sure that the Canadian felt the same.

'We-ell, they do say lightning never strikes twice in the same place.'

'We know all about what happened yesterday, but there's no alternative. The Japs are using that field and they've got to be stopped. It's as simple as that.'

Bennett wondered if the CO had already made another protest. If he had, it had obviously made no difference.

'You'll have our own Corsairs with you this time, so there should be no repetition of yesterday's mix-up. Just go in, bomb, and get out fast.'

Bennett, Moose and Collis solemnly shook hands with each other before climbing into the aircraft, but yesterday's debacle lay as a great unspoken shadow over them all. Once they might have joked about it a little, in the savage black humour of the fighting man. 'Made your will yet?' 'I'll have your Port Said postcards if you don't get back.' A square metal patch had been riveted over the hole in the wing, its paint a slightly different shade from the rest of the wing.

Low down over the sea they could see one Corsair squadron providing high cover above them. The other squadron would take off from *Inflexible* twenty minutes after them and rely on their superior speed to be over the target and dealing with the flak positions at the same time as the Avengers were on the run in. The nine Avengers droned on – one which had been unserviceable yesterday had been repaired in time to be included in today's operation. Collis fired a burst from his guns, the red blobs of tracer describing a gentle parabola before dropping into the sea. The Japanese coast appeared ahead of them, the same low cliffs and strip of beach as yesterday.

The routine was exactly the same: watch for the landmarks as they appeared and plot the position on the Bigsworth board, warn Moose in good time as a turning point came up, mark them off, get out his penknife to put a better point on the pencil, the blackish flakes of graphite scattering over the white surface of the chart. A brief burst of flak came from an AA position over to port. Moose swung the Avenger over to starboard. Collis fired a burst, and the guns fell silent as the Avenger's speed carried them out of range.

'Ten minutes to target.'

'Roger.'

Moose opened the throttle, eased the stick back and the aircraft began to climb, tucked in on the CO's port wing, exactly in formation. There was another Avenger on his starboard wing, and the other six were grouped into two vics of three astern, one to starboard, one to port. Yesterday they had begun the bombing run with four of those vics, twelve aircraft in all. Once more he found himself checking that his parachute was in its place, tugging on the straps of the harness to make sure it was fully tight.

Five thousand feet. A gentle turn to port, a few degrees only, to line up with the main runway, a deep breath as the nose went down and the run in began. Black smoke appeared below them as the flak opened up.

'There they are!' Collis shouted, as half a dozen Corsairs shot across the field at right angles to them and almost at ground level, red tracer streaming from their guns. It made Bennett feel a little better.

There was a sudden jolt, and black smoke issuing from the engine cowling.

'Pilot to crew,' came Moose's startled voice over the intercom. 'We've been hit!' He was doing things with stick and rudder to keep the aircraft in its dive.

'Better get rid of the bomb load,' Bennett heard himself saying.

'I'm going to hang on for a minute. Don't want to waste them.'

Two thousand feet; the grey concrete of the runway still ahead. The Corsairs had come round in a hundred-and-eighty-degree turn and were making another run, almost certainly against orders, but Bennett was grateful to them for it. Sixteen hundred feet; another movement of stick and rudder as Moose brought the aircraft on to the exact line of the runway. Another jolt and 'Bombs gone!'

Black smoke was streaming from the cowling, but the Avenger's engine continued its reassuring roar.

'I'm going to get a bit of height and try and get out to sea,' Moose said.

'I'll second that,' said Collis.

They all knew what the Japanese were supposed to do to their prisoners and without saying anything this

422

had become the uppermost thought in their minds.

'Blue Two, this is Blue Leader. Are you all right?'

'Blue Two, I think so. At the moment.' Moose's Canadian voice contrasted with the CO's South London grammar school.

'Blue Leader, can you make it back?'

'Blue Two, I'm not sure. Going to try to make the coast.'

'Blue Leader Roger. We'll stay with you.'

The squadron reformed around them; it was reassuring somehow to be inside their protective ring. But the smoking continued, and an acrid smell of burning was stealing back into the cockpit. Bennett remembered a chap who had been a couple of years ahead of him at school and gone into the RAF, coming home on leave and telling him that the German FW 190s were buggers to shoot down. 'You can knock chunks off the engines and they still keep going. Air cooled. If you hit a 109 they seize up solid as soon as the glycol starts to leak.' The Avenger had an air-cooled radial engine and that made him feel a little better, until he remembered that he had found out later that Dick Chivers had never seen action and could not have been speaking from experience.

The minutes crawled by, each one drawn out as long as possible. Bennett tried to concentrate on the navigation, but their progress across the chart was equally slow. He looked again at his parachute. *Clip it on to the harness, make sure it's the right way up. Push the canopy back, release the seat harness, take hold of the ripcord with one hand and jump. Shout 'Abracadabra! One! Two! Three!' and pull the ripcord.* Someone else from school had been a Bomber Command navigator and had baled out of a Lancaster over the Ruhr. He had lain up by day and walked by night, and walked into Holland or Belgium in three or four days. He'd knocked on the door of a farmhouse for help, the people had given him food and civilian clothes and given him directions to another farm a few miles away. Somewhere along the line he had made contact with one of the escape lines and had been passed along it all the way to the very south of France and over the Pyrenees into Spain. But this was not Germany, with nothing worse than a POW camp if you were picked up. Down there was Japan and the Japanese beheaded those who fell into their hands alive. Japan was hilly and there were villages dotted about below them, an occasional small town further off.

The Avengers were back at six thousand feet, to give the crew of the damaged aircraft a chance to glide as far as possible if the engine seized, or room to bale out if it came to that, so they must be visible to the enemy radar, and any minute a flight of Japanese fighters could appear in the sky ahead or astern. The Corsairs were above them, but fifteen thousand feet higher, seemingly too distant to offer any protection.

'Coast coming up,' Moose said briefly.

At that moment the engine stuttered and missed a few beats, then just as suddenly picked up again. The sea was in sight, pale blue and rippled, stretching away towards the horizon, with no sign of life upon it.

'There they are!' Collis shouted into the intercom, the proper procedure forgotten.

'There who are?' Moose said irritably.

Bennett craned his head round as far as it would go, his seat harness preventing him from turning his upper body too, and the cold hand clutched once more at his windpipe. Four Japanese aircraft above and behind them, their silhouettes instantly recognisable from the models and posters on display in *Inflexible*'s briefing room.

'As if I didn't know,' Moose said into the intercom.

Far above them the Corsairs were peeling off one by one from their formation, diving into the attack.

'I'm going to try full throttle, try to get right out to

sea at least.' Moose's hand pushed the throttle lever forward, the roar of the engine became louder and the needle on the airspeed indicator jerked upwards.

The sharp nose of a Japanese fighter appeared behind the formation, and each of the nine Avenger gunners opened up, still much too far away, the tracer curving down harmlessly beneath the fighter's belly.

'Shit!' Collis cursed briefly.

The Avenger's engine missed again. Bennett wondered how long it could last with the additional strain on it of running at full throttle. He tried a brief glance downwards. They were over the coast now, but with the Japanese fighters on their tail it hardly seemed to matter. Where were the Corsairs? The Japanese guns opened fire; Collis was replying, hurling his turret from side to side and keeping up a continuous burst of fire. Moose was jinking the Avenger about, never holding the same course for more than a second, trying to make them a more difficult target, but at the same time making an unsteady gun platform for Collis. *Where were the Corsairs?* A jolt as something hit the fuselage. For a moment he thought Collis had been hit but the gunner continued to fire. The engine coughed, seemed to pick up again for a moment, coughed again, then two or three more times, and stopped completely.

'Shit!'

There at last were the Corsairs, coming down on the Japanese from out of the sun. The Japanese which had been firing at them dropped away, streaming the white smoke which meant that his radiator had been punctured. Moose had throttled back, trying to persuade the dead engine to restart, but to no avail.

'Okay guys. Stand by to ditch.'

Bennett seized the Bigsworth board, scrabbled to lay off a course with the parallel rule. 'Observer to Pilot, steer one-six-zero degrees towards the Fleet.'

'Roger. Steering one-six-zero degrees.'

'Mayday, Mayday, Mayday, this is Blue Two. We have engine failure, preparing to ditch. My heading is one-six-zero degrees, over.'

The CO's observer checked back the message, added 'Good luck' on the end, a final acknowledgement of the seriousness of their situation.

They were losing height rapidly now, the propeller still windmilling in the slipstream to drag them down. The battle was still going on above them, but the Japanese seemed to have decided that they were not worth following to finish off. Lower down the sea seemed much rougher than it had from altitude, waves marching in steady succession across its surface. Moose was speaking into the intercom, telling them to make sure their straps were tight and to be ready to get out as soon as the aircraft touched down on the water. Bennett looked up again. The battle seemed to be over, the remaining Avengers back in formation and heading away towards the fleet, the Corsair squadrons climbing back towards twenty thousand feet.

Canopy back.

'Blue Leader, this is Blue Two, my position eight miles from coast, heading one-six-zero, about to ditch, ditching – now!'

The Avenger hit the water on its belly, pitched forwards so that for a moment Bennett thought it was going under, then rocked back on to an even keel. He released his harness, then jerked the radio lead out of its socket as he stood up. They had gone through the drill in training. The pilot went out on to the port wing, the gunner jettisoned the side panel of his turret, climbed out to join him, and together they removed the panel on the fuselage above the wing, pulled out the three-man dinghy which was stowed there, inflated it and climbed in from the wing; the observer went out on the starboard side, inflated the one-man dinghy carried on his parachute harness and paddled around the air-craft's stern to join them.

The aircraft rocked precariously as Bennett clambered out, made clumsy by the need to hurry. He found the dinghy pack, pulled off the tab on top of the CO_2 bottle and watched as it expanded in a series of jerks. The dinghy settled on the water. Bennett started to climb down, remembered to pull off another tab to inflate his Mae West. He dropped down from the wing, but the dinghy had drifted away at the last second and he found himself suddenly in the water, the Mae West carrying him back to the surface before he had time to swallow more than a mouthful. The dinghy floated tauntingly a few feet away, he struck out, thought that he would get to it in a couple of strokes, but it drifted further off, perhaps impelled by his own efforts to reach it.

'Ben, are you okay?'

The other two were only feet from him, but in his own struggles he had almost forgotten about them.

'Aw, forget that thing. We've got the three-man ready over here.'

Bennett watched the dinghy slide another foot further from him, and gave it up as a bad job. He struck out in jerky strokes once more, finding that the Mae West impeded the full movement of his arms. It was only a few yards but it seemed an age before he reached the Avenger's tail, and more minutes before he rounded it and began to swim towards the dinghy in which Moose and Collis were now sitting, maddeningly dry.

'All aboard for the Skylark,' Collis said.

They paddled the dinghy towards him, laboriously and with much splashing, then hauled him over the low rubber side.

'Never realised you were such a weight,' said Collis.

Bennett found a space, and sat getting his breath back for several minutes. The Avenger was lower in the

427

water now, and drifting away from them, or perhaps they were drifting away from it.

'Okay now, Ben?'

They scrabbled about inside the dinghy and found a small rubber-covered package attached to the side with a sealed container of water, several lengths of fishing line with a variety of hooks on the end, two compasses little bigger than a button, chocolate, chewing gum, a map printed on silk with the winds and currents marked, a flare pistol and half a dozen flares. There was a bailer, made of rubber stretched over a metal frame, a miniature aluminium mast and a bright red cotton sail. The amount and variety of the provisions cheered them. They had got the Mayday signal off, the squadron had seen them go in and must know where they were. It would not be long, perhaps only an hour or so if they were lucky. Bennett looked out over the wide circle of sea around them, noticed that in one quadrant the horizon changed from blue to dirty white, and realised that they were still in sight of the Japanese coast and only a few miles from it, that it was as likely that the Japanese had plotted their position, and were even now sending out a fast patrol boat to pick them up.

'That's not the only thing,' Moose said after looking at the white smear for several minutes. 'Aren't we due another replen tomorrow?'

Chapter Thirty-Two

'Macpherson and Bennett, and Leading Airman Collis, sir.'

'Did anyone see them ditch?'

'No, sir.'

'You were fully occupied at the time, I take it?'

'Yes, sir.' The Avenger CO sounded relieved at not having to explain himself. 'The Japs jumped us and by the time we'd got away from them there was no sign. We did pick up an R/T message that they were ditching, but no one actually saw them go in.'

Thurston looked out over the bridge screen to starboard. There was a fair sea running, nothing like the huge mountains of water the typhoon had created, but still a fair swell, and the sky remained grey and overcast, so that it was cooler than it had been for several days.

'They should have made it into their dinghy, sir, given ordinary luck. The Avenger's not a bad aircraft to ditch, and it's got flotation bags so it should stay afloat for long enough to get clear.'

The Avenger CO sounded anxious, almost as though he was pleading with Thurston to do something. Lieutenant Hurst seemed very young, with lank brown hair and a thin intense face, not yet sure of himself in his new position. Until Sydney he had been just one among the squadron's pilots, then the Senior Pilot had gone sick with a bad recurrent attack of malaria and had had to be left behind. Hurst had just been getting used to his new responsibilities when he had found himself promoted again and leading the squadron. He had not yet been twenty-four hours in command, and already one of his crews had been shot down.

Thurston moved a few paces and bent to study the chart spread out under the Perspex sheet which covered the chart table. 'If you were in that area when the Jap fighters jumped you, they must have ditched pretty close inshore.' He indicated a shallow arc with a pair of dividers. It all depended on the currents, and the way the tide was running, whether Sub-Lieutenant Macpherson and his crew were carried safely out to sea or drifted inshore to be taken prisoner by the Japanese. If they had made it into their dinghy at all. He took the bulky volume of the *Pacific Coast Pilot* from its stowage and rifled through the pages, came to no obvious conclusion. 'We'll keep looking for them. Chances are they'll be picked up in a few hours,' he said with a cheerfulness which did not seem to carry conviction.

The day went on as usual. Both Corsair squadrons had landed on, refuelled and flown off again, one on another Ramrod, the other on CAP over the Fleet. No one reported seeing a dinghy. Of course the Ramrods flew out virtually at sea level, and the pilots were concentrating too much on their flying to spare much attention for anything else. They flew back much higher, but in the sea that was now running a dinghy would be a difficult object to spot. The Americans had been alerted, as had the lifeguard submarine which patrolled ahead of the Fleet. The men would have sufficient food and water to last them several days; the weather was relatively good.

Are you all right, West? Are you all right, Macrae? Are you all right, Sanderson? and a dead Royal Marine band corporal slumped against his chest in the last cold hour before dawn. Four days, in which one by one those of *Connaught*'s men who had been able to jump into the sea in the three minutes' grace given the ship

430

before she went down had succumbed to exposure and exhaustion of the will. He was standing up against the bridge screen, found that both his hands were gripping its top edge, the knuckles whitening with the tension. He screwed his eyes up, shook his head slightly as if trying to drive away his ghosts. But when he opened them again the ghosts were still there, turned now into three men in a yellow rubber dinghy, drifting in towards the shore and the Japanese guns.

Dusk came, and the smear of Japanese coastline merged with the red, gold and broken grey cloud of the sunset and then disappeared. They opened one of the tins of water, each drank a carefully measured ration from the bailer, stopped up the opening of the tin with some of the chewing gum and ate a couple of squares of the chocolate. They had set the fishing lines with bits of an old envelope Moose had found in one of his pockets as bait. Bennett and Collis had ragged him a little about this; the rule was that anything which might identify the ship or anything beyond name and rank, or name, rate and service number in the case of the TAGs, had to be left behind.

But that had been much earlier, when the prospects of being picked up that same afternoon had still seemed good. Since then aircraft had flown over them several times – Fireflies from *Irresistible*, Avengers, Corsairs, and once an American flying boat which might have been specifically there to look for them. They had fumbled with the signalling mirror, tried to reflect the sun towards them – they had decided to conserve the flares as there were so few of them – but each time the aircraft had continued on their original heading. Each time, too, there had been the nagging fear that the Japanese had seen their signals, a fear which only gradually ebbed as the hours passed and the Japanese did not come. They had dropped other pieces of the envelope over the side of the dinghy, and Bennett had tried to calculate which way the drift was carrying them, but the heavy swell made it impossible; the coast seemed to come no nearer, but neither did it move further away.

With the coming of night it grew cold, and they huddled together in the bottom of the dinghy for warmth, the rubber sheet which had been rolled up and secured to the side with press studs pulled over them and keeping the worst of the water out. From *Inflexible*'s deck the sea had not seemed particularly rough, but the frail dinghy was at the mercy of the waves, rolling and pitching and sometimes carried round in complete circles. They had stepped the aluminium mast in the slot provided for it, and hoisted the sail, which lessened the motion, but the wind seemed to be carrying them inshore, so they had had to take it down again. With the unfamiliar motion all three had been seasick, almost as soon as they had got into the dinghy and again after they had eaten.

Bennett felt a hand on his shoulder, came out of the half-doze which passed in these circumstances for sleep.

'Your turn on watch,' Collis told him.

Bennett moved away from Moose, trying not to wake him, and stretched his cramped limbs. 'What time is it?'

Collis had the only watch which still worked. 'Just coming up to 2200.'

'See anything?'

'Not a sausage.'

Bennett groaned. 'Don't start me off thinking about food. I could just about eat a horse.'

'Not out here you couldn't. You'd throw it all back up.'

Despite the circumstances they both managed to grin.

Bennett moved to the stern of the dinghy and swung his arms across his chest several times in an effort to

432

warm himself. His flying suit had not quite dried out after his period in the water and the night wind cut cold through the damp cotton. He envied Moose, who seemed to have fallen asleep as soon as Collis had taken over from him earlier, and still slept on, mouth opening slightly, front teeth showing whitely in the darkness, even snoring a little from time to time.

Collis seemed in no hurry to get some sleep. 'They must be pulling back by now.'

They had known at sunset that there would be little or no chance of rescue before the next morning – the dinghy would not show up on radar and even if it passed close by the lifeguard submarine would not see them – but the knowledge that the Fleet was withdrawing south-eastwards for a planned rendezvous with the Fleet Train had induced a profound sense of depression until Collis had reminded them that they had supplies for several days, 'and some Chinese steward from a merchant ship lasted four bloody months on a life raft by 'imself. Something like four months anyway. And that was way down in the South Atlantic. Here we've got aircraft going over all the time. One of them's bound to spot us.' Neither he nor either of the other two would allow himself to speak of the possibility of being picked up by the Japanese.

Thurston lay on his bunk, listening to the night sounds of the ship, the regular clicking of the fan on its bracket standing out above everything else. The padre had been up earlier, had sat on the chair opposite him and asked whether he wanted to talk about his father, whether he would like a short memorial service in the ship's chapel. But a memorial service would have been an artificial thing; of all the men on board only he had known his father, and so any mourning was and must remain a private thing for him alone. He had thanked the padre, assured him that he would come to him if he felt the need. The padre was just doing his job, of course – how many times had he, Thurston, told an officer or rating under his command who had lost a relation to go to the padre if he wanted to talk to someone? They would have buried the old man by now, today or yesterday, in the church of which he had been vicar for thirty years, where the names of two of his sons appeared on the memorial to the dead of the last war, with a trumpeter to sound the Last Post and cavalry Reveille over him. George would have been there – he had been appointed to a training submarine at Blyth after leaving the Submarine School at Fort Blockhouse and would have no difficulty in getting a day's leave now that the war in Europe was over; Kate too, despite the lengthy journey it would have involved. Alice would have left her post in one of the Newcastle hospitals to organise her stepmother in the aftermath of her husband's death.

He was an executor of his father's will, and no doubt the solicitors would be writing to him soon enough. But there was little he could do from this distance; he supposed that Alice could take over from him. He was the old man's only surviving son, but he was right out on the periphery of things. He did not know, and would not know for at least another week, assuming that Maud or Alice had written to him immediately, how he had died, and in what circumstances. The letter to his stepmother was done, and would go with the mail tomorrow, but it would be a month before the answer came. Meanwhile, twelve of his men were dead, and three more might or might not be in their dinghy, perilously close to the enemy coast. The fan continued its clicking. He set his teeth, then finally stood up to switch it off. But even with that source of irritation gone it was a long time before he slept.

The sun came up out of the eastern sea, a great red ball lighting up the water. None of them had slept for long;

434

even Moose had been brought awake in the early hours by the cold, and not gone back to sleep again. The white smear on the horizon had disappeared and now there was only a great blue circle of sea around them.

'That's something, at least,' said Moose briefly.

But their throats were too dry for any of them to feel much like talking, even after another tiny ration of water. No aircraft passed over them. They saw a squadron of American Avengers a long way off, and the white condensation trails of the high flying B29s, on their way to bomb Tokyo or some other Japanese city, tried flashing them with the signalling mirror, but with faint hope only. Bennett got out one of the button-sized compasses, and decided that the wind was blowing westerly, away from the Japanese coast, and that it was worth hoisting the sail again. It seemed to take much longer than yesterday to get it up, and the realisation came that even after less than twenty-four hours in the dinghy they were already much weakened by the seasickness, the lack of food and water.

As the sun rose higher it grew warmer, the warmth welcome at first after the long cold night, drying their clothes out at last and inducing a short-lived sense of well-being. But soon the sun grew too hot to be enjoyed, beating down on their heads and reflecting back off the sea and the yellow rubber of the dinghy. Chaps had lasted several weeks in boats and on rafts in warm waters like this; they had food and water and none of them was injured; but even yesterday, when aircraft had passed over their heads several times, they had not been sighted, and the wind and currents, while taking them away from the Japanese coast, might be carrying them out of the zone over which Allied aircraft operated. The dinghy was less than ten feet long, a minute object in all the vastness of the ocean.

There was a letter in the mail in his father's familiar copperplate hand, dated sixteen days earlier. It was just as usual, a few remarks about the weather, acid comments on the Labour Party's success in the General Election. *After what Mr Churchill has done for this country, to dismiss him before the war is even over. Of course, the people here seem to regard the war as being done with now that the Germans are defeated and quite forget about the Japanese*. It was a strange sensation to read the letter, knowing that the writer was now dead.

'Any more news about your father?'

'Not yet, sir. I'm not really expecting anything.'

'Bad business.'

'Yes, sir.'

The Admiral had been careful and conciliatory around Thurston for the last couple of days, as if he had appreciated that he had made a poor job of breaking the news to him and was trying to make amends. But it was easier for him to restrict himself to monosyllables, to carry on outwardly as though nothing had changed. He had had the same sensation before, of being two men, the outer man wearing the uniform and carrying out his duties automatically, as he had been trained to do, the inner man cut off to some extent, gone away small inside himself and prey to a jumble of confused thoughts. But there was a war on and private troubles had to be subordinated to that. It wasn't as if his being at home when it had happened would have made much difference, he told himself. His father would still be dead.

He looked through the other letters. Three from Kate, one from Helen to say that she had passed all her exams; *it was a bit of a near thing in Anatomy, but at least I've got through*.

'My daughter's got through her first-year medical exams.'

'Must be a clever girl.'

'She's always wanted to be a doctor. When she was small her dolls seemed to spend all their time in

436

bandages. And my sister's a doctor, which is probably what started her off.'

Alice had been perhaps the most single-minded of the four of them. It had been expected that after she had finished school she would stay at home for a few years to help her stepmother before getting married. But when the war came she had announced that with two of her brothers going into the army and the third already at sea she was not prepared to spend her time working out menus and arranging flowers, and had disappeared to London to spend four years as a VAD. The war over, she had caused still more consternation by announcing that she intended to train as a doctor, that she had already been accepted as a student by a hospital in Edinburgh, and there was sufficient of the money their mother had left in trust for her to pay the tuition fees, if her father would allow her access to it, and as for the rest, she would manage somehow.

In the end they had all chipped in. Maud had had some money of her own, Thurston had lent Alice part of his share of the Navy's wartime prize money, and their grandfather had given her the money which had been earmarked for Edmund's final year at Oxford. The old man had continued to disapprove, declaring that women doctors were all very well, but as soon as she had qualified she would get married and waste it all. But Alice had remained unmarried and the old man had been won over to the extent of referring with paternal pride to 'my daughter, the doctor'.

Alice had always taken a particular interest in her only niece, and so it was not very surprising that Helen had decided early on to follow her into medicine. She had also shown a streak of her aunt's determination. As she was only seventeen it had been thought by her parents that it would be sensible for her to train in Newcastle and live with her aunt, but she had insisted that she wished to be an 'ordinary student' and had duly

437

applied to and been accepted by the same hospital where Alice had gone.

One letter from George, which was unexpected as he had always been an erratic correspondent, except at prep school and Dartmouth when he had been required to write to his parents every Sunday. George was still in the training submarine but hoping to be appointed to an operational boat within a few weeks, and trying to wangle himself a place in one which was going to the Far East – there was a submarine flotilla based at Trincomalee and another at Fremantle. Kate had remarked in one of her letters that George seemed to have a girl-friend among the Wrens at Blyth; the last time he had been on leave there had been veiled references to a Jane, and a photograph of a Wren had appeared on his chest of drawers. It all seemed a very long way off, and quite separate from the war he himself was involved in.

In the dinghy time dragged past very slowly. Bennett tried to remember when at any time in the past he had spent an entire day doing nothing, and with nothing to do, without book, newspaper or anything else with which to occupy himself. They rested in the bottom of the dinghy, moving as little as possible in order to conserve their energy and to prevent themselves sweating and using up any more liquid than was absolutely necessary, without any of them speaking for long periods. They had leant over the sides, and splashed themselves with seawater, but as the water evaporated their skins had broken into angry rashes from the salt left behind. Once or twice they had seen triangular fins above the water, a hundred or more yards off but still far too close for comfort, apparently circling them, waiting for the moment to close in.

Bennett rubbed his chin, a day's growth of bristles rasping against his hand, looked out over the water. The sea was much flatter than yesterday, and in the bright sunlight visibility was better, though blue heat haze draped the horizon. The compass told him that the drift was carrying them north-eastwards, roughly parallel to the coast of the main Japanese island but still out of sight of it, and so out of the main zone of British and American operations. 'Keep going like this and we'll finish up in Alaska,' Collis had said. 'Turn right for Vancouver,' Moose had replied. That was the last thing anyone had said for a long time. They had made various experiments with the sail, but it was quite clear that the dinghy would not steer, was only capable of running with the wind and current further out into the vast Pacific. He shifted uncomfortably, his head pounding from the glare and from dehydration; he rolled it slowly from left to right, shutting his eyes automatically when the sun grew too strong.

'You all right, Ben?'

'Just about. How about you?'

'Just thinking I should have joined the army instead. You don't have to go messing about in boats in the Seaforth Highlanders of Vancouver.'

'I'm not sure I fancy your knees in a kilt.'

'You wouldn't have to. I'd have my feet under the table in a nice German household right now, with a couple of buxom Gretchens to look after me, waiting for my demob number to come through. And you'd be stuck with some Limey prune who couldn't manage a deck landing to save his life.'

'Perhaps I should have done what my brother did and failed the medical. He's a clerk in the civil service, spends all his time complaining about the paper shortage and how he has to go and train with the Home Guard two nights a week. He doesn't even have to do that any more. And all that's wrong with him is that he couldn't read the bottom line of the eyesight chart.'

'Neither could I.' Moose grinned. 'So I got there early, before they started the medicals, chatted up one of the nurses, managed to sneak into the room where the chart was, and learnt it all off by heart. Doctor was real impressed.'

'So that's why your landings are always so bloody awful,' said Collis.

Moose leant over the side, gathered up some water in the bailer and flung it over Collis, who responded in kind, so that a water fight went on until the three of them were thoroughly soaked and the dinghy had to be bailed out once more.

'That'll teach you to have some respect for your superiors,' Moose told Collis with mock severity and in a parody of an upper-class English accent.

Hardly had they settled into their former positions once more when Collis was shouting, pointing up into the sky to the south.

'Look, there's another aircraft!'

Bennett and Moose both followed the direction Collis was pointing in, but could see nothing.

'Look! I saw the sun flashing off it. I'm sure I did!' Collis grabbed the mirror, and started to line it up, catching the sun in it and trying to reflect it towards the aircraft.

'There it is again,' he insisted.

This time Bennett saw it, a single bright flash some ten miles off and perhaps two thousand feet up, just on the edge of the heat haze, which was what had made it difficult to see.

'Shall I try one of the flares?' Without waiting for a reply Collis pulled out the flare pistol, broke it open and inserted one of the six miniature flares.

'Don't waste them,' Moose counselled.

Collis raised the pistol and pulled the trigger. The flare soared up into the air, then burst into bright red flight and floated gently down, trailing grey smoke behind it. Bennett picked up the mirror, turned it this way and that until the sun flashed from its centre. Not

440

morse, just a ragged series of flashes that the crew of the aircraft might see.

For a long moment the aircraft remained on its course, so that it seemed as though its crew could not have seen anything. Then back from the blue haze came an answering flash, a series of morse dots and dashes from the signal lamp in the aircraft's nose. Laboriously Bennett spelt out an answer. *British. Hit by flak yesterday forenoon. Flying Avenger. Three.*

It was an American Mariner flying boat, and it was only minutes later that it was landing on the water a hundred or so yards from them and taxiing towards them with engines idling. A door in the fuselage opened and a man in flying suit and baseball cap leant out. Moose, Bennett and Collis found the paddles lying in the bottom of the dinghy and tried to make some headway towards the aircraft, but the drift seemed to carry them further away.

'Gonna throw you a line,' the man in the doorway shouted.

A coil came flying out over the water, and landed a good six feet from them. Bennett did not care any more. He dropped over the side, forgetful even of the sharks, reaching the monkey's fist at the end of the line in three or four strokes. Meanwhile, Moose and Collis had managed to paddle the dinghy a few feet towards him so that he was able to turn around and push the line through one of the d-rings in its bow.

'Have you got it? Okay, we'll haul you in.'

A second American appeared in the doorway, and the two hauled the line in hand over hand in a series of jerks.

'Okay, it's just one step.'

Standing upright for the first time in many hours, Bennett felt suddenly giddy, swayed dangerously and might have fallen into the water had not one of the Americans grabbed a handful of his flying suit and

441

pulled him up inside. The interior of the flying boat was very dark after the bright glare outside. He swayed again, one of his legs gave way and he toppled sideways on to the metal floor, greyish and filmed with oil.

'Okay, pal, take it easy.'

One of the Americans steered him further into the fuselage. He looked round, saw Collis and Moose following behind him, then the second American bringing the dinghy on board and shutting the door.

'Now let's just hope we can get off again. It's kinda rough today. But we wouldn't have done it at all yesterday.' The American's words came out through a wad of chewing gum. 'Too goddamn rough to do anything.'

The Americans, who seemed to be the flying boat's navigator and wireless operator, produced thermos flasks of hot coffee, sweets and chocolate from what seemed to be their own rations for the flight, found some blankets and spread them out on the fuselage floor for them to sit on.

'Were you actually looking for us?' Bennett asked.

'Hell, no. We're looking for a couple of our own F4U guys who got shot down this morning. Couldn't see anything where they were supposed to have gone in, so we went downwind a bit in case they'd drifted, then Mac – he's the pilot – started shouting that some guy was dazzling him with a signalling mirror, so we thought we'd better have a look-see, and that was you. We were expecting one of our guys, not three Limeys.'

'Lucky for us that you did take a look.'

'Yeah. Well, it's what we're here for. We're starting to get low on gas so we'll take you back to Okinawa with us, and we'll get a message to your ship so they know you're okay, and then we'll figure out how you're going to get back there.'

It had only been the day before that they had left *Inflexible*, but already it seemed a lifetime ago. The flying

442

boat made the slow flight back to Okinawa, they disembarked, were ferried ashore in a motorboat the Americans called a gig, and were taken to the American shore base thrown up by the SeeBees as soon as the Japanese on Okinawa had been defeated. 'You've got to be a bit careful. There's the odd sniper still holed up further inland, and we haven't finished clearing all the minefields yet, so stick to the sidewalks and don't go wandering off by yourselves.' They were given American uniforms to wear, shown to a large American 'mess hall' for a meal of fried chicken and ice cream, medically examined, allocated bunks for the night, given ten dollars each, and told that they would be flown out to their ship the next day. It was all very efficient, and obviously something the Americans were well practised in.

The relief at being safe and looked after was overwhelming.

Chapter Thirty-Three

'Hello, strangers.'

'We were just getting ready for your memorial service when we heard the Yanks had got you. The padre was frightfully disappointed.'

They had been woken soon after dawn with the news that one of *Inflexible*'s Avengers had arrived at the airstrip near the American shore base to pick them up, and had barely had time to gather up their few belongings before piling into a waiting jeep. Moose sat in the observer's seat for the flight back, Bennett in the seat by the main wireless set which the TAG used when not in his turret, and Collis on the floor between them. It was overcast again, and began to rain heavily as the Avenger taxied out to take off, heavy drops of rain stinging off the outside of the canopy.

It was strange now to be returning to the carrier, having been accepted as dead by the rest of the squadron and the ship's officers. *Inflexible* was cloaked in rain; the Avenger had to stooge about over the fleet for almost an hour before the visibility cleared enough to permit an attempt at landing, and was waved off twice before finally landing on. They were debriefed, told several times by various people that they looked like a bunch of Yanks in the American uniforms they had been given, medically examined a second time, and told that they would not be required for flying until the following day at the earliest. Bennett went to the ready room, almost empty as all three squadrons were flying on various

444

sorties, sat in one of the chairs and leafed idly through the magazines, and the latest issue of the ship's daily news sheet. Only two days ago he had been doing the same thing, in the same chair, but a great abyss seemed now to divide the two, so that it was as if he was looking back at a different life. While he, Moose and Collis had been in their dinghy, the daily routine on board *Inflexible* had gone on as usual. The news sheet, which had gone to press at 1800 the previous evening, reported that a further replen had taken place, that intelligence reports suggested that the American B29s had done further heavy damage in their raids on Tokyo, and their own attacks on the Japanese airfields were having the desired effect. The Avenger crew shot down the day before was still missing. There was Bennett's name in black and white, along with those of Moose and Collis. A memorial service would be held in the ship's chapel at 1900.

Bennett could not concentrate on the magazines any further, so he went aft to the cabin he shared with one of the other observers, an awkward journey at Action Stations, with a heavy watertight door to be opened every few yards and then clipped shut behind him.

The cabin was very tidy. The Marine who acted as servant for himself and his cabin mate had been in to clean as usual. Both bunks were made up with immaculate mitred corners, all clothes and shoes put away in the lockers. He turned one of the taps on the washbasin, and turned it off again when only a thin trickle of water emanated from it. The sameness of it all should have been comforting, but in some peculiar way it now seemed to threaten him. He pulled himself up on to his bunk, sat on it for a moment with his legs swinging, looking across to the photograph of an actress in a bathing suit that the other observer had cut out of a magazine and stuck on the bulkhead. It was a long time until

445

lunch, and that in any case would be action messing, soup and sandwiches, and he could not think of any way to occupy himself until then. He was still sitting there ten minutes later when Moose pushed aside the curtain and stepped over the coaming.

'You okay, Ben?'

'Yes, I think so. Funny, though, I can't think what to do with myself.'

'I can't either. I'm trying to remember what we normally do to fill in time, and it just seems unreal. Real strange business, coming back from the dead.'

'I wonder if Lazarus ever felt like this.'

'Yeah, that's what I'd really like to know.'

'Ship's turning into wind. Someone must be on the way back.'

Bennett cocked an ear to the approaching sound of engines.

'Must be our lot.'

'Yeah, sounds like them. It's going to be kind of funny to see them all again.'

'Didn't you think we'd make it?'

'No, it's not that. Hell, with all the aircraft we've got flying over that bit of sea I thought we'd have to be pretty unlucky for nobody to spot us. I don't really know what it is.'

'Lazarus again.'

'Yeah. Come on, Ben. Time we did something about it.'

Bennett dropped down from his bunk, felt Moose's large hand clap him across the shoulders.

'Come on, fella. Let's go see how much Coke it takes to get drunk.'

A signal arrived from the Americans without warning, cancelling all strikes and ordering the entire fleet to withdraw two hundred miles to the east because of a 'special operation'.

446

'The buzz is going round that there's going to be a secret commando raid on the palace in Tokyo to kidnap the Emperor, so we can hold him hostage and the Japs will have to surrender,' Spencer told Thurston when he came up with his supper tray that evening. 'After all, they think he's a god, don't they, sir. Either that or we're goin' to use some kind of secret weapon on them.' Spencer waited until Thurston had begun eating before asking curiously, 'Do *you* know what all this is about, sir?'

'No more than you do, Spencer. I'm not in Admiral Halsey's confidence any more than you are.'

The cloud and overcast continued all day. During the afternoon the air grew heavy and thundery, and soon after dark the first bolt of lightning split the sky in two, and a brief but fierce tropical storm raged over the fleet, bringing thunder which rolled close overhead, so close that for a time the storm seemed almost on top of them, and rain which rebounded in heavy droplets off every flat surface and streamed down hastily donned oilskins. On the flight deck the hangar party worked on, oilskins pulled up over their heads so that they looked strangely misshapen and gnome-like in the darkness, trying by sleight of hand and movements of their bodies to keep the water from getting inside the open inspection panels of the aircraft or the magazines in the wings, where hundreds of rounds of ammunition now lay sleeping, ready to be wakened into deadly life the instant the pilot pressed the red button on the stick.

For perhaps an hour the storm lasted, then the fleet was on the other side of it, beneath stars which had broken through the ragged shreds of grey-black cloud. On the bridge all was ordered calm, as it had been while the storm lasted, but now it was over there was a comfortable sense of peace as men settled down to the uneventful remainder of their watch. Dimmed lights showed at

447

the binnacle and the various indicators, circles of red amid the grey darkness, whilst the gyro repeater ticked on in its usual metronomic rhythm. There was an occasional exchange of words, but mostly there was the companionable silence of men who knew what they were doing and who knew with absolute certainty that they could rely upon one another. Most of *Inflexible*'s complement had been in her for at least two years, had joined her before the long refit in America. At this stage of the war the majority of the ratings were Hostilities Only, stiffened by a hard core of chief and petty officers and regular RN ratings who had joined as Boys, but they now had the experience of anything up to six years at sea. The new arrivals had been absorbed by the old hands, had been trained and initiated by them, so that by now they were virtually indistinguishable from the rest.

Spencer's prediction was more accurate than he could have known. There was a brief signal the next morning: 'Little Boy Compels Sugar How Mike Able.' Sugar How Mike Able was the Japanese town of Hiroshima on the Inland Sea, which *Inflexible*'s aircraft had flown over a few weeks earlier. All anybody could say about the place was that there had been a lot of flak around the outskirts. What Little Boy meant nobody knew.

For the rest of the forenoon watch the task force zig-zagged over the same few miles of sea, waiting for the signal to end the impasse, sending them back into position off the Japanese islands to renew the strikes, or ordering a further withdrawal. The rumours became wilder. The Emperor had committed suicide in Hiroshima; the American Marines had landed at Hiroshima – 'And they're welcome to it,' declared a pilot who had lost part of a wing tip to the Hiroshima flak a fortnight before. Surrender negotiations were starting in the Town Hall in Hiroshima. 'Do the Japanese have town halls?' queried one doubter.

The news finally came through at lunchtime, on a signal form brought up to the Admiral from the main wireless office.

'So this is it.' Winthrop passed Thurston the signal.

'D'ye hear there? This is the Captain speaking. President Truman has just announced that at approximately 0800 this morning an American aircraft dropped an atomic bomb on the Japanese city of Hiroshima. This is an entirely new type of bomb said to have the explosive power equivalent to at least twenty thousand tons of TNT, and therefore many times more powerful than any bomb used by the RAF or any other air force during the war. The United Nations have again called on the Japanese to surrender unconditionally, but the Japanese have not yet responded. Until the Japanese do surrender the war goes on, and there will be no let up in the offensive against them. That is all.'

After the ship's broadcast had clicked off Thurston stood for several minutes looking out to sea, screwing his eyes up against the glare off the water. Last night's storm had cleared the overcast, so that the day was as hot and bright as any day in the Far East had been. It was far more than he dared allow himself to hope, that the war which he had come to accept would drag on for another year, perhaps two, and involve a bloody struggle against Japanese troops fighting in defence of their own land, might come to a sudden end as the result of the dropping of this mysterious American bomb.

'Like nothing you or I have ever seen,' the Admiral said that evening in a rare thoughtful moment. 'There was some very vague buzz going round the Admiralty when I was there that the Yanks were working on some fantastic new bomb made with uranium, and a lot of the best scientific brains seemed to disappear to America suddenly, but nothing more concrete than that. I wonder how many of the things the Yanks have got.'

'Hope they do surrender, sir,' Spencer told Thurston. 'Then me and Rosie can start being married properly. You know, sir, me coming home regular and all that.'

If the war did end he and Kate too could go back to being properly married, at least for a couple of years while he put in his time ashore. He could try for command of the Navigation School when he left *Inflexible*, or an air station perhaps; Kate could find them a house nearby and he could go off to work in the morning and come home at night as he hadn't been able to do since before the war, get to know George and Helen again, and try to be a proper father to Thomas and Andrew. He might accept Masters' offer, make a fresh start away from the Navy and put down some roots at last.

The thought of Kate reminded him uneasily of Jane, made him wonder what effect his affair with her would have on his married life with Kate. Jane had stirred something inside him which had lain dormant for a long time, something which he had not even been aware of until he met her. He realised that the affair had changed him, in a way he could not precisely pin down, and knew too that nothing in his relationship with Kate could be quite the same again. But many other things would not be the same after a long war. Perhaps the changes had begun to show themselves already, in the wholesale rejection of the old order by the people who had elected a Labour government with the biggest majority ever seen.

But no further news came, only orders for a return to the operational area and a renewal of the air strikes. *Inflexible* turned her head westwards and pitched into a short steep sea as the sun set once more in a blaze of colour. Perhaps it was all too good to be true, the idea that the war could be brought to an end by the dropping of a single bomb, however awesome its destructive power.

Chapter Thirty-Four

As his aircraft roared over the strip of sand Petty Officer Takashima turned his head for a last look at Japan. The beach and the low cliffs which rose behind it looked as they always did, as did the fishing village which straggled along both banks of a small river where it cut through the cliffs. Another quite ordinary day for the unknown fishermen who lived in that village five hundred feet below, though they now ventured out in their boats only at night, so as to escape the British and American aircraft which flew over that area in their attacks on Japan.

But this was the last hour of Takashima's life and everything around him was a little more vivid, a little more precious than usual. Three days ago he and nine others had been called to the Wing Commander's office to be told that the time had come for them to die for their Emperor and for Japan. Takashima had been a fighter pilot for a little more than a year, and as the war had gone on more and more of his time had been spent in flying escort for other pilots who had been chosen to die, defending their bomb-laden aircraft from the British and American fighters so that they could make the final dive on to the deck of one of the warships which now threatened Japan. As fuel and ammunition grew more scarce he had known that his own time would come. The kamikazes had become the sword, and other pilots and aircraft could not be spared to escort them but must now die with them.

He and the other nine had been given forty-eight hours' leave in which to bid their families farewell. In the disruption caused by enemy bombing it had taken Takashima almost twenty-four of those hours to reach home. It had been late in the afternoon when he arrived, his father just home from his job in an ammunition factory, his mother preparing the evening meal. They had known instantly why he was there. His mother had insisted that he have the best and crispest pieces of meat and fish, the largest helping of the soup. His sisters, too young to appreciate the situation, had merely watched in silence as he ate, seated cross-legged on the floor, chopsticks poised over their bowls, exquisite bone china which Takashima remembered from earliest childhood, rich and spicy smells rising out of them. They had pressed him to stay a little longer, but the journey back would take as long as the homeward journey, so he had left them before midnight, travelling back to the airfield by a succession of delayed and diverted trains.

It had been afternoon when he returned, to be told what had happened that morning after he left Hiroshima. A single American bomber had dropped a strange new weapon, the like of which no man had ever seen. A large part of the city had been reduced to rubble. There was no news from there; the information had come from aircraft flying over the city. His family, a few among many thousands, were almost certainly dead; they had lived in one of the most devastated areas. Better in any case to believe them dead and that he would join them in paradise after this last mission. His hatred of the British and Americans was no longer a boy's immature rage against a vaguely known enemy, but a slow-burning hatred for the men who had killed his family and destroyed his home.

This morning he and the other kamikazes had been briefed for their mission, had made their final prayers

453

in the shrine erected to the gods, drunk the cup of sake before their comrades who had yet to be chosen and had been saluted by their commander. In his aircraft, not the streamlined Kawasaki fighter which he normally flew but an old Zero with a five-hundred-pound bomb at its belly, he had gone through the cockpit check as usual, fidgeted with his straps until he was comfortable, tied the sacred headband of the rising sun above his brows. The mechanics had come to lock the cockpit canopy, but he had waved them away. He was ready to meet death of his own choosing, as a warrior, a warrior of Japan.

The ten aircraft flew low over the sea, below the enemy radar so that they should not be seen until the last moment, a trick they had learned from the enemy themselves. The afternoon sun came hot through the cockpit canopy, making him sweat inside his flying suit. He looked out to his right, saw Hosoya, whom he had trained with and who had been his closest friend since they had joined. The others he did not know; they were all volunteers from the army and from civilian life, given only the brief training which now sufficed for a kamikaze, their aircraft wandering away from their course and jerking back in the other direction as the pilots overcorrected. It would not be long now. There were the British fighters, the elegant Seafires and the bent-winged Corsairs climbing away from the carriers which lay below the horizon. It had been an American bomber which had destroyed his home, only the island bases from which the B29s operated were far beyond the range of the kamikazes. Takashima had asked that he might be permitted to carry out his mission against an American ship, but the commander had reminded him that the British carriers with their heavy deck armour were more difficult to destroy or disable and that there would be greater glory and greater reward for a pilot who succeeded.

454

There were the British, coming in to intercept. He and Hosoya, the only fighter pilots among the kamikazes, peeled off from the formation, climbing up above them, ready to defend them. Fear now, not of death, for he had accepted that and welcomed it provided he met it in the proper way, but of death at the hands of a Corsair or Seafire before he reached his target. Sun flashed from their wing tips as the enemy aircraft came in to the attack, red tracer streaming from their guns. Old and bomb-laden, the Zero was sluggish and clumsy, but Takashima found new skill as he flung his aircraft about to escape the guns, managed to evade one aircraft and get himself into a firing position astern of a second. He pressed the gun button, shouted exultantly as his rounds punched into the Seafire's rear fuselage. But the Seafire was faster and drew out of range before Takashima could get in a second burst. Below him a Corsair came down on a Zero, flames creeping along its fuselage as the bullets found their mark. Takashima saw the pilot's head jerk back as the fire reached the cockpit, and then the bomb at the aircraft's belly went off. The force of the blast flung the pursuing Corsair on to its back and Takashima got in another brief burst as the pilot struggled to right it, but was frustrated again as superior speed took the Corsair beyond his range. He looked round for Hosoya, could not see him. The British were among the Zeros, the half-trained pilots unable to manoeuvre to protect themselves, and were picking them off so that one by one they went down into the sea.

There were the British ships, a great grey mass of them, their guns sending up a curtain of fire, puffs of black smoke stippling the blue sky. Takashima selected his target, the aircraft carrier nearest to him. No British carrier had yet been destroyed or even disabled by a kamikaze; to do so would bring him immortality, and the vengeance for his family which he now craved. To hit the armoured deck would be ineffective; the only vulnerable part was the island which towered unarmoured above the deck on the starboard side, which had the bridges and operations rooms, the ready rooms where the pilots waited between sorties against Japan. The British ship maintained her course, white water creaming along either flank, water turning to froth and foam astern of her.

Takashima's headband had worked loose. He pushed it up out of his eyes, felt sweat stream from beneath it, the salt prickling his eyelids. The small anti-aircraft weapons opened up, blobs of red tracer coming up at him. He jinked, never holding the same course for more than a couple of heartbeats. Perhaps the other Zeros had all been shot down into the sea, for he saw none of them; but he did not care about them any more. It was between him and the great grey carrier he had selected and on whose decks he would die as a kamikaze. The British fighters, too, had gone, pulling away as their own anti-aircraft fire began. Tracer exploded around him, a jolt as a cannon shell from a British Oerlikon gun hit home in the engine cowling in front of him.

He pushed the nose down into the dive, taking aim on the open bridge halfway up the island, acrid smoke beginning to come back into the cockpit. The big ship was holding her course, the guns training round to pour their fire into his Zero. Takashima jerked stick and rudder to follow the ship as she turned.

The British captain was good; he would hold the same course until the final seconds before impact, then put his helm hard over, to send the kamikaze either plunging into the sea or smashing into the armoured flight deck where his bomb and his courage would be wasted. Takashima knew this, and was ready.

Cannon shells were striking on the wings, black smoke

coming out of the engine. Takashima prayed that in these last seconds the engine would not seize and prevent him from fulfilling his mission. Another impact; a cannon shell coming up through the cockpit floor and exploding beneath him. He felt the metal shards slam into his body and legs, looked down to see blood welling up out of his wounds. Petrol spilled into the cockpit from a punctured fuel tank, rising to his ankles, surprisingly cold, the fumes catching at his nostrils. The white ensign with its bold red cross streamed back from the masthead, apparently rigid in the slipstream, a second and smaller flag beneath it and to one side, with another red cross and one red ball. This was a flagship, he realised.

There was the bridge, men in white overalls and steel helmets standing on it, more men on a second bridge on the deck above. They were his enemy, the closest he had ever been to them. The petrol caught fire, and his legs and lower body were wreathed in flames. He screamed, saw the grey steel island rising up in front of him, the lower bridge exactly in his sights. He screamed again and went on screaming as the flames laid his flesh bare, felt a sudden shock of shame at this betrayal. But nothing now could defeat him. There was a heavy-set man directly in front of him, face almost entirely concealed by his steel helmet and white hood, standing quite still, his gaze turned directly at Takashima, knowing that with the impact would come his own death.

The big ship was beginning to turn, the bridge and the thickset figure sliding away to one side. Takashima whipped the stick across, kicked the rudder and felt the battered Zero respond.

'*Banzai!*'

The sudden change of course hadn't worked. The kamikaze was still coming on, oblivious to the gunfire being poured into it from every close-range weapon which could be brought to bear, yellow fire burning inside the cockpit, the pilot's face, contorted in agony, surrounded by flame. No one could live through that storm of fire, but the aircraft still came on, still under the pilot's control. Thurston saw the midshipman beside him frozen to the spot, mesmerised, gave him a violent shove between the shoulder blades so that he went sprawling on the deck plates. As the kamikaze ploughed into the Admiral's bridge ten feet below there was a searing wave of heat, and he staggered backwards, off balance, as the blast shock hit him. Something struck him high on the left thigh in the same instant, knocked the leg from beneath him so that he crashed into the man behind and went sprawling on top of him. Somewhere near he heard someone screaming, a high unnerving sound which cut through the fuddle of the blast and went on and on. The kamikaze, burning from end to end, toppled down on to the flight deck with a crash, landing half on top of the Corsair parked there.

The man beneath him grunted. Thurston half-rolled himself off him, saw another man staggering blindly about, his head wreathed in flames where burning petrol had hit him as the kamikaze's fuel tanks exploded, a bright splash of blood all down one side. Thurston grasped the binnacle with both hands, pulled himself up on it, managed a couple of paces with his left leg trailing behind him. The man's arms were flailing wildly about his head. Instinctively Thurston grasped him by the arms, pushed him down on to the deck, then dropped down beside him and rolled over so that the weight of his body would smother the flames, noticing even as he did so the pungent smell of petrol which hung around him. There wasn't enough space for him to turn him over more than once in either direction, so he had to roll him back again, attack the last of the fire with his hands, trusting to his asbestos gloves to protect

458

them. Someone else came up, unrecognisable in his anti-flash gear, a fire extinguisher in his hands. Further off he could hear another man, Bingham or the Navigator from the voice, talking into the telephone and asking for a first-aid party on the bridge. The burnt man stopped screaming quite suddenly, began to whimper, his head rolling convulsively from side to side, blood soaking one side of his hood and the shoulder of his white overalls, his left eye hanging from its socket like some huge squashed fruit. The circle of bare flesh within the hood was red and black and unrecognisable; it was only the Navigator's name above the breast pocket which told Thurston who he was.

'Oh my God.' It was almost a sigh.

The smell of burnt flesh was suddenly in Thurston's nostrils, overlaying the petrol smell of a moment before. The man with the fire extinguisher was talking to the Navigator at a soothing pitch, telling him that all he needed to do was to hang on a bit longer until the first aid party could get to him. Thurston pulled himself upright once more, rested one hand on the binnacle to steady himself, relieved to be able to leave the Navigator to someone else.

'The Admiral's dead, sir. I think they must all be dead.' It was Bingham's voice, and Bingham was standing in front of him, swaying a little.

Thurston took a couple more steps and looked out over the bridge screen. The Admiral was quite dead, there was no question about it, half propped into a sitting position, his head lolling to one side, the crown of his tin hat split open and grey brain showing through the blood and splintered bone. One of his legs was gone almost at the hip, the other a reddish pulp, white bone showing through the blood and mess. The blond Flag Lieutenant lay next to him, chest stove in and sightless eyes staring upwards into the sky. Thurston heard someone throw up, felt saliva flood his mouth and turned away.

'Are you all right, sir?' Bingham was asking him.

He felt the blood running down his leg inside the overalls, but the answer was automatic. 'Quite all right, thank you.'

Around Thurston the rest of the bridge watchkeepers were picking themselves up, several of them marked with fresh blood where splinters of flying metal from the explosion had hit them. The Navigator was sprawled on the deck plates, a signalman bending over him, trying to calm him as he began to scream again. A second signalman lay near by, huddled into a foetal position with his legs drawn up into his belly, a long splinter of bone sticking out of his overalls below the knee. He screamed once as the Chief Yeoman knelt beside him and started to apply a field dressing to the wound, then set his teeth and lay still, his face chalk-white and his freckles standing out as dark blotches.

The Admiral was dead and the senior captain must take over the squadron. 'Get *Imperious* on the TBS and say I want to speak to Captain Strickland.'

The Gunnery Officer picked up the handset and translated briefly into the TBS argot.

'Through, sir.'

He told Strickland in a couple of short sentences that the Admiral was dead and that Strickland was in command of the squadron.

'What's your other damage?'

'Not sure yet. I'll give you a full report as soon as I can get it.' He was aware that he was speaking in plain language on an insecure link, that the Japanese might well listen in to British signals traffic as the British listened in to theirs, aware too that his voice sounded strange, almost disembodied, especially through the distortion of the radio.

'Bob, are you all right?' Strickland asked anxiously.

'I just got in the way of something. I'm all right.' He looked down, saw the spreading red stain on one leg of his overalls, blood running over the top of his boot and on to the metal plates. He was leaning against the bridge screen, realising now that it was himself and not Bingham who was swaying.

'All right, I'll wait to hear from you. Out.'

A sick-berth attendant was on his knees beside the Navigator; another was dealing with the injured signalman, deftly applying bandages and lashing the man's legs together as a crude form of splinting.

'Now you, sir.'

A youngish sick-berth petty officer was standing in front of him. There was shouting on the flight deck and sounds of hoses as the fire party got to work on the burning aircraft, and other aircraft were trundled clear of them. Thurston moved back to the binnacle, let himself down on to the raised monkey's island which surrounded it, relieved to be able to sit and rest for a moment. But there was so much to think about with all three squadrons airborne and due to land on in the next hour and a half, damage assessments to be made – on which would depend the matter of whether the squadrons could land safely on board *Inflexible* or would have to be diverted to the other carriers – repairs, burials for the dead and succour for the wounded, the transfer of command and what was left of the Admiral's staff to *Imperious*.

The sick-bay Petty Officer had taken a clasp knife from his haversack and ripped open the leg of his overalls as far as the knee.

'Looks a bit nasty, sir. Looks like it's gone in deep.'

The two halves of the overall leg had been pulled apart so that the wound lay exposed, a ragged gash perhaps an inch and a half long and a third the width. No pain; that would come later, when the shock of the impact had worn off.

461

'Only a little bit, probably, but gone in pretty deep.'

'Just tie it up.'

'Aye aye, sir.'

Someone had come up the bridge ladder and was talking to the Commander (Air).

'Captain, sir, Lieutenant-Commander (Flying) thinks we have an unexploded bomb on board.' The tone was strangely formal in the circumstances. 'It looks as though the Jap's bomb didn't go off.'

It hadn't struck him until then, but that was the reason the serious damage had been confined to such a small area, to the Admiral's bridge which the kamikaze had actually hit. A five-hundred-pound bomb, had it gone off, would have destroyed half the island; certainly nothing would have been left of men standing a mere fifteen feet from it.

The Petty Officer SBA was busy wrapping the bandage around Thurston's leg when the Lieutenant-Commander (Flying) arrived on the bridge proper, his trade nickname of Little F laughably inappropriate as he was six foot three and a formidable rugby player, with a bushy reddish-blond beard jutting out from his chin.

'Yes, sir, the bomb's still there. God only knows why it hasn't gone off, but it hasn't.'

'Can you get it over the side without it going off?'

'I'm not sure, sir. It's stuck between the wreckage of the Zero and the Corsair, so we'd have to get the wreck off it before we could hope to move it. The mobile crane won't have the outreach to get anything that size over the side. We'd have to shift it all aft, then use the boat-deck crane like we did the last time.' Little F appeared to notice Thurston's appearance for the first time. 'Are you all right, sir?'

Thurston felt rather foolish as he sat on the monkey's island with his overalls cut open and the sick-bay Petty Officer fiddling about with the gash in his thigh. 'Quite all right, thank you,' he said for the third time.

Little F went on. 'We could bring the mobile crane up from the hangar and use it to get the wreckage aft to where the boat-deck crane can pick it up, or it might be better to use the dodgem.'

'I'd better take a look at it for myself.'

The Petty Officer pushed a safety pin into the layers of bandage. 'That should be all right for now, sir, but the PMO ought to have a look at it.'

'Thank you.' Thurston hoisted himself to his feet, stepped out cautiously towards the ladder. Supported by the bandages the leg felt less fragile, more capable of use. He slid down the ladders on his hands, Little F and Boy Maxwell at his heels.

Inflexible's few parked aircraft had been trundled away to the forward lift and struck down into the hangar, leaving the wrecked Zero and the Corsair it had crashed on to in a grotesque tangle of metal in the centre of a circle of water and foam which slowly expanded as the ship rolled. The Corsair was on one wheel, its folded wings bent into strange angles, the remains of the Zero on top of it. The Japanese pilot was still strapped into his cockpit, his face a blackened skull, teeth set in a rictus of a grin where the flesh had been shrivelled away, a strong smell of excreta hanging in the air where he had fouled himself before the impact.

'Nice-looking little bugger, isn't he, sir,' Little F remarked almost casually. He considered the problem of moving the wreckage in silence for a little longer. 'I think it had better be the mobile crane, sir. If the Jap'll lift off, the bomb may come up with it. If not, we should be able to lift it clear and move it away by itself.'

'You'd better ask for a volunteer to drive it.'

'I'd rather do it myself, sir, if that's all right.'

'Are you sure?'

'Yes, sir. I've had plenty of practice at driving the thing, and, well, sir, to be quite honest, I don't think I could bear to watch someone else doing it.'

'All right. Don't try to rush it. Take all the time you need.'

Thurston pulled up the chin strap of his tin hat, lifted the helmet clear of his head, felt sweat run down inside the anti-flash hood he was still wearing. He mopped at his face as best he could, put the tin hat back on again. They would have to evacuate the island and get everybody below the deck armour which an exploding five-hundred-pound bomb would not penetrate, leaving Little F alone with the bomb.

'I will, sir.'

Ten minutes later Thurston, the Gunnery Officer, Bingham, Midshipman Jacobs, the Chief Yeoman and Boy Maxwell were standing at the secondary conning position, a small platform on the port side abreast the island, normally used only for berthing port side to, but from which the ship could be commanded in the event of the bridge becoming untenable. The rest of the deck was quite empty, appearing much larger than it did when occupied with aircraft and men. The other three carriers remained in their usual stations, but now seemed to be further away than usual.

Inflexible had turned into wind with the rest as the aircraft had begun to return from their sorties, but her own squadrons had been diverted and would divide themselves between the other three, returning only when the bomb had been safely dealt with. *If* it could be safely dealt with. He had been able to push to the back of his mind when talking to Little F the fact that they were standing within a few feet of a quarter of a ton of high explosive, the bomb's fuse almost certainly rendered highly unstable by the impact on *Inflexible*'s deck and the petrol explosion. Now the danger they were all in as Little F drove the mobile crane up the deck from the after lift and halted a couple of feet from the piled wreckage was only too apparent. He had to concentrate on keeping his left leg braced, praying that it would not suddenly give way beneath him; his head had begun to ache from the glare and the pressure of the tin hat on the old scar.

Little F dropped from the driving seat on to the deck. They could see him fiddling with the lifting hook, finding something in the wreckage to attach it to. It seemed a long time before he was satisfied, then he was climbing back into the seat, switching the engine on again. The wire cable tightened, and some of the wreckage began to pull clear of the rest. Something – it looked like part of a wing – fell back on to the deck with a clatter, and Thurston held his breath, his heart thumping against his ribs. The bomb was clearly visible now, a long grey cylinder, rounded at one end, with white-painted Japanese lettering on the uppermost side. The mobile crane was reversing aft, slowly at first, then increasing its speed as it moved further from the bomb, its load of twisted metal screeching horribly on the steel deck and leaving deep parallel score marks on its surface.

The mobile crane came back up the deck. Little F got down once more and walked up to the bomb, stood studying it for a time with his hands on his hips, then came walking across the deck.

'I think it would be the best thing if I moved the bomb by itself. It's pretty finely balanced where it is and if I tried to move the whole lot it'd probably fall off. I think I should be able to get a couple of slings underneath it and then hook them up to the crane.'

'You're going to need someone to give you a hand with them.'

'I think I can manage it by myself, sir.'

'Rot,' said Bingham. 'You can't move the crane and hook the slings up at the same time. I'll come and give you a hand.' He said it so decisively that Thurston had to let him go.

He watched again as they walked back towards the island, saw Little F select a couple of wire strops from the locker at the back of the mobile crane. Sun flashed off the bright edges of broken metal as the two men picked their way over the piled wreckage, one on each side, leant over the bomb and began to thread the strops beneath it. Little F's body was resting on top of the bomb, his hands working out of sight, Bingham crouched opposite. Bingham's mouth was moving, but he was too far away for the sound to be heard. Once Bingham's foot slipped and he went down on top of the bomb, a piece of metal dropping on to the deck with a clatter which was unnaturally loud in the silence.

The afternoon sun beating down and reflected off the steel deck was unbearably hot, the air heavy with heat and barely stirred by the ship's movement. Thurston looked aft, saw the ship's wake was a little crooked. 'Watch your steering, Quartermaster.' It was said more to distract himself than for any solid reason. Little F dropped on to the deck once more, cautiously moved the mobile crane a few feet further forward, stopped. Bingham was standing atop the wreckage, legs set wide apart astride the bomb itself, leaning forward to attach the metal rings at the ends of the strops over the hook. There was a splash of red on the back of one of his asbestos gloves, stark against the white as he held his hand up to show Little F that all was ready.

Thurston found his heart was thudding again as the tension came on the wires and the bomb began to lift clear of the wreckage. It was unbalanced, the rounded end several inches lower than the end which narrowed towards the fins, and he found himself praying silently that it would not slip out of the slings. Little F reversed the crane slowly down the deck, Bingham walking along beside the bomb, putting an arm out to balance it when it threatened to swing. Blood from his hand was spreading up his overall sleeve towards his elbow, his face, like Little F's, entirely hidden by his helmet and

466

anti-flash gear. The wrecked Corsair was innocuous now, all eyes on the bomb as it moved slowly down the deck to where another party waited for it. Around *Inflexible* the rest of the squadron steamed serenely on, all their aircraft now on board and struck down into the hangars.

The mobile crane stopped, gently lowered its burden on to the deck. Someone else stepped astride the bomb, hooked it up to the long boom of the boat-deck crane waiting for it, and quite suddenly the thing was swinging out over the ship's side and dropping towards the water at the slowest speed the crane could operate. The nose of the bomb met the ship's wake, made a small wake of its own for a few seconds, then the crane operator heaved on the backstay to trip the hook, and the bomb disappeared from sight. Thurston looked around him, realised that the Chief Yeoman had had his eyes shut for the last few minutes. Suddenly everyone around Thurston was smiling and laughing, the tension of the last half-hour, the five men killed on the Admiral's bridge and the damage the kamikaze had caused, entirely lost in the flood of relief. Little F and Bingham were walking back up the deck, quite casually, as if this was something they did every day of their lives.

'I could do with a drink after that,' Bingham said when he reached the secondary conning position – Little F was already calling his flight-deck party up from below to begin the main work of clearing up. Bingham was bareheaded now and looked rather pale, his languid front maintained with an effort.

'You'd better get that hand seen to.'

'Oh that's nothing, sir. I just caught it on a sharp edge somewhere. Didn't even realise I'd done it until Little F told me.' He gave a tired smile. 'I hope I don't have to do that again.'

Chapter Thirty-Five

Normality was restored to *Inflexible* in a few hours. Damage control parties made temporary repairs, shored up what needed to be shored up with heavy baulks of timber, removed the dead from the Admiral's bridge and carried them below to the sick-bay flat to await burial. Containers of tea found their way up to the gun positions, and the crews were stood down a few at a time for a mug of tea and a cigarette. *Inflexible*'s aircraft made the short journey back from the other carriers, and the hangar party set to work on them in preparation for the next day's sorties. The wreckage of the Zero and the Corsair was unceremoniously tipped over the side, the dead Japanese pilot still strapped into his cockpit, his blackened skull bearing the same maniacal grin, and spat on one by one by the flight-deck party before being pushed into the sea with his aircraft.

The First Lieutenant had taken over from the Gunnery Officer as PCO, and Carstairs had relieved Bingham as Officer of the Watch, standing in his usual position on the bridge with the Midshipman of the Watch beside him, almost as if this was just another day. But the bridge screen was pierced in many places by ragged splinter holes, and there was a pool of tacky blood on the port side where the signalman had been hit. Carstairs had been in the Plot when the kamikaze hit, and now seemed almost unnaturally clean and untroubled, a creature from another world. The blood, dull-coloured, drying gradually from the edges of the pool, where an uneven brownish crust floated on it, seemed somehow sinister now, everyone on the bridge taking elaborate care not to step in it, or in the blood streaked elsewhere on the metal plates.

'Have someone clean that up, Carstairs.'

The Commander came up to the bridge to report on the progress of the repairs.

'I take it you're going to recommend Little F and Bingham for the VC, sir. I didn't see much of it myself, of course, but from what people have been telling me . . . '

'To be honest, Commander, I hadn't really thought about it as yet.' There had been so many other things to think about in the last few hours.

They moved into a corner of the bridge, and lowered their voices so that the watchkeepers could not hear them. 'But you will do, sir? Wings is very keen that Little F should have proper recognition, and I should say Bingham too, of course.'

'Yes, of course, Commander. I'd say they'd both earned it twice over. I didn't have to think about what I was doing. They did.'

The Commander thought for a moment. 'It's just occurred to me, sir, perhaps it should be the GC rather than the VC. That's what chaps usually get for bomb disposal.'

'I think that's because bomb disposal is not "in the face of the enemy", but Roberts and Petty Officer Gould both got the VC for those bombs, if you remember.'

'Yes, sir, but weren't they just outside an enemy harbour, and the submarine could have submerged at any moment?'

'Yes, you're quite right. I'll have to think about it a bit, and have my secretary check up on the regulations. But it'll have to be one or the other.'

'Yes, sir, and thank you.'

469

Once more a funeral took place at nightfall, with a row of canvas-wrapped bodies on the deck in the stern, four Marines resting on reversed arms ('When you receive the order to rest on your arms reversed you will rest on your arms reversed and assume a mournful and melancholy haspect. Mournful because your shipmate's gone to a better 'ome, melancholy because he 'asn't paid 'is mess bill'), the gun salute which was the dead Admiral's due booming out over the black water.

The exhilaration of relief had worn off, to be replaced by something else: shock, anger, disbelief. They had been extraordinarily lucky once more, Thurston knew. Had the bomb gone off when the Japanese intended it to, he and all the bridge watchkeepers would have gone the way of the Admiral and his staff, many more would have been killed and wounded inside the island, and *Inflexible* would even now be on her way back to Sydney for repairs. Yet only yesterday there had been the brief rush of hope that the war might suddenly end, and even this morning some of that hope had still been there. But not now, not any more. The Japanese would not surrender simply because of one bomb, and the war would drag on as they had always expected it would.

Thurston was standing apart from the rest as the padre stumbled through the burial service once more, leaning on a stick which Spencer had found for him, pain beginning to claw now through the numbness in his thigh, his face set into grim lines against it. He thought how the void left by the Admiral's death was even now being closed. Strickland had temporarily taken over command of the squadron; in a few days or weeks another Rear Admiral would arrive to take over. The Admiral's secretary would go through his effects, and in six months' time a couple of tin cases of uniforms would reach his family in England. Thurston supposed that he would have to write to them. Although the Admiral had stamped his personality on *Inflexible* in

470

the short time he had been on board, he had let slip nothing about his life outside the service. Thurston had a vague idea that there was a sister in Hampshire somewhere; the Admiral's secretary would certainly know, and it would be on the Admiral's next-of-kin card anyway.

The last of the five bundles went over the side, the Rear Admiral's flag came slowly down from the masthead. Thurston found to his embarrassment that his eyelids were wet, and that he had to screw his eyes shut to hold back the tears gathering there. It was all such a bloody bloody waste, the more so if indeed the war was almost over. The Japanese, too, cold-bloodedly inducing their young men to smash themselves and their aircraft on to their enemy's decks for a tainted ideal.

The burials ended, and Thurston limped back up to the bridge, negotiating the ladders in a slow and awkward dot-and-carry-one fashion now that his leg had begun to stiffen, the pain in his thigh intensifying with each forced movement. The Officer of the Watch handed him a signal. 'The Russians have declared war on Japan, sir.' Thurston did not care enough about it to try to work out what it might mean for the conflict. 'I'll be in my sea cabin.'

Thurston went into the tiny bathroom off his sea cabin, studied himself in the mirror above the basin. He had not had time to clean up and shift into khaki before the burials. There was a long streak of black across the bridge of his nose, paler where sweat had spread it over one cheek, and gritty to the touch; there was more blackening on the front of his overalls, scorch marks on the sleeves in several places, and the left leg was gaping open to the knee, stained liberally with dried blood.

He turned the cold tap, found to his relief that the water was back on, splashed some over his face and neck, watched it run back into the basin and form a

471

dirty greyish puddle in the bottom. He was very tired. Weariness hit him like a hammer now that he no longer had to keep himself going; he was too weary even to have a shower and shift out of the overalls he had been wearing all day. He should find out how the Navigator and the wounded signalman were doing. He should go to the sick bay and have someone look at his leg, but that could wait a little longer.

He lay back on his bunk, unfastened the front of his overalls and scratched at the rash on his chest in what was now almost a reflex action. The fan in the corner clicked as it reached the end of its traverse and turned, as usual doing no more than stirring the overheated air in the tiny cabin. He shifted his damaged leg, trying to find the least uncomfortable position for it, moved it again as the talons began to claw at the muscles once more. Click. The scuttle was wide open, but there was only hot air for the fan to draw in from the outside. Billy Bones landed on the bunk at his feet, sniffed cautiously, then came forward to be stroked. He rubbed the kitten between the ears, Billy purred and then settled down beside him.

Shutting his eyes, he tried to ignore the throbbing pain in his thigh, saw again the kamikaze, smoke and flame coming from its engine and wings, the pilot holding his aircraft on her course, his face visible above the flames which now filled the cockpit, becoming a blackened and grinning skull as he came on. He opened his eyes, found that he was shaking, the sweat of fear trickling off his forehead and into his eyes, the salt stinging on the raw flesh. He turned his head, saw Kate's photograph on the desk opposite, unreal in the red half-light of the cabin. Click. Kate was smiling, serene and lovely, but she was ten thousand miles away, far beyond his reach, and he had been unfaithful to her. Click.

There was a list on the Court and Social page of *The*

472

Times, his own name and the name of his prep school appearing near the bottom, between those of W. D. Tatham, St Peter's Court, and J. F. Tuck, Heatherdown, heavily circled in red ink in his father's unmistakable hand, and then a few days later a large cardboard box, heavily secured with string and sealing wax, from Messrs Gieves of Bond Street. Gieves' representatives had been present throughout the interviews and exams, and had measured all the candidates for their uniforms, but it was only now, looking at the items wrapped in their tissue paper, immaculately pressed and folded into stiff lines, the shirts, collars, long trousers – both blue and white for working rig – the round jacket and the brass-buttoned waistcoat which went with it for Number One dress, the two caps with their gold-embroidered badges, the white cap covers to be worn between 1st May and 30th September, it was only now that it began to be real.

He stood for a long time, not wanting to disturb the perfection of it, a little apprehensive at the thought of what it all meant, the turning aside from what had been planned for him – Wellington, then Woolwich and the Royal Artillery – oblivious to his father standing next to him. 'Well, aren't you going to try them on and make sure they fit you?' Strange, too, to look in the mirror in his bedroom a few minutes later and see the naval cadet who looked back at him, feeling immeasurably older, already halfway to manhood, no longer the Robert Thurston who had idled his way through five years at prep school until the fact that there was a stiff series of written exams to be surmounted if he was to have any hope of getting into Osborne had impelled him into work. He combed his hair, parting it precisely down the left side of his head, put on one of the caps, tilted it back and a little to one side like the naval officers he had seen, and grinned at the image in the mirror. The cadet grinned back. He contorted his face into a grimace; again the cadet returned it. He was beginning to

473

become used to this strange new self, less uncomfortable with him. He walked down the stairs, carefully in the stiff new boots ('three pairs strong black boots of uniform pattern, soles at least half an inch thick'), knocked twice on the door of his father's study.

'Enter.' His father was sitting at his desk beneath the window, the newspaper open in front of him, taking off the spectacles he used only in private, looking him up and down and smiling in warm approval, so that for a moment there was a sense of his father's affection for him. 'There are some fingermarks on the peak of your cap.' And then came the first words of the lecture, of the same kind as he had heard so often before, that this must not be a mere flash in the pan, that he hoped the Navy would inculcate in him a proper sense of duty and responsibility, that naval discipline would undoubtedly be good for him, taking the sweetness out of his triumph and turning all the bright glory into tarnished brass.

It was always the same with his father. A year later he came home on leave from Osborne eighth in the term, with a prize for navigation and a Very Good for conduct, and all the old man had done was to ask why he hadn't managed an Excellent for conduct, adding that with the brain he had he could surely have done better than eighth if he had really applied himself, et cetera, et cetera. It was pointless to say that almost nobody had got an Excellent – a couple of chaps had, but they were both complete drips. Mrs Forsyth, who was about to become his stepmother, took him aside later on to tell him that she at least thought he had done extremely well, and his grandfather said much the same, but it didn't make up for it.

Click. The muscle on the front of his thigh knotted up suddenly with cramp. He worked the knee back and forth, as far as it would go now, in an attempt to relieve it. Sweat stood out on his face again. The Admiral had been a dozen feet from him when the kamikaze hit, and it was only because the Japanese bomb had failed to go off that he and the rest of the bridge watchkeepers had lived through it, and only because Little F and Bingham had got the bomb safely overboard that there were not many more dead men to be buried, and more mutilated bodies for the surgeons to salvage as best they could.

He shuddered, remembering the narrow escape that he and the rest of them had had. He was getting too old for this; each close shave took a little more out of you, something that could not be regained; the blind sense of immortality which, once destroyed, could not be re-built. You lived with death, violent death which came without warning, and learnt to accept its prospect so that most of the time it was only a thread running through the back of the mind. Some, particularly the aircrews, became superstitious, convinced that they would be all right provided they carried the lucky coin, wore the scarf the girlfriend in England had given them, or continued to put the left flying boot on before the right. Others, and Thurston counted himself among them, were fatalistic – 'If the bullet's got your name on . . .' Still others shut their minds to the whole business. But when other men died beside you and you lived on, or the cannon shell smashed through the bulkhead you had moved away from a moment before, the comforting illusion of your own invulnerability was torn away, and you had then to steel yourself to go on, remind yourself that this was what you were there for, that you had a job to do, and other men were relying on you to do it.

He heard footsteps in the flat outside, then a knock on the bulkhead, pulled himself up into a sitting position, carefully, so as not to disturb his leg.

'Come.'

It was the PMO, grey and stooped in the doorway,

475

one hand still on the bulkhead as the other pulled the curtain back.

'What brings you here, PMO?'

'I came on deck for a breath of air and then I remembered I hadn't seen this splinter wound of yours, sir, so I'm here to repair the omission.' Grant took a couple of paces across the cabin. 'Mm, I'll see things a lot better in the sick bay.'

Now his weight had been off the leg for a time it seemed an enormous effort to get down from the bunk and have to walk again. The leg had stiffened in a partly bent position and was reluctant to straighten again.

'Can you manage?'

'Yes, of course.' With the stick Spencer had found it was a little easier, leaning heavily on that and allowing the toes only of his left foot to make contact with the deck. He still had his boots on; he had been too weary to bother with taking them off earlier.

'How's Pilot?' Thurston asked when he was sitting on Grant's examination couch with the Surgeon Commander unwrapping the dressing the sick-bay Petty Officer had applied earlier.

'Very lucky.' Grant's accent was noticeable once more, so that 'very' had a double or even a treble 'r' and came out almost as 'vairry'. 'He's lost an eye, and he'll aye live.'

Grant stopped speaking for a moment. The Navigator was RN, and the eyesight requirements for the Executive Branch were stringent. Thurston found himself wondering what they would make of a navigator with one eye, his mind wandering a little in its weariness.

'The burns look a bit nasty, but they're actually fairly superficial. He had his hood up, which saved most of his face, and you managed to put the flames out before they had time to do much damage.'

'I didn't think about it. I just knocked him down and rolled him about. I didn't even stop to think whether it was the right thing to do.' He was saying too much, thinking of the Navigator swinging slowly round, hands plucking at the flames around his head, the bloody socket and the eye bouncing grotesquely on his cheek. He grimaced, and looked away from Grant in embarrassment.

'Lucky for him that you didn't stop to think, and lucky for you that you had your gloves on and didn't do yourself any damage. Let's see your hands.' Thurston held them out, palms uppermost, turned them over as Grant looked, heard him grunt in satisfaction. 'A bit pink, but nothing to worry about.'

'Can I see him?'

'Let's get this leg of yours sorted out first.'

Thurston winced as the last turn of bandage was ripped away from his leg where it had stuck. A small rivulet of fresh blood began to trickle down the thigh towards the inside.

'Well, sir, ye're a lucky man. If you weren't as tall as you are, and the splinter had come a little more towards the inside, I think it'd have done you some serious damage.'

Thurston managed a weak grin, looking down at his leg and thinking that there really were only about four inches in it. If he'd been turned a little more towards the port side, and he'd been half a head shorter. That would certainly have been a rich vengeance for his dalliance with Jane Roper. 'Still, a miss is as good as a mile,' he said with forced cheerfulness.

'And there you have it.' Grant was prodding at the swollen flesh around the wound, telling him to bend the leg and straighten it again. He straightened up at last, leaning back against the bulkhead. 'This is one that's better out than in, and the sooner it's out the better. I'll get hold of Stockley to do it.' Grant picked up the telephone and spoke into it.

Surgeon Lieutenant Stockley arrived a few minutes later, conferred briefly with Grant, then said with the usual surgeon's heartiness, 'No problem, sir. We'll just give you a quick whiff and we'll have it out in a couple of minutes. No worse than having a tooth out.'

'I don't want an anaesthetic.'

'Sir, it'll hurt like hell if I try to do it without.'

'It's hurting like hell now, and I don't want to be knocked out for the next three days.' He had to be awake and alert in order to do his job, not fuddled with ether at this of all times.

'You'll have to have something, sir. I'd defy you or anyone else to keep still enough without, and I could do a lot of damage to your quadriceps if you shifted while I was doing it. I'm not prepared to take the risk.'

Thurston saw Grant beckon to Stockley with one finger, and the two surgeons drew away into the shadows in one corner of the compartment, moving close together and conferring in voices too low for him to hear.

'Well, sir,' Stockley said when he returned at last, 'we could try filling you up with local and hope that'll be enough. I'm prepared to give it a try, but I must warn you it may not be entirely effective.'

'In plain English,' Grant said with a thin smile, 'it'll still hurt like hell.'

Twenty minutes later he was lying on the operating table at the other end of the sick bay with a gowned and masked Stockley bending over him. He had insisted on seeing the Navigator first, propped up in a narrow pipe cot so that nothing came into contact with his bandaged shoulders, one side of his face untouched, blackish beard shadow visible against the skin, the other entirely hidden by more bandaging. His remaining eye had been very bright in the half-light cast by the lamp in the corner of the compartment, the pupil reduced to a pinhead by the morphine he had been given. 'I'm sorry, sir. I made a bit of a fool of myself.' The Navigator had sounded embarrassed.

'I think most of us would have done much the same in the circumstances.'

'Yes, sir.' He had hesitated for a moment before speaking again. 'They tell me I've you to thank that it wasn't any worse, sir.'

The Navigator had turned his bandaged head towards him, the one eye meeting his. He had felt the blush spreading across his face, said something vague and indefinite, remembered Grant standing in the doorway. 'I'll have to go, Pilot. I'll come and see you again.'

'I suppose they'll be sending me across to the hospital ship next replen. Everybody keeps telling me that Nelson seemed to manage all right with one eye.' The Navigator's voice had broken, his face jerking convulsively back towards the far bulkhead, a single tear visible as it coursed down his cheek, leaving a glistening trail behind it.

Stockley was leaning over him, a syringe in one hand. 'What a bloody enormous needle.'

'It's a buttock needle, sir. Only one that's long enough to get right in.'

Spencer's face suddenly appeared round the door.

'No, Spencer, you're not coming in here,' Grant said firmly.

'Sir?'

'Go and find me some clothes, Spencer.'

'Aye aye, sir.'

It hurt, as Stockley had prophesied, first as the surgeon circled his thigh with a series of injections, then as he selected an instrument and began to probe downwards into the wound, the clawing pain breaking through the numbness the injections had created. It was very hot, the air in the small compartment heavy with humidity, and the lights above painfully bright. Sweat coursed off Stockley's forehead as he concentrated on his work, ran down inside his mask and gathered in large droplets on the point of his chin. Thurston found himself gripping the edges of the table with both hands, concentrating his attention on the drops falling from the surgeon's chin in a slow and absolutely steady rhythm, creating a spreading damp patch on the green towel which had been spread over his legs.

There was a tugging, an intensification of the pain, and a grunt from within Stockley's mask. The instrument came up, out through the layers which were still numb from the injections, dark now with blood. The SBA standing at his head wiped his face with a damp cloth. Another instrument, like a narrow and long-handled pair of pincers, was slapped into Stockley's hand by the SBA standing next to him. The thing went in, there was more tugging and an explosion of pain which brought tears into his eyes and made him clench his teeth together to avoid crying out, his back jerking six inches clear of the table.

'Nearly there, sir,' the SBA said.

Another grunt from Stockley, and then he was holding the instrument up, something small and round clenched in its jaws.

'There you are, sir.' Stockley dipped the thing in a kidney dish which the SBA was holding out to him, held it up once more. It was small and round, gently curved on one side, a rivet head from the Zero's metal skin, and must have been blown from the aircraft with tremendous force to embed itself so deeply in his flesh.

'Keep it for a souvenir.'

But Thurston had pulled himself half upright, twisted over on to his right side, and was being sick into a bucket one of the SBAs had jammed beneath his mouth.

Chapter Thirty-Six

The Americans dropped a second atomic bomb at 1100 the next morning. A few men allowed themselves to wonder whether this further demonstration of Allied might could induce the Japanese to sue for peace, but after the previous anticlimax nobody could really believe in the prospect. It had begun to be accepted once more that the Japanese attitude of no surrender would prevail, and that the war would drag itself out to 1947. The Americans attacked the few remaining Japanese heavy ships in harbour at Kure, immobile now from lack of fuel and reduced to floating gun batteries, wreaking a rich revenge for Pearl Harbor and relegating the British to secondary targets ashore. But the Japanese showed no sign of giving up yet. Their flak was as heavy and accurate as ever, and *Inflexible* lost two more of her Corsairs.

Yet surely the Japanese couldn't go on much longer. Their surface fleet was all but destroyed, their armaments industry was being bombed flat by the Americans, their armies everywhere on the retreat – in Burma, where the British and Indian Armies had retaken Rangoon and bottled up the surviving Japanese forces; in the islands, which were being recaptured one by one; and in Manchuria, where the Russians had launched a sudden and overwhelming offensive a few hours before the second bomb had been dropped. Their air force, which one Sunday morning less than four years ago had destroyed an entire American fleet and the Americans' illusion of invincibility in a few minutes, was reduced to hastily recruited young men trained and prepared for one mission only, mostly to be shot down into the sea long before they reached their target.

Thurston, as usual, spent most of his time on the bridge, sitting with his gammy leg stretched out in front of him and his foot resting on one of the projections on the bridge screen in front of him.

'You must be magnetic, sir,' Spencer had commented. 'You seem to pick up any bit of metal that's going. Could just about paper Rosie's front room with your Hurt Certificates.'

Thurston, like everyone else aboard *Inflexible*, wanted above all else for the war to end, found himself praying that the dropping of the two atomic bombs would finally lead the Japanese to surrender, but a small hard voice inside told him not to hope too much, for those hopes might still be dashed.

They pulled back for another replen, and the letter he had been waiting for arrived at last. Refuelling was in progress, and he pushed it into his pocket, telling himself that he would read it later in private.

> . . . *I do not believe that your father suffered at all, which is some comfort at least. The weather has been rather damp in the last week or so and your father's chest had been bothering him again, but yesterday was a most beautiful sunny morning and he insisted on taking Omega out. He came home in fine fettle, but I think the outing must have tired him rather, as he fell asleep in the drawing room after lunch. He must have died in his sleep, quite peacefully. Dr Harrison said it must have*

*been a heart attack, and that in all probability
he knew nothing about it, which we must be
thankful for, at least.*

*Dr Harrison telephoned Alice, and she
managed to catch the last train so that she
arrived just before eleven o'clock yesterday
evening. It is a terrible shock for her, poor
girl, but she is a great comfort . . . The funeral
is on Friday, and it is such a pity that you cannot be at home for it . . .*

There was a letter, too, from his sister, and as typical of
her as Maud's was of his stepmother. Their father had
died from a heart attack, and the post-mortem had confirmed it. The whole business had been a terrible shock
for Maud, finding the old man dead in a chair opposite
her, and Maud was herself in her late seventies and not
in the best of health. Alice was trying to take as much
of the responsibility for organising the funeral and so
on out of her hands, and once the funeral was out of the
way she was going to insist that Maud went away for a
good long break, which would be easier now that the
war in Europe was over. Kate was coming for the
funeral and bringing the boys with her, which should
help to provide a distraction. She had started to go
through their father's papers, and was putting to one
side the things which she thought he should see before a
decision was made about them.

*There are his South African War diaries and
all sorts of lecture notes from Sandhurst which
you might find interesting, as well as all your
reports from Osborne, and quite a pile of your
letters from when you were a midshipman. He
seems to have kept almost everything anyone
sent him. It's quite strange to see it all, and
makes one think about him rather differently.*

Alice had never married, and perhaps through having

to compete with three brothers, and perhaps also through making her way in her chosen profession, she had become a rather brisk, no-nonsense sort of woman, highly respected among her medical colleagues but close to none of them. Thurston could well imagine her organising her stepmother and the necessary obsequies for their father.

There was a small object wrapped in several layers of tissue paper in the corner of the envelope which had contained Alice's letter. He unwrapped it carefully, smoothing each sheet out on the desktop, almost sure what was within but not yet certain. Footsteps sounded in the flat outside, two voices were arguing at a rising pitch. He shouted to them to pipe down; the voices were suddenly quiet, then continued again in fierce whispers as the footsteps moved further away. He unwrapped the last sheet of paper, found what he expected, the old and now rather worn signet ring that used to be on his father's hand and on his grandfather's before him. He hesitated a little, then pushed it over the knuckles of his little finger and held it up towards the light. It was a little tight, the red light glinting on the device engraved on its face, a mounted Indian cavalryman, lance in hand, a tiger turning at bay, a brief inscription in Persian, in characters too small to read in comfort, running round the edge – *Where Duty may call, there will the faithful servant go* – the same device and words as were on the cigarette case his grandfather had given him for his twenty-first birthday.

His thigh was beginning to cramp again, he moved his left foot forward a few inches, rubbed at the muscle around the wound. The pain eased, but only for a moment. He stood up, limped the few paces to the door and out into the flat beyond. As usual at this time of night it was very quiet, lit by the same dull red bulbs as in his sea cabin, all the doors open and hooked back for maximum ventilation. The Admiral's sea cabin was empty, of course; so too was the Navigator's, each bunk stripped, folded sheets piled on top, the drawers beneath no doubt emptied, ready for the next occupant when he arrived on board.

That morning there had also been a terse, formally phrased letter from the commanding officer of the Naval Detention Quarters in Sydney, informing him that Signalman Norton had flung himself down a stairwell a week earlier. They had become concerned about him and had sent him to hospital; he had broken away from the SBA who was watching him while being escorted to the heads, and had gone over the banister before the man could catch up with him. Norton had died instantly from a broken neck. How much longer, Thurston asked himself, and how many more?

'This is it, chaps! This is what we've been waiting for, the Yanks are letting us have a piece of the action at last!' The Ops Officer rapped his wooden pointer on the briefing room blackboard. 'I don't need to tell you all to pay attention, I'm sure. The *Hikyu* is a Japanese eight-inch cruiser, similar in size and dimensions to our County class, but a good deal more modern.' He indicated the silhouette pinned to the blackboard.

'Four eight-inch turrets, quite a variety of smaller weapons, and capable of thirty-odd knots flat out. She was badly shot up by the Yanks at Leyte, but managed to limp back home and she's been in dry dock ever since. Word has just reached us, and photo recce has confirmed it, that the Japs have moved her out of dry dock and are making her ready for some sort of sortie. What you chaps are going to do is stop her. The Yanks have finally realised that we are actually on the same side as them. They've stopped hogging all the juicy targets and given us the *Hikyu* to deal with. This is going to be a maximum effort, chaps, every aircraft we can get into the air. The attack will take place in three waves at ten-minute intervals. We are going to form the second wave, and go in straight after the Seafires and Fireflies from *Irresistible*, who are going to soften up the flak positions.'

He indicated the row of aerial photographs which were pinned along the top of the blackboard. 'These were taken at first light this morning. The *Hikyu* wasn't here yesterday, so the Japs must have moved her during the night, when we were all tucked up in our bunks. As you can see, she's moored close in under this cliff, and the clifftop itself is stiff with flak positions, so you're going to have a tricky bit of flying to get at her, and your bombs will have to be dropped at low level to make sure of hitting her. You'll all be carrying bombs on this trip, the Corsairs included.' There was a chorus of groans from the Corsair pilots. 'Don't be so ungrateful. This is the first time since we joined the Yanks that we've had anything like a real target to play with.'

The rest of the briefing was soon over. The aircrews crowded round the blackboard for a few minutes, intent on the aerial photographs which showed their target, the long grey shape below the dirty white of the cliff, the flak positions clustered above.

'The Japs sure don't want to lose this one,' Moose Macpherson said.

'Not surprising, since it's the only thing bigger than a bathtub that they've got left.'

On the flight deck outside, Sub-Lieutenant Broome climbed up into his cockpit, busied himself with his harness, fumbling with the shoulder straps and swearing at the mechanic assisting him when one of the straps accidentally went out of reach behind him. Broome had been on board *Inflexible* for four months now, two of them in action, and he had changed considerably from the eager boy who had first flown on to join the ship. He was thinner, and looked much older than his years. At night, in the cramped and overheated cabin above

486

the screws which he shared with another pilot, it was difficult to sleep; he shut his eyes and would be flying again, evading a Japanese fighter coming in for the kill, flame spouting from its gun ports, or making his final approach to land on, the carrier's deck rolling and pitching ahead of him, the bats moving in all directions, too fast for him to react to. He would waken shouting, to be cursed by his cabin mate, a replacement who had only joined on the last replen but one, and then lie awake again for a long time, wishing he could turn the light on and read for a while, but that would keep the other man awake.

He reached into his breast pocket, felt for the coin which was in there, an old one-rupee piece with a hole through the middle which someone had given him as a swap when he was a boy and he'd carried round ever since. He went through the cockpit check, reminding himself to check that the bomb circuit was working, waiting for the order to start the engine and watch the great propeller in front of him turn slowly round and then disappear in a blur. Another order came, the Corsair ahead began to move forward. A mechanic whipped away the chocks, and ducked beneath the port wing as Broome let off the brakes and the Corsair started to roll forward. *Open the throttle, see the leading Corsair lift clear of the deck and the main wheels rise up into their wells.* Then he was off the deck himself, dropping sickeningly into the shadow ahead of the carrier's bow before the Corsair gained flying speed. *Turn away to starboard to clear the take-off area, tuck into place in the formation.* As always he was calmer now that the waiting was over and they were flying towards the target, enjoying the brief spell of calm when all he needed to do was concentrate on flying his aircraft and maintaining his position on the CO's starboard wing tip.

The Corsair, laden with the five-hundred-pound bomb, was heavier and more sluggish than usual, reacted less positively to the controls. The day was overcast and muggy, the sun breaking only occasionally through the grey veil of cloud, a brief rain shower rattling on the cockpit canopy as the squadron sped low over the sea. The slower Avengers had taken off ahead of them, fired one by one from the catapult in *Inflexible*'s bow, and would rendezvous with the Corsairs a few miles short of the target. The second Corsair squadron was visible over to starboard, right down at sea level, the fitful sun reflecting off the wing tips.

The nose of the CO's Corsair went down, taking them lower still, so that the whirling propeller seemed to reach down into the troughs between the white wave crests. Voices spoke over the R/T, the Seafire and Firefly pilots already nearing the target, the FDO on board *Irresistible* giving them their final instructions. *Not long now*. Broome fidgeted with his straps, in the way which had now become a habit, running his fingers down the inside of his shoulder straps, first the seat harness, then the parachute harness beneath, released one side of his oxygen mask, pulled a plastic bottle of water from its stowage, uncorked it between his knees and tilted his head back to take a long drink. The CO was indicating with his hand, in the same old *piano, piano* motion. Broome had drifted a little high while he was drinking; he eased the stick very gently forward, then back again almost immediately as the Corsair found its correct position.

They could see the Japanese coast coming up now, Shikoku, the smallest of the main Japanese islands, a long dark streak rising out of the sea, long columns of grey smoke coming up from it and spreading into a pall which merged with the grey blanket of cloud. The chatter on the R/T was excited staccato as the Seafires and Fireflies made their attack. Someone was shouting; he thought he recognised the voice, a chap who had been on the same course in Canada, tall, with fair hair, who had smoked a pipe, whom he hadn't known was out here. He tried to remember the chap's name, and then the voice was abruptly cut off.

The CO was altering course, leading them round to port, and there were the Avengers ahead of them, ungainly and lumbering with their large bellies, each filled with two thousand pounds of armour-piercing bombs ready for a warship target. The Corsairs throttled back to avoid overhauling the Avengers, and the whole formation flew on, skirting the island and keeping out over the water. The Japanese radar would pick them up as soon as they passed through one thousand feet, so the climb to altitude before the Avengers made their attack must be left to the last possible moment.

Over to starboard a flak post opened fire, but the rounds burst far short of them, and soon ceased. A small and rather scruffy-looking fishing boat was crossing from starboard to port ahead of them. It wasn't really a worthwhile target, but the CO gave it a brief burst, and Broome saw the bullets striking on the wooden hull and ricocheting into the water. There was land visible on either side of them now, the width of water beneath them narrowing very gradually. They began to climb, the CO giving final instructions over the R/T. Broome adjusted his straps once again, hot and sticky inside the confined cockpit.

There was the target, lying at anchor beneath the cliff exactly as the aerial photographs had shown, the whitish cliff towering above, flak beginning to hose up from camouflaged positions on the clifftop. The CO gave another order, and Broome peeled off into a dive in obedience to it. The Avengers were diving too, the bomb doors opening in their bellies. The big ship was in his sights, exactly central; his hand was on the button, ready to release as soon as he was close enough.

The ship's guns were firing now, smoke billowing upwards from her four main turrets, and smaller puffs coming up from the close-range weapons scattered over her decks. There was a bang, and he saw the Corsair ahead disappear, had to jerk the aircraft over to port to avoid flying into the debris. He had lost the ship; there was only water and cliff ahead of him. He risked a glance around, found the cruiser once more, got himself lined up with it. Not long now; flak bursting all around, red and green and smoke-black. He was firing now, the rounds striking the ship's deck or into the sea around her.

A Japanese staggered across the deck, clutching his chest, swung slowly round and went down, his body hanging half over the rails, jerking again as the Corsair's guns pumped more bullets into him. The ship filled his sights; he pressed the release, felt the aircraft bounce upwards as the five-hundred-pound weight fell away. The cliff towered above. He jerked the Corsair round in a split-arse turn to port, seemed to miss the cliff edge by inches, clawed his way upwards with the stick back in his belly and the supercharger engaged. The cliff edge, and flak, came at him horizontally. He turned to port again, pushed the throttle right open, trying to put as much space as he could between his aircraft and the flak positions. He saw another Corsair, guns blazing as it roared across the clifftop, felt slightly ashamed at his cowardice in not taking on the flak positions with him. The flak was still heavy; he remembered that the Seafires had been supposed to soften up the gunners before the main attack went in, wondered what had happened to them.

He was clear of the cliff now, catching his breath, looking round for the rest of the squadron, when there was a bang beneath him, a heavy blow in the Corsair's belly. His first thought was relief that the bomb wasn't there any longer. The aircraft responded heavily, which meant that the wings, rudder and tailplane must be intact. Undercart probably shot though; he was going to have trouble landing back on, might be better to try ditching alongside, where a destroyer could pick him up. Someone was shouting over the R/T: 'We got her, we got her!' He risked a look down, saw the Japanese cruiser, lying right over on her beam ends, a long swathe of red lead running along her side. 'Got the bitch, got the bitch!' someone else was shouting in exultation. But it didn't seem so important now.

He checked the altimeter. Fifteen hundred feet – enough room to bale out if it came to it. Airspeed a bit slower than usual – of course, the damage, whatever it was, would increase the drag and so slow things down. He was thirsty again, but needed both hands for the controls now. He touched the rupee coin in his pocket and felt a little better. The squadron was regrouping, voices asking him over the R/T whether he was all right, commenting on the state of the Corsair's belly. The flak had fallen away behind and there were no more Japanese fighters left to harry them on the way back, only the kamikazes, who could be shot out of the sky like turkeys by any half-trained pilot.

Fifteen minutes passed. Broome had to concentrate on flying the aircraft, keeping it on course and maintaining his altitude. He looked around, saw the metal skin bubbled around the starboard wing root, the paint flaking away, wondered whether the wing really seemed more bent than usual or whether it was just his imagination. The Corsair lurched as his concentration lapsed for a second; his right arm was beginning to ache from the effort of holding the aircraft on course. He smelt burning, wondered where it was coming from, thought of the petrol tanks around him, some at least filled only with the petrol vapour that was many times more explosive than petrol itself, felt fear clutch coldly at his vitals.

He was watching the starboard wing root now, concentrating less on keeping the Corsair on her course with the rest of the squadron. It probably would come to a ditching, easier than trying to land on with a dodgy wing and an undercart which might not go down, and, if it did, might not stay down. He thought of one of the prangs he had seen: the pilot had tried to land on after being shot up, the starboard leg had collapsed first and the Corsair had slewed round to port on the remaining wheel before it too collapsed, ploughed into the barrier and caught fire. He found himself praying silently that he wouldn't burn, he didn't want to burn, anything else, but he didn't want to burn.

The burning smell was stronger. He wondered whether he was going to make it back to the carrier. There was an awful lot of sea below. The rest of the squadron were around him, shepherding him back towards the ship, but he felt himself to be alone with the aircraft; it was he who had to get the Corsair back and land her on or ditch her alongside.

Bang!! There was another lurch, and he saw the starboard wing separate from the fuselage and fall away. Instantly, the rest of the aircraft went into a tight spin to port. He reached for the canopy locks. The canopy did not budge. He tried again, felt it move slightly, got his fingers into the gap which was beginning to form, dragged the canopy back inch by inch on its runners. He tried to stand up, remembered that his harness still secured him to the seat, yanked the safety pin out, then the radio lead. He glanced at the altimeter, below a thousand feet now and unwinding fast.

He squeezed his head out into the gap, feeling the four-hundred-mile-an-hour slipstream buffet him. He fought the rest of his body out, feeling the great bustle of the parachute jam against the lip of the canopy, shoved with all his strength to get it free. The slipstream caught him, his legs slithered out, he felt one shoulder strike against the rudder. He remembered his training, the instructions given long ago with his first parachute, put his right hand out to the ripcord, gabbled 'ABRACADABRA, ONE, TWO, THREE!!' and pulled.

The handle came off in his hand. This was it; he'd picked a parachute which hadn't been packed properly. He shut his eyes, then felt a jerk, a slowing in his headlong fall, opened his eyes again and looked up to see the glorious white canopy mushroom out above him. Just in time; he must be below three hundred feet now, the white crests below. It was going to be rough. He heard an engine, saw a Corsair slowly circling above him, close enough for him to read the identification letters on the fuselage. Q-Queenie – Ted Edwards. It made him feel better, less alone. His feet felt cold, the slipstream had taken his shoes off. Oh well, it would be easier to swim without them.

The water was much colder than he expected. He hit it with his knees surprisingly hard and went deep, tried to claw his way upwards and found himself enmeshed in the rigging lines of the parachute. He fumbled with one hand at the release box, while with the other he tried to fight his way clear. The box wouldn't budge. He had to use both hands, twisted it, and then pressed in hard. The harness fell away, but the canopy and its rigging lines were still all around him, preventing him from swimming, the silk collapsing all around him.

His lungs bursting, he twisted away and dived deeper, counted five strokes and turned upwards again. The canopy was still there, but he seemed to have reached the edge of it; in a couple more strokes he was clear of the enveloping silk, the buoyancy of the water carrying him back up towards the surface. His head came up in a trough, he drew in great lungfuls of air, remembered his Mae West and pulled the tab on the CO_2 bottle. The Mae West firmed up around him almost instantly and he found himself floating quite comfortably, with his head well clear of the water, but the waves sloshing into his mouth and nose.

Dinghy. He pulled the tab on the second CO_2 bottle, watching the yellow dinghy thrash like a live thing as it inflated. It floated on the surface, secured to him by a length of line, inevitably upside down. It took him a long time to right it, and longer still to get into it as it kept drifting away capriciously to the full length of the line. He lay in the bottom of the dinghy, vomited almost immediately with the unfamiliar motion, watched as the foul-smelling stuff slithered back and forth with the rolling of the dinghy. At last he roused himself, baled out the dinghy with the bailer which had been supplied, waved to the pilot of the Corsair still orbiting above him. The pilot dipped his wings, which cheered Broome up, made him hope that he would not have long to wait.

He did not. His watch had stopped when he hit the water, but it could not have been much more than an hour later that a biplane shape appeared in the sky to the east, instantly recognisable as the Walrus amphibian which *Inflexible* carried for air-sea rescue purposes, and only a few moments after that before the Walrus was landing on the water upwind of him, taxying slowly towards him.

'You chose the right time to be picked up,' the observer shouted above the noise of the engine. He was from the Avenger squadron, and Broome knew him only by sight. 'We sank the *Hikyu*, and Nimitz sent a peace warning just as we were setting off to pick you up.'

'A what?' Broome said stupidly.

'A peace warning. We got this signal, just as we were getting briefed. "*This is a peace warning*."'

It didn't really sink in. Broome was lying on the floor

494

inside the Walrus, with the observer patiently getting him out of his sodden flying kit.

'What it means is, the Sons of Heaven are throwing in the towel. The war's over. Or nearly over,' the observer added as an afterthought.

Chapter Thirty-Seven

'Isn't that the most beautiful sight you ever saw, sir,' Spencer commented.

It was 0600 on 15th August 1945, the sun had just risen, aircraft bombed up and ready to go on the carriers' flight decks, the warships at Action Stations, as they had been every dawn at sea for the last six years.

The signal flying from the flagship's halyards read simply, CEASE HOSTILITIES AGAINST JAPAN.

'Lot of good chaps not here to see it,' Thurston said slowly.

'No, sir.'

Thurston found that there was no sense of triumph, only relief that after six long years it was all over. He got down from his chair, limped a few paces to rest his arms on the top of the bridge screen, looked across the water lit up by the rising sun, and thought of all the men he had commanded who had not lived to see this moment; the three hundred and eighty-two who had gone down with *Connaught*, the men killed in the *Seydlitz* action or during that last convoy to Malta. He could remember the names, and the faces, grinning beneath their uniform caps, young men and mere boys, and the older, more experienced men with wives and families at home. There were the men who had gone down into the icy darkness of the Barents Sea with *Crusader*, the aircrews, lost by the steady attrition of landing accidents as often as by enemy action, the men killed by the kamikazes over the last few months, and

496

those who had died when *Persephone*'s 5.25-inch shell smashed into the island. And all the other young men left scarred and maimed, altered in ways they might not be aware of by the war they had fought in, separated for the rest of their lives from those men, even servicemen, who had spent their war at home and not seen action. And there was, too, a lurking undercurrent of pride in having been at sea on the last day of the war as well as the first, that he had not taken the easier way offered to him after his breakdown, but had clawed his way back to command, and played his part in the great enterprise which had finally defeated both the Germans and the Japanese.

Dawn Action Stations ran its course.

'Secure from Action Stations, but keep the guns' crews and damage control parties closed up, as we don't know what the Japs might do.'

'Aye aye, sir.'

There had been a warning earlier that the surrender might lead the more fanatical Japanese to launch another kamikaze attack. Already there had been rumours of mass suicides ashore.

'Hands to Defence Stations. All guns' crews and damage control parties remain closed up.'

From the flight deck below there were sounds of cheering and shouting, men tearing open their overalls, running to the deck edge and casting their tin hats into the ship's wake.

'Shall I put a stop to that, sir?' asked the PCO.

'No, leave them to it. After all, it's not every day they win a war.'

> *And gentlemen in England now abed,*
> *Shall think themselves accursed they*
> *were not here,*
> *And hold their manhoods cheap while*

any speak,
That fought with us upon St Crispin's Day.

And now, he thought, he really would have to make up his mind about Masters' offer.

Historical Note

It is all too frequently assumed that the role of the Royal Navy in the war against Japan began and ended with the series of humiliating reverses and desperate rearguard actions which took place in the period from December 1941 to May 1942, in which the capital ships *Prince of Wales* and *Repulse*, the aircraft carrier *Hermes*, the cruisers *Cornwall*, *Dorsetshire* and *Perth* (RAN), were destroyed by Japanese carrier-borne aircraft, proof, if any were needed following the devastating attack on Pearl Harbor, of the potency of the aircraft carrier in modern war. Now, almost fifty years after the event, it is usually considered that the naval war, and indeed the land war, in the Pacific, was entirely prosecuted by the Americans, and the role played by British and Commonwealth forces is virtually forgotten.

A British aircraft carrier appeared in the Pacific as early as March 1943. In October 1942, following the Battles of Midway and Santa Cruz, when the Americans were left without a single operational carrier, the US Chiefs of Staff asked the Admiralty for the loan of one aircraft carrier, or, better still, two. The Royal Navy, itself lacking sufficient fleet carriers and with many other commitments, in particular the 'Torch' landings in North Africa of November 1942, could not spare a carrier until December. HMS *Victorious* reached Pearl Harbor in March of the following year, and after a period of training to accustom her aircrews to American practices, joined the US fleet in May, operating with the Americans in September and forming part of the covering force for the landings of MacArthur's forces in New Georgia.

The turning of the tide in the war against Germany, and, in particular, the crippling and eventual sinking of the German battleship *Tirpitz* by a series of attacks by the Fleet Air Arm and RAF during 1944, freed the bulk of the Home Fleet for service elsewhere, and Churchill was able at the Quebec Conference of 1944 to offer President Roosevelt a British fleet for service in the Pacific.

Roosevelt accepted the offer with alacrity, but many Americans had to be persuaded that a British force could make a significant contribution to the war effort, a situation not eased by the notorious anti-British stance of the US Naval Commander in Chief, Admiral Ernest J. King (it has been suggested that King's Anglophobia stemmed not only from his Irish ancestry, but from having found himself under Royal Navy command in the last months of World War I). In particular, it was considered that the British aircraft carriers, with their heavy deck armour, could not carry sufficient aircraft to make their presence worthwhile, that they had insufficient anti-aircraft armament and that conditions aboard them would become intolerable in the heat and humidity of the Pacific.

The British Pacific Fleet was formed in November 1944, partly from the more modern units of the Eastern Fleet, partly from ships released from the Home Fleet, and reached Sydney, its main base, in January 1945. Overall command was vested in Admiral Sir Bruce Fraser, who remained (much to his personal regret) in Sydney, and command of the Fleet at sea in Vice Admiral Sir Bernard Rawlings and Rear Admiral Sir Philip Vian, flying his flag as Rear Admiral Aircraft Carriers. That the Fleet managed to operate successfully in conditions far removed from those for which many of the ships had been designed was due in large measure to the unquenchable spirit and high morale among the aircrews and ships' companies, the great bulk of whom, by this stage of war, were not regular servicemen but wartime volunteers and conscripts.

Admiral King, fearing that a British fleet would act as a drain on American resources, had insisted that the British be self-sufficient in logistical matters, which meant that the Fleet had to operate at the end of very extended lines of communication – by July 1945 the Fleet was operating more than four thousand miles from Sydney, and over two thousand miles from the advanced base at Manus in the Admiralty Islands, just north of New Guinea, having to 'make do and mend' with a fleet train which John Winton aptly describes as 'possibly the most motley collection of vessels ever assembled', comprising ships of several nationalities, with crews serving under an even larger variety of Royal Navy regulations and Merchant Navy articles. It worked, but, indeed, 'God alone knew how'.

While *HMS INFLEXIBLE* is, of course, a work of fiction, the operations of the British Pacific Fleet between May and August 1945 were much as described here, and readers may be interested to learn that many of the incidents described actually occurred, though not always to the same ship. The carrier damaged by fire from another ship of the task force was HMS *Illustrious*, hit by two 5.25-inch shells from the cruiser *Euryalus* on 29th January 1945, suffering eleven men killed and twenty-two wounded, one of whom died later. The incident is graphically described by Norman Hanson in his book *Carrier Pilot*, and is also mentioned in *Admiral of the Fleet*, Oliver Warner's biography of Admiral of the Fleet Sir Charles Lambe, who was in command of *Illustrious* at this time. I have been unable to discover what, if any, action was taken by the Admiralty in connection with this, and the Board of Enquiry and associated events are entirely the products of my imagination.

Several of the British carriers were damaged by kamikaze attacks, the armoured decks proving their worth. After the Americans' initial scepticism it is interesting to quote the remark of an unnamed American liaison officer on board one of the British ships: 'When a kamikaze hits a US carrier it's six months' repair in Pearl. In a limey carrier it's "Sweepers, man your brooms!"' Or, as another American put it to Captain Philip Ruck-Keene of HMS *Formidable*, the only British carrier to take two kamikaze hits: 'Sir, they're a honey.' The words 'Ask them what typhoon' were uttered by Captain Q. D. Graham of HMS *Indefatigable*; may the shades forgive me for making use of someone else's line, but the temptation was irresistible.

It is sobering to record that many of the Fleet Air Arm's casualties, in the Pacific as elsewhere, were not due to enemy action but to flying accidents, mainly in the course of deck landing. Hanson records that a total of thirty pilots flew with 1833 Corsair Squadron from *Illustrious* between August 1943 and April 1945, of whom a third were killed, half of them in accidents.

The attack on the *Hikyu* is based on an attack on the Japanese training carrier *Nagato*, which took place much as described, though I have exercised some artistic licence in altering the date by a few days. It was this which brought the Royal Navy the last Victoria Cross of the Second World War, awarded posthumously to Lieutenant R. H. Gray RCNVR, on 9th August 1945. Mention of the VC leads me to Lieutenant P. S. W. Roberts and Petty Officer T. W. Gould, who both received this supreme award for their cold-blooded courage in removing two bombs which had penetrated the outer casing of HM Submarine *Thrasher*, on the night of 16th February 1942, all the while knowing that the submarine could have submerged without warning at any moment. Gould recently found himself obliged to sell his VC in order to provide for his own and his wife's old age, a sad commentary on the way this country treats its former servicemen.

The 'Bennett' referred to disparagingly by Jack Roper was Major-General H.G. Bennett, GOC 8th Australian Division, who was villified by his fellow countrymen and never re-employed after making his own escape from Singapore in the confusion which followed the surrender, rather than going into captivity with his men, whom he had ordered *not* to escape.

The '*Royal Oak* affair' was a cause célèbre of the late 1920s, having its origins in an incident at a wardroom dance in which the Rear Admiral of the First Battle Squadron of the Mediterranean Fleet, observing that few of the lady guests were dancing, berated the bandmaster of his flagship, HMS *Royal Oak*, for his apparent failure to provide appropriate music, and was heard to declare 'I won't have a bugger like that in my ship'. Following a series of incidents which must to outsiders have seemed farcical, and worsening friction between the Admiral on the one hand and the *Royal Oak*'s Captain and officers on the other, the Captain and Commander wrote letters of complaint to the Commander in Chief Mediterranean, passing through the proper service channels, whereupon they were both court-martialled on charges which were technical to say the least, found guilty and sentenced to be dismissed their ship. The careers of all three officers were ruined by the affair; the Admiral was never re-employed, the Captain was retired shortly afterwards, and the Commander felt constrained to resign his commission. An entertaining, if perhaps partisan, account of the episode is given by Leslie Gardiner in *The Royal Oak Courts Martial*.